HINDER

A BENDER'S NOVEL

KRISTIN PING

Fire Quill Publishing
www.firequillpublishing.com
All rights reserved, including the right of reproduction in whole or in part in any form. All graphics and text associated with Fire Quill Publishing.
Formatting by FQ Design
Manufactured in South Africa.
First Fire Quill Publishing edition April 2018
ISBN-13: 978-1-947649-15-6

To Maddy and Jellybean

ACKNOWLEDGMENTS

First of all I would like to give God the thanks that I could write this story. I am grateful for everything you have given me in life.

To my family, my husband and children, for giving up time spending with me so I can write. For your love and support.

To my editor, Jess Campbell, you are seriously a master when it comes to tweaking sentences and words, and thank you for being so passionate about my stories.

To Monique Fischer, who proof read my word. Thank you so much for always willing to grab another one of my stories.

To the big support at Fire Quill Publishers. You know I couldn't have done any of this without you. Your hard work and dedication goes above and beyond.

To my cover artist, Joemel, thank you for this brilliant concept. You have such great talent.

To Leandri, thank you for helping me with the spells in the book. I suck at rhyming. You have a great talent.

To everyone reading this, thank you for purchasing, reviewing, my novel. Your support means so much to me. And remember, Witches are vain.

Take care till next time
Kristin.

1

JEFF

AWE FILLED me as I watched Ethan playing in the garden. Though only ten years old and scrawny, he was... a wonder.

The farm was the safest place for him. A few miles from the city and its prying eyes. Less danger here.

His hands lightly stroked the rosebushes as he walked past them.

It wasn't time for them to bloom yet, but at Ethan's tender touch, pink and white rosebuds opened and expanded into the most beautiful roses I'd ever seen.

"Ethan," I called from the porch, warning in my tone.

His blond head snapped toward me. He pulled his hand to his chest. "Sorry, Dad."

"Be careful." I spoke as if he was pulling the cat's tail—not lending nature a hand.

With one flutter of the newspaper, I pretended to return to reading. After a few seconds scowling at the small black letters, I peeked over the top of the page and stared back at Ethan.

Natalie his mother, never let him explore. She worried about the *others*. That they would see.

Ethan walked over to the willow sapling Natalie had planted a few weeks ago. It wasn't tall; the top barely reached Ethan's waistline. He stumbled and fell with hands first—diving right into the willow.

It started to grow... and grow. In a matter of seconds, it was a full-grown tree. Slender, silver-green leaves swayed in the lazy breeze.

The newspaper fluttered as I set it aside and stood, mouth agape. Not many could do that at his age.

Surprise galloped on the heels of awe, followed by a dash of fear—okay, more than a dash— as Ethan stood and brushed himself off.

So this was what Natalie felt most of the time

My eyes darted this way and that. What if anyone saw?

Everything was exactly as it had been a few moments ago, except for the mature willow in the middle of the yard, its graceful branches lazily stroking the earth. A few cows grazed serenely in the green pasture. The chickens clucked in their pen. The ginger tomcat lay on the opposite chair to mine.

Behind me, the door opened. Natalie gasped. She smacked my shoulder with a dish cloth—hard. I scrambled back from her wrath.

"I told you to watch him!" she hissed. She ran down the steps with huge eyes and long strides. She reached him and crouched down in front of him, almost pulling the boy down with her, scowling.

Rubbing my shoulder, I watched the expression on my son's face. He hadn't meant to do it. It was an accident. Ethan never asked to be born into our family of Benders.

Ever since he got a taste of his element, well, he'd just been so damn curious.

He would need to find his match: an earth Wielder.

Earth Wielders rarely reached their fifteenth birthdays. And just because of what Ethan would become one day, his life was in mortal danger.

Benders were born to protect Wielders. The payoff was being able to manipulate the Wielder's element. To use it to their advantage. To, well, *bend* it into whatever they wanted the element to do. Whether it was to make a tree grow or a fire burn or the wind blow... Wielders could start the process, but the Benders performed the magic. They told the flame how to crackle, or the earth how to quake, or the gale how to waft.

Without a Bender, Wielders would cause chaos.

If a water Wielder or an earth Wielder had no Bender, then a tsunami was inevitable.

Wielders and Benders were a mechanism, an interdependent team that functioned as one. They benefited mutually from one another and kept each other safe.

It had always been this way since Wielders were labeled as Witches. Now they had plenty of names—alchemists, spellbinders, and shifters, to name a few.

On Ethan's tenth birthday, exactly at the stroke of midnight, he had received his earth element. The connection between the earth and Ethan was so powerful, it had triggered an earthquake for a full three seconds.

Benders always received the full dose of their Wielders' ability. For the next few years, Ethan would be able to wield the earth Element as well as bend it. For the next four years, we not only needed to find his Wielder, but also to keep him safe from the *Others*.

Earth Wielders were a force of balance. They were the true leaders of all supernaturals. They had to stay pure. They carried within them the power for immense good... or if they fell, immense evil. If they lost their sense of balance, they could become Necrocretors. Necrocretors didn't play by the rules. They broke and bent them as they pleased.

Everything Natalie and I did aimed toward keeping Ethan balanced and on the side of good.

The hardest test Ethan would face in his entire life would be if his Wielder turned out to be female. The resistance. Wielders and Benders could never be involved as a couple. And yet the pull is addictive, and strong. Even though it's against the law many Wielders and Benders failed. I know, I was one of them...a long time ago.

The rest of the supernaturals consists of what humans would call monsters, myths, and paranormal beings that makes great characters of monst fictional tales.

Ever since the jinns lost the chalice, they were no longer part of the race. Lowest on the totem pole were the shifters. Once a shifter went rogue, and became a Necrocretor, there was no turning back. Shifters were vicious and could turn into anyone with the same anatomy as theirs. Necrocretors loved gaining shifters.

It's why earth Wielder never reach that age, the age where their magic matures and stabilizes. The phase where they magic was powerful enough to reset the balance, to wipe the earth clean from all the evil inside the Necrocretors, from all the ugly, and to start uphold the law of not just the elements, but of all the supernaturals.

There hadn't been someone like that in the past four hundred years.

It was why the Guardians, a supernatural human race, started with the Sentinels.

A group of five that would jump in when things get out of hand.

Sometimes I think they were a myth, as they haven't jumped in yet.

Before Sentinels it was just earth Wielders. That was how powerful they were and Ethan was the lucky boy that was going to be part of that. He was going to become the next earth Wielder's protector in every way possible.

Tears formed in Ethan's eyes, but he refused to let them roll down his cheek. He tried so hard to live up to his element, to be strong and special.

Sad that the boy didn't know how strong or special he already was. Maybe it was my fault as a father, as a parent.

I wanted to tell Natalie that she should stop making him feel so terrible. He was just exploring. But what good would that do? We would just end up fighting again. I was so tired of our fights. Shoulders slumped, I turned to go inside. That was when I heard the roar of engines.

The hair on my arms and neck stood straight. Adrenaline poured into my blood like jet fuel and my heartbeat skyrocketed as I turned to see Natalie running toward me across the yard, jerking little Ethan along by the hand.

"Get rid of them. Now." She shouldered past me into the house.

No one had seen what Ethan had done, right? No, it wasn't possible. Was it?

Three black Jeeps and a silver one careened into the driveway, spitting gravel behind their shiny black tires. I leaped off the steps but then composed myself. With great effort, I slowed to a sedate walk. I had to try to make this farmhouse seem like any other sleepy home on this continent—even though it was far from it.

Who are these people? What are they doing here?

They weren't Necrocretors. Necrocretors didn't use Jeeps or SUVs to make their entrances. Whoever they were, they were driving fast. Too fast.

As they pulled closer, the sun glinted off the tinted windows and blinded me. Then when they turned an angle, I saw it. It was the outline of a barrel.

I dove for the willow. Bullets shredded bark above my head. Splinters and sawdust flew everywhere.

My back was firmly against the tree, safe from the bullets, or so I hoped. *Thank goodness he grew a fully mature tree,* I marveled. *Otherwise I'd be dead.*

I recited words that hadn't touched my tongue in years. I carried them in my skin on my tattoo, across my chest, close to my heart. A phrase scribbled in Latin that I've learned at a very young age. : Estque vel me vel

Its meaning was simple: *It is either them or me.*

If someone had to die, it wasn't going to be me.

I took out the Zippo in my back pocket, closed my eyes, and used my diaphragmatic breathing exercises to calm my heart.

More gunshots sizzled overhead. Bits of the porch railing and the willow bar exploded. The air filled with the scent of sulfur and singed wood.

I took a deep breath.

Then I flicked the flint.

WITHOUT MY WIELDER, I was jack shit. But I could manipulate. I could bend a flame if there was one to begin with.

The seductive odor of butane filled my nostrils as I bent the flame that burst from my lighter.

I expertly tossed two fireballs and felt the warmth of satisfaction when they rolled right where I wanted them—directly underneath two of the Jeeps. They exploded. A concussion of pure sound preceded the greasy cloud of black smoke and metal debris.

The other Jeeps squealed to a stop, spinning out of control in the gravel. For the next few minutes, fireballs and gunshots flew through the air. The gunmen used the cars as shields. They started firing relentlessly. I hunched behind my puny tree. They didn't give me a second to throw another fireball.

One man stopped firing for three seconds. I took the opportunity and whirled out to hurl another attack. He released his empty magazine; it clattered to the ground. He whipped up a new one—a sleek, black metal box—and clicked it in so fast, I might not have noticed it if I hadn't been facing him to throw a fireball. Tactical reload. They had plenty more where that came from. He was shooting again before I even formed my next attack.

It was raining gunshots.

This tree couldn't shield me much longer. Pieces of bark shaved off by bullets showered down on me.

The door to the farmhouse opened. Natalie walked out with a shotgun in her hand. Her hair was wild and her eyes wilder.

She aimed her gun at the two men approaching the house. It went off. *Boom, boom.* Two shots echoed in the air. One of them hit its mark. One of our attackers screamed in pain. Still bullets showered the porch as Natalie dove for cover.

She yelped and grabbed her stomach. A slim copper cartridge connected with her body at twenty-five hundred feet per second, but it might as well have been slow motion for me. She let out a yelp of surprise—then an involuntary groan of pain. She toppled to the ground behind the porch railing. Out of sight.

I cried out and flicked on my zippo again. Blindly, I threw six fireballs into the direction of the Jeeps. *Natalie.* One after the other, I hurled flame and destruction.

The earth started to rumble through the soles of my feet. Horror crept into my rage. "Ethan!"

He was crouched down by the porch steps. Tears streamed down his face, but the emotion was hard. Not delicate grief but anger. He was livid and the world would know it soon.

Both of his fists hammered down on the ground.

I shut my eyes as the current of it rushed deep underground. *His power.* I realized that this would be the only window to get to my son and up to that porch where there was a half a wall to hide behind.

I got up and didn't look back; I had a mental picture of what I would find.

The earth making a wave out of dirt and rock and grass. A terrifying wall rose and rolled toward the two Jeeps left standing.

I darted from the cover of the willow tree toward the house as fast as I could. Shots still whizzed past me.

I grabbed Ethan as I passed and pulled him toward the porch.

He grunted and growled. Feral. Furious.

We had to get to safety from whatever he conjured. I lost my balance as the earth wave crashed. A stray bullet in the shoulder. A spasm of agony traced its patch across muscle and sinew. I ignored it.

I dove with Ethan behind the porch railing. My gaze skittered across the porch floor, looking for her. A trail of crimson liquid led inside.

Still the bastards didn't let up. Bullets flew over our heads. I shoved Ethan ahead of me and crawled in behind him as glasses shattered overhead.

Natalie lay a few paces away. We both crawled to her.

Her eyes were still open. A tear rolled down her cheek. A sticky red bloom marred her t-shirt. Blood seeped out of her and pooled onto the floor.

"Babe, I'm..." Tears welled up in my eyes.

"Shh," she said softly. "It's going to be okay."

How? I wanted to say. She wasn't looking so good. She wasn't even in the same universe as okay.

I peeked over the railing. Grass, rock, and dirt were strewn everywhere. A gaping chasm yawned in the earth. One of the Jeeps had fallen into it; only the top of the roof stuck out. Another teetered half in, half out. They had no were to go, our attackers. They couldn't escape. Then one of the men stirred.

I ducked back down as a scream left his mouth.

Can't they just die?

Fingers of wind started teased my hair.

"Finally," Natalie whispered. "Jeff."

I opened my eyes. A part of me knew what she was going to say, and I didn't want to hear it. "What is it?" I asked anyway.

"Take Ethan and go."

"I'm not leaving you here."

"You have no choice. You need to go. I'll deal with this."

"How?" It slipped out as tears rolled over my cheeks.

"Just do as I ask for once," she begged. A beatific smile spread over her face. "Promise me that you will find his Wielder, that you will make sure that he fulfills his destiny and becomes the man I wanted to raise."

I nodded. Tears blurred my vision. I kissed her knuckles in succession, one through ten and ten through one. Salty sweat and coppery blood mingled on my lips. Ethan huddled next to his mother. Crying. She touched his face softly. "Ethan, be a good boy for your dad. I love you." She looked at me. Her eyes nailed me to the wall. "You too," she mouthed.

"I love you more."

She smiled, then her face froze. "Now go."

I got up and yanked Ethan up behind me. The boy screamed, not wanting to leave his mother's side. But we had no choice. I had to protect him.

Bullets missed us by inches as we ran deeper into the house.

Bullets still followed us. A potted plant exploded, spilling black soil onto the coffee table a few feet from me. An arc of violent holes peppered the drywall of the hallway beside Ethan. I pulled him into the sitting room around the corner a millisecond before the carved crown molding shredded away as if bitten into by a vicious giant with tiny missile fangs. I came to a halt.

Bullets hit part of the opposite wall. My shoulder was soaked in my own blood. I had the shakes. Bad.

Ethan was behind me. His face was covered with snot and tears. He was still bawling, but he knew his mother's fate.

The gunfire ceased.

I peeked around the corner and saw Natalie getting up. I knew she'd told me to run, but I couldn't leave her.

One of her arms clutched her stomach wound; the other was starting to spin around in a circular motion. Like a lopsided windmill. Ethan sobbed for her. "Shush," I ordered. I heard magazines sliding into rifles, several all at once. Not a reprieve. Just a reload. She wasn't going to make it.

The movement of her hand finally caught the wind. It was blowing now. Stronger and stronger.

Objects moved in the air, debris from the exploded cars or the damage from the gunfire or the loose earth and rocks from the earth wave. I heard the groan of something that wasn't... natural.

We had to get out of here.

My wounded wife was busy bending the wind to form a tornado.

I grabbed Ethan and shielded his body underneath mine. Natalie's tornado picked up momentum. It was a funnel now. Wind and earth and sheer destruction. It marched toward the gunmen like a sentient being. The screams of our attackers mixed with the howling of the wind. Trees, the shed, and even the teetering Jeep groaned and squealed as the wind tore them apart. The remaining shooters screamed as it took them. Their voices were drowned out in the gale.

But it started to come back in the direction from which it had come. Like a demented boomerang, the tornado was headed right for us.

"No!" I yelled. I covered Ethan's head but my eyes remained glued to the scene.

Natalie flung her hands back and I watched in horror as she levitated and blew away.

"Natalie!" I cried. My body shook with Ethan's. I just sat there holding my boy until I realized that the tornado wasn't moving away. It still came for us.

I grabbed Ethan. "Run, boy, run!"

"Not without Mom," he yelled back.

"Your mother is gone." The angry tornado she'd bent from a slight breeze drew closer.

It was eating the front part of the house. We slipped out the back.

I sprinted toward the truck and pushed Ethan in first. I told Ethan to get behind the seat. The boy listened.

The tornado was starting to feed on the farm house. She'd created it in desperation. It was a wild thing. We weren't going to make it. I wasn't going to fulfill my wife's last wishes.

I cranked the ignition but the junk engine wheezed and coughed. The truck didn't want to start, no matter how hard I tried.

"Start!" I cussed and swore. I turned the ignition again. *Start, damn you!*

The entire vehicle was being dragged across the ground toward the hungry tornado now. I closed my eyes and started to pray.

"Our God, who art in heaven, Thy Kingdom come, they will be done... forgive us our trespasses as You forgive us."

The movement of the truck stopped and just like that, the tornado shifted.

My heart stopped. I held my breath. As unpredictable as my Natalie, the tornado changed course.

Leaving us and the detritus of what was left of our lives behind.

2

7 YEARS LATER
ETHAN

"C'MON, YOU NITWIT," Sedgwick yelled. He was the drill sergeant from hell. But luckily for me, I wasn't the nitwit of the moment.

"You have your Element. Take him down!" he spat at Ed, my opponent.

Ed came for me as Felix wielded him fire from the sideline.

I ducked the searing balls of flame that he threw at me. I jumped on him, pinning him down. Cheers erupted from the bleachers.

He tried to go with a burning technique, but I saw it coming. I pinned down the hand that was stretched to grab my arm. The heat in his palm scorched the hair on my legs, but it was nothing I couldn't handle.

Soph's shrill whistle overrode Sedgwick's shouts. I looked up as a fire extinguisher left her arms and came hurtling my way.

I launched to my feet, caught the extinguisher, and in a few seconds, white fluff covered Ed's entire face, and torso, cooling him down.

Ed grunted, fuming. He wiped his face from the foam.

The class burst out in laughter.

Ed flung white foam on the floor. I kept the empty extinguisher in my hands, the sides of my mouth curved slightly as he threw another bitch fit about how I, a common guy with no ability, beat his ass once again. "That is cheating," he insisted.

Sedgwick scowled at Ed with his arms folded. "You have an ability you can use, yet Ethan still gets the upper hand each and every time. How is that possible?" he grunted, inches from Ed's face.

"He's fast and slippery like a slug."

"Then become a slug," Sedgwick roared. One of his veins running from his neck to his temple was going to pop at any moment.

Ed flinched, which made all of us suppress our laughter.

"Get out of my sight," Sedgwick said through gritted teeth.

Ed ran in the direction of the locker, cussing all the way. Felix followed close behind, shaking his head.

Sedgwick looked at me, his expression dead serious. Then he smiled. "The fire extinguisher," he said and turned to the Californian babe slash tiger I had the pleasure of calling my girl, "was a brilliant move, Soph. Don't let me catch you helping him again."

"He would've found a way to get to the extinguisher eventually," she sang with her hands in the air dramatically.

Everyone laughed again. Sedgwick addressed the class. "Go take a shower. It was entertaining. Don't forget, practice patience. The Wielder and Bender Annual Celebration is weeks away, people. We have investors to impress."

Students scattered in the direction of the showers. I was on my way to pursue them when a meaty hand hit my chest and pushed me to stop. Sedgwick blocked me. Our faces were inches from one another. "I'm counting on you, Sutcliff."

I grinned, cocky. "Don't you always?"

"There is always a time for firsts. Don't disappoint me."

"Never," I said.

He lowered his hand from my chest and jerked his head toward the showers.

Soph leaned against the wall in front of the girl's locker rooms, speaking to Leanne. She slapped me hard on the ass with her towel. "Nice moves, Golden Boy," she flirted. She disappeared behind Leanne into the girl's showers, her pale blond locks bouncing against her shoulders.

I grinned from ear to ear. I knew Ed wasn't going to let me forget it that easily. I'd have to find a way to make it up to the poor soul eventually... or not.

He called me a cheat.

He had an ability where I had none.

I sauntered into the locker room. The five guys in the club cheered. I lifted my hands and took the win with pleasure. A few slap shakes and shoulder jabs and I was free to take my shower in peace.

I let the steaming water rush over my body.

The institute looked to outsiders like a boxing club, and not a place where Benders and Wielders Trained. It was protected by a glamour that would vanish if you recite any spell. They taught us everything from how to block a punch to bend an element. Okay, so it looked like it was built in Roman times, had a bit of a Greek architecture, but that was as special as it went, if you didn't count the glamour

I wasn't always gift-free.

I used to own an element just like all of them.

When I was ten years old, I got the element of earth to play with. I could wield it, could make flowers grow, even trees—a willow to be precise—even if it was by accident.

For four years, I learned as much as I could from the element I had to bend one day.

It was a strong ability. Everyone had wanted to train me, and that was how I ended up here with Sedgwick and Mira, two Benders who were part of the Peer program. A program that would look awesome on my résumé one day.

I even at one stage had the Sentinel's attention. Dad still believe that they weren't real, a myth to keep the Necrocretors at bay. But I knew they were out there, watching for the right time to intervene. I felt them close by, saw them in the form of a raven or a bat watching me. They were there.

I built a name for myself among my own kind.

In class, when someone asked me my bend (which was a smart word for element, really), I would say earth. Gasps always followed.

I was kicking ass everywhere I went. And then just before my fifteenth's birthday it all disappeared because I didn't find my Wielder.

I didn't even know if he or she existed. That was the crappiest part of this duo, this team, a greater power forced together.

Benders couldn't do shit without their Wielders. There was nothing to bend if the Wielder couldn't wield it.

Well, Dad could, and Mom could... but it was a loophole. They'd discovered that they didn't need their Wielders. All Dad needed was his Zippo and Mom, nothing more than a light breeze.

But I was out of luck. There was nothing that could manipulate the growth of a plant or moving of tree roots burying deep in the ground, apart from their own, very slow process, growing. Nothing accept a Wielder.

So, for the past almost three years, I had gotten used to

being normal—or as close to normal as I could. The day I lost my ability to bend earth was the day I became disabled. It felt as if someone had cut off one of my limbs.

I had to keep my name high somehow. I clung to that old saying. *It's hard to get what you want, but harder to keep it...* Well, it was something like that.

The only thing I could do was to fight my way through the old-fashioned way: by kicking the living shit out of whoever I faced in the ring, with or without my bend.

News spread even faster.

I was the boy without an element, and I still whopped the snot out of my opponents. I became what Sedgwick and Mira called their Golden Boy.

At the annual WABA Celebration, investors would come and we would update them on why they paid good money to keep our institute, one of many, open. I usually was the cherry on top. This year wasn't going to be any different.

I finally finished with my shower and went to my locker to put on my sweats and muscle tee.

I was one of the last ones to leave. As I exited the lockers, I found Soph waiting for me. She wore tight jeans and a tank top and was biting her lower lip in that way that drove me crazy.

Could she be any hotter?

I grunted. She laughed, standing on her tiptoes, reaching up to kiss my lips.

"You need a ride?" Her voice was filled with double entendre.

"If you don't mind," I mimicked her.

She laughed and wrinkled her nose. "We are talking about just a lift, right?"

I chuckled and nodded.

"Well, then I'm sure Leanne would do it for that beautiful smile of yours."

I blushed and her laughter chimed in my ears. Incredible how she still found a way to make me blush.

I texted Dad that I was getting a lift.

Leanne was waiting for us outside. She was an air Bender. Red hair and light blue eyes. I put her into the pit bull category. She was always backing Soph up with vicious barks.

Her Wielder was Annie. Those girls had been paired as a team longer than any of the rest of us. Annie was an even feistier redhead, her eyes green. In the caricatures of my mind's eye, Annie's pit bull had two heads.

Soph's Wielder was Sam. He was one of the royals—or at least, his family saw themselves as royals. Yes, the witches and warlocks had them too, but Sam's family wasn't really in that category. They just thought they were.

Soph liked him, but I had no idea what she saw in him. Except maybe that he let her play with his fire in a nonsexual way.

I climbed into the back of Leanne's convertible with Soph. The evening had that warmth in the air. The humidity was high, typical for a Summer night in Billings, Montana.

Annie hopped in front. An alternative rock band I'm sure would be famous one dayblared from the radio as Leanne spun away.

My lips found Soph's. I could kiss this girl forever. She could easily become my forever too.

The car came to a stop but we didn't. A few seconds later I got hit on the arm by a baseball cap. With a wet suction sound, we disengaged from each other as I rubbed my shoulder in mock pain.

Leanne and Annie laughed. "Bye, Ethan. See you tomorrow," they sang. Tomorrow was the first day of school again.

I got out and leaned over to say goodnight to Sophie. "Text me... all night," she said. I winked and the car peeled away.

I sighed contentedly and walked toward the front door of our black coal, that sometime have the ability to change my mood just by staring at it, two-bedroom house. We'd lived here for the past seven years. Ever since Mom died.

I missed her. Dad didn't speak much about her.

I opened the front door and walk in.

The smell ofspaghetti à la Jeff, more like a spaghetti à la mess, came from the kitchen Between stirring the red tomato slop in the steaming pot and sipping a bottle of beer, Dad was watching the news.

I sighed as the woman speak about another missing person. Something horrible was happening with the Supernatural race. Guardians are going missing and vampires. Most of the vampires are known in the human race, it's their way of blending in, hiding myths humans thought were only real in storybooks.

Peter St. Clair, a very respectable business man and also a royal among the vampires went missing.

Dad believed with all of his heart that Necrocretors was behind this, and that witches was going to be next. He kept taps on this since the second it started.

What did they wanted with Guardians and vampires. Was the Necrocretors behind this?

Dad switch off the T.V the minute he saw me standing in the door way. Why he always tried to protect me from all the shit, I don't know?

"HOW WAS TRAINING?" He opened the fridge, took out a soda and threw the can my way.

I caught it and opened it in one flick. "Good. I kicked Ed's ass." I slurped my Coke.

"The fire Wielder." Dad had a huge grin on his face. "That's my boy." He leaned forward with his fist suspended in the air. "Fist punch."

I gave Dad my best unimpressed-Ethan-Sutcliff glare. "Dad, you just hold out your first, you don't need to say fist punch."

"Don't let me hanging."

I shook my head and punched his fist. "It's *leave* me hanging."

"You hungry?" He took two deep ceramic bowls out of the cupboard.

I gestured at my sweats. "Mind if I change?"

"Sure, go ahead."

I went up to my room and put on my PJs. Just as I pulled a worn cotton tee over my head, the buzzer of my phone went off.

A smile spread on my face. It could only be one girl. I fell on my bed and opened her text. It was a picture of her wearing those sexy new PJs of hers.

She was perfect. Perfect hair. Beach blonde with sun-kissed skin. It's why I called her a Californian babe. She had a body of surfer girl and the look of someone who spent hours every day on the beach.

I typed back, *Mmm*. And sent it.

My head fell on the pillow and for a second, just a second, I closed my eyes.

I didn't even hear the second buzz from my phone.

I was just too tired. I fell asleep.

A SOFT COLD breeze brushed against my cheek.

I opened my eyes immediately as it was wrong to feel this cold during summer nights, which was usually sticky and make one feel the need to take more than two showers a day.

I thought I would find myself in a dark room, on my bed, with probably a window open, slight drool patch on the covers, but no.

I found myself outside. Somewhere in the woods. Woods that didn't look familiar.

I rubbed my arms as the cold spread into my bones. A puff of smoke leave my mouth as I breathed.

Where the fuck was I?

I scratched my head, frowning blearily. I remembered going to bed, seeing that hot picture of Soph. Then I must have fallen asleep.

Pine needles poked me in the back of the head and I pulled them out, wincing at the sting of their sharp tips. The scent of earth, a scent that called to my soul, was thick in the air. I wasn't dreaming. This was too real for a dream. I got up.

The only light in the sky was the moon. I hadn't seen the moon that big or that bright in a long time. The stars glimmered brightly too. There were so many. *Where am I? How did I get here?*

A rustle in the trees caught my attention. Wary, I turned to look. But I saw nothing. I seemed to be deep in a forest, right on the edge of a huge clearing surrounded by stately oaks and graceful maples and stubborn pines.

Hey, I was an earth guy. I knew this kind of thing.

Then in the distance I saw something. The dark silhouette of something flying toward me. Something big with rapidly flapping wings. A bird? An eagle? Definitely bigger than a bat. I squinted, but the more I focused, the less clearly I could make it out.

I ducked behind the fat trunk of a pin oak and watched as the bird came to a perfect landing in a nearby tree.

It was an owl, and it wasn't really that big. It had seemed so huge as it neared, but so small when it landed... Shivers rose on my arms. This was more than a little freaky.

The owl looked around. Its luminous gold eyes scanned the woods and gave me the creeps. I stayed hidden; something deep inside me didn't want to be found by that owl.

It stopped looking around, spread its wings, and took a few awkward steps forward.

Faint light glinted from something around its neck, but that wasn't the freaky part. I sucked in my breath as the bird started to grow—and grow, lengthening and tripling, quadrupling, quintupling in size.

My mouth fell open. A young woman replaced the owl's form. She was a shifter. Another race in the family of the witches. They shifted into animals, mostly owls or ravens.

I had never saw one up this close. Only my dad ever spoke about the witch shifter race. He's known one a long time ago.

I couldn't see the woman's face. Despite the crazy big moon, she was under dappled shadow of a hoody, and the blinding light in the locket around her neck looked as if it was getting anxious to escape the golden trap.

I took a step to the side and a twig snapped under my shoe. The woman's head jerked my way. I hunched behind the tree and held my breath.

She spoke softly to someone. Someone who wasn't there a few minutes ago.

I went down on my haunches and retreated further behind the tree. I held my breath.

Rapid footsteps pattered over leaves toward me. Then, inches from my hiding place, it stopped.

I could smell something, like dirt and dust and fur. The image of a vicious animal formed in my mind. Fear I never felt before rippled goosebumps all over my flesh.

Puffs of hot breath in the chilly night air as something breathedright next to my tree. Yet... nothing was there.

My heartbeat felt louder than a drum.

Then the footsteps padded back to the woman.

I breathed out and my burning lungs thanked me. My heart steadied. I rubbed my arms again trying to get warmth into my body.

I peeked around the tree once more. The woman no longer peered into the woods and seemed satisfied that there wasn't anyone around. Sweat beaded my brow. *Close one.*

She opened the locket and a shaft—no, a beacon—of intense light flooded the clearing and illuminated the trees.

I shielded my eyes and sought refuge a few more trees deeper into the woods.

What *was* that?

I felt like we were standing on top of a disco ball. Bright colors—greens, pinks, purples, yellows—all danced off the trees around me. It was as if this woman had stolen the northern lights and trapped the entire phenomenon in her locket. And now she was finally setting it free.

I gaped at the spectacle of the woman—now just an outline against the light—walking forward as the light poured from her locket.

It was simply amazing. I couldn't take my eyes from it. I'd never seen anything like it.

Something trickled against my calf and I glanced down.

Fog and mist covered the ground. It ran unnaturally fast toward the lady. My eyes widened as the smoky tendrils swallowed her first, then the light.

White fogwas sudden and complete. I couldn't even see the tree I was hiding behind. I couldn't see inches in front of me.

Everything vanished in a blanket of white clouds.

Rumbling approached. Flashes of light shine through the

fog. The colors still seeped through here and there, mixed with the lightning.

The rumbling became stronger, louder. My brain tried to process what was happening..

The earth quivered. Hard. The force made me lose my balance and I grabbed onto the tree trunk. My breath came in short, excited bursts. This was what I had been born to do. What I had lost.

I hugged the tree as it vibrated right through me, to my bones. It shook so hard, I felt as if it was going to wake up my lost element.

That thought elated me. I hugged the tree harder. I shut my eyes. The earth bucked. My ears filled with the sound of something heavy dragging across the ground.

I felt suddenly small. I didn't know why. What the hell was this?

The earth shook for a long time. Then it stopped. My eyes snapped open. Nothing happened. Slowly I could make out the rough bark in front of me.

The fog started to retreat. The outline of the woman reappeared, but she wasn't alone.

She had brought something with her. From... wherever she'd been in that roiling cloud of fog and light. Something humongous lurked right behind her.

I gasped as I realized the woman had conjured a castle from the fog—or maybe the fog had brought it. You never know with witches.

"What the fuck?" My voice popped out much louder than I'd intended. I hid behind the tree again.

The woman yelled a command. Footsteps scurried fast toward me again. I wasn't going to be as lucky this time. *This might be my only window to escape.*

I started to run as fast as I could. Fleeing something I couldn't see.

My heart raced. The adrenaline that pumped through my veins lent me strength and my legs pumped faster. Still the foot-steps were right behind me... and then the sound vanished.

Something hard connected with my back and I sprawled to the ground, arms and legs askew.

I jumped up, and found myself in my bedroom. *What the...* Still panting, I patted myself down for injury. What just happened?

It was a dream.

You had a dream.

But if that were true, why was I still so terrified? Was it because of the invisible creature that hunted me, or the woman who dragged an entire palace from the fog? It had been so vivid. Something lingered around that type of magic.

I didn't know what the dream meant. Or what was chasing me, pouncing on me just before I woke up. It had felt so real.

I went to the bathroom and splashed my face with cold water from the faucet. Droplets clung to the whiskers along my jawline.

The clock told me it was three. I huffed. Ironic. It was called the witching hour.

Back in my room, I plopped down my chair behind my laptop and started hammering at the keyboard.

This had to mean something. A quick keyword search and I opened a few tabs on dreaming about owls. In another tab I searched for witches and invisible pets.

I clicked on a few of the dreaming sites. None of them was what I was looking for. A bunch of New Age nonsense. I cleared the search and typed in another short description. Back to the other tab, I clicked a promising link about witches and invisible pets.

Buried low on the page was something the site authors referred to as a wisp. It was a cat, but not a cat. The artist's rendering showed something more or less the height and build of a great dane. That was one mother of a cat.

Wisps were rare, the page explained. Only one would be born to any given witch family. They were hunted like demons in the Salem witch trials. They'd been wiped out almost to extinction.

I scowled. Mankind was so stupid.

They could go invisible, spy on humans in their catlike forms, or carry messages between witches in times of danger without being detected.

In some cases, wisps were guardians, too. One photograph was of a cat sitting on a chair, glowing in the dark.

Had it been a wisp that attacked me?

I exited that tab and went back to the results for owl dreams. I finally scored. I read the words on my computer fast and as I kept going, the fine hairs on my arms started to raise.

I looked up from the computer and stroked my stubbly jaw.

It said here that dreaming about owls meant a change. More drastically, my life was about to change.

3

ALEX

"ALEX," my mother's voice called from the hallway. "Get ready, sweetheart."

I glanced out the window to the garden, where my cat was playing with a butterfly. She had to glamour here true form. Half the size smaller than what she truly was, more the height of a cocker Spaniel, as she was actually not a cat at all. She was our family tree's Wisp, had been since the beginning of time and she was well, almost a thousand years old if not older. At this very moment she was glamoring herself as a black cat, but her true form was quite the opposite.

I had never owned a pet before in all my sixteen years.

My cat's name was Fibbs—because she was a bit of a lie. She had been my aunt Ariel's companion for a long time.

There weren't many wisps left. They were ancient. Some saw them as protectors to witches and warlocks. Many saw them as bad omens

Fibbs was sort of a generational hand-me-down, having

belonged to the first in our branch of the family tree, don't know how many generation ago.

Seeing Fibbs play like a normal housecat in a garden was magical all by itself. The garden was far from lifeless. Butterflies fluttered like bits of colorful paper on the wind. Dewdrops formed perfect spheres on the leaves. The early sun refracted rainbows of color in the thousands of pearls. It looked like we were growing diamonds among the fragrant flowers.

For the past two weeks, I couldn't stop staring. At everything. Just the sheer joy of observing everything that was going on around me had become one of my favorite things.

For sixteen—well, almost seventeen—years, I lived in aunty Ariel's locket.

I know if I said this aloud to a human, they would think it bizarre, crazy... impossible. But it was true. I had existed inside a locket that hung from a thin golden necklace.

It wasn't just me: my father and mother; Louis, Dad's hard-headed Wielder; and a couple of tutors lived there too. Inside, the locket was spacious. It housed a sixteenth-century palace with a garden, an indoor pool, and the woods where I could wield my ability.

But there was no wind. No seasons. No change other than sunshine and nighttime. The sun didn't provide any warmth. Sticky, hot, stuffy, stale air threatened to choke every breath I took.

Artificial air conditioning and the swimming pool were our only ways to cool off.

Beyond the woods, it just ended. It was a wall that ran up as far as I could see. No one could go futher. At times, it felt so small. Cramped. As if I couldn't breathe.

And that was it. My life inside a locket.

I knew my parents tried to make it feel real, and it sort of was real.

Aunt Ariel shared a name with the titular character in my favorite cartoon growing up. But she was no mermaid. She was an owl.

She was part of the shifter witch race and could transform into an owl at will.

Her sister and my mother, Meredith, was a fire Wielder who had lost her Bender a long time ago. He didn't die... their story just didn't end on a happy note.

My life may have been sheltered, but even I understood that it was rare in the community of witches to have one Wielder daughter and one shifter daughter.

When I was born, it made things even more uncommon. My very existence shone a spotlight on our entire family. Put a target on us. Because I was the rarest witch of all: an earth Wielder.

Earth Wielders were powerful. We could tap into Nature itself. We could see through animal eyes, communicate with them as we aged. We could manipulate trees, plants, and the very earth itself.

I YAWNED AND STRETCHED, watching the sunlight shimmer in Fibbs's sleek coat. Despite Mom's nagging call, something about watching the breeze in the flowers, the sun in the dew, and the lazy circuit of the butterfly made me reflect on all the global and historical circumstances that had led me to this moment.

Witches and their cousins, the jinns, had been the very first supernatural beings. Through witches, vampires were created, potions went horribly wrong, werewolves were born. Humans caught in the crossfire crafted garbled, untrue stories to explain things. They blamed the Egyptians' god, Ra, but in fact it was the fault of witches.

Jinns, the wishing masters, lost their chalice, and lost the ability to grant wishes. They were no longer seen as part of our race. Dad said that they lost their will to live; some committed suicide while others went stark raving mad.

Wielders and shifters weren't the only witch races, for that matter. Alchemists concocted warlock potions that could brew the end of the world or foment world peace if they wanted. Both deadly spells that one should not mess with, not if you want to become a Necrocretor.

Spellbinders were the final witch race. They wrote spells, wove magic, and used words to manipulate the fabric of reality. They even made the alchemists' potion recipes rhyme. Spellbinders and Alchemists clicked together and were protected by a complete different guardian race, other then what Wielders have.

And earth Wielders, well, we were supposed to rule all of them. To keep the balance between all of them.

Pretty much all the supernatural races that didn't want to be bound and tight down, saw earth Wielders and earth Benders as a threat. We were too powerful. We could limit them. And so, for centuries, my kind was exterminated by supernaturals jealously guarding their own sovereignty for fear of being controlled or brought to justice for misdeeds. No one loves the certainty that there was someone else far more powerful than they. And so my very existence made it a near certainty that we would be targeted by assassins and mercenaries every waking moment. The Necrocretors,. the evil ones. The monsters that didn't play by the rules, that didn't want to be ruled. They were mainly behind our murders. Necrocretors consists of a group of rogue supernaturals.

The vampires that didn't want to feed under the radar and

hide; they wanted humans to know they existed as they preyed on fear and weakness.

Werewolves hated being forced into lockdown when they grew crazy every full moon. They felt it particularly unjust since they'd been valiant protectors until an unbreakable curse had been placed on them. They loathed the suffering and the stigma of having to be caged when the curse reared its ugly head every twenty-nine days. Some called it balance as the werewolves were just so damn perfect, protecting humans from vampires. So, after the curse, they had to go on lockdown every full moon; otherwise they would kill innocents.

Another shifter race that Mom said wasn't beautiful to look at also comprised this group of evil rebels. They could shift into any human form. Most had violent tempers and didn't like to be told what they could and couldn't do. Necrocretors groups with these shifters were the biggest threat, because the shifter could pretend to be your best friend and you wouldn't know it until it was too late.

Some witches had gone to the dark side, too. Alchemists who couldn't master the true potions they wanted. Spellbinders ordered to burn their destructive spells. Shifters forced to give up a life of frolicking with humans unwilling to keep our races a secret. Wielders because of their dark Benders.

Every single monster had a weakness, and the Wielders' weakness came in the form of their Benders. This was called the resistance.

I sighed. Thinking about this made me anxious.

Though it seemed stupid to me, not resisting our Benders opened Wielders—not just earth Wielders but all the element Wielders—to dangerous heights of power. Wielders who didn't resist became drunk on that power, felt like gods, made godly decisions about who lived and who died.

I wouldn't be able to resist my Bender; and he or she wouldn't be able to resist me either.

The part that sucks the most, loving your Wielder, getting physical, took its toll on us Wielders. We labored under our own draconian rules: it was forbidden to love our Benders. That was the resistance, the test that I was destined to fail, the test that could make me descend to be a Necrocretor.

Mom worried constantly about that too. She said whoever my Bender was would never be able to resist me. That I had to be the strong one. Because earth Wielders were blessed—cursed?—with unnatural beauty.

I had raven-black hair with midnight blue eyes. My skin that had never seen real sunlight looked sun-kissed. I was tall and slender, more like a runway model than someone who'd been on the run most of her life.

The reason my mom and dad and aunt Ariel decided to imprison us in her locket for sixteen years was to protect me from the Necrocretors. And to prepare me for the time that I have to meet my Bender. Whoever they were.

Aunt Ariel became our Keeper until it was time for me to find my Bender. If I found him or her—if he or she had not already been slaughtered—together we could grow stronger and fulfill our destiny.

Mom's favorite hobby outside wielding fire was spellbinding; she had a special knack for glamour conjuring. Between the two sisters, they devised a con when I was just a baby. A plan to protect all of us until my seventeenth birthday.

Mom hexed Ariel's locket. She gave Aunt Ariel part of my earth element, which she took to an alchemist to make a slam—temporary empowerment.

All witches could use slams in any form. Alchemists brewed them, spellbinders usually conjured them, and the others? Well, like my mom, they could watch and learn.

We were all born into a certain race but most of us could study and learn a secondary or tertiary power. Like mom loved spellbinding, even though she was a Wielder and aunt Ariel loved brewing potions, easy ones though.

"Alex!" Mom's voice was right behind me. I jumped. "Earth to Alex. We need to go."

AROUND FIVE, just as the afternoon sun was starting to set, I started to get ready for tonight's WABA Celebration.

I scurried to my bathroom and washed my face. I rushed back to my bedroom to step into the indigo dress that mom planned me to wear to the Wielders and Benders Annual Celebration—the WABA Celebration.

Aunt Ariel made plenty of jokes about that name. I smiled as I thought about my aunt. She was so much younger in spirit than Mom. She was carefree, even though she'd protected all of us for almost seventeen years.

I had never seen her before she pulled us out of the locket two months ago. But because she had been temporarily gifted my earth wielding powers, we'd had a special bond. Because of that, I'd always heard her. Her voice was the one in the back of my head. The one that sometimes sang to me, or told me stories about the world, or even peppered my dreams with the things that she saw. I'd lived through many of her stories.

The day I'd finally met her was a day I would never forget.

It had been late at night. That entire week before we escaped Aunt Ariel's locket, I had suffered insomnia. I was too excited to sleep.

Excited to be finally become part of the world I'd been learning about my whole life.

It felt different as we all exited.

The air was hot but fresh, not as stale as the locket.

A soft, breeze blew in my hair. The stars glimmered brighter, and the moon too seemed vibrant. Not even Mom could conjure the beauty of the real moon.

And right underneath it, yards away from all of us, stood Aunt Ariel in all her glory. Tears stung my eyes. I ran as fast as I could toward her.

Mom called me back in a scolding tone, but her voice trailed off as she realized whom I was running to. A friend. Our keeper. Our blood.

I connected hard with Ariel's body and she wrapped her arms tight around me. She spun me around. "Look at you!" She pushed me away and grabbed me again. "You are gorgeous!" she yelled.

"Ariel," my mother hissed.

She rolled her eyes at mom and waved it off. "Oh, Meredith, still as pruney as ever. We are safe. Fibbs and I made sure of that. Nobody for miles, sister. Stretch out and enjoy the night. Welcome back to reality. How was the locket?"

Mom didn't say anything. She just grabbed her sister and held on. It was clear she never wanted to let go.

Fibbs? Mom had mentioned her, and I couldn't help but wonder where she was.

The outline of an animal figure appeared behind Ariel. It became clearer as it walked toward us. At first I thought it was a small jaguar. But then the form of a huge spotted cat leapt into Mom's arms. She hugged it awkwardly. I could tell Fibbs was heavy.

Her paws were around Mom's neck as if hugging her back. They pressed their foreheads together. A loud purr rumbled from the gorgeous cat's belly.

"I missed you too," Mom said. She introduced her to me as our family wisp who would play the part of a normal pet. Or sort of normal, anyhow—as she could only hide herself as a medium size dog other then her humungous jaguar size, when we were in the company of humans.

Fibbs bowed in front of me..

"Her bowing toward you is a promise to protect you and to serve as a companion for as long she may live. You need to bow back if you accept her promise, Alex," Mom explained.

I LOOK at this giant cat, still in the bow position, and then I returned the gesture.

I was jolted back to the present by the touch of hands on my back, zipping up my dress. I turned around and found my aunt.

She was by far my favorite person in this world.

Her lips curved into a radiant smile. Her light brown hair was gathered up into an elegant bun with the lower part of her hair hanging in curls over her shoulder.

She wore one of Mom's diamond necklaces and a pale yellow satin dress that caressed her skin.

"Why do I have to wear this poufy one, and you get to wear that?" I pointed at her dress.

"Because I'm not the one who has to make an impression."

I looked at the ceiling. *Do I really have to do this tonight?*

"I know that look. C'mon, you'll be fine. Just smile. They'll be eating out of your palm in no time, or so Fibbs says. I happen to agree. You will come to see very soon that Fibbs is usually right about these sorts of things."

"Seriously, it can't be that easy."

"Honey." She pulled a stray curl back behind my hair. "Tonight you are going to learn just how easy it is for woman born with earth."

I hated that saying.

Mom said it, Dad said it, even my tutors said it all the time.

No, my sarcastic voice chided. *I don't look anything like them, even though father has my dark hair and blue eyes. No, I was born with earth.*

Whatever.

ETHAN

ONLY MINUTES BEFORE MY FIGHT.

I sat inside the locker room with a photograph of Mother in my hand.

I didn't know why I was thinking of her so much lately. But I missed her.

The way she used to chase me around the house, playing hide-and-seek. The way her pancakes tasted on a rainy day. The way we snuggled up and watched movies together under a blanket. The way she tucked me in at nights, telling me dazzlingly creative bedtime stories.

Dad wasn't bad. He just wasn't Mom.

I kissed her picture and sighed. I was sure that when she made my father promised to look after me, she hadn't pictured this.

The WABA Celebration had finally come.

Sedgwick had drilled us the past few weeks. Hard. Some of the Benders had passed out from exhaustion. No joke. Many parents weren't very happy with him.

The celebration was a black-tie event. Ice sculptures glittered under tasteful spotlights throughout the ballroom. A five-course meal was served on silver platters by a white-gloved staff.

Dad had a secret name for this special night. It wasn't the WABA Celebration. We called it the SUKA Celebration. Sucking Up and Kissing Ass.

Before I found myself in the locker rooms, dressed as someone who belonged in a fight club and not the Benders' Association, I too, had been wearing my tuxedo and black tie, smiling at the Wielder community, and sucking up to people in high places.

That was when I saw her.

She was chatting to Old Man Gezler, one of the Benders' Association chairmen, in a small group a few feet away from the one Dad and I huddled in.

I didn't know who she was, but I couldn't take my eyes off her.

I'd attended WABA every year and assumed after seven years I knew every single witch, warlock, and Bender there was.

Her, though... I'd never seen her before.

She was stunning. That was a word I didn't even use to describe Sophie.

No, this girl was not just beautiful. She took my breath away. I devolved into a stuttering zombie, addicted to her angelic face.

Her raven hair flowed in curls over a deep blue dress that matched the most magnetic eyes I've ever seen.

I stared at her like an idiot. When she finally looked at me, I just kept staring. I could tell that I was making her uncomfortable with my gawking.

Her gaze skittered away. From her polite but bored expression I could tell she was pretending to listen to one of Gezler's war stories from eons ago.

After the fifth or six time she glanced at me and found me still gaping, a soft smile tugged at the corner of her lips.

My own mouth mimicked her smile.

My father called my name. It was time to get ready for the tournament. For a split second I looked at him and nodded my consent. When I looked back her way, she was gone.

I sighed, a goofy grin plastered on my face. Who was that nameless fox?

I knew it was wrong to label girls as animals the minute I saw them. But it was a habit. And she was truly a fox.

For the first time, I was glad that I came to the WABA Celebration. I hoped to get another chance to see this fox and to learn her name.

But first I needed to re-kick the living shit out of Ed while Felix fed him fire to bend on me. It wasn't as scary as it sounded. I'd been training with the institute for so long without my element that it was a walk in the park.

Dad didn't want me to get my hopes up of receiving my element again. He figured my Wielder was already dead. He had a point. They never made it to their sixteenth birthday.

Even so, I sometimes secretly watched from the sidelines at the Wielders and Benders training together.

I envied Sam and Soph, although I hated Sam with every ounce of my body. He thought the sun shone out of his ass. It wasn't the sun, it was the devil with a torch.. Very easy to get the two mixed up.

Still, I would have given anything to get unstuck from this stage I was glued to and go somewhere in the direction of forward.

At least the institute wasn't my whole life. I still had a normal life away from the Benders' Association. Away from the paranormals I was born into.

Blend in, that was the rule. Ever since Mother's death, well, father thought it was safe to blend in closer to the Association Headquarters in Billings, Montana.

I was a senior at Sky View High, a jock to be exact. I played Varsity football and tried to be a regular human, even though I was far from it. If I was honest, I wasn't doing such a bad job at fitting in.

Wielders like Sam attended the private school up the mountain. Only witches and warlocks got in there. No need to advertise on billboards and in magazines.

Witches and warlocks were known to be vain. They loved limelight and praise. So yeah, they loved to tout their school as an elite private school. Their waiting list to get in probably stretched down to Florida.

The green light above my locker went on. Showtime. I prayed that tonight I wouldn't see my ass. Not with Miss Foxy sitting somewhere in the crowd.

4

ALEX

I LET out a long exhalation through my teeth. I didn't want to offend the Chairman of the Benders' Association who droned on and on about the fifty previous WABA Celebrations before this one. So boring.

Aunt Ariel had a smile I'd never seen on her face before. Her eyes traveled between me and the big-bellied, mustachioed man. I don't think that it was a genuine smile.

I tried to extricate myself as the Chairman laughed. But he touched my arm.

"Yes, yes, darling. I do remember that specific Celebration too. Old Ruckus was so intoxicating," he carried on, laughing with the woman who clearly wanted his attention. I wished her success so he would stop torturing me.

Over his shoulder, Aunt Ariel smiled again. I narrowed my eyes at her. *This isn't funny anymore. Rescue me from this overgrown potbellied pig!*

I cast my gaze around and found a guy staring in my direction. He was extremely tall and kind of cute with his messy dark blonde hair. I looked immediately away. My heart started to beat a few beats faster. *Keep it together,* I told myself sternly. I couldn't go mooning after every cute boy I saw now that I was outside the locket.

I shifted my eyes past the Chairman, whose name I had already forgotten. My mind whirred. Was that guy still watching me? It was hard to keep pretending to listen. I couldn't help it; my gaze found its way back to the cute guy. To my surprise, he was still staring.

What was he staring at? It couldn't be me. I didn't know him from Adam.

Chairman What's-His-Name laughed and the woman laughed too. I pretended to find his comments funny. I kept nodding but his words fell senseless on my ears.

I glanced in the guy's direction again. This was ridiculous. Was something stuck in my hair, some gigantic bug? Maybe I had spinach in my teeth. My tongue glided over my teeth, probing for any stuck food. It was a hopeless case.

I examined my dress. Nothing wrong or torn, no skin showing that wasn't supposed to, nothing hanging out.

I took another breath.

"Just enjoy it and work it, baby," Aunt Ariel had said while extolling the mumbo-jumbo perks of an earth Wielder.

Perks of an earth Wielder—was that what this was? I stared at her as she glided away from the woman she'd been speaking with, a half-empty glass of glittering champagne in her hand. She was supposed to grab me on the way.

My eyes caught the guy again. Still staring at me. There was something wrong with this guy.

"So you see, the decorations this year are made of plastic that is only glamourized to look like glass," prattled on Chairman What's-His-Name. "We couldn't risk the same catastrophe twice."

Please shoot me now, I begged as polite titters erupted around me. I stared straight at my mother, who had just joined our group.

Involuntarily, my eyes boomeranged back in the guy's direction.

"Ethan," a voice called. Nobody responded. The guy still stared at me, mouth agape. "Ethan," the man beside him yelled again. I couldn't help but start to smile. If Ethan was his name, this was getting awkward, yet a little flattering too.

Mom dutifully engaged Chairman What's-His-Name and I seized on my chance to escape. At that moment, I saw how a middle-aged man with dark brown hair yelled the name Ethan again and grabbed the staring mystery guy.

I couldn't help but laugh. I sucked out of the cluster of people fast and strode purposefully in the wake of my aunt. I doubted I'd get another chance to escape the clutches of boredom.

I reached her where she stood chatting with another group. They were a blur of well-bred smiles, diamond brooches, black bowties, and crystal goblets of cognac and champagne. The scent of floral perfumes mingled with the fumes of expensive alcohol.

She smiled serenely. "You made it."

"I thought he was never going to stop talking."

"Poor Meredith." She looked back at Mom. "You think we should go on a rescue mission?"

I searched for my staring cute guy. Ethan. He was gone. My gaze landed on Mom, who was laughing. "Nah, Mom can take care of herself." I hooked my arm with my aunt's.

She smiled at me and took another sip of her bubbly. "What was going on between you and that hottie?"

My eyebrows rose. "You saw that?"

"Honey, everyone saw that."

Heat flooded my cheeks. "Ugh, how embarrassing."

"I told you, the perks—"

"Yeah, yeah. Whatever," I cut her off.

A voice came over the sound system, instructing us to go find our tables.

Ours was way at the back. Mom joined us, playfully chiding us for leaving her with Old Man Gezler, right, that was his name.

The lights dimmed and the evening program was underway.

TO THINK that I'd been excited to come tonight. I eyed my aunt's disregarded glass enviously. Anything to stop the incessant boredom.

Speaker after speaker took the stage to delicate applause. Official after official prattling on about Wielders, rules, regulations, the however many thousandth year this had been. Dad and Mom soaked up each word.

There was an increasing chance that my brain was going to ooze out of my ears. I stifled my millionth yawn. But then a man came up and said, "Now the moment we've all been waiting for. Are you ready for some real Bender sparring?"

The crowd roared, the first time it had shown any liveliness all night. I perked up. What was this?

Two chicks took the stage and attacked each other, their Wielders feeding them their elements. Despite the excited cheers from the audience, the spittle and sweat flinging through the air, the sudden blast of screaming wind and rush of torrential water, I fell back in my chair, disappointed.

I couldn't watch these people beat each other up. To prove what? That they were worthy of being our protectors?

It was stupid.

I looked at Mom and wondered what she was thinking. Did she approve? I couldn't help but to wonder if *he* was here—her Bender.

She had been one of those Wielders who couldn't resist. Well, he couldn't resist either. They had fallen in love. Mom didn't care that it was forbidden. She loved her Bender as much as she loved my father. Maybe more.

His name was Jeffery Sutcliff. Their story was achingly lovely and sad as hell.

She'd shown me a picture of him once. Only once. He was a looker. Chestnut hair, eyes the color of chicory grounds, lean and powerful physique.

Never in history had one Bender paired with two Wielders... until Jeff Sutcliff. He could bend both Mom's fire and that of her best friend, Siobhan, at the same time. He was a badass from hell.

Just imagining what he looked like with both their fires in his hands, crawling up his torso, caressing his face, made me feel my mom's loss.

Siobhan, whom my mom referred to as a fiery redhead who was as stubborn as an ox, used to be Mom's best friend. Born from a rich witch family just like she was. But when it came to Jeff, the two couldn't find mutual ground.

Jeff had stood between Mom and Siobhan like a lightning rod.

The first time she told me that she was a Bender who had lost her Wielder, I'd thought she was pulling my leg.

Siobhan wanted him all to herself. Mom didn't want to share him either. It was an endless trio of who wanted whom.

Jeff saved Mom's life once. She refused to tell me how. After that, they both found it harder to resist the chemistry they shared. They stepped over the line. They got physical. They were crazy for one another.

She really thought he was going to choose her, but in the end Jeff chose Siobhan without giving Mom a real explanation, and the last Mom heard, Siobhan died because she was reckless and didn't listen to anyone, not even Jeff.

Mom ended up with no Bender. Each Wielder only got one Bender and that was that.

Dad—Frederick Burgendorf, whose family was viewed like pseudo-royalty among the Wielder race—took his opportunity in the wake of Jeff's abandonment and that was how they ended up together.

Tonight Mom was elegant as always. Mom paged through one of the program booklets that had been placed on the tables.

She wore a green gown tailored to fit her body like a glove. Her blonde hair sparkled with a discreet net of emeralds that matched her eyes. She looked like someone in her mid-twenties, and not a woman of almost fifty.

Dad was just as freakishly handsome. They fit so well together.

Aunt Ariel was speaking softly to Louis. He almost smiled, which would have been a first for my father's Bender of nearly thirty years.

None of them seemed to pay much mind to what was happening in the fighting ring on stage.

A blonde girl threw a redhead over her shoulder with a fierce yell. The other girl's body connected hard with the floor. I looked away again, my stomach uneasy. I flinched every time flesh slammed against flesh, every time someone dropped to the floor.

The reason why I'd been so excited drained from my mind. I clung to it now, trying to reclaim some of my former hopefulness. After all, Mom had assured me that if I have a Bender, he or she would be here tonight.

A PART of me was scared. Everyone that I knew kept telling me how hard it was for earth Wielders and earth Benders to pass the test of resistance. That if we didn't, we'd both be in danger of going dark. Really dark.

I still didn't understand why it would be so hard. Over the pastfew weeks, Mom and Dad had taken me to parties and introduced me to a lot of good-looking Wielders. They'd captured my attention for like five seconds until I realized they were all as shallow as the birdbath in the garden.

But battle after battle played out in front of us, and my optimism sputtered. Every one of those girls on the stage tonight showed their abilities, which meant that their Wielders were close by—and therefore none of them could be my Bender.

I sucked in breath as the blonde girl took a bad blast of wind. She couldn't breathe. I wanted to yell, "Enough!" But then the redhead finally relented.

The girl panted, gasping for air. She kneeled, her palms flat on the floor, her body heaving.

Applause filled the room. The referee strutted out on the stage. The blonde went over and helped her up. They shook hands and bowed. Everyone kept clapping as the air Bender was announced the victor of this round.

I hate this. Why do they let them fight and show off what their abilities can do?

They both headed down offstage. A teenage boy with dark hair walked up. The speaker introduced him as Ed Dreary. His element was fire.

My air pipe closed. I had witnessed what Mom could do with her fire... and that was with no Bender. It scared me at times. I saw another guy wearing a tuxedo. His hair was neatly comb. He was introduced as Felix Manfred. His wielder. Felix took off his jacket and tie and rolled up his sleeve as the speaker announced the other team.

"Facing the one and only Ethan Sutcliff."

Mom sucked in a sharp breath as the crowd started to cheer. A favour among the crowds I assume. Mom's fingers clenched the pamphlet as she searched it with urgent eyes. Then it hit me. He said Ethan. As in the guy who stared at me, and Sutcliff, as in Jeff Sutcliff?

Even Aunt Ariel craned her neck as she looked at the guy.

The guy sauntered out on stage.

My cheeks burned; I was glad for the dimmed lights. It was my creepy stalker from earlier. Okay, not creepy. The rather cute kind-of stalker. The one whose body went on for days. He was shirtless. His chest gleamed, the spotlight glinting over his eight-pack and rippling biceps and bulky pecs. *Oh my word.* My eyes scanned over every perfectly formed muscle.

Both guys were barefoot. His opponent's body was almost as chiseled. I could barely blink. I looked for his wielder. Nobody was in sight.

"What is Ethan's ability?" I whispered to my mother, as I'd been too busy drooling to listen to the referee.

She frowned at the booklet. "It says here he doesn't have an ability."

"What?" I whispered a tiny bit louder. Now even Dad was scrutinizing his booklet with intensity.

"He has no ability," Mom said again, sounding alarmed. "How can they do this?"

"A normal guy," I mouthed.

"Calm down, I'm sure it's just an error," Father said. All the same he angled toward the stage so that he could watch this fight.

I was getting nervous for this guy. *Fire against nothing? Is the Association insane?*

The bell gonged. The two guys faced off and circled each other.

Ed attacked first, but not with fire. With punches and kicks.

Ethan ducked and dove, rolling out of his grip like he was smeared with oil. Ed couldn't hold on to him.

Even from back here, I could tell his skin shone with sweat, not oil. In fact, his body was perfect. My eyes traveled lower, following the v-line of Ethan's Adonis belt that disappeared into his shorts. I found myself biting my lower lip. I shook my head to get out of this daze.

What the hell was happening to me?

I JERKED as Ethan jabbed a two-punch combo at Ed. It was so fast. The crowd cheered as Ed went down.

Felix was feeding finally fire, which made the crowd gasped more.

Ed's arms lifted and caught Felix's fire. It grew and grew until a fireball flew in Ethan's direction.

Ethan ducked and rolled. The fireball missed him by an inch and sizzled harmlessly against some invisible barrier that protected the crowd. Ethan went for Ed again.

"Show your ability. C'mon, where is your Wielder?" I muttered. Desperately searching for anyone feeding any form of element to him from the sidelines.

Still nobody showed. I couldn't watch but couldn't keep my eyes off them either. I craned my neck to see where Ethan's Wielder was one more time. Why did I even care? Was it his staring from earlier? His perfect body. This wasn't like me.

I grabbed Mom's arm and squeezed as he avoided another fireball. "Why isn't he showing his ability?"

"I don't know, unless..." She shook the pamphlet. "Unless this wasn't a typing error."

My father didn't take his eyes off Ethan either. Aunt Ariel and Louis watched the battle with rapt breathlessness.

Why on earth would they put a normal guy against a fire Wielder?

Ethan rolled out of the path of two more fireballs and onto his hands and feet. He leaped on Ed with his massive legs around his neck and threw him hard to the floor.

I gaped at his monkey moves. *Okay, that was hot.* I had to admit, this Ethan had some scary tactics.

He got up but Ed didn't. He prowled like a predator, waiting for Ed to stir, and when he finally did, Ethan went closer.

A referee climbed up on stage and took the mic to speak. Behind the referee, Ethan lent Ed a hand up. I couldn't believe how a normal guy with no ability had just beaten a guy who could bend fire. Fire, for crying out loud!

Ed slapped Ethan's hand away. Ethan shrugged with the same smile he'd bestowed upon me earlier. He faced the crowd, whose roaring applause nearly drowned out the referee's following words: "The winner of this round!"

A fireball the size of a soccer ball formed in Ed's hands. Before the referee let out another sentence, the flames left Ed's hands.

I jumped to my feet. "Behind you!"

Ethan turned around. He opened his hands to block the flames and the earth shook.

I fell back into my chair.

Everything that held me up waned underneath me. My head spun like crazy. A migraine, full-blown and searing, pounded in my temples. I grunted, growled through clenched teeth, and must have hissed a few words at my mom.

Energy drained me like someone had turned on a devastating spigot. I couldn't even lift my pinkie finger. What happened? I had no idea.

Sounds filtered through a long tunnel from far away, like I was miles from a concert listening to scraps on the wind. Voices were hollow. All I could see was the silhouette of my mother hovering over me as I lay in my chair. She touched my face, speaking to me though I couldn't make out the words.

My parents' blurry figures pivoted back to stare at whatever was happening on stage.

"Mom?" I said in a tired voice.

"Take her. Now," my father ordered Ariel in a grave voice. Then to Louis: "Make sure nobody follows you."

"It's going to be okay, Alex," Aunt Ariel said. She was so close to me. Louis picked me up. She looked past me, back to the stage. We moved fast in the opposite direction.

"What is going on?" I glimpsed the exit sign shown above my head. "What happened?"

Louis didn't answer me. "Bring the car around." He still sounded far away, ordering someone over his earpiece. Soon I felt cold air on my face.

Why was I so tired?

What happened?

Was Ethan okay? Did he stop the ball of fire?

I needed to know, but my questions didn't get answered. I was bundled into the back seat of the car, and before the vehicle hit the road, I slipped into unconsciousness.

5

ETHAN

MASSIVE, jagged cracks split the stage into three uneven pieces.

A huge tree—I shoved a fist into my eyes to clear them, but it was true—a tree—had shoved straight up through the platform and snatched my opponent in its rapidly growing, revolving branches. Ed's body levitated, trapped in branches and roots twirling around him like voracious snakes. One root jabbed him through the foot.

He screamed like a pig at slaughter. Tears streamed down his cheeks.

I couldn't think with the noise. My mind tried to make sense of what the hell was going on. Nothing fit. A million questions, one after the other, raced through my mind at the speed of light.

What was this? How? What happened? How? What does this mean? How?

Nothing made sense. *I am a Bender, not a Wielder?* How was this possible?

A slap to my back brought me out of my string of thoughts.

My dad had joined me on the shaky third of stage. He was... laughing. The head-back belly laugh. He hadn't laughed like that in a very long time. Maybe not since Mom.

I stared at him, mouth agape. Funny was the last thing this was.

"Dad," I finally mustered. "Why are you laughing? Ed's hurt."

"He is a weasel, trying to attack you from behind."

I shook my head. I remembered what I'd heard seconds before the earth had started quaking. I touched my head. Pain scissored across my temple.

"What is it, son?" Dad tone turned serious as he put his hand on my shoulder. It felt so cold. "You are blazing hot."

"What the hell is this?" I asked again. "I'm no Wielder."

I spun in a slow circle. The curtains in front of the stage podium were drawn shut. I didn't even notice when that happened. The fabric practically vibrated with the sound of a stampede of footsteps and shouted demands.

"Come, let's go to the locker room." My father led me out as couple of teachers from the institute started cutting Ed from the tree or the tree from the stage, whichever was easier.

"Dad." I couldn't wait until we were in the locker room. I had to know what the heck was going on. *Am I a Wielder?*

"Just wait two seconds, Ethan."

I nodded and followed him dumbly. He took me to where my tux hung still neatly inside my personal locker. He gently shoved me down to sit on the wooden bench. He left, told me he will be back in a sec. I obeyed. My mind reeled, trying to make sense of this. It couldn't.

A wail announced newcomers. Five men wheeled a stretcher attached to half a monstrous tree through the locker room to the physical therapy room way at the back. Ed writhed on the stretcher. They'd cut the tree from the stage; a root still protruded from his foot.

A trail of crimson blood marked his path. I could smell the coppery liquid and the earthy odor of sawed tree.

I felt bad. It had all happened so fast.

He was still screaming that deafening, chill-to-the-bone type of sound as if he was being burned alive.

Medical staff tried to calm him as they wheeled him into the farthest room way at the back. His screams died out as they closed the door.

They wouldn't be able to take him to the human emergency room. *I mean how on earth are you going to explain a tree growing around his body and one of the roots piercing him through the foot?* Luckily, doctors from the Association were on standby at WABA Celebrations, in case shit exactly like this happened.

My father came back in, carrying a bucket of ice cubes. He set it on the bench next to me. He took out a plastic baggie. I shook my thoughts away from the ice cubes. "Dad, how?" I demanded.

My father filled the plastic bag as he spoke. "I was on my way to the stage to congratulate you. It was probably one of the most brilliant fights I've seen in a long time, son." He sounded excited. "A fire Wielder and he didn't touch you once."

"I know, I was there." Annoyance, rather than pride, colored my voice. "What happened?"

Dad frowned.

I pressed my palm to my forehead. "One minute I'm up there listening to Sy announcing the winner. The next, something tells me to turn around and I see this huge ball of fire hurtling toward me."

"Son, everyone was yelling for you to turn around."

I shook my head. "No, this was different."

My father stared at me, not putting ice cubes in the bag anymore. "Was the voice male or female?"

"I don't know. I can't remember. But I listened. It was as if I had no choice." It had been the strangest sensation.

My father squinted and then a smile turned the corners of his lips upward. "Your Wielder finally came home."

I narrowed my eyes. "*What?*"

"It's the only thing that can explain any of this, Ethan. The signs are all there. The bending of earth. Why it's finally listening to you again. The spike in temperature of your body." He zipped the ice pack up and pressed it in the tense, hot space between my shoulder blades. I shuddered at the cold. "It's normal," he reassured me. "The extra source of power caused your core temperature to rise like that. It is power you could only have gotten from one supplier: your Wielder."

Shock trickled across my skin faster than condensation from the ice pack.

My father held my gaze. "The voice you heard. It's your Wielder guiding you, son. Even if that person had no idea that he or she was guiding you. Your Wielder is here tonight. We just need to find who it is."

MEREDITH

"IS SHE OKAY?" Frederick kissed my shoulder as I stared into Alex's room from the hall. She was asleep. Fibbs lay next to her. She'd grown fond of her the past few months.

I nodded.

"So it's *him*?" He had that tone in his voice.

I closed my eyes and sighed. "Frederick, I can't do this with you now. Please."

"I'm not picking a fight, Meredith." He sighed. "Isn't it

strange, how out of seven billion people on the planet, out of hundreds of millions of witches, the bigger power has to choose *him*?"

Huffing, I faced him with my arms folded. "You can say the name. A Sutcliff. It's not so hard, Frederick."

He pointed a finger at me and spoke in a hard whisper through clench teeth. "I have every reason to be affected by this, Meredith."

I took a deep breath. This was why I hadn't wanted to start this conversation. He would always find a way to turn everything around and make it about him. "I'm tired. Fight with me tomorrow over things I have absolutely no control over, please. Because tonight, I don't give a fucking rat's ass." I stormed past him.

I didn't even know if Ethan was related to Jeff at all. I knew that he'd gotten married a good twenty years ago after Siobhan's death to another Bender, but other than that, I was just as clueless as my husband.

Ethan could have been his if Jeff fathered a child. And that was what Frederick's problem was. That Ethan could be Jeff Sutcliff's son.

Jeff had always been an obstacle in Frederick's life. Ever since we were teenagers. Constantly fighting for my heart. Sometimes I wondered if Frederick wasn't still fighting for my heart.

I shrugged out of my dress and took a long shower.

Seeing Alex tonight in that royal blue dress had brought back a lot of memories. Where did all the time go? It went so quickly.

The other day she was still a baby crawling around in the house. Tonight she was a comely woman and no one could peel their eyes away from her.

When Ethan strode out on that stage, I had seen the hunger

in her eyes. The way she looked at him. Had they had some sort of a moment before that? Did she know him? It looked like it.

The minute I saw in the program that this boy had no ability, I was certain he would be my daughter's Bender.

The Association wouldn't put a normal human in the ring with a Wielder. No, this boy was far from normal. He'd merely lost his bend for lack of a Wielder.

Then they announced his name. I'd always known fate was a cruel mistress.

Two weeks ago, we'd decided it was time to emerge from Ariel's protection and into the open. To find Alex's Bender. To train the two to fend for themselves and protect each other.

I still had hope, though, that it wasn't him. That he wasn't an earth Bender. But then I saw how worried she got. The attraction was already there. I didn't want this fight for her. It was going to be already so hard, fighting off all the assassins sent to kill the earth pair.

The lights flickered off.

Silence.

I turned off the faucet, searching for my towel in the dark. My heart beat a thousand beats.

It's just a power outage.

We'd been so long under Ariel's protection, so far away from danger, that anything out of place made me paranoid.

I wiped the steam off the bathroom window and peered out. The closest house to the plantation was about a mile down the road. Their lights were shining in the distance.

My stomach churned. I didn't like this feeling.

I wrapped the towel around me and opened the door.

Everything was pitch dark, the hallways, the staircase. Not a single sound reached my ears. Frederick and Louis wouldn't have been this quiet if it was just an electrical problem.

The hair on my arms raised. Goosebumps flushed over my

skin. I looked toward Alex's room. Fibbs was at least protecting her. It wasn't far. If I ran really fast, I would make it in no time.

I took a deep breath and listened for any noise that could tell me my fear was only my imagination. That we were safe. That nobody was hunting my daughter. But then again Frederick would've found me already if it was just a blackout.

I sprinted to Alex's room.

I heard the power whooping in my ear, making that hollow sound before a Bender releases the Wielder's ability. It was strong. That type of power only belonged to one group: Necrocretors.

A fireball lit up part of the stairs and flew right at me.

I blocked it with my own fire, but a part of my power dribbled to the floor, making me stumble. I kept my balance and ran harder.

I slammed into Alex's door, opened it, and closed it hard behind me. She was still sleeping on the bed. Fibbs lay on top of her, hissing.

"It's only me," I said to the wisp.

She started to glow. Fibbs began forming a shield around Alex. I began an incantation even as I pushed all the heavy furniture I was strong enough to move against Alex' door.

It wouldn't help much. Maybe it would slow whoever wanted Alex down a few seconds, but with the spell I was reciting, it should be enough to buy me some time in figuring how to get my daughter to safety. How to save her life and help her see her seventeenth birthday.

A tapping at the window made me jump. A owl owl hovered in the air.

Where the hell were Frederick and Louis?

I opened the window and let Ariel in. She shifted back into her human form. Her feathers became the sixteenth-century dress that artists still loved to portray witches in. The garment fell over Ariel's body. We both rushed over to Alex's bed.

Ariel opened her locket and joined me in reciting the words of the conveying spell. I concentrated on Alex, and I knew Ariel did too. This spell only worked with utmost focus. I pictured where she had to go in mind's eye.

A time for everything
And to everything in its place
Return into the locket, where you'll be safe.
Through time and space.

Alex's body started to fade lighter and lighter. She was turning into shimmering dust, getting ready for the transport to the locket.

The first pound came from her door. I looked over my shoulder and stared with grave eyes at it. *How long before it shatters?*

Fibbs's shield wasn't nearly in place, but the cat was glowing like never before, protecting the family she was born and sworn to protect.

Ariel's soft hand touched my chin and turned my head to look back at her. We kept on reciting the spell.

More pounding at the door. It was so hard to concentrate. Alex wasn't fading fast enough.

I spoke the spell faster, with more meaning. As the door exploded into splinters, Fibbs's shield vanished. She turned invisible. She pounced on the attacker, a man in all black whose features I couldn't quite make out. He screamed as bloody slashes appeared on his cheek.

I fell on Alex's body to protect her... but touched nothing.

Ariel closed her locket. She spun around, shifting back into an owl. Two flaps of her wings and she was out the window. I could breathe again. My daughter would live to see another day.

The Necrocretor bared his teeth. A furious scream left his mouth as he hurled an angry fireball at me.

I blocked it. Barely. My strength waned. He was so strong and I had spent so much energy on the conveying spell. I fell to the ground.

Louis and Frederick loomed in the hallway behind the intruder, unseen. They stealthily made their way toward him. Over his shoulder, Louis nodded.

I met the gaze of the Necrocretors who stood over me. I mustered my little remaining power and hurled it past him.

He thought I'd missed my target and laughed an evil, gleeful laugh. The sound seeped through my bones. I shuddered.

Frederick wielded his water, and Louis bent it to swallow my fireball without killing it, making the impact of the shot so much stronger. The water would hit the Necrocretor first and then my fire would explode.

It was something Louis had picked up through the years. He couldn't bend my fire the way Jeff used to, but he could bend Frederick's water to transport my fire where he needed it. A handy trick for a Wielder without a Bender.

It hit the attacker straight into the back of his head. The blow flung me backward through a pane of glass and out onto Alex's balcony.

Frederick cried out my name, but Louis barked at him to stay his ground.

I could hear the Necrocretor pull himself up. They never died easily.

I hear the rush of Frederick's water as he wielded it, the power behind Louis's bending techniques.

Somehow, I started gaining some of my strength back. An annoying scream escaped me as I got up and started throwing my fire back inside Alex's room for Louis to use as he needed it. Frederick's water swallowed some of it, other bits exploded against the wall. I didn't stop.

Something hard collided with me. Both of us rolled down the stairs to the first-floor deck outside the kitchen.

It was the Bender.

I landed a few paces away from him. Without pausing to think, I pushed myself up and went into the kitchen through the door—how had that been unlocked?—trying to put as much distance as possible between Bender and Wielder. Not that it looked like this Wielder needed a Bender.

The Bender followed me, taking the bait. For such a powerful couple, they weren't that smart. You never split up the Bender and Wielder. It was rule number one. Then again, these two were dark. Like all Necrocretor witches, they believed they possessed the power of gods; why would they think that this rule ever applied to them?

I opened the fridge and the Bender hit it face-first.

My foot connected hard with his chest as I gave him a back-kick. He fell backward and crashed into the chair, toppled over it, and landed hard on the floor.

Freon-cold air poured out of the open fridge around me like mystical fog. I grabbed the tray of ice. In Louis's hands, ice was another weapon.

I turned to retreat and to my surprise almost slammed into the Wielder. He'd brought the fight closer to his Bender.

I froze.

He wrapped his gloved hands around my neck. The power that squeezed through his hand was strong as it closed my air-pipe and picked me up from the ground.

I couldn't breathe as my feet dangled in the air.

The ice cubes clattered to the floor. They weren't going to make it to Louis and Frederick.

"I will find your daughter," he intoned, his gruff whisper hollow. "She will die."

Suddenly ice cubes hovered in the air. *Fibbs.* The Wielder didn't notice. Spots assailed my vision as my body used the last of the oxygen trapped in my lungs. Frederick appeared behind the Wielder, reaching down and picking up the ice cubes.

Life was pulling away from me. My attacker's fire heated up through his hands and gloves to the naked flesh of my throat.

Then he grunted. The heat vanished. I dropped to the floor, coughing and hacking. Only then did I realize that his grip around my neck was gone. It still felt so tight.

Frederick was the first to reach me. Louis extracted one of the ice spears that stuck out from the Wielder's body that my husband wielded. It was slick with warm, thick blood. He pierced it through the attacker's heart without saying a word.

The double glass door in the living room shattered. Louis jumped up like lightning, this time taking his forty-cal pistol with him.

Frederick hugged me tight. "Please tell me Alex is safe."

"She is," I wheezed. "Ariel took her."

We lay there together. Fibbs showed herself again. Frederick stroked her head. "Good girl," he said. She meowed.

We couldn't do more. Everything around us was ruined so the best option was just to wait for whoever returned first.

ARIEL WAS FIRST. Louis was still out there searching for the Bender. It would not be good news if the Bender escaped and told whoever was searching for Alex where to find her.

We waited for proof that danger was over before reverting the spell and bringing Alex out of the locket. The way I felt now, she would never come back until she is 2 1.

We called the authorities—the Association.

Clive was the first to show. He was tall, slender, auburn hair, and soft eyes, He worked in a very special devision inside the special forces of Billings. There was a stage I would have trusted him with my life, but now, I wasn't so sure. He found us in what was left of the living room. He looked around. The house inside was a mess. Half of one wall was destroyed by fire and water; the other half was knee-deep covered in snow. "What happened?"

Ariel stood by the fireplace, Frederick leaned by the window, and I sat on the chair with Fibbs next to me, her head on my lap.

"Necrocretors found us." Ariel started to pace.

"Where is Alex?" Clive wanted to know.

Ariel just looked at him. "Safe for now. Did you know anything about this? Are you sure that your men can be trusted? They must have seen her tonight at the WABA Celebration..."

Clive lifted his hands in defense. "Ariel, calm down. I'm on your side."

"Are you?" she demanded.

"Enough." Frederick stepped in. My sister fell silent. Frederick looked at Clive. "She has a point. I thought you said you were doing thorough checks on attendees this year."

"We do, Frederick." Clive looked devastated about this news, that there was a leak somewhere. "Tell me what you all want me to do and I'll do it."

A pregnant silence suspended between us all for a moment.

Finally my husband said, "You are good at forgetting spells."

Clive squinted. "How do you...?"

"Doesn't matter," Frederick interrupted. "It's my job to protect my daughter and I would do anything to ensure her safety. Erase the memory of her presence tonight from everyone she spoke to.. Then I'll know we have your goodwill to help us."

Clive thought about this hard. After a few moments he nodded.

Just then the door opened. We all jumped ready to fight again.

Louis stood in the doorway and we relaxed once again. He looked exhausted. He was panting as he slouched in.

Grasped in his grip was the Bender's head. Detached from its body.

6

MEREDITH

WATER WASHED OVER MY FACE, pouring out of the faucet of the sixteenth-century castle that existed in Ariel's locket.

My daughter still hadn't woken. We didn't dare revert the spell. Instead, Frederick and Louis had guided us into the locket to be with her.

I needed to keep her safe. How had the Necrocretors found us so fast? Somebody was helping them. They must have seen Alex at the celebration when Ethan bent earth. *I mean, it was spectacular enough to get people talking.*

I had no idea if only those two had followed us, or if there were more out there keeping tabs on us.

At this exact moment, the only idea that I was open to saying screw Ethan and just keeping Alex inside the locket until she reached her twenty-first birthday, when her wielding ability would be fully matured. Then nothing would be able to hurt her.

Right?

"She's awake." Ariel appeared in the bathroom doorway. "She's not happy, Mer."

I dried off my face in a hurry. I walked with huge strides past my sister to Alex's room. I found her standing at the window. "Sweetheart," I said.

She faced me. She gave me one of her fuck-you-Mom stares.

"I had no choice," I said.

"You always have a choice," Alex yelled. "You and Daddy have taught me that from a young age."

"You will understand one day, baby. When you have a little one..."

"Stop saying that I would understand when I have children of my own. How is that even possible if I never get out of this prison? I can't live in Ariel's locket anymore." She looked at Ariel apologetically. "No offense."

"None taken," Ariel chirped with her hands spread out in defense.

"It's no life, Mom."

I took a step closer. "Necrocretors almost killed you. They found you."

She squinted. "You think I don't know that? There will always be some sort of danger that wants to hurt me around the corner. I know you try to keep me safe, but do it in the real world, please! Not in this one where nothing is genuine." Bitterness laced her tone.

I appraised her, eyebrows up. When did she become so brave, so passionate in the things she wanted? So grown up. I sighed.

"I'll help, you know I will." Ariel approached me. "You can make Alex's and my bond stronger for now until Ethan learns more. Fibbs will help, too. She vowed to Alex to keep her safe."

I give her a withering look. I wanted to tell her that Alex would not pass the test of resistance. I had already seen it in her eyes. She wasn't strong enough. I didn't even want to put her up to the test.

"Ethan!" Alex yelled and we both fell silent. Shit, she didn't know. "Ethan is my Bender. Offcourse he is my Bender." She sounded scared. She took a deep breath. Silence linger in the air. Maybe this fear of resistance would make her stay in this locket. Then she took a deep breath.

"Is Ethan okay?" Alex asked. I closed my eyes in exasperation.

"Are you okay?" I ignored her question.

"He's fine," said Ariel. "In fact, that boy is more than just fine."

"Ariel," I scolded. Alex didn't need to be reminded how beautiful her Bender was.

"Just saying."

Alex suppressed a smile.

"I'm fine mom. If he is my Bender then I need to face him sooner or later right. He can help with protecting me. I mean we can protect each other...you know what I mean."

Ariel raised her eyebrows. She was getting the same vibes from Alex as I was, that this was going to be the hardest test of her life. The risistance.

I nodded. "So, what do you suggest, sweetheart?" I asked. "Because I don't know how many Necrocretors saw you. I don't know how to protect you in the real world. They were only two and it took three of us *and* a wisp to kill them."

A tiny frown formed between her eyebrows. "Do they know where we live?"

I shrugged.

"They might not," Ariel said. "You killed both that were there."

"We don't know," I said firmly. "We might even need to move."

"No, Mom!"

"Alex, I can't..."

"And I cannot run and hide like a scared little mouse anymore." She stamped her foot in defiance. "I need to learn how to wield my earth properly. Ethan needs to learn how to bend it." She sounded so frustrated. "Get more guards, more cameras, ask the Benders' Association for more Wielders, take my element and strengthen the bond between me and Ariel... If losing me is really scaring you, hell, conjure a glamour to hide my face. But I'm not going to hide anymore."

I stared at her. Took another deep breath. I could force her to stay in here if I really wanted to, but I didn't want to see my baby so sad all the time. So angry. She loved the real world, loved Fibbs and her aunt. Neither of them would be able to come with us. I couldn't do that to her again.

"Okay, baby, but we do this my way or you can..."

She careened into me and flung her arms around my neck. "Thank you, thank you, thank you."

"Alex, you need to realize the danger here."

"Mom, I do. Dad and you... everyone has prepared me well for this. But I should train with the right people now. For real."

I nodded and tucked a stray lock of hair behind her ear. She was so beautiful. Ethan would never be able to resist her.

Then I remembered what she'd said about conjuring a glamour. *She's right.* Maybe there was a way to protect her, not just from the Necrocretors but from Ethan Sutcliff too. Maybe, just maybe she wouldn't have to fight the resistance after all.

"Oh, I know that look," Ariel said, watching my face.

"What is it, Mom?" Alex wanted to know.

A smile spread on my face. "Toil and coil and trouble, my brewing pot is going to bubble."

ALEX

I WAS SITTING at the kitchen table. The kitchen in the real world and not the one inside Aunt Ariel's locket.

Dad popped in and planted his lips on my head. He smiled, stroking my cheek.

"You sure you are up for this change? Your mother's glamours are very strong, Alex."

I nodded. *If this is what it takes to get a chance in the real world, then bring it on.* I glanced at the door that led to the basement. She'd been down there with Ariel the past forty-eight hours. Working straight through.

"How long does a glamour spell take?" I had to know.

"A good one? Easily a few days. The kind your mother wants to conjure? I don't know. Just be assured that it will be something to admire."

I laughed at the way he said it. "She's really that good?"

"Your mother should've been a Spellbinder. She was always better at spells then wielding." He waggled his eyebrows playfully. Still, his tone was sad. I could only imagine what it was like for him growing up with her and Jeff.

Dad had never liked Jeff, that much I knew. Whether it was because he broke my mother's heart when he chose Siobhan, or whether he was jealous over the two of them, well, I still had to figure that one out.

I got up to head to my room and passed the fresh drywall and paint tarps in the destroyed part of the living room. The fumes of paint made me lightheaded.

I gestured for Fibbs to follow. She did. I loved her so much. I'd begged Mom for the incantation for seeing through her eyes, but she still haven't given it to me. *One victory at a time, I guess.* She said that I should be careful using it on Fibbs as she wasn't really a cat, but part of the witching race.

I threw myself on my bed, my thoughts already obsessing about Ethan. These days my mind rarely strayed from him.

What was he feeling at this very moment? I knew he was okay; Mom and Ariel had recounted everything that had happened the minute I'd slumped in my chair, drained.

He had blocked the fire with my Earth. I had wielded, and he had bent. I didn't even know that I wielded it. Ariel was more wowed at the distance I wielded it, then anything else.

Poor Ed had gotten badly hurt. They said everything had happened so fast, Ethan didn't bend it properly. It was everything at once and too much all at the same time. A piece of the tree that split the stage in three stabbed Ed through the foot.

I couldn't even remember his screams. Aunt Ariel had said it sounded like he was being eaten alive. Not a pleasant image. I had asked how she knew what that sounded like.

A smile had tugged on the corner of her lips. "I've seen plenty in my years," she had pronounced with an air of great mystery.

I could just imagine. Not only had she experienced many things, she'd traveled almost the whole world. Never staying in one place for too long while protecting us in her locket.

The specter of Ethan forced its way back into my mind as if he was adamant to be the only one occupying my thoughts.

I hated that already.

I couldn't wait to start school. Mom wanted me to go to the one in the mountains just for witches, and warlocks but Dad had refused. The Necrocretors would look there first, he'd argued. Sending me to the witch school just wasn't thinking smart. So I would enroll at Sky View High soon. Well, as soon as Mom and Ariel emerged from the basement with a glamour.

I'd never tried on a glamour before. It wasn't like I'd ever needed one until now.

I was nervous as hell.

The way everyone had stared at me the night of the WABA Celebration. I was going to stand out like a blobfish among fluttering betta fish. The way Ethan stared, I didn't know if I was strong enough to resist him.

I would try my utmost best.

Maybe I would. I didn't know him. The guy I imagined from only a stare might not even exist.

I WAS STANDING in front of the mirror. My heart was beating from excitement, fear, anxiety.... *All of the above.*

All those emotions combined to make my stomach slosh uncomfortably.

When Dad had said that Mom's glamour was something to admire, I didn't imagine anything like this. It had taken her a full four days to conjure this.

"So," my mother said. "What do you think?"

I examined the girl in the mirror again. Her hair was pure white, frail-looking sticks that hung to her shoulders. I was afraid to touch it; they might break. Screwy teeth slightly outthrust from underneath my lips, making them flat and thin, resembling the shape of a beak.

"I look like a duck," I said as my eyes lingered on my mouth.

Dad's shoulders bobbed behind me in silent laughter. His hand covered his face as he peeked at me with big eyes every few seconds.

Aunt Ariel had no words. Just worried eyes with raised eyebrows.

Mom? Mom loved every minute of this.

The glasses were the first thing to notice. It was as if she'd taken two bottoms of beer bottles and stuck them to my face.

Not to mention the zit the size of my fingernail on the tip of my nose. It scared me.

Aunt Ariel finally cleared her throat. "Mer," she said. "You've always been brilliant at glamours, but this is social suicide."

"That pimple," my father added. "It's a bit too much, dear. Just a tad less... cruel?" He held his finger and thumb two inches apart as if to say exactly how much less.

"Thank you," I mouthed in the mirror at both Ariel and Dad. He winked.

Mom's face said it all. She was not impressed with the response she was getting. Her arms folded across her chest. She glared at my aunt and father. "Fine. Next time, you conjure it." She snatched the glasses off my face and huffed out the door.

My old self was staring back at me. Those glasses were seriously powerful.

"Everyone knows about the wonders of Pantene, too," Aunt Ariel yelled after her. Mom grunted.

All three of us suppressed laughter.

I found my old self still looking back at me. I could breathe again. "That was scary."

"She's usually not that dramatic, but taking that it's you... I mean, she locked you in a piece of jewelry for sixteen years, sweets. My advice? Just go with it." Aunt Ariel gave me that concerned look again and sighed deeply.

"So what? I'm going to become Ducky?" The name just slipped out. All three of us laughed.

"It's a catchy name." My father kissed me on my forehead. "You'll be okay, whatever she is going to do next. It won't be the end of the world, Alex. And know she has the best intentions. She loves you."

"I know," I said. But that girl in the mirror seriously scared me.

7

ETHAN

I SNAPPED OPEN MY LAPTOP.

The past week I couldn't stop thinking about my Wielder. Who was he? Why did he leave? We'd tried to find him. We'd asked around if anyone had met an earth Wielder at the WABA Celebration, but nobody fessed up.

It was as if he'd vanished into thin air, and it was working on my nerves because of antoher thing that happened the night on the WABA celebration. Two bodies were discovered. One without a head, and another that was labeled as John Doe. Was it my wielder, and whoever were protecting them? I was crazy with worry. I just felt that power again and to think that I might have lost it this time forever was seriously too much to handle.

Seeing that both bodies were male, Dad strongly believed that it was a he, and the fact that I couldn't remember the gender of the voice that had guided me. .

Was this what that owl dream meant? That my life was about to change?

I'd spent the last few days searching for the Wielder

through the Association network. Well, he wasn't the only one I was searching for. The network was a complicated platform. It was disguised through an online retailer that sold everything from electronics to clothes.

We would type in a certain product, and once we were on that product page, we hit Ctrl and the six key. It then redirected to the home page of the Benders' Association website. It documented witches back to the seventeenth century. Famous witches, evil witches, witches they thought turned rogue.

All the witches were nicely categorized. Then there were vampires, werewolves, and shifters. Last came the jinns, but their section was password-restricted.

Ryan, one of our other fire bender buddies, Ed, and I used to try and guess the passwords to get into the jinn site. We'd always been curious about what was written about the jinn race; they were a mystery to us all. But no luck so far, and eventually the burning desire to know had petered out.

I pressed the Wielders category and it took me to many subcategories.

There were the obvious ones: earth, fire, air, and Wind.

Below each element was a category for Benders.

Mom's photograph was in deceased folder under air. Also the way she died and whom she was protecting—me.

I was on here too, under earth. There were only a few of us, not many. All dead except me. It was depressing and the reason I rarely ventured into that category anymore. It made me feel like soon my number would get punched too. Then that would be it. My date of death would be typed in with all the others.

I sighed, scanning the earth Wielders. All dead.

Why did the Necrocretors kill us? Theories abounded. One was that they hated to be controlled. Something told me it wasn't that simple. There was already some control among them; they still operated under the radar and no earth pair existed to keep them down. So, what was it?

I didn't find anything new.

Instead of looking for my mystery Wielder, I scrolled through dozens, maybe hundreds of photos. Acres of them. Trying to find the foxy girl from that night.

Again, everything led to nothing. It was fruitless. I even called up Old Man Gezler, but he couldn't remember her. He acted like I was crazy, speaking a different language. I just shook my head. Something was wrong with that dude. How could he not remember such beauty?

I covered my face with my palms and took a deep breath.

A faint knock came at my door.

"Come in."

It opened. Dad hovered in my doorway. "You need to eat something, Ethan."

"I'm fine."

He pursed his lips into a thin line. "You are not fine. Sedgwick is worried about you. Let us help you find him."

I sighed. "How?" I felt so defeated. I'd looked at every possible angle the past week. Nothing. "What if..."

"Don't think like that Ethan. Carry on with your training. Something tells me that you don't need to go and look for them. They will find us."

They?. I didn't ask this time what my father meant by they, as he explained it to me so nicely.

It takes a team of people to keep someone as important as an earth Wielder alive for this long. "

"Come eat, please." My father shut the door.

I thought about what he said. To be honest, I didn't know if I could wait for them, whoever they were. I was ready to move forward. Why had they taken so long to begin with? Why hadn't they shown themselves this week? Why hadn't they made contact?

I was sure I wasn't the only one who felt this stuck, this ready to learn more. I took another deep breath, as if it could calm my nerves. It didn't. I didn't think it ever had.

I snapped shut my laptop and headed to the door. Dad was right. They'd have to appear at some point. They had to come to us. I would just love to know when.

ALEX

I STOOD in front of my locker, struggling to get the stupid thing open. Today was the first day of school. So far it was horrible.

We decided to wait a week or two after the attack before mom send me to school, to make sure that whoever sent those two after us, would have moved on from its search or just taking it a bit easier, making the ones that has to protect me, jobs easier. It's also the reason why we haven't came in contact with Jeff and Ethan, letting them know that I was here. Dad and Louis think that they might still be keeping taps on them. I was glad too for my own personal reasons. I could find out what type of guy Ethan really was. Who knows, maybe he would show me exactly who he was and I wouldn't like him that much, it would make resisting him so much easier when I do come out and show him who I truly was.

I closed my eyes.

Faces were imprinted on my mind. Kids could be cruel. Dad had warned me last night. Mom had gotten mad at him for it.

I was Ducky, and I hated it.

It was as if Mom wished I were ugly. As cruel as it sound but still, it was as if she knew why I'd agreed to this. That I wouldn't be able to resist Ethan's stares and eventually the flirting and wanting more would make me fail. It's as if Mom had seen straight through my reasoning and agreed to obscure my true appearance from Ethan.

I felt like a coward. I was a shallow, vain witch like all my ancestors. Pathetic.

Still, I'd never attended public school. Or school of any kind, for that matter. I couldn't stop wishing for something to look forward to. I punched my locker. Nothing. The damn thing refused to open.

Another guy passed me, making a perfect imitation of a duck.

It was the third time this morning. I pulled up my hoody to hide my hideous face. He wouldn't be quacking if he knew what hid behind the beer bottoms. Then I would be the one braying like a jackass.

That thought put a smile to my face.

I smacked the locker again. This was useless. I'd never get to get this thing open.

Then I felt it.

It was a decrease in power. And impossible drain on my energy. My legs wobbled like they'd give in any second.

I didn't understand.

My heart felt on the verge of exploding. A fist slammed hard on the edge of my locker and the door flew open, inches away from connecting with my face.

"Hard," said a male voice. I looked up and saw him. Ethan. He grinned, slung his backpack over one shoulder, and wrapped arm around the waist of a girl with bleach-blond hair.

"Oh," I mouthed.

That was why my energy waned. Ethan. I wanted to crawl into my locker and take a nap. I rested for a few seconds with my forehead against the locker. Slowly the strength he'd stolen returned as he disappeared around the corner.

I closed my eyes and took deep breaths. His face. The one from the other night at the Celebration, devilishly handsome in a tux, just staring at me.

It was a weird feeling.

That girl he was staring at that night? Yeah, she was gone. Only Ducky stood in her place.

I opened my eyes and wearily stacked my brand-new text-books in a neat row. An old mirror was taped to the side of my locker. Inside it was Ducky's brittle hair hanging unevenly above huge brown eyes protruding behind the beer bottle spectacles. And that mouth. Luckilly the pimple was gone.

I hated this glamour. I slammed the door of the locker hard.

The first period bell rang. I slung my backpack over my shoulder and hunted down my first class.

I MUST HAVE WALKED up and down a dozen hallways today. It was the period before lunch, and I still had no idea where I was. I had plenty help from the janitor this morning. Pity I couldn't get him to chaperone me the whole day.

Maybe because of my new dorky identity, few offered me help. It was like I was invisible to them. Teenagers, I had discovered, were shallow and mean. Something Mom had been counting on, I was sure.

With a frustrated sigh, I looked at the letters above the class-room doors. They were labeled H, I, and J.

I was looking for classroom 4.

I glanced down at my schedule again. It was a mess. A frumpy woman at Reception had given me a crisp sheet of paper with a map of the school on it. The school was big. I struggled to figure out where I was. Was this stupid map some horrible trick? My fingers traced the labyrinthine hallways on the now-crumpled paper. I couldn't see H, I, or J anywhere.

They just didn't exist.

Where the hell was this class?

I even contemplated doing a hex to show me the way of my new class. The idea took hold. Just a small one. Nobody would know.

I glanced around. Dingy white tiles lit by clinical fluorescent light, worn wooden doors, brown metal lockers adorned with scratched graffiti either proclaiming eternal love between sets of initials, or insults at hated students of eras long gone. Not another person in sight.

Screw it. I took a steadying breath.

> *Bound and binding, binding and bound.*
> *See Room 4, so freakin' late.*
> *Can't be lost, finding the room would be great.*
> *Bound and binding, binding and bound.*
> *Please help Room 4 to be found.*

A trail of silver dust formed. I had to concentrate hard to see it moving in the direction of where I should've been fifteen minutes ago. Room 4.

I followed it out of the building, past another boxy brick building. A trail of gray fog slithered around the corner to intersect with my silver spell.

My breath seized in my lungs. My mind went back to one of the lessons my tutor Wendy had given me a few years ago. It had been my favorite subject—evil spells—although Mom didn't like it.

This spell was a dark one, conjured through fog. One that evil used to find something. It worked similarly to my silver dust. But the difference was that the fog was ten times stronger than my silver dust.

I slipped through the first door and shut it softly. I prayed that it would follow my trail, and not me. I hoped Mom's glamour was working. She'd said it wouldn't just hide my appearance. It would also throw every Wielder and Bender off. Supposedly it put a lid on my power as well as my looks.

Did I just make a terrible mistake? It was just one stupid location spell.

The fog trailed behind my spell.

The safest path was to go the other way. But I really wanted to be among my classmates and not in the open where Necro-cretors could find me.

I followed the gray fog from a distance as it snaked around corners. It slipped underneath a door. I went up to it. No numeral hung over the worn wood frame, but it had to be number four. I waited a few minutes. The fog would encounter a classroom full of people and hopefully dissipate among them. Used up. Harmless.

When I suspected that danger had passed, fooled by me, I resolved to go inside. I was already more than twenty minutes late. *I might as well just sit this one out*, but I had to go to class scared that I would get the D-word.

I didn't want to get punished on my very first day.

I turned the knob. Light filtered from the classroom with the jumbled voices of a dozen people speaking at the same time.

The room was filled with students... but no teacher. Everyone stopped and stared at me.

Creepy.

I stepped inside, uncertain, and closed the door to the hall behind me with a metallic click. And then the distinct sound of a heavy deadbolt sliding into place.

Instinct took over. I turned my back on the classroom full of students and hammered on the door. *To hell with this. I want to go home.* I pulled fruitlessly on the doorknob, my heart racing.

Someone had locked it from the other side.

The kids behind me went super quiet.

The hair on my arms raised.

Everything went dark.

8

WHEN I TURNED around the classroom with the sunlight streaming through the window was gone. The students were gone. I couldn't see anything. Just dark outlines.

I huffed. This wasn't even a classroom to begin with, it was a trick. One that lured me to where it wanted me to be.

There were never a classroom to begin with.

This was some sort

of a storage closet. The air was hot and unbreathable. Clammy. Trying to suffocate me.

Where was I?

The fog was clever. It knew that I was following it. It led me where a hunter wanted me to be. And I had followed it like dumb prey.

My heart beat fast. Something up ahead clanged to the floor. Then came the distinct thud of footsteps. Someone was running away.

"Is anyone there?" I yelled. The fog wouldn't follow me if some other entity were here with me. It's not how the spells work, well, not finding or locating spells. It was part of the blend in architecture. If I wasn't alone, it would disappear, the location spell would evaporate, leaving whoever created it blind.

No answer came.

I tried the door again... to no avail.

The words of an unlocking spell reverberated through my skull, ready to spring to my lips. But then, that was what had gotten me into this mess the first place. A location spell.

I knew the minute I'd seen that fog. Casting that spell had been a terrible mistake.

Mom had made me promise yesterday to stay hidden. I'd broken that promise with the spell.

Whoever was searching for me was alerted the minute I said those words.

I rolled my eyes and slammed my palms against the unyielding door. Why couldn't my parents just be direct? "Don't use spells or the bad guys are going to find you" would have been nice and clear.

The stuffy air started to get colder. Goosebumps flushed over my skin.

I pressed myself against the useless door and peered into the darkness. The outline of objects big and small faded into an inky darkness.

My breathing became faster. *Protect your identity, Alex, even if it's Ducky.*

"Found you."

I jumped at the hard whisper in my ear. My hand lit up with light.

Fight darkness with light, Wendy had taught me. Especially evil in the form of fog or mist. It wasn't a lot. I covered my face with my glowing hands.

There was a screech. Then a hiss. The suffocating feeling started to back off.

Nausea threatened to make me lose my breakfast. My

energy waned. I hoped Ethan might listen to his instincts and come to my rescue. But he didn't show.

The glamour didn't just block my identity. It dampened my power.

The darkness was feeding off anything that was alive to gain strength. This moment, as it retreated from the light in my hands, was my only chance to escape. Otherwise I was a goner.

I ran through the darkness. Legs pumping. Breath coming out in gasps.

Where was I? Earlier I saw objects in the room. Now, nothing. Blindly, I stretched out my glowing hands in front of me to avoid running into anything.

Something burned my shoulder. I fell to the floor. A scream left my mouth. Brilliant light poured out of my palms, a sudden involuntary beacon of pain and panic. Light cut into the shadows. Whatever was chasing me backed away immediately, hissing and screeching.

I still lay on my back. Light shone from my hands and pooled over my face. I felt drained, even more than when Ethan had walked past me.

Don't pass out. Don't lose consciousness.

My light started to fade, fainter and fainter until it was gone. I blinked to adjust my eyes to the sudden blackness.

After a few minutes or so, the outlines of objects started to show themselves again.

The inky thick darkness was gone.

Taking huge breaths, I got up and felt my way forward, searching for an exit.

I was in a dark hallway now. What was this place? Was I still at school?

Something behind me clanged to the floor. Figures darted toward me again.

My heart beat like crazy and I ran as if my life depended on it. Because... it did.

Up ahead, a thin white rectangle stood stark against a wall. A door. Would it be locked? I wasn't going to take my chances. I wound up all my strength and smashed into it.

The door shattered; my body hurtled through air and connected hard against the floor.

Light bathed me and it felt as if I could breathe again. My glasses were still firmly on my head. When I uncovered my eyes, a hundred faces stared down at me.

My eyes caught something past their legs. A buffet line bordered the room.

I was inside the cafeteria.

ETHAN

I BELCHED AND GRIMACED, fighting the urge to throw up. Was I coming down with something?

Then the door that they'd closed up when Block D shut down smashed into a million pieces. A figure toppled through the space and landed at weird angles among the splinters of wood.

My entire table of Benders—Soph, Ryan, Leanne, and myself—all jumped up. Ready to attack.

It wasn't just me that was jumpy, the news about recent deaths and bodies washing up wrecked everyone in the wielding Bender community. Leaving us all on edge. Constantly alert for danger.

Everyone went quiet and gaped at the girl. I knew her. The Ugly Duckling I'd helped with her locker this morning.

She uncovered her eyes and looked around.

Then two dark figures exited after her. Soph whipped out

her lighter, but I grabbed her arm in warning. There was no danger. "It's only Wes and Phil."

The boys in question were disguised in flowy black robes and self-satisfied smirks. They grunted like apes and everyone laughed. I let go of Soph when she subsided.

The girl sat straight as everyone started to laugh—this time, at her. Ryan joined in, then so did Leanne and Sophie too.

Idiots. I smiled just thinking how wrong this could've gone if the cafeteria had been set on fire by two Benders. I took a deep breath.

The girl cast her gaze like a piteous net in every direction, her huge eyes protruding from behind those glasses. It looked as if she wanted to cry.

Soph pressed her lips together.

Wes tried to help her up. He looked guilty now for scaring her shitless.

She slapped his hand away. "Idiots." She got up and ran out the cafeteria.

Some of the kids shook their heads and walked out. The rest all applauded. Wes and Phil took a bow. They would get at least two weeks' detention for this, that was for sure.

"Poor Ugly Duckling," Leanne said with a mocking tone.

I hated that I had been the one to give her the name this morning. After I helped her, Soph had teased me of always being everyone's knight in shining armor. The girl who leaned daydreaming against her locker wasn't helping my position; I hated that I had that effect on so many of them. "What, Ugly Duckling?" I'd sneered. "I'm just a nice guy, Soph. I only have eyes for you."

Now everyone was going to call her that.

I huffed and glanced at the utilitarian clock on the wall of the cafeteria, grimy from years of hanging above the buffet line.

The bell would ring in a few minutes. I got up to put my tray on the drop-off area.

As I walked passed the open gap in the wall from which the new girl had toppled, I felt it. A strong, suffocating vibe.

Soph and Leanne just carried on walking, laughing about the prank and how evil Wes and Phil were.

Ryan halted. "You okay, Ethan?"

I squinted at him. "You don't feel it?"

He looked at me strangely and then to the hole. "Feel what?"

I stared at the opening in the wall and shook my head. "Maybe it's just my imagination. Let's go."

And with that, the bell ring.

I went to biology class, still confused. Why hadn't my friends felt that eerie sensation that came from the closed-off Block D.

Was it connected to the girl? Had Wes and Phil really scared her that badly.

She didn't look as terrified once she realized that she'd been punked by two guys dressed in theater robes.

For some reason, I couldn't shake this weird feeling in my gut. It wasn't so bad that I wanted to puke. But something was not copacetic.

Mr. Gorge entered the classroom. "Turn to page one hundred fifty-four. No talking. We have plenty to cover today."

The room filled with the soothing rustle of dry pages. I reached the assigned page and frowned. A drawing of a huge onion stared up at me.

The sprinklers went off. I gasped as ice-cold water rained down on us. Girls shrieked and everyone ran for the door.

"No running," Mr. Gorge yelled.

I got up. So much for biology. I followed everyone back outside to the assembly block.

There wasn't a teacher or student who didn't get soaked. The teachers herded us outside to the front of the school. Lucky for us it was summer and everyone enjoyed the cool down. Girls wearing white tried—a little too obviously—to hide the color of their bras as their tops clung to them like a second skin. Boys couldn't stop looking.

I shook my head as my eyes caught Soph. She looked delicious. She wore her wet clothes with confidence. She came next to me and I shook my wet hair at her, which made her shriek playfully.

She laughed that sweet laugh of her.

Behind her sulked the Ugly Duckling. She wasn't wet at all.

I frowned. Her eyes caught mine and she looked away. She slunk away in the direction of a big-ass SUV parked at the bottom of the stairs.

I found Soph staring at me as I stared at her climbing into the SUV.

"What is it with you and Ugly Duckling?" Soph asked.

"I don't know. Something about her feels out of place."

Her eyes were as sharp as razor blades. "Like what?"

"I don't know, Soph."

9

ETHAN

I SPOKE to Sedgwick and Mira in the office at the institute that night. I hadn't been training the past week, which had Dad worried.

"I think your father has a point," said Sedgwick. "Just carry on as you do every day and they will find you one of these days. I don't think you need to go look for them."

I nodded. "My dad also thinks Necrocretors are behind the recent spate of murders."

"Searching for the earth Wielder?" Sedgwick sighed.

"It must be," Mira agreed. "We haven't had this much action around here for years."

"You don't get it. What if those guys was actually my Wielder."

"I don't think so Ethan. Whoever is protecting your Wielder is not going to let them find them now. They've been doing a great job till now."

"Once again, Mira has a strong defence going. I doubt one of them was your Wielder. For all we know it could be the introdors trying to kill your Wielder." Sidwig said and a cold finger rushed up my spine. Mira just stared at him as he walked away.

"Creepy thought." Mira said and I laughed.

Still, I didn't like this. I could protect him if only they would let us know who—and where—he was.

It made me feel so helpless. So useless.

"Go train. Maybe you'll feel better." Mira must have sensed my mood. She gave me one of her super punches on the shoulders. The one meant to get us riled up but only ever left us with a numb twinge for at least half an hour.

An hour into my training, I had to admit, Mira was right. I felt better. My mind wasn't clogged up anymore. The ball of nerves I'd felt the week since the Celebration was loosening in my gut. Once I was good and sweaty and exhausted, I put away my gear and showered, feeling more clearheaded.

Leanne took me home again. When we pulled up to my house, I slid out and thanked her.

"You sure you are okay?" Soph asked.

"Aren't I always?"

She sighed. "I worry about you, you know."

"Don't." I touched her cheek. She turned her face to kiss the palm of my hand.

"See you tomorrow."

"Text me before you go to bed," she said.

I smiled.

"Bye, Golden Boy," Leanne sang.

I waved sauntered to the front door. The crunch of gravel and asphalt punctuated their departure.

I found Dad sitting at the table, staring at a piece of paper. His face looked hard and ashen.

"Dad?" Maybe there was something in the air; maybe my

feeling something in the hole in the cafeteria wall was just my imagination after all. "What is it?"

He shook his head, gaze glued to the paper on the table.

I leaned over and reached for it. It was an invitation.

My eyes caught the name first. The only name that had the power to put Dad into this nostalgia.

Meredith.

She was one of my father's former Wielders, from a long time ago.

Dad was sort of a legend himself, having once bonded with two Wielders at the same time. No one else in the history of Benders had anyone else done that. Siobhan Miller was one, the one I had grown up knowing. She stayed with dad and then got herself killed because she was stubborn. I think I was seven, maybe eight? He took it hard as she was the only Wielder in his life now. The other one was Meredith Warner, now Meredith Burgendorf. For a long time Dad had no idea where she was, it was as if she just vanished.

"When did she came back?" I scrutinized the invitation. It was a coming-out-to-society type of invite. Something witches did to introduce their children to the Benders' Association.

"A couple of weeks ago, almost a month now."."

I froze on the precipice of my next question; how could he know its answer? "You think her kid is the earth Wielder?"

"The invite was here when I came home, right after I walked into her this afternoon. She acted surprised when she saw me, Ethan, but I know her too well. She wasn't surprised. She was hiding something. I can assure you: her kid is your Wielder.."

Faith was cruel.My ability return to me the night of the celebration. Why didn't my father saw Meredith that night. I need to know for sure.

The invite was on a pure white eggshell card stock, glossed

over with a white and silver shimmer with flamboyant silver script. It requested the presence of our family to attend a formal introduction. It failed to reveal who was being introduced, or even if it was male or female. Just that it was time to introduce someone special.

My heart thumped with conviction. They were going to introduce the earth Wielder. My Wielder really wasn't dead.

They didn't give much information on here, probably afraid it would get into the wrong hands and spelled out that an earth Wielder had moved to town. Something I suspected they already knew.

The Benders' Association was doing this on purpose.

Date, three weeks from now.

Time? Seven o'clock in the evening, for half an hour. Place? The old Buchman plantation—though it was more of a castle than a plantation. For years, it had stood empty, except the rare rich businessman who briefly rented it out.

It wasn't a wonder that the Burgendorfs had rented it. They were seen as royals when it came to the Benders' Association. And not like Sam's family. That was just how rich Frederick Burgendorf was.

A part of me was excited to attend a rich man's party. Those were the best.

But a part of me was nervous as I would finally meet the Wielder who carried all the power for me to bend.

"Son," my father said. "We will deal with it as it comes."

I didn't like his answer.

He'd said it was a he, made me believe that it was a he. Why was I getting a different impression now? I had a funny feeling that he knew Meredith had only one kid... and the kid wasn't male.

But I nodded. "I need to go take a shower," I lied. I wanted to get away. Needed to get my head around this.

Meredith might be my Wielder's mother.

I knew Dad had a romantic history with her. Forbidden between Wielders and Benders. They called it the Resistance. Dad had failed the test. Still, he chose Siobhan at the end. Nobody knows why?

I opened my bag and took out my trainers, my gloves, and the ointment I dabbed on my knuckles before each fight to prevent blisters.

My Wielder might not be male. I sighed. It was impossible to stop thinking about possibility. And the girl. The one at the WABA Celebration. The one I couldn't take my eyes off. The fox whose name I never got, and somehow managed to vanish from everyone's memories like a puff of smoke.

Everyone's but mine. I huffed.

It would make my day if this Wielder did turn out to be a girl—and it was her. Then I would finally believe the earth Element attraction everyone had drilled into my cranium since I was little.

The attraction that I would need to resist, since the earth's survival depended on it.

Benders were the only ones who could keep their Wielders in check. But they could also destroy them if they disobeyed the rules. I still had to figure out that part. The institute was impenetrably silent on the subject as to how it all came together or fell apart.

They were stupid; how could anyone know what we were doing wrong unless they taught us?

That type of responsibility lay on my eighteen-year-old shoulders.

Then it hit me.

I definitely didn't want my Wielder to be her.

ALEX

THE NEXT DAY I walked into school and found everyone staring at me. No, *gawking*.

Some of them, mostly the girls, murmured to each other behind their hands. The majority of the boys laughed. Hard.

Before they could detect the hot tears that sprang to my eyes, I yanked the hood of my sweatshirt up to cover my head. I tried to make myself smaller. This glamour was the opposite of invisible.

A spell could help, but yesterday had scared the living crap out of me. I knew the fog was real, and was under the impression that the class was too. It was so vivid, but it ended up to be another spell, fooling the one that casted another. It was in fact some sort of room where they stored everything and that was connected to other big rooms. Part of it had just been a mean prank, but the threat was real. It was hard to determine what was scarier. Either way, I didn't want a repeat.

I knew I should've told Mom, but she would freak out and homeschool me again.

I found my locker and hit it as hard as I could in the precise spot Ethan had pointed out yesterday morning. There was zero strength behind the punch, thanks to the glamour.

I hit it again. My locker flew open.

There she was. Ducky, staring back at me out of the mirror. My identity ninety percent of my day now. Avoiding her gaze, I took what I needed and closed the door.

A girl my height materialized where my locker door had been. I jumped

"Sorry, didn't mean to scare you." She had long, dark hair and goggles like mine.

The corners of my lips turned upward. "It's okay. Just a bit jittery."

"Who could blame you? After what Wes and Phil pulled off yesterday... those idiots."

Wes and Phil. "I take it they are the ones who..."

I didn't need to finish my sentence. Everyone knew that I had been the target of yesterday's prank. After all, I had tumbled right into the cafeteria at lunchtime. No way anyone had missed it.

If only they knew what had happened before Wes and Phil. Well, I wouldn't have been the only one freaked out. And no one would think me such a scaredy-cat.

"I'm Cynthia." She stuck her hand out sideways, awkwardly shifting some books in her arms.

"Alex." I shook her hand and flung my own backpack over my shoulder.

"What do you have first period?" Cynthia asked.

"Math."

"With Tradaux?"

I thought that was the name on my schedule. I pulled it out and showed it to Cynthia.

"Oh, well you can just follow me."

A little bubble of hope rose in my chest as we made our way through the thinning crowd as students rushed to beat the bell. We entered a classroom. My eyes remained fixed on the floor as I followed her in, avoiding the gazes of the students as a hush fell. I plopped down in the empty seat next to Cynthia.

Tradaux reminded me of a hawk. He had a long, beak-shaped nose with gray hair protruding from his nostrils. What little hair on top of his head remained, he combed sideways in a vain attempt to cover his shiny skull. He wore an ugly brown tweed, bowtie and all.

Even I could see that he should have retired a long time ago.

Looking at him actually hurt my eyes... until I remembered what I looked like. *You're no one to judge, Alex,* I chided myself, pulling out my behemoth trigonometry textbook from my backpack.

Math was a subject that came easily to witches and warlocks. All the potions we brewed revolved around arithmetic. The measure of how much poison to add to a love potion in order not to kill the victim, and at what temperature it had to reach for consumption. Not that I would use it, but I loved numbers.

Class was a breeze and Tradaux eased off my after trying to startle me with a trick question—and I got it right. The next class had Cynthia again, and it was awesome having someone around who wasn't just staring at me. When we didn't have the next period together, she took me to the right place and then, smiling, said, "I'll meet you after, right here."

It was like she knew how much I needed a buoy. I guessed she was one of the few who felt sorry for me. She made sure I didn't get lost or become a victim of another prank. It was sweet.

I followed her toward the cafeteria at lunch. I couldn't help but to stare at the jagged hole in the wall that someone had tried to close with a sheet of opaque plastic.

The hair on my arm rose as I thought about the entity that was attach to the fog, tricking me, trying to seclude me off hoping it would find me, that part had really happened—as opposed to what everyone thought happened in there: Two stupid boys wearing stupid robes. They could be glad that the entity disappeared the minute they showed up scaring the crap out of me.

"We can go and sit outside if you want," Cynthia offered.

Ethan walked in.

My energy waned sharply. He was worse than an incubus. I tried to ignore the laughter at his table. Jerks. I had to admit, I felt disappointed in Ethan Sutcliff as he grinned in response to the others making fun of the hole in the wall.

I walked as far as possible past Ethan so I wouldn't fall on my ass and drop my food this time.

A girl sniggered. "Is that the Ugly Duckling of yesterday's prank? Don't you think that's just the cleverest name Ethan ever came up with?" My feet, up to know racing to get away from Ethan's energy, plodded to a halt at the sting of her words. "Still, Phil and Wes seriously didn't deserve two months of detention."

Ethan had called me that—Ugly Duckling? It was one thing to think it myself. Quite another to know it came out of the mouth of my future Bender. Betrayal was an icepick in my heart.

Cynthia stopped in front of me. She must have realized that I wasn't behind her anymore. She came back to where I stood, my hands shaking and my milk carton thudding on the plastic lunch tray.

The blabbermouth finally stopped chattering as she noticed me standing right in front of her table. Her eyes were as round as quarters, and just as lifeless.

I swallowed. "What did you call me?"

"Nothing," the girl said.

"Nothing." Now my fork rattled against the plate, I was shaking so badly. She was lucky that Ethan Sutcliff was so close to me. Otherwise, she would've gotten attacked by tree roots, strung up by her toes, or squashed like a pumpkin. Then again, it wasn't this girl who had first dubbed me Ugly Duckling. Ethan would be squashed with her like the giant bug he'd turned out to be.

"Come on, Alex. Don't pay them any attention." Cynthia led me by the arm toward the courtyard.

Behind me, laughter erupted. Starting with the girl and her table.

People could be so mean. I felt like crying.

I officially hated school.

10

ALEX

THE FINAL BELL RANG. *Thank heavens this horrible day is over.*

Nobody except Cynthia bothered to learn my name. Everyone else had called me Ugly Duckling. Mom was going to love Ethan Sutcliff for that.

I reached my locker and slammed my fist as hard as I could against the spot that would make the stupid thing open.

Ethan was close by. He had to be; I felt it. When I looked up he was standing next to the same blonde girl he was always with, leaning against her locker. Flirting with her, judging by the look of things. Her coy titters said it was more than welcome.

He didn't look like a Bender now. He looked like a jock. Like an idiot jock made of muscle and zero brains.

Cynthia followed my gaze. She smiled, not unkindly. "Ethan Sutcliff," she intoned. "The girls all want him and the guys want to be him."

I rolled my eyes. *As if.* I tried again to open my locker, but nothing. Day two and I was so tired of this stupid thing.

A guy with red hair walked past me. He coughed a word: "Fuglies."

Cynthia's expression was blithely unimpressed. "Seriously?" she yelled. "So old, dude. Think of a new one."

I couldn't help but to laugh at her. I wasn't so sure what the word meant—but obviously it had to do with being ugly.

His friends thought it was hilarious and chortled as they trailed behind him and out the side door.

"Idiots." Cynthia seethed.

"Thank you for being so kind to me today." Who knew? Maybe she would realize that I was a loser and wouldn't talk to me tomorrow.

"C'mon. You seem like such a nice person. We nerds need to stick together."

I laughed. She was referring to my glasses, ones I didn't really need. Suddenly I felt sorry for her. Still, I really liked her a lot.

She had a knack for drastically changing subjects. Out of the blue she started carrying on about chess and that she had practice this afternoon from three to four and if I would like to go with, I was more than welcome.

They sort of needed extra players on their chess team, but I told her I would have to ask my mom.

I hit my locker a third time and to my surprise it finally swung open and hit me in the face. Laughter rippled through the hallway around me. Even Cynthia had to suppress a giggle.

"It's fine," I said. "You can laugh."

She just smiled. Such a nice person.

"You'll get the hang of it," she promised. She left me to handle things and went over to her own locker. It was across the hallway, a few lockers down from California Barbie's.

Power seeped out of me as if my shoes were sieves. I needed a nap, stat. Better yet, I wanted to clock this guy with one of my heavy books and steal back my strength. He still leaned against the locker chatting up his girlfriend. Seriously, didn't he ever get enough of her? *Just leave already.*

My gaze lingered on him.

Despite my rage, there was no denying that he was a beautiful guy with his blond, scruffy hair and bright green eyes. Well, the latter I couldn't exactly see from here. I'd picked it up by poring over his picture in Mom's booklet from WABA.

One of the girls walked over to the blonde girl and grabbed her around the neck in an embrace and whispered something in her ear.

The blonde girl looked past her friend—straight at me. My blood chilled. She chuckled, sizing me up. I spun back to my locker and shut the door.

Cynthia was back at my side. She leveled a long stare at them before turning to face me. "If I were you, I would not get on Sophie's bad side. She belongs to some club that teaches her all sorts of fighting techniques. It's where she and Ethan met. She scares the crap out of me."

So, this Sophie was a Bender too. Why hadn't I picked up on it?

That was what they told the normal kids Benders do. Learning the art of fighting at the boxing club.

"I'll try to remember that," I said with a curve of my lips. What would Cynthia do if I showed her what I could do? She would probably run screaming, and I would never see her again.

I shouldered my bag. Cynthia pulled me by my arm toward the incubus and his girlfriend.

My knees shook with every step I took closer to Ethan. I closed my eyes, concentrating on not falling flat on my face.

Cynthia let go of my hand.

A door fell away before the weight of my body and I tripped and fell. My eyes shot open as I tumbled outside. My backpack skidded off the stairs. My phone went flying and there was a telltale crunch as the screen shattered. I was chased by Sophie and her friend's cruel cackles.

I didn't care about my backpack or my phone. All I cared about was my glasses. They were the key to my glamour. Mom had warned me that if I broke them, the glamour would break too. Praying that they were firmly on my face, I reached a tentative hand up. They were. I could breathe again.

The door opened. The sound of laughter intensified.

"Ethan, seriously," Sophie yelled.

"Are you okay?" Cynthia was already picking up some of my books that had escaped my unzipped bag.

I felt my power draining again, crashing to the floor. I looked up... right into Ethan's face.

He lent me a hand as I shook my head. "Are you okay?" he echoed Cynthia.

I nodded without a word and took his proffered hand. Energy poured out of my body. I winced.

He looked concerned, thinking I was hurt. "Do you want me to take you somewhere?" he asked, ready to lift me up.

"It's fine. I'm fine," I said in a tired voice. "Just go. Please."

He frowned. "Okay." He went back inside, looking bewildered.

I saw Sophie walk up to him and fold her arms around his neck, kissing him on the lips.

I took a huge breath.

Why couldn't he feel the zap in his energy levels. Was it different for them? This was so weird.

"Are you okay?" Cynthia touched my arm and handed me my backpack and my broken phone. "You look so tired."

"I am tired," I barked at her and felt immediately sorry.

"Sorry," I said and she shook her head as if to say, *no worries.* "Sorry," I repeated. "I have never felt so embarrassed my entire life."

She started to laugh.

"I didn't take him for the helping kind of guy," I said, raising my eyebrows to the door where Ethan had disappeared.

"Yeah." She sighed loudly. "Exactly why every girl wants to be with him. Because he is just perfect. A real knight in shining armor."

Yay me. I didn't say that aloud.

I just hoped Mom had been right when she'd said that things would get better every day.

FOR THE NEXT FEW WEEKS, I tried to stay away from Ethan Sutcliff. But it was a lost cause.

Every time I thought I was clear of him, he would appear around a corner and slam into me, or open a door and hit me in the face. I would cuss, really cuss, loudly, while desperately clinging with my life to my glasses so that the glamour didn't falter.

It was hard to imagine what that would look like to bystanders—the Ugly Duckling turning into a swan in less than a minute. I doubted that there was a witch in the Association who could conjure a memory spell that would work on so many people at once.

Ethan was always nice. He'd help me up, joke that we should stop meeting like this. I would laugh it off and hurry off to get as far away from him as possible.

A few hours later, without fail, I would fall victim to a prank or a freak accident—a leg stuck out to trip me, a water fountain that sprayed my face, or just a particularly nasty verbal jab-- and

Sophie Rutter would always be close by, high-fiving her girls at a job well done. The message was clear: *Leave my man alone, dork.*

I didn't know what to do. Anger fizzed up inside until one night a tree root smashed through my bedroom window and my room turned into a jungle.

My parents listened. Aunt Ariel too. Dad suggested that I find something to funnel my anger, something like running. Track would be perfect.

Tryouts were starting soon.

I signed up the next day

What I didn't know at the time I signed up was that the track field was adjacent to the football field... where Ethan practiced four times a week.

This afternoon was my first practice. I put on the way-too-big tracksuit and t-shirt Mom had bought for me at the last minute. She'd said the poor fit would suit Ducky's identity.

I *hated* Ducky.

At least Mom had bought a sports bra too, so that nothing would jiggle while I ran. Then again, I didn't have much that could jiggle to begin with.

I hated this glamor. I couldn't wait to get home, but if this was how it was supposed to be, then so be it.

I sighed and walked out of the locker room.

I could hear the cheerleaders practicing their chants for the next football game. Sophie and Leanne were both on the squad.

I tried to steer clear of Sophie because wherever she was, Ethan was sure to follow. Besides, she had a predatory look in her eye every time she looked at me. I chose the route farthest away from them.

I wasn't scared of a little Bender, no matter what her element. I was scared that I might slip up and reveal myself as the earth Wielder. Not just to her but the rest of the world.

That kind of mistake would bring a load of trouble to me, my family, and my future Bender. I tried not to show who I was before the right time came. Dad was still not sure if they were keeping taps on Ethan and his father, or not.

I jogged past them without giving them too much attention, but I could hear their sniggers quacking.

Someone's shadow caught my eye, slanted long against the polyurethane track by the sun behind me. I turned around. The mascot, a falcon, was following me, flapping his arms like a chicken, mimicking Sophie's quacking noises. I ran faster, but he kept pace. When I next glanced back to see if he had gained ground, I was rewarded with the sight of a brown blur hitting his big stuffed face.

With a squawk, he fell flat to the ground.

The thing that had hit him rolled to a wobbly stop nearby. A football. I looked back and saw a couple of guys high-five Ethan.

The cheerleader girls cheered and he took a bow.

Why did he just do that?

Uneasy, I kept jogging until I reached Coach Delaroux, who trained the track team.

"Name?" he yelled like a boot camp instructor.

"Alex ," I said. "Alexandra B...,"

"Have you done track before?" He interrupted before I could say my last name. He sized me up from top to bottom, which made me feel extra uncomfortable.

"Does the treadmill count?"

He let out a huge breath. "Three laps should be enough to warm up." He blew his whistle.

I started to run as well as I could. Despite the drain of energy from Ethan over there on the football field.

Mom hadn't been wrong when she'd said it would get better... but she wasn't entirely right either. Every time I walk past Ethan, he felt like a magnetic field pulling me toward him.

The first lap was fairly easy. I ran it in about four minutes. The second round was harder; I could feel blood pounding in my cheeks. Coach yelled to go faster unless I wanted to be here until doomsday.

I pushed harder.

My feet pounded against the rubbery material. My bones reverberated with every stride. My breath burst from my lips in anguished puffs, scraping from my lungs. Why my father had suggested track beat me. It was *not* as easy as it looked. Well not in Ducky's form.

By the beginning of the third lap, I thought I was going to pass out.

Then something hard collided with the side of my head and I was literally thrown off my feet. I fell to ground in a crumple of sweaty limbs. The first thing I reach for was my glasses on my head. They almost slid off, I pulled them into place just in time.

Laughter erupted from the cheerleaders' stand. A shrill whistle tweeted in the distance. A few jocks' faces blotted out the sun, hovering over me.

"Are you okay?" Ethan's voice. With it, a distinct lessening of energy to the point that I was gasping for breath.

"Yeah," I whined.

He and a few of his teammates were clustered around me, their helmets tucked under their meaty arms.

"You took a bad hit." Ethan sounded apologetic. "Maybe you should stay down for a while."

"No, really?" Sarcasm dripped from my voice. "I would never have thought of that. Which direction did that ball come from, anyway?" I slapped his hand away.

"Ooh, Ugly Duckling is feisty," one of his teammates said.

"Guys," Ethan said. "C'mon."

Why did he have to be so perfect?

He offered me a hand again. I smacked it away a second

time. "Just don't, okay?" I said, stern. "If you haven't figured out by now that something bad always happens to me every time you're nice to me, then you are dafter then I thought."

Ethan's gaze moved to the cheerleaders' stand. I got up myself and limped away.

"Ooh, she thinks you're *daft*, Ethan," one yelled.

"Sure, it's just a cover-up," another said and Ethan laughed.

I stopped in my tracks. "A cover-up?" A mirthless laugh escaped me. "What—" I looked at Ethan—"You're so vain, you think all girls want to be with you?"

His friends chortled gleefully.

"If you must know, I'm weary of you," I said. "That is it."

I whirled around and hoped he'd read between the lines and understood my message.

"Ooh, *weary*," the guys mocked.

I limped off. My head pounded like mad. that Ethan could just go to hell, as nice as he was trying to be. It was all for show. He was as shallow as his stupid girlfriend after all.

ETHAN

I watched the Ugly Duckling walking away.

Even as I thought it, I felt guilty. It was stupid to label girls as animals. First the fox, now the poor Ugly Duckling. I never thought everyone would start calling her that. After almost a month of school, I still didn't even know her name.

What did she mean by weary? *She's weary of me? Why choose those words?*

It wasn't against the rules to go up and ask her what she meant. It would, however, lead to more questions. Questions that could lead to discussing the world of witches. Those kinds of questions would break a shit-ton of rules with consequences if she had no idea what I was talking about.

"Ethan!" Coach yelled.

My teammates didn't desist, pretending that my heart was beating wildly for the Ugly Duckling. I just shook my head. They could be jerks, but it was these jerks my neck depended on.

For the final thirty minutes, Coach drilled us hard, working out some new plays focusing on how we could score in less than three seconds. At last the whistle blew. I tossed a towel over my shoulders to soak up the rivers of sweat, my chest heaving.

Tomorrow was Friday. My favorite day of the week. Saturday was the big party, the one that would reveal my future Wielder—or so I hoped.

As I plodded tiredly off the field, my thoughts strayed to the Ugly Duckling. What had she meant, "weary of me"?

I wasn't the only one who was still thinking about her. Inside the locker room, Pete, Ryan, and Joe were still joking about how she'd been thrown off her feet.

I didn't see who threw the ball. All I saw was the ball flying at the speed of light in the wrong direction and smashing into the side of Ugly Duckling's head.

As I rummaged through my gym bag, I couldn't help but laugh at Joe's recap. He was a hilarious impersonator.

Steven let a towel fly and whipped Ryan on the ass. "Nice shot, Ryan."

Steven and Joe high-fived. "Yeah, man," Steven jeered, "that chick saw her ass hard."

"Nice shot?" I asked, looking at Ryan. "*You* threw that ball?"

His grin faded when he saw my serious expression. "Relax. I didn't think it would knock her off her feet."

"Why do you do that?" I had to know what was going through his mind. Had the dumb jock taken too many hits? "What if she got hurt?"

"Chill, dude," he said, getting defensive. "What's your problem?"

"You don't think, Ryan." I tapped a finger against my temple. *You are a fire Bender.* I wished I could say it out loud. I shook my head, took my towel, and headed to the showers.

"What is his problem?" Steven demanded. "I thought it was hilarious."

"Don't." Ryan sounded pissed-off. Their voices were drowned out when I turned on the water.

What was it about the Ugly Duckling that made me so upset? *I'm weary of you.* What did she mean, and why did she choose those words? Was she weary of me, or weary around me?

I hated not knowing what people meant. I hated misunderstandings. Clearly this girl misunderstood everything about me.

WORDLESSLY I GOT DRESSED and picked up my bag. I didn't speak, pissed at my team for being so cruel today. Why did Ryan throw that ball?

I felt sorry for the Ugly Duckling. No one should get hit with no warning like that. It was a wonder that she'd gotten up and walked away.

I exited the lockers and walked with huge strides to where my Jeep was parked. I always drove the Jeep on days we practiced. It was just easier than waiting for Soph to finish drilling the cheerleading squad. I rounded the corner and smacked right into someone.

"Fuck, fuck fuck, fuckity fuck," she cried, clutching at the thick beer-bottle glasses on her face.

"I'm sorry," I said. "I really didn't see you."

She looked as if she were about to cry as I helped her up.

She spoke more slowly. "It's fine. I should look where I'm going anyway. It's not your fault."

"Nice to know, thank you." I didn't keep the sarcasm out of my voice.

Someone honked. She picked up her backpack and limped toward an expensive Porsche SUV. It wasn't the one that usually picked her up. I struggled to see the driver through the tinted windows.

She climbed in and it drove off.

I shook my head once and headed in the direction of my own Jeep.

Who was this girl?

11

ETHAN

FRIDAY WHIZZED BY. I didn't see Ugly Duckling anywhere. Maybe her parents had spotted the egg growing out of her head and decided that the world was cruel enough and kept her home.

I felt bad the minute that thought left my brain. It wasn't her fault that she looked the way she did. She probably had an amazing personality.

I groaned when I pulled my tie knot and saw the skinny end was a good two inches lower than the fat end. I untied it and vowed not to let my mind wander; my tie needed to be perfect. It was already Saturday. The party—and my future—awaited.

My dad appeared behind me in the mirror. He lent me a hand. "I miss your mother when it comes to things like this."

A smile tugged at the corners of my lips. "Me too."

"Son," Dad started. "Whatever happens tonight, know that you will be okay."

I frowned. Why was he always saying that?

He tapped me on my shoulder hard and picked up his jacket.

It was time to head to the party. Everyone I knew—everyone who had been around since I was ten years old—would be there: Sophie, Ryan, Leanne, Annie, Ed, Felix, and even Sam.

Tonight was a beautiful evening. The sun just set and there was a warm breeze in the air. The humidity not too high. The ride to the old Buchman plantation was a quiet one. We weren't guys of many words, Dad and me. We didn't need to talk much.

I knew Dad was just as nervous as I was. He was going to see one of his Wielders tonight. One with whom he still shared a deep bond. The one he once loved with his entire being.

I wondered from time to time what it felt like to love someone with your whole self.

The massive gray stone wall of the plantation came into view. Four towers were visible behind the wall, scraping into the sky. It had a vintage feel to it. Since it had stood abandoned for so long, I wondered if the Burgendorfs had updated the interior décor to look modern when they moved in.

Dad came to a halt behind the Rolls Royce in front of us. The driver gave the guard his invitation. After consulting a board and a clipped exchange over a handheld radio, the guard let him in. The big gates clanged open, revealing a mother of a courtyard with a grandiose fountain and manicured shrubbery.

Our turn. Dad presented our invitation.

The guard barked into his walkie. The other one was taking his time to confirm. Dad gazed up at the guy with a wondering expression in his eyes.

The guard muttered a few things and then, more loudly, said, "Over and out." The ornate gates opened.

"What was that about?" I asked as Dad drove past the gates.

"Let's just say Frederick and I weren't each other's favorite people."

"Dad, that was twenty years ago."

"Time doesn't always change people, Ethan."

Illuminated by warm lights, the courtyard sprawled over several acres of land. Guards patrolled everywhere, sleek and menacing. Dad stopped in front of the door. A valet took the keys from him as we got out. He slid in and parked the car on our behalf.

A whistle left my mouth.

"It's overpowering, I know," Dad said. "But if this is the house of the earth Wielder, you need to get used to this, son. It would be your life till the day you part."

I stared at the plantation, giving a barely perceptible nod. As we approached the heavy doors that were a good fifteen feet tall, I took a deep, steadying breath. I needed to clear my head and calm my heart, which was beating entirely too fast.

ALEX

GUESTS WERE ALREADY TRICKLING IN. I was nowhere near ready. I was still my outfit from earlier today. The top resembled the uniforms of the waiters wo would serve drinks and hors d'oeuvres tonight.

Mom had tried everything to heal the blue smash of a bruise on my head. I was just glad that I didn't grow an extra head.

I hunkered in the kitchen, munching on a sandwich. I wasn't in the mood for a party. At all.

Yesterday I had looked forward to this because we'd been planning to do this as me—no glamour.

But then Dad received word through one of his close resources of four murders closeby. Kids aged between fifteen and seventeen. Their corpses were torched. They hadn't yet been identified.

I knew without having to ask that they were female, and that they had dark hair. All beautiful girls, all resembling me.

It was the work of a Necrocretors, and the reason I didn't go to school yesterday. Well, that and the terrible bruise where a ball had clobbered me on Thursday afternoon.

If the Necrocretors continued, I wouldn't be able to keep attending school. Dad hired a platoon on top of the one Louis had already hired after the attack.

The extra security was only working on Mom's nerves. If she could have things her way, tonight would've been canceled. But the entire witching world was intrigued about the presentation, more so by the omission of my name. Practically everyone had RSVP'd yes. Dad wasn't one to disappoint an audience. So the party was still on. He promised nothing would go wrong tonight.

The Necrocretors might feel like gods, but there were too many Wielders and Benders tonight for them to do anything stupid.

Ariel loved the extra guards. "Finally, I have something yummy to look at," she teased.

If anyone asked me what I thought, I would tell them exactly what a stupid tradition this was. Parading your kids like trophies in front of important Association members bordered on exploitative. A dumb tradition that happened to witches and warlocks for the last four hundred years, if not more. I hated it.

Wielders and Benders would be in their best attire, dripping riches. And the stuffy plantation that resemble a freak'n palace we were renting only made it worse.

My parents were forcing me to wear my glamour in the midst of all these prissy swans. It was all the Necrocretors' fault. Mom and Dad had commanded me to wear it at all times. Starting now.

Mom was like, "Sure it will work. earth Element Wielders

are so beautiful, Alex, and they would look for a beautiful Wielder. Finding Ducky in your place will make them just walk on by."

Just walk on by? Puh-lease.

Dad thought it was brilliant. The only one who felt my pain was my aunt. Mom and Dad didn't give a crap that they were ruining my life.

I took another giant mouthful of ham and cheese just as the doors opened to reveal Etan Sutcliff. I closed my eyes in frustration as a wave of fatigue washed over me in his presence. First school, now home. I set the sandwich on my plate and swallowed the suddenly dry lump in my throat.

He looked surprised to find me here. "I won't tell," he said with a conspiratorial wink. "Your secret is safe with me." He came to sit across from me.

I narrowed my eyes. My secret safe with him? What was he on?

"I get it," he said in an understanding tone, oblivious to my confusion. "It might be the only time you get off to eat something all night. You have no idea how demanding guests can get, serving at parties like this."

I looked at my lap. I got what he was implying. *He thinks I'm the help.*

"So, you work this sort of function a lot?"

On a whim, I decided to play dumb. He thought I wasn't a witch. Would he reveal our existence to an outsider? "What sort of functions would that be?"

"What do you think is tonight about?" He gave me a dazzling smile.

Smooth. "Don't know, don't care, and I don't give a shit. Just as long as I get paid." I decided to keep humoring him as he swallowed a sip of champagne. "It could be a swingers' party for all I care."

He spewed out his drink. White foam fizzed on the table between us. My lips curved upward. I got up and walked to the door. "Duty calls," I said and left.

I hated it when people made assumptions.

Outside I almost bumped into Sophie and Leanne with Ryan. The whole motley crew was here.

Leanne shoved an empty champagne flute in my hand.

"Ugly Duckling, what are you doing here?" She plopped her glass in my hand too. "I would like another, please."

"Sure, on its way." I walked toward the hallway. I put the empty glasses on a passing waiter's tray. I slipped up to my room.

Mom was there waiting. "Alex, where the hell were you?"

I rolled my eyes and said sarcastically, "Entertaining guests."

"You know how late this is. Your revealing is in half an hour."

"No Mom. Ducky's revealing is in half an hour." I felt like crying. This was so unfair.

"I know it's not easy, Alex, but we made a choice."

"I didn't think that it was going to lead to this. You think I love being her?" I whined. "I hate it."

"Why, because of how little people are reacting to her?" she asked. "It's not a bad thing, Alex. At least you will know who your real friends will be one day."

"Oh, and I'm sure Grandma conjured some hideous beast to find out who *your* real friends were. Is that why Siobhan left you a long time ago?".."

Mother's face fell. "Do not speak of the dead like that Alex."

I felt bad the second she said it. It just slipped out.

She shoved the dress into my hand. " You will be putting on this dress and will be doing what you were told, what you rehearsed with your father—showing them what your Element is," she hissed through her teeth.

I wanted to pull my face but was already playing on thin ice , so I sighed instead. *Yes ma'am*, I chided in my head.

Her eyes bored into my soul for a moment longer. Then she strode out, smacking the door closed behind her.

My dress awaited me on the bed.

I pulled it over my body—Ducky's blindingly pale body. I hoped the guests brought sunglasses.

The dress was way too long. Mom had made last-minute alterations, especially around the sides, and forgot to cut from the hem of the dress. Even with high heels, the dress brushed the floor.

I missed my height.

I turned sideways in the mirror.

I missed my ass and my sun-kissed skin. I missed my blue eyes, my dark hair, my plump lips... I missed me.

I wanted to scream, trapped in this ugly duckling's skin. I didn't know how long I looked at my reflection, but it felt like a long time. Tears formed in her eyes. Not my eyes—my reflection's. I felt ashamed that I had called her that. I sighed and wiped away the wetness.

Ethan's face jumped into my head. My stomach fluttered slightly. Even if he was an idiot, he still had an effect on me.

Mom was right. Dad was right. I was way over my head with him. The worst part was that he still had no clue who I was.

I didn't need my true appearance to do this. I needed to protect myself, protect what was waiting up ahead. And Ducky was that shield.

She wasn't ugly. She wasn't weak. That was me. I was the weak one, the shallow one. The pathetic one.

"I'm sorry," I whispered to the mirror and took a deep breath. In my mind, Ducky accepted my apology.

I uttered an old incantation to help with my hair, twisting it into the bun I always loved and in a few seconds, it was up and beautiful, even with the dry sticks Mom had given me for hair.

I pleated out my light blue dress, slipped on my elbow-length gloves, and stared at two huge brown eyes through thick glasses.

I was as ready as I could be.

I opened the door and waited to hear my name.

ETHAN

SOPHIE, Leanne, and Ryan stood by Dad and me, close to the wall by the stairs.

Sam was speaking to Soph in sign language, from the opposite side to where all the Wielders stood.

Flirting with her was more like it. She suppressed her laughter.

I had one sign for him; I raised my middle finger.

She slapped me playfully as the smile on Sam's face disappeared.

"He's an idiot. Just go talk to him." I looked at her.

She didn't appreciate my tone. Tonight we would probably fight again over me being too jealous and possessive. As if.

I just didn't like idiots or snobs. And Sam was a snob and a big fucking idiot.

She stomped off with Leanne on her heels as my father just shook his head.

I looked at Sam, who just stared at me with a blank expression. I raised my eyes at him and he finally looked away.

Jerk.

Clustered around him was every single Wielder who could be here tonight. It seemed everyone who lived close to headquarters had come. They were the most sophisticated Wielders, the ones whose forefathers could be traced to the eighteen-hundreds.

Beside me, Dad froze. I followed his gaze and saw her.

Meredith.

She was radiant, he skin almost resemble a pure satin by the way it sort of glow. Her hair was blonde, light blonde and taken up high into a bun. She was wearing a long flowy dress that fell over her curves elegantly. She couldn't be older then thirty but Dad was almost reaching his fifties. Why the fuck did my father chose Siobhan when he could have been her wielder.

Behind her was a handsome man with dark hair and midnight-blue eyes. They greeted all their guests with gracious smiles and soft-spoken words.

My heart started to gallop as I thought about the Fox again. Dad always said that earth Wielders were beautiful.

They approached Dad and me. "Jeffery!" Meredith sang Dad's name with a dazzling smile, kissing him on each cheek.

Frederick's jaw muscles pumped as he shook my hand.

"Thank you for inviting us." Dad bowed his head with a weird expression on his face. I couldn't interpret it, but it looked like Meredith could.

She avoided his gaze and turned to me. "You must be Ethan." She shook my hand gently.

"Yes, nice to meet you."

"Pleasure is all mine."

"Jeff," Frederick mumbled.

"Fred," Dad answered.

Both of their jaws pumped now.

Frederick addressed me. "Ethan, you fought well the other night. Let's just hope your bending technique is as great."

"Frederick," Meredith scolded him and Dad had to suppress his smile.

"What? I'm just saying."

"You need to excuse him. There is no filter from his mind to his mouth." She rolled her eyes.

"No offense taken."

Frederick huffed as he walked passed. His kid was the earth Wielder, all right. Dad couldn't keep his smile at bay anymore.

When Meredith and Frederick both reached the staircase, Sophie hooked her arm into mine. I sighed. Girls were so weird. I could never tell what mood they were in.

Someone clinked a silver fork against a crystal goblet. Everyone fell quiet.

Frederick boomed, "It is a delight to welcome all of you to our fine establishment tonight. And to show you our gratitude for coming, we would like to present you all with a gift that you can pick up later before you depart."

Everyone applauded. After it fell silent, he carried on. "Sixteen years ago, my wife brought the biggest joy of my life into this world. And tonight, it would be my pleasure to introduce you all to our daughter."

It felt as if my blood left my body. He said *daughter*.

Dad gulped his entire glass of champagne.

My Wielder was female.

"The reason we couldn't introduce her on the invitation is simple. She will show you all what she can do. I'm sure you will understand why we had to break tradition."

He had no problem with speaking in front of crowds. He lifted his glass of champagne and we all did the same.

"I present you my daughter, Alex Burgendorf."

Everyone's gazes lifted to the top of the stairs. A girl appeared.

My mouth fell open. It was Ugly Duckling.

I had made a total fool of myself. She wasn't a servant; she was merely just having a snack before her big night. I chuckled ruefully under my breath.

"What is it?" Dad asked me with a frown.

"She is the new kid at our school."

"She goes to Sky View?"

I nodded.

He huffed. His gaze lingered on her.

I wondered what was going through his mind. "What is it, Dad?"

"I don't know. earth Wielders are usually the opposite of... *that*."

"Maybe she's not the earth Wielder," I said hopefully.

"Maybe not."

We applauded as Alex reached her father and kissed him on each cheek. She kissed her mother too and took off one glove.

A servant walked toward them, a covered tray balanced on his hand.

"Alex has prepared something special for tonight," Frederick announced. "I'm quite nervous as she has been upset with me lately and I'm her lab rat for tonight."

The crowd ate it up and laughed appreciatively.

With a flourish, he removed the lid from the platter. On the platter rested a tree branch.

It was my turn to frown. She was an earth Wielder.

Alex started to spin her hand in the air. Everyone was mesmerized as tiny roots sprang from the branch and spiraled in the air. A single red rose blossomed atop the writhing mass of roots and leaves.

It deserved a gasp... and the crowd obliged.

I couldn't stop staring at her wielding this rose just from a branch.

I wanted to help when it spiraled too much to one side.

My father felt my anticipation. "Easy, Ethan."

I pulled myself back under control.

She plucked the rose without even touching it. It hovered in the air.

She gave her father a wicked smile.

"Easy now, darling," he joked. Breathless laughter erupted around me.

She stepped back and lifted both her hands. She made vigorous gestures in the air. The roots wove perfectly into a braided, earthy rope. It spiraled around her father and twisted tightly around him, pinning his arms to his sides and lifting him off his feet.

Everyone stared wide-eyed at the show.

Then it just stopped. Everything was still except Mr. Burgendorf's chest as he breathed hard. He didn't seem scared, just excited.

"You sure about that last statement, Daddy?" she said cunningly. Everyone laughed again.

She went sidled up to her father. The rose floated closer to his face and touched his cheek. Her lips moved. A tiny groan emitted from Frederick.

She stroked the side of his cheek in long, elegant movements, from his jawline to his temple. Everywhere she touched revealed a beast. As if Frederick was a beast hiding in human skin.

Gasps filled the air.

Alex blew on the velvety crimson petals. They flew into the sky toward the windows way up at the top and kissed her father.

The roots retreated slowly back into the branch that lay on the silver tray.

Frederick was put back onto his feet. When all the roots disappeared, the lid went back on the platter.

"Alex Burgendorf," Frederick cried. The room thundered with applause from all the Benders and Wielders, the ladies' gold bangles jangling merrily.

My father smiled but his eyes were narrowed. Something bugged him.

"What don't you buy, Dad?"

"Everything. I told you that earth Wielders are far more attractive than this little duck."

I couldn't help but smile. "I don't understand."

"Something is not quite right here, son."

"Dad, it is what is, remember? You're right. I will be okay. Besides it's just what people are saying, maybe this attraction between earth Wielders and Benders isn't what people say it is."

My father laughed. "It's not that simple, Ethan. Every single earth Wielder in history, as well as every earth Bender, has failed. It almost led to world destruction. Who do you think laid down the rule that Wielders and Benders are not allowed to cross the line."

I looked at Alex skeptically. No way was I going to fall for *that*.

"It isn't that easy," my father said, eying Alex with suspicion.

THE PRESENTATION WAS FOLLOWED by a night of fine wine and dining. The party moved into the ballroom and sat at round tables.

Alex was at the farthest table from mine. I didn't look much her way.

Sophie got extremely quiet after the presentation. Ugly Duckling was more than just that. She was a powerful earth Wielder behind that pair of glasses. Sophie's thoughts were brewing almost audibly.

My father still didn't buy all of this. I could see how desperately he wanted to know what her parents was hiding.

To me, though, it was simple: Alex was the first earth Wielder that wasn't breathtakingly beautiful.

No, her beauty lay in the wielding. One couldn't take one's eyes off her when she wielded earth.

Frederick and Alex opened the dance floor. For all her awkwardness, she moved with a certain grace... at least until she stumbled over her too-long dress. Sequined women and tuxedoed men rose and followed their steps.

My father slipped out the back. He never was one for this sort of thing. Always out of place.

Around eleven, I saw Alex standing by the punch. I walked up to her. For the first time since we met, I looked—really looked —at her. Her knees started to shake. She immediately looked up, found my gaze, and held it with her own.

I frowned. Could it be me that...? Then I felt it. A current of energy flowing through me. Soft, but it was there. Why didn't I felt it before?

Her words from that day at the running track jumped into my mind. She'd said she was weary of me. *This* was what she meant.

I stopped right next to her. "You could've said something, you know."

"And take all the fun away from every assumption?" she scoffed.

"You like it when people make asses out of themselves."

"Ah, so you know what 'assume' means when you break it down. You seem to forget, you weren't the only one who was made out to be an ass. I was too."

"Then why didn't you say something?"

"Like what? Who I was? Do you know the danger that's out there, Ethan. I guess not. My dad had to make sure that it's safe before telling anyone about me."

"We could've..."

"Besides," she interrupted me. "Nobody buys it."

I stared at her. She looked away. "I think my appearance summed everything up, don't you?"

I huffed. "It's just looks, Alex."

"Yet everyone seems to call me nasty names about what I remind them of."

It slipped out in a harsh bark. "They are just people." I felt super bad. Ugly Duckling was just a cute name for someone whose beauty still needed to be discovered.

Her jaw was set. "Easy for you to say, Ethan."

"How long have you known?"

"Since the night of the Celebration."

I squinted. "You were there?"

"I was there, hiding in the darkest corner."

"It's not what I meant."

"Oh, no. Sorry, I guess I assumed." She raised her eyebrows and started to walk away as Sophie reached us.

She stopped as she passed Sophie. "Tell your friend next time he should think twice at who his target is. Doing things to gain pretty girls' trust isn't very manly or sexy. I will hang him by his toes next time and the one who ordered him to do it.. And I will make sure there is an audience."

Eyes round, Sophie swallowed hard. Alex turned around and walk away, more like gliding away.

The corners of my lips twitched, but I didn't dare smile. Alex truly blamed Sophie for everything. I nudged her. "What did she mean, 'doing things to gain pretty girls' trust'?"

She looked away, guilty.

"Soph, please tell me you didn't ask Ryan to hit her with that ball."

"I didn't think he would be spot-on," she protested. "I just wanted to scare her. I didn't know who she was, okay?"

I felt pissed-off. "Still, why would you do that?"

"Oh, please, Ethan. It's not like you're innocent in this whole thing."

She was referring to my ugly nickname.

"I felt bad about that, okay?"

"Still, it didn't stop you." She stormed away.

I glimpsed Alex walking toward her room. I wished it was that easy—to say what was on my mind and head off to bed.

It was time to hunt my father down and go home myself. I'd had enough of balls, legends, and girls with glasses.

12

ALEX

I HANDED in my art project. It was a mess. When I'd left the house in the morning, it had looked great—a scale model of uptown complete with tiny houses and pristine streets. I'd felt positive that it would get me an A+.

That was, until I "bumped into" Sophie. "Bumped into" belonged in quoted because there was no doubt that she'd done it on purpose.

My project tumbled from my grip and somersaulted in the air. I lost my balance, frantically grabbing my glasses. The replica clattered to the floor before I recovered.

"So sorry, Alex!" She knelt down and picked up my project —and I didn't miss it when she squeezed the crumpled pasteboard, further damaging the small houses before she handed them over.

"Just leave it!" I yelled, making another scene.

She lifted her hands in a defensive gesture. Leanne and the cheerleading squad suppressed giggles.

Cynthia lost it. "You are all evil. The devil's spawn." Her

dark hair fell wildly across her googly glasses as she gave them a filthy look. She knew how dangerous they were, but she stood up for me. It made me feel good.

Sophie got all up in Cynthia's personal space, shoulders back, boobs out like weapons. "Oh? And what are you going to do, freckles?"

"Enough," I yelled.

Sophie leveled her wicked smile on me. She came super close, staring down at me. My true self was just as tall as she was, but Ducky was no contest.

"Remember where you are, specs. I'm not afraid of you," she whispered.

"Be careful," I spat back. "There's no holding back at the institute."

For a split second I could see fear in her eyes. Then she regained herself, lifted her hands, and backed away with an evil grin adorning her face. Her friends surrounded her like a patch of cattails and they drifted off.

Cynthia looked at me with huge eyes. "What the hell just happened?"

I fumbled for a quick lie. "Nothing. My mom is sort of a karate freak. She's sent me to lessons since I could speak. Sophie there just met her match at the institute the other day."

"You train with them." Admiration dripped from Cynthia's tone. "You go, girl. That one getting her ass kicked is something I so want to see." She jutted her thumb over her shoulder in the direction the cheerleader demons had left.

Uh oh. I had to steer her clear of that kind of thinking. "Rules of the institute. No fighting out of class."

"Do you think they will take on new students?"

Oh, crap. "No, I think they're full at the moment." *Lie better Alex.* It would be a disaster if Cynthia's mom phoned asking difficult questions. "My mom pays loads of money just so they could accept me, and I have to prove that I'm worthy."

Cynthia's eyes grew big again. "Okay, maybe it's not for me. I'm not good when it comes to proving myself to anyone."

I jostled her shoulder with my own. "Don't say that. You would be surprised what people can do when opportunity presents itself. I mean, just look at what you did standing up to those girls."

"Yeah, that felt pretty radical."

I laughed at her word choice.

"Sorry about your project." She leaned down to help me to pick up the houses as delicately as possible. "You know that wasn't an accident, right?"

I nodded. "I know."

"Why does she pick on you so much?" Cynthia wanted to know.

"Because she's insecure," I said.

"Sophie, insecure?" Cynthia's eyebrows shot up.

I laughed. "It's hard to explain. I'm better than she is at something, and that always makes people like her insecure."

"Got it." She mimed writing a note in the air. "Find something you are better at than Sophie Rutter."

The rest of the day, whenever I had free time, I tried to save my project and put it back together as best as I could.

Ethan came over as I was standing at my locker. I felt him before seeing him. Cynthia's mouth almost hung on the ground when he spoke to me.

"I'm sorry about this morning."

"Why are you sorry? You didn't break my project."

He scowled. "Alex, you're always so defensive."

"Fine, apology accepted. I hope you know why she is doing all of this."

He shook his head.

"Thought you were smarter than that, Ethan."

"Just tell me." He sounded defeated and annoyed.

"Because of you. Just stay away from me, please," I begged.

"You know it's not going to be that easy, Alex. We have a lot of training to do."

I closed my locker and shrugged. I was done with this. I spun on my heel and left him standing there.

Cynthia's footsteps stomped behind me. "What the hell?"

"Oh, he is sort of my sparring buddy. Hate that," I said softly.

"You practice with Ethan Sutcliff."

I smiled. She made him sound as if he was her moon, sun, and stars.

"Now I get why Sophie hates you so much."

I laughed. "Yeah, I wish he got it too."

"Seriously," she asked and I nodded. "I guess you can't have everything. Right?"

I laughed. She was right: Ethan Sutcliff wasn't very bright sometimes.

AFTER SCHOOL, I fled the disapproving glare of my art teacher to find Louis waiting for me outside. I offered Cynthia a ride, but she eyed Louis, whose demeanor screamed no-nonsense-goon-squad, and declined. I gave her a cheerful wave and hopped in the SUV.

I slouched into the house after a boring drive home. Louis never talked much other than polite answers when he was asked a direct question.

My foot was on the first stair when Mom's voice called out, "Alex."

I sighed. I just wanted to go to my room and forget about the art project Dad and I had worked on the past week.

I slunk into the dining room, where she was having a cup of coffee at the table.

Her face brightened with a smile. "How was your day? How did the art project go?"

My face fell.

"Uh oh," Mom said. "What happened?"

"Nothing expected," I said sarcastically. "Just Sophie smashing into me while I was carrying it."

"So, it's Sophie who has been giving you a hard time. She is a fire Bender."

I shrug not knowing how mom even knew that or if Soph was a fire bender at all.?"

"Mom, please. I can take care of myself."

"I'm so sorry, sweetheart." She got up and give me a hug. "You worked so hard on that project."

I sighed. "I know. Good thing Cynthia actually stood up to them."

"Cynthia, your new friend?"

"Yes." I still couldn't believe it myself.

"You can invite her for a sleepover, sweetheart."

"You kidding me, right? And how do I explain to her the miraculous transformation when I take off my glasses, Mom?"

Mom froze. "Okay, I didn't think about that one. Well, why not invite her for an afternoon or go watch a movie or something?"

"I'll think about it." Suddenly I felt crabby all over again.

"Alex, there's something else we need to talk about."

I sighed. *What now?*

"About spending time with a certain earth Bender."

Incredulous, I laughed. This was just my luck. I'd told him today to stay away from me, and here Mom wanted to push us together.

"What is it?"

I shook my head, gazing at the ground, my arm on my hip. "Nothing. So, what is the plan?"

"You have to start training with him at the institute."

"When?" I asked. Maybe I didn't lie to Cynthia after all.

"Tonight, around five."

I nodded and stared into nothing. I shook myself under the sullen mood that had settled around my shoulders. "Anything else?"

"Nope, you are free to go." She shooed me out.

I rushed up to my room. I fell on my bed, took off my glasses, and watched my old self with her long legs and lean body snap back into place.

I wonder what Ethan Sutcliff would do if I showed up as myself tonight and not as the Ugly Duckling. But Mom and Dad would have aneurisms, that was for sure.

ETHAN

I FOUND Dad again at the table reading a newspaper as the sun caught that side of the house. Mom used to tease him that he was a shifter in his previous life. A cat to be precise. He did love the afternoon sun, always baking and purring away.

He looked up as I entered.

"Good, you're home. We need to talk."

"About what?" My voice was tired.

"Alex."

"It's useless, Dad. She made it crystal clear today that she wants nothing to do with me."

The newspaper crinkled in his hands, leaving a faint black stain on his fingertips. "Ethan, it's not up to her. I already spoke to her mother, getting a few things out of the way, making sense of a few too."

"You met with her mother?" I wondered what Dad's agenda was behind this.

"Don't look at me like that. I'm much wiser then I used to be. The attraction isn't that strong anymore."

I didn't bother hiding my skepticism. "If you say so."

He narrowed his eyes. "And what is that supposed to mean?"

"C'mon, Dad. I saw the way you looked at her at Alex's party. You still like her. More than you let on."

"She is married to Frederick, Ethan. I had my chance and I chose Siobhan.

"Yeah, and then she died. I felt bad at times for my father. He didn't speak a lot about his choices and why he chose Siobhan and not Meredith.

"Getting back to you, you start training tonight with her at the institute."

"The institute. Are you guys insane? There isn't enough space for us at the institute."

He thought about it. A dazed look fell across his eyes, the corners twitching. I saw the memory occur to him: my eleventh birthday party. Thank heavens it had only been Benders and Wielders and not normal kids in attendance. "Then where do you suggest?"

"In the woods. It will give us space to expand and explore with the earth Element."

Nodding, Dad slipped his phone out of his jacket pocket. He dialed a number and said hello to Meredith. I left him a little privacy as he grappled with how to argue over the danger of a confined space when exploring with earth Element.

A smile tugged at the corners of my lips. Ducky was not going to be happy about this. Not one bit.

13

ALEX

"HELL NO. We are training at the institute, Jeff, and that is final." Mom slammed down the phone and cussed under her breath, something about confined spaces.

So Ethan wanted to take our sessions closer to our Element. I huffed. I knew how to handle my Element. He probably wanted more space for that ego of his.

Mom knocked on my door at fifteen minutes to five.

I had on my trainers and T-shirt. In my real body, up in my room, it hadn't looked so bad, but the minute I put on my glasses, I drowned in them. The T-shirt was practically a sail. My entire body deflated. I gave my best pleading expression to Mom.

"You know why we are doing this, sweetheart."

"Yeah, I know." I said. "Still, she's a lot to get used to. I feel so puny."

"You are, babes." She put her arm over my shoulder and pulled me close. She gave me a sweet smile and handed me my favorite jacket.

I shrugged out of her embrace and pulled it over my head. Even my jacket was too big, the arms way too long, and it strained over the muffin top pooch of my waistline.

Alex was graceful, athletically built, and lean. She had a fast metabolism. Ducky was short and clumsy, and her metabolism moved at the speed of a slug.

I gave up on the zipper and followed Mom out to the car.

The drive to the institute made my stomach turn. Mom had made an add-on to the glasses, a charm to make them stay on my face. It felt now as if I was wearing swimming goggles. I didn't know what to expect, but Mom promised she would be with me every step of the way.

There weren't a lot of cars as she pulled up to the parking lot. A yellow Jeep, a convertible, a Cherokee SUV, and a Mustang.

I climbed out. The minute my feet touched the ground, I could feel the incubus starting to drain what little energy I had.

"Are you okay?" Mom frowned at me.

"I'll live," I growled.

We went to the front of what looked like a boxing club.

"You sure we are at the right place?"

"Yep. The institute has done wonders to make this place to blend in, Alex." She opened the front door and I could feel a strange tug, an invisible barrier like I imagined a magnetic field would be. Something that wasn't Ethan.

"What is that?"

"Another glamour, for when normal folk walk in here by accident."

We entered a gray lobby paneled with faded inspirational posters and the same dingy fake-pebble rubber flooring that every cheap community gym had. Dusty fluorescent lights with bulbs glared overhead, making the poor receptionist look gaunt and zombielike.

We went to the front desk and waited for what felt like forever. Then a lady who seemed to have the flu walked out and planted herself at the squat reception desk. She blew her nose with a ridiculous honk. "Can I help you?"

Mom intoned,

> *Magic mend and candle burn.*
> *Sickness end, good health return.*

The glamour fell away the minute Mom uttered the spell. A shimmer washed away the ordinary-looking boxing club. White marble columns flanked an elegant, arched doorway behind her. A gleaming oak floor and a utilitarian but tasteful desk replaced what had been there before.

A repeating motif chased itself along the floor, the crown molding, the columns, and even the baseboards. It was an emblem of two crossed swords and a chalice. The chalice made me think of the Jinns.

The muffled but distinctive sounds of fighting in were no longer blocked by the glamour.

The hacking, coughing lady transformed into a fetching woman whose long, dark hair and creamy garment made me think of a Greek goddess.

Mom cleared her throat. "I'm here to see Mira Garland."

"One sec," she said and sashayed through the archway.

"This place is something else." Why was I so nervous? It was just Ethan Sutcliff. With that sculpted body and V-line... Ah, I should not have gone there.

A woman with pink hair and the stern face of a drill sergeant walked straight up to Mom while the receptionist glided back to her post.

"Mira." Mom smiled from ear to ear.

The woman with pink hair grabbed Mom in a bear hug and

squealed like a teenage girl. "I thought I was never going to see you again. You haven't changed a bit."

"You are too kind. I've changed plenty, believe me," Mom cooed. "This—" she pointed at me— "is Alex, my daughter."

Mira turned around and her face fell. It was something people did lately when Ducky got introduced as Mom's daughter. This woman hadn't attended my revealing; otherwise she would've been ready to hide her shock.

"Oh." Her confused gaze darted between Mom and me.

"Alex," Mom said as if I were the dumbstruck one.

"Nice to meet you," I said through gritted teeth.

Mira shook herself. "How rude of me. Alex, nice to meet you. I'm Mira. I'm a bender and one of the Peers of this institute. Come. Ethan is waiting."

Mom held out her arm toward the entrance and I followed Mira through it.

I couldn't help but to whistle under my breath. Something told me that this training was going be disastrous.

ETHAN

LATE. And not just by a few minutes. Dad and I had been waiting for more than a freakin' hour. He did tell them four, right?

I hated that her mother had vetoed my request to train in the woods. Dad wasn't too happy either.

Something told me tonight was going to be chaotic.

I just hoped that, by tomorrow, there wouldn't be a huge tree growing through the middle of the arena.

Finally, Alex and her mother showed up, tagging along behind Mira.

"It's about fucking time," I mumbled.

"Easy, Ethan. You don't want to start this session the wrong way."

I rolled my eyes. I wasn't scared of the Ugly Duckling. She had this thing about her, thinking that she was smarter and better than everyone else. Sure, I'd made a mistake and assumed the wrong thing about her, but jeez. *Give me a break.*

Mira finally reached us. She raised her eyebrows, a mischievous smile curving her mouth. "You ready, Ethan?"

"I've been ready for the past hour," I grumbled. I could feel my father's eyes on me as I started doing windmills with my arms to warm up my muscles again.

"Are we late?" Meredith consulted her watch.

"Not a lot," Dad demurred. It was his turn to receive my glare.

Alex cowered behind her mother.

"Shall we begin?" Meredith asked.

Yes, please, if you don't mind... your highness, I thought snarkily. They sure acted like royalty.

"What is wrong with you?" Alex demanded.

I leveled a look at her too. *I've been waiting for you for a fucking hour. That's what's wrong. Learn to be punctual. Better, ask your mother to turn your ass into a clock.*

I should've said that. It would've been the best comeback of the year. But I behaved. "Nothing. Can we start?"

She nodded and wriggled out of her ill-fitting jacket. The sleeves covered her hands but the front part didn't want to close. Dad made a slight noise, his attention fixed on her jacket too.

What was it with him?

I shook it away; whatever it was, it had to wait for another time. Right now, it was Bending time.

Finally.

14

ETHAN

ALEX WAS EXTREMELY WEAK. Never thought I would say that about an earth Wielder.

Legend had it that they were the most powerful of all the Wielders. Classes extolled the unbelievable feats of earth Wielders from eras past. But here she was taking breaks almost every fifteen minutes.

Her legs wobbled, and it was worse when I touched her arms to help her to wield.

My father just shook his head.

We weren't going to get anywhere at this pace.

The umpteenth time Alex failed to wield earth like she had done that night with merely a branch, I shook my head. "What is up with you?" I asked.

"I'm tired." She staggered to the sidelines, where her mother sat holding a tablet.

"Alex, we are not going to get stronger if you keep taking breaks."

"I can't help it," she said, a few octaves higher than strictly necessary. "I'm not the incubus here." She scowled.

"What am I missing here?" I asked Dad, who was standing off on his own, staring at the floor, his jaw muscles pumping.

Alex's voice was snide. "What, you think I'm weak at the knees every time you smile at me? Or wait, it must be that gorgeous body of yours."

I frowned. What was wrong with this chick?

"*You* are what's draining me." She sounded so frustrated. "You keep stealing my energy like a blood-sucking leech." She pantomimed claws in the air.

"Is this true?"

Meredith didn't look up from her tablet as she answered. "Alex will get used to it, Ethan, but yes, what she says is correct. You drain all the power she has."

Alex glared at her mother but it went unnoticed.

I was starting to understand her frustration. No attention at home—not me at all. I lifted my arms in defeat. "We might as well bring the tents and sleeping bags next time, because at this rate, I'm afraid we won't get far."

Alex grunted and pushed herself from the spot she had just claimed next to her mom. She strode over to me and poked me in the chest. "I have a better idea. Let's call it quits, because I doubt I would be able to learn anything from you."

"What is your problem? Because I didn't get the memo."

"*My* problem? I'm afraid that *you* are too daft and won't get it."

"Alexandra," Meredith finally interrupted. "What is this?"

"I'm tired, Mom," she yelled. For a second I thought she was going to cry. "I can't do this anymore." She reached up to take off her glasses and her mother suddenly had all the attention in the world.

She shot up and grabbed Alex's wrist. "Okay," was all I

heard. "Is there an office where I can speak in private with my daughter?"

Mira nodded. She picked up her handbag and led Alex by the arm to Mira's office.

My jaw dropped open. Literally. *They waltz in here an hour late, we haven't even trained for a full hour, and now they are going to leave again?*

Dad watched them walk away with narrowed eyes. Mira came back toward us.

The minute she was in earshot, I sighed. "So what, that's it?"

"It looks like it, Golden Boy. What is that bad energy between the two of you?"

"It's a long story." I pulled my hand through my hair.

The three of us turned toward Mira's office. Meredith closed the blinds.

"You getting the same feeling?" Mira asked my father.

"I don't know. Something doesn't add up."

My father has said this from the minute he saw her.

"They usually aren't this tired."

"Exactly my point," he agreed.

"What do you think is wrong?" I was intrigued.

"I don't know, son, but I'm sure as hell going to find out."

The door finally opened. Meredith came out alone, serenely slipping something into her blazer pocket.

"I'm afraid that is all for tonight. I'm so sorry, Ethan. I'll see if I can give her a tonic or something before she comes to train next time."

A faint flicker of concern hit me. "Is she okay?"

"She's fine. Just tired." She said the word tired as if it was code for something else. She nodded as she walked past. "Jeff. Mira." And just like that she was gone.

I slouched to the showers. Tonight was a complete waste of my time.

Dad waited for me outside in the Jeep while I got my bag and got lectured by Mira about being more patient. "Maybe you'll learn more if you're patient," she said.

Whatever that meant. If the Ugly Duckling could be here on time, then I could turn down the volume on my grouchiness.

I left her standing there and blew past everyone I saw without a word. I just wanted to go home.

Why did my Wielder hate me so much?

Did she know that I had been the one to give her that nickname everyone was calling her? Shit. She probably found out and that was why she was so pissed.

Dad was waiting, Jeep idling, in front of the club. I got in.

He pealed out the minute I slammed the door. He drove fast.

"Something chasing us?" I asked, pulling on my seatbelt.

"No, but tonight I'm going to get answers. Meredith is hiding something big." He emitted a manic little laugh I'd never heard out of him before. "I can feel it." That laugh again. Like it was a game.

I don't have time for this shit.

He dropped me off and left as if the devil was chasing him.

I unlocked the door and went to my room. I just wanted this day to be over. Mira wanted me to be patient with her.

Yeah, Christmas was coming too.

ALEX

TONIGHT HAD BEEN A COMPLETE MESS. Every time he touched my arms it was as if he deliberately stole all my energy.

I'd never felt so drained my entire life. I couldn't do it anymore. I had to get out of there, had to get rid of the glamour.

The second Mom closed the blinds, I took off the glasses and returned to my real form. I started to feel better, but it wasn't enough for my bad mood to disappear.

I took it out on Ethan. I shouldn't have, but I was so mad at him. It was so unfair that he could just take my energy and use it however he wanted, wasting it on frivolous things.

Why didn't I had that power over him?

It didn't escape me that Mom didn't even introduce me properly to Jeff Sutcliff. I guessed he also had that ability to crawl under her skin.

"Go, Alex," Mom held out her hand for Ducky's glasses and I surrendered them without hesitation. I'd happily throw them into a volcano at this point.

"How?" If that door opened now, anyone on the other side would get a heart attack.

She walked to the window and opened it. "Just go. I'll apologize."

"Apologize? I can't do this."

"We will speak later tonight. Go," she ordered again.

I shrugged and jumped through the first-floor window with my hoodie pulled up to obscure my face. A convenient hedge of juniper bushes encircled the building, and crept along the side of the building until I was in view of the parking lot. There I knelt in the dirt behind a bush among wrinkled purple berries, trying not to get the sticky sap all over my clothes. A bright, resinous smell filled my nose and helped clear my head.

I waited for what felt like forever.

Mom finally came out, but still I waited. I wasn't surprised when she opened her car door and Jeff's voice called her name.

He jogged into view, standing a few yards away in the parking lot. I couldn't hear what they were saying, but by Mom's hesitance and tense body language, it was clear that yeah, he had the same effect on her that Ethan had on me.

She finally climbed into the SUV as Jeff went back inside. She reversed out of her parking spot toward to where I was hiding.

I sprinted to the car, opened the passenger door, and jumped in.

Mom drove away so fast, the tires squealed. Wordlessly we watched the unremarkable sunset drain out of the sky and shadows deepened among the suburban homes that got bigger and more expensive as we neared our neighborhood. I was still quiet when we pulled up to the Buchman plantation.

Dad and Aunt Ariel both gasped when they saw me and not Ducky's face. I shook my head and ran up to my room without preamble. Mom could take the job of recounting the utter failure that had been my training session.

How the hell were we going to fix this?

I was about to stick my earbuds in and turn on my mp3 player when I heard Jeff's voice. Curiosity got the better of me. I tiptoed to my door.

I cursed the creaky wooden floors. The entire house made noise. It worked on my nerves. I opened the door.

Jeff's voice, low and insistent, floated up the stairs. "I want to know what you're hiding, Meredith."

"We are not hiding anything," my father said.

"Please, Jeff." Mom's tone was sweet.

"Don't you dare!" No longer keeping quiet. "That's my son. He needs to learn how to protect her. *That* up there is *not* the earth Wielder."

"Leave my house," my father yelled.

"I swear to you Meredith, if you have been wasting our time..."

"You do what?" Mom shrieked. "What, Jeff? You've done

everything you could possibly do to me twenty years ago."

"Leave, or I'll make you leave," my father threatened.

"I want to see her," Jeff insisted.

My feet moved as if of their own volition. I was already walking down the stairs.

"She is sleeping. Please, just go," Mom begged.

"I'm not going anywhere. You had your kid go out the freakin' window, for crying out loud."

Dad mumbled something and could hear his footsteps stomping off.

Aunt Ariel joined the fray. "Jeff, I really think..."

"Stay out of this, Ariel," he growled.

"Don't tell my sister to stay out of this," Mom spat.

"Enough!" I said. All of them turned to me at once. "You're acting like a bunch of spoiled brats."

Jeff gaped at me, then at Mom and back at me again. "Who is this?"

Mom didn't answer. No need in trying to lie to him, so I walked up to him, held out my hand and introduced myself as I'd wanted to do this evening.

He took my hand, mouth opening and closing like a fish. I knew what was whirring through his mind. This was the look of an earth Wielder. "Why?" Jeff managed at last.

My father came back and stopped, thunderstruck.

"It's okay, Daddy. He's right, he needs to know."

"Then he should have some manners and not come into my home and demand answers."

The vitriol between the two of them was intense.

"Let's go. I'm sure Mom can explain why she did this." I met his bemused gaze. "And I will just have to trust his judgment to keep it to himself until the right time."

With that, I hooked my arm into my father's and we went to his room to watch some classic movies.

15

ALEX

FOR THE NEXT FEW DAYS, school continued to be terrible and training after school was the same. We no longer used the institute during off hours, and other individuals and bender/wielder pairs worked in the giant room. Sophie made sure she was never far away. Sometimes Mira or her partner, a red-faced, blustery man named Sedgwick, held group training sessions at the same time we practiced.

This made everything worse, the awareness of an audience.

Jeff didn't even look at my mother. He was still pissed off about the glamour. I didn't know what Mom told him, but for some reason he didn't tell his son about my true appearance behind Ducky's beer-bottle lenses.

Ethan still acted like it was the end of the world every time I ask for a break. I could see he was anxious to learn how to bend earth.

I felt his pain, really I did. Because away from him, I made the most beautiful art with my Element. Somehow, I could bend it too. I would never be as good as him, but I missed it, especially when I was this close to him.

Mom gave me a bottle of water.

"Unless there is some special potion giving me extra strength in there, it's not going to do shit," I said.

Her eyes bored into my skull. "Language," she admonished.

I didn't give a shit anymore. I was tired. I was always tired.

"Ugh, enough," she barked. She yanked me up from the bench. For a second, I thought she was going to show the entire club who I really was. She pulled me to the padded ring where Ethan stood and bounced on his toes. Like he was flaunting how much energy he had. Jerk.

We stopped in front of him.

Mom stuck out a finger at him. "Take off your shirt."

Ethan looked wary. "Excuse me?"

"You want to bend earth?" she asked. "Then take off your shirt."

Oh no. I closed my eyes. This was not going to end well. I remembered the body hiding underneath that shirt... and its effects on me.

He took off his shirt real fast, as if bending earth was something he had to do, no, something he needed to do. As if Ethan Sutcliff's survival depended on it.

Mom stared at his torso a little bit and I blushed. *Seriously. He's, like, seventeen.*

She snapped out of it and whirled on me. "Okay, Alex."

Jeff approached, hands out as if calming a feral animal. "What are you going to do?" He voiced the question that buzzed in my mind.

"Shush." Mom pushed me right in front of Ethan. His pecs were in my face. I stepped back.

This was so awkward.

"You want your energy back? Then take it. Stop whining about how tired you are and take it back."

"How?" I whined.

She took me gently by the arm and pulled me away from Ethan. *Thank heavens.* It felt as if I could breathe again.

Everyone who was supposed to be training stared at us. A part of me believed it was because Mom was going to teach them something about witch power, or maybe it was because Ethan took off his shirt. It was a fifty-fifty situation.

"Like this," she said. "Repeat after me. Oh, and as for you," she said to Ethan, "this won't affect you since I'm a fire Wielder."

He gave a noncommittal shrug. "Okay."

"Candle burn, consumed by fire," she intoned, placing both her hands on his shoulders. She stroked gently from his neck, over his shoulders, down his arms.

I'm going to die.

"And come to pass what I desire." She changed direction, palms on his stomach headed upward to his chest and stopping below his chin.

What the fuck? Mortification paralyzed me. Ethan looked horror-struck. *Please, just kill me now*, I prayed.

"Flames creep down to iron pin." She repeated the first movement. *"Release the power contained with in."* She touched his torso again.

Jeff started to chuckle. "Are you mad?"

Thank you! I could have kissed him right then—if that wouldn't make both of us look mad.

She arched a cocky eyebrow. "He is so desperate to bend, I'm giving him a chance to show me if he is really ready for this."

I knew I certainly wasn't not ready for this, but it seemed my opinion didn't matter here.

"Bring it on." Ethan was so full of confidence.

The corners of her lips curved. "Okay. Alex."

"Do I really have to do that?" I asked.

"Yes, you do." Mom pushed me toward Ethan again.

"Is this going to hurt?" he asked his father.

"Just be prepared." Something told me she'd used this on him before. No wonder they couldn't fight the resistance.

I took a deep breath. My hands hovered in the air over his shoulder. His gleaming skin called to my fingertips.

Ethan started to bark like a rabid dog. I pulled my hands back as if burned. Mom jumped from the sudden outburst. But then everyone laughed.

So immature. "Har, har," I said.

"I won't bite. Just touch me." He took my hand and placed it onto his body.

"Okay, fine." I yanked my hand back again and got ready.

I did what Mom said, reciting the first line of the spell. But then I didn't do the second part correctly and she stopped me.

"Like this," she said and touched his wrists. "When you reach his hands, make a circular movement toward his stomach as you want the energy to move in a circular direction toward you."

She wasn't making any sense. I suspected she only wanted to get her hands on his perfectly sculpted body, but okay, I'd go with it.

I took her place again, rolled my eyes, and started over.

Nothing happened. This was a waste of my time, not just my energy. But she insisted I try again. And again.

Then it happened. The fifth time I felt up Ethan Sutcliff, a strong current jolted through my body. I couldn't stop it. It was electrifying. The floor shook underneath my feet.

I tried to stop, but I didn't have any control over it. What the hell was happening?

Royal blue and crimson mats stacked on the floor burst into

pieces. White foam puffed into the air as big branches sprouted from underneath the caramel wood floor.

Screams reverberated off the walls. People scattered to escape the three—no, five—tree roots that punched up through the floor.

Mom was gone, Jeff was gone, and worst of all, Ethan didn't Bend shit. It was just him and me and a violent forest threatening to consume us and drag us down to hell.

"Ethan, bend!" Mom's shout sounded far above me, like way up, the ceiling up.

I heard a grunt from Ethan.

The roots were forming a massive tree. I wished I could stop. It was never like this. Why wouldn't my Element just stop? What the hell did my mother do? But the energy just filled me, as if I were nothing but an overflowing pitcher of light.

Glass shattered. Peopled yelped and cried out. Wood splintered. Light faltered as the tree reached the ceiling and burst the fluorescent bulbs.

I couldn't look. I couldn't stop it. I couldn't do anything.

Abruptly the earth stopped rumbling.

The roots came to a halt as if someone had pushed the off button on nature.

I strained my eyes. Something sparkled in the gloom. My heart raced. My chest heaved.

"What the hell!" Sophie screamed from somewhere on my right. Probably against a wall. "You want to kill us?"

I blew my hair out of my face. I didn't want to touch any part of me right now. I clearly didn't have control as well as I thought I had.

"Ethan," my mother's voice said. "Are you okay?"

"Yep, I think I have it." He sounded like he was flat on his back.

"You finally got it?" I yelled. "You got shit."

ALL THE OTHERS who had been training dissipated. From the looks of things, their training would be out for a few weeks.

The club was ruined. A massive tree towered in the center of the practice space. Its heavy boughs were adorned with bits of flooring and workout equipment, bizarre Christmas ornaments. It was a sycamore, I was pretty sure, with its verdant foliage and mottled, flaky bark in alternating brown, gray, and greenish-white.

Mom stood off to one side, promising the two grim-faced Peersthat she would get them a glamour in the next few hours and chanted a spell that would hold until then,so normal folks wouldn't see a tree growing through the middle of the boxing club. "And of course I'll pay for the damages," she vowed.

I hadn't wanted Ethan to be right, but he was. He'd suggested practicing in our natural habitat.

This was what Ethan had feared. Mom just had to prove a point, that he wasn't ready for earth.

He was lucky that my glamour dampened most of my power. Otherwise every single day would've probably ended with him lying flat on his back and *not* in a sexy way.

Still, touching him tonight like that had been... I shivered. I hoped never to have to do it again.

I'd never felt so embarrassed in my entire life. Sure, he had a hot body. Many girls, my best friend included, would have killed to touch him the way I had tonight. But doing it in front of our parents? Awkward!

I made sure to get out of there first.

On my way out, I apologized to Sedgwick, the guy who ran the place with Mira. He looked like one of the GI Joe action figures that Dad collected.

Pushing through the front door, I took big gulps of the warm evening air. Thankfully night had already fallen. I went straight to Mom's SUV and leaned against it. I was scared to look up, scared to find out just what damage me element had caused, but saw nothing, when I finally did. Mom was really good at spells.

Finally, she showed, climbing through the tangled roots that blocked the entrance. She closed the door and had a huge grin on her face. "That was..."

"Not amazing. What were you thinking? Did you know that was going to happen?"

She stopped. Her smile disappeared. "I didn't think it would be like that the first time."

"Mom, did I have to touch him?"

"Oh, c'mon, Alex. It's not the end of the world. Unless you feel something for the brute."

"No," I lied. Any girl in their right mind would feel something toward Ethan Sutcliff, physically at least.

"You did terrific. You should be proud of yourself."

The car chirped as she unlocked it and we both got in. "Mom, there is a huge tree growing through the roof of the institute. How the heck are you going to make a glamour big enough so that everyone else who isn't like us sees a normal building?"

She smiled again. That confident grin of hers. "If I can make the prettiest girl in town look like..." She sighed. "Well, not so pretty... I can glamour a stupid building."

She put the keys into the ignition and stepped on the gas.

I pulled my hoodie up and took off my glasses. Everything grew, shrunk, and fell back into place as the real Alex took over.

My hands still tingled. I closed my eyes, only to be met with Ethan and his semi-naked body standing inches from me.

16

ETHAN

I HAD TO ADMIT, I'd never felt this drained before. "Well that was different," I said as Dad drove out of the parking lot. "Did you know that would happen?"

"No, to be honest, I... didn't think she would be able to do that yet."

"What, taking energy?" It was a strange pull. I still didn't understand half of it. Or what it even meant. It was as if some magnetic force had awakened and pulled all my strength out of me and into her.

It had knocked me on my ass. I wasn't prepared. I almost passed out, or would have if not for everything starting to rumble and shake.

Screams filled the place. A humongous tree was sprouting—no, punching—out of the ground. Alex disappeared fast. I covered my face as it hit the lights mounted into the ceiling.

I completely forgot to bend. Didn't even try.

When I eventually registered what I had to do, well, the tree had already crashed through the ceiling and damage was done.

One thing was finally proven: I was right about training in the woods, far away from confinement. Small comfort to be right about something, at least right.

The thing that I didn't bargain on was the power Alex truly had over me. Never would I have thought that Soph's insecurity was founded. Until tonight.

Every time she touched me, I felt something growing in my stomach. It didn't hurt, and it wasn't an unpleasant feeling either. Quite the opposite.

I could feel that little Ethan was waking up too. So embarrassing. I had no control over the way she made me feel with every stroke.

Thinking about it now, I was confused. Did I like Alex in that way? I couldn't have.

Was this the resistance everyone talked about? Maybe it didn't matter what she looked like; she could find a way to become irresistible to me.

I didn't like that. It felt as if I had no choice and that this test was already lost before it even began.

Dad pulled into our driveway. The garage door opened to admit us. "You okay?"

"Just tired."

"I have to say, it's a miracle you're still awake, Ethan. You're so much stronger than I was at your age."

I squinted at him. I could barely keep my eyes open anyway.

"The first time she did that to me," he carried on, "well, I passed out before I even hit the ground and only woke up the next day." He laughed. "Go to bed and sleep it off. You'll feel better in the morning."

I didn't argue this time. I climbed out of the Jeep and shuffled toward my room.

I really didn't think I'd be able to climb up the stairs, but I made it. My body fell like a sack of flour on my bed and just like that, I was gone.

ALEX

I STRUGGLED to fall asleep that night. I had way too much energy.

A knock came at my door. Aunt Ariel popped into my room and closed it behind her.

I pushed myself up from my bed. "How did you know I was awake?"

"You know I have an owl's hearing." She smiled. "I heard what you did today."

My entire body deflated. I was desperately trying to forget about tonight's events and here she came and reminded me of it.

"Alex, sweetheart, what you managed to do tonight..." She shook her head. "It's pretty insane for a witch your age."

It came out of my mouth before I could snatch it back. "I had to touch him, and it was a bit embarrassing, to be honest."

She snorted, which made me laugh.

"Why, he has one of the most amazing bodies I have seen in a long time. I wouldn't mind getting my hands all over that."

"Ariel!" I scolded.

She threw her head back and laughed.

"Shh, you're going to wake Mom up."

"Oh, you are as big of a prude as she is. You need to get out, girl. And Saturday night when your folks are on their date, it's you and me and the club called V."

I squinted at her. "The club called V?"

"It's my favorite," she sang.

I sighed because I knew I wouldn't be allowed to go in my true form, but hey, why not? A night out was a night out.

"Fine. Saturday, then."

She winked, kissed my head, and got up. "Sweet dreams, Alex, unless they are going to be about Ethan..."

"Ariel," I groused and hit her playfully.

She laughed and walked to the door. "Just joking. Your mother will kill me if she hears me mentioning his name." She opened my door and slipped out.

I turned over her last words in my mind. What did Ariel mean by that?

ETHAN

"C'MON," Garret wheedled, as Ryan and Joe mimed begging. They wanted me to come with them on Saturday night to Club V.

That club was always so crowded. The music was so loud that I could hardly hear myself think. But maybe they had a point. Maybe not thinking wasn't such a bad idea.

Soph and the girls weren't invited, though. "Boys only," Garret promised. I knew for a fact Soph wasn't going to be happy.

"Fine, anything to get you off my back. What time?"

"Pick you up around seven."

"No, I'll meet you there."

"You don't trust me, Ethan." Garret had a mock-wounded expression, his hands in the air.

"If I want to leave, I want to leave."

"Now why do you say that? Starting a night out with the boys with that attitude isn't going to go well." Garret laughed and Ryan high-fived him.

"My rules. I'm driving my Jeep."

Garret took me by both my shoulders. "It's going to be epic, dude." He whooped loudly and headed to the shower with his towel wrapped around his waist.

After football practice, I went home before bending training. I passed the institute on the way.

From the outside it looked like nothing major had happened. But once I focused and used my energy to look past Meredith's glamour, I could make out the tree peeking out of the rooftop.

I huffed, impatient for the traffic light to turn green.

They should've listened.

The same thing happened at my eleventh birthday party. It was a mess. My ability was still too strong for me, and as I sneezed, my hands shook. Leafy branches crashed through all our windows. The others dove for cover. Dad pushed me hard to the floor, and everything came to an abrupt stop.

Ryan got hurt badly as a tree branch smacked glass into his face. He still had faint scars across his eyebrow and hand to prove it. He called them his battle scars.

It wasn't such an awesome birthday party.

A honk brought me back to reality. The light was green.

When I got home, I found Dad in the lounge, watching a baseball/footballmatch on ESPN.

"I'm home," I yelled, making a beeline for the stairs.

"Ethan," he called. "Come here."

I stepped off the bottom stair and turned around. I was already going to be late.

"Mira called. They are still busy fixing the club."

"I know that, but surely Meredith has agreed to train in the woods now."

"She said Alex needs time."

Again. I sighed loudly.

"You need to be patient with her, Ethan."

"Dad, I've been waiting patiently for her for three years. I don't know how much more patient I can be."

I stomped up to my room to decide what I was going to do with myself tonight. I wasn't used to staying home.

We usually practiced nights at the institute till seven and from there either went to the smoothie hut or grabbed a pizza at Ernie's diner.

I wished that we were already into football season. We were still in training for now, with our first game coming up in a couple of weeks at homecoming. At least during football season, I had games I could go to on Fridays and not stay at home, working on my own nerves.

I texted Soph. She told me that they were at Wesley's, a hangout that sometimes sold beer to underage kids. Soph and Leanne had fake IDs. Maybe, just maybe, I needed some quality time with Soph to get my anxiety under control. So I told her that I would meet her in a few minutes.

I yelled at Dad that I would see him later tonight and was out the door before he could ask me where I was going.

SPENT, I finally rolled off of Soph. We were both sweaty and hadn't bothered to take off our shirts. The Jeep was not the most comfortable spot to have sex, but it was good as any. After all, it was sex with the hottest girl in school. What more could a guy want?

I zipped up my jeans while she pulled up her panties and climbed over me into the front seat.

I maneuvered behind the steering wheel and turned on the ignition.

She pulled out her phone with a distinctly unsatisfied little "Huh."

"Are you okay?" I asked, still grinning. *What's not to smile about?*

"My mother's called eleven times. Really, when is she going to give me a break? No trust at all."

I arched an eyebrow. We just did something untrustworthy and she felt upset about lack of trust? Sometimes Soph didn't make any sense.

"Just be patient. One more year and we can go wherever we want."

She smiled. "With Ugly Duckling and Sam in tow."

"Don't call her that, please." I feel so bad about that.

"It's not like it isn't accurate," she said cruelly, flipping a sweaty lock of blond hair out of her eyes.

"It's not right. She has feelings and they bleed into me when I'm around her," I lied. I would say anything to make them stop calling her that.

She went super quiet. "You feel something for her?"

I narrowed my eyes and wondered if I'd heard correctly. "Like what?"

"I don't know. Everyone makes such a big deal about the Resistance."

"Well, you feel something for Sam." There was a better chance of Soph crossing that line than me.

"No." She spoke too fast. "I already told you I don't."

"Well that's my answer too." Annoyance at Soph started to overpower the lingering orgasmic tingles. How could she even think that? She was Sophie Rutter, for crying out loud. The most beautiful girl at Sky View High.

Too frustrated to talk, I took her back to the diner, where her Volkswagen stood in the parking lot.

I waited until she was safely in her Beetle. She revved her engine, reversed, and drove off. I followed her until our paths diverged near the lake.

How could she think that I felt something for Alex? She was *Alex*.

I used the remote to open the garage door and parked the Jeep next to Dad's black one. I entered and found only the lamp in the living room on. Dad must be already asleep.

I switched everything off, made sure everything was locked, and went up to take a quick shower. Warm water sprayed over my face as thoughts jumbled and tumbled through my mind.

When were we going to take up training again?

When was Alex going to be strong enough for me to actually bend something? Would she touch me like that again.

I didn't like the touching. It made me feel funny and... I just didn't like it.

Worse, how could Soph think I felt something for her? Was Alex telling the truth when she said that every time I was nice to her, Soph punished her? Why was she so insecure? It was Alex Burgendorf, for crying out loud. The Ugly Duckling of Sky View High. And there was no contest at all between a duck and a tiger.

17

ALEX

MOM AND DAD left on their date, and Ariel just came to tell me that I had a few minutes to get ready. That was ten minutes ago.

I was standing in front of my closet. Had been for ten minutes. Nothing fit Ducky. Everything was tailor-made for Alex, or the real me with her long legs and lean ass.

I couldn't imagine going to this Club V in sneakers.

Ariel came back in, wearing a skimpy yellow dress stunning pair of heels with laces that crisscrossed each other attractively up her ankle.

"What didn't you get when I said a few minutes, Alex?" She sounded as if the Zombie apocalypse was upon us.

"I'm just going to stay in. I have nothing to wear," I said, defeated. "Well nothing for this form."

"You can always—"

"No," I interrupted. As much as I hated Ducky, I hated Necrocretors even more.

"Fine. I'm sure we can come up with something between

our two closets." She planted herself in front of mine and started to search for who knew what.

She took out some stretchy black pants and put them on my bed. She eyed my closet again with her hand on her hip and then bolted out of my room and down the hall.

I started to take off my sweatpants and pulled on the stretchy black ones. I had to jump into them and pray that I didn't rip them.

When they were finally over my bum and on my waist, Aunt Ariel came back.

"Wow, that actually looks nice, Alex."

I turned around and wiggled my ass at her. She narrowed her eyes and walked toward me.

"Okay, so we both know that your mother was a little bit overprotective when she conjured Ducky, but who could blame her? You are her one and only baby. So, we will work with what she left us. You can relax, missy. Your mother might be excellent at glamours, but I am a master of fashion." She raised her eyebrows playfully and handed me a flowy black top, and a cute pair of open-toed ankle boots.

I pulled on her blouse as delicately as possible. To my surprise and delight, even though it cut into me, it looked amazing. The flowy parts hung over Ducky's curves. I zipped up the shoes and examined myself in the mirror.

I wished I could take off the glasses.

Aunt Ariel took out my elastic band and ruffled my hair.

"Even with those beer bottoms, we are going to give Ducky her chance to shine tonight."

ETHAN

I PARKED behind Club V. It was packed. I wasn't in the

mood to be here at all. Just as I told myself that I was going to pull out and go home, Garret and Ryan tapped on my window.

Garret howled as I pulled my keys out of the ignition. No escaping tonight.

I got out and greeted them with our custom greeting—a handshake combined with high fives and a chest bump. I followed them into Club V.

I presented the fake ID Soph had gotten me today. She wasn't happy about me going out without her, but she got over it fast, saying Leanne had suggested a girls' night in with Annie anyway.

The bouncer admitted us with barely a glance and we pushed through the crowd. Garret and Ryan had become regulars. Both guys looked like they were in college already. We got three beers and perched on stools at the oblong bar.

Club V was always brimming with sweaty, gyrating dancers. Dancing was really a trance anyway. Everyone was possessed by the thumping bass.

My gaze caught a woman on the other side of the dance floor. She wore a bright yellow dress. She had a baby face that made me think of an owl. Owl lady.

A snow-white head bobbed next to her. I squinted. Was that Alex? What was she doing here, and who was the Owl?

"I'll see you guys in a few," I shouted in Garret's ear. The noise in this place always overpowered my senses. It made it hard to wind down.

I pushed through, stepped on toes, almost made a girl fall on her ass, spilled a drink, and jostled so many people. Finally I reached them.

Owl's dress was short. Her legs went on for days. Who was she?

She was chatting up a much older gentleman, flirting with

him. As I neared I realized Owl wasn't my age but closer to mid-thirties.

Alex froze when she saw me. Now that I knew to look for it, I saw the tremble in her knees as I unwittingly drained her energy.

I shook my head with a smile on my face. She threw her head backward and looked as if she was going to cuss.

Owl leaned in to say something to her and then spotted me. A beautiful smile spread across her face.

"First time I'm seeing you here, Ethan Sutcliff."

How the hell did she know my name?

"Here I was trying to give my niece time away from you and all that wielding crap." She stuck her hand out to me. "Name is Ariel. Ariel Warren."

I shook it. "You are Meredith's sister?"

"Guilty," she sang.

I looked at Alex. "Good evening Alex."

She looked at me with sleepy eyes. I couldn't help but to laugh. "You know I don't do that on purpose, right?"

"You sure about that? Because to me you are a freakin' natural, like you've done this since the day you could walk."

I laughed. "Sorry." I took a sip of my beer.

"C'mon, lighten up." Ariel shook Alex. "It's not the end of the world. Maybe the two of you will find some common ground tonight."

A small smile tugged on Alex's mouth. I wondered why her mother never got her a pair of contacts.

Ariel led Alex by the hand to the dance floor. "You coming, Golden Boy?" Ariel shouted.

How the hell? Witches.

I followed them and we bobbed around like idiots under the strobe lights.

Garret, Joe and Ryan found us during the second song.

Miming and shouting, I introduced them to Ariel. When I mentioned Ryan's name, she looked past him at Alex, who nodded once, grimly. He received a smack on the head out of nowhere.

"Don't throw balls at people!" she yelled. I burst into laughter.

We all carried on dancing until a song came up and Ariel started to do different moves. She rolled her belly and waved her arms like a hippie or a belly dancer. The whole combination was mesmerizing. I couldn't stop looking at Ariel, and by the look of it, neither couldany of the guys..

She swayed completely off beat, yet it put me in a trance. Was this some sort of magic I didn't know about?

Alex, however, stared with a raised eyebrow at her aunt and stopped dancing altogether.

"Okay," she yelled at Ariel. "You're going to dance like that? I'm going to find a booth to hide." She took off into the crowd.

I laughed.

"What is wrong with my dancing?" she yelled back with a surprised look on her face. She surveyed me and the guys. Ryan and Garret put their thumbs up. Joe just had a sheepish grin.

"I'm no dance expert." I pointed at Alex.

"Just go," she mouthed and waved off Alex's reaction to her dancing moves. Garret, Joe and Ryan stayed.

Typical.

Ariel had confidence, that much I could say. I liked confident women.

It was easy to find Alex. Her snow-white hair glowed like a beacon under the black-light.

She was tucked into one of the booths. The bench opposite her was occupied by a guy and girl who needed to get a room.

"May I?" I yelled, pointing at the open seat next to her.

"Last time I checked it's a free country."

I sat down, smiling. Would we ever find some sort of truce, the way Ariel suggested? "So, you always come here?"

Alex chuckled. "You think? My mom would kill my aunt for bringing me to this place."

"Ah," I finally get it. "She sneaked you out?"

"No, the 'rents have their monthly date night." She sipped her cider.

Got it. I looked in Ariel's direction. "So how do you explain Ariel and your mother and... you?" I knew I sounded shallow but couldn't help it.

Then something hit me. Dad backed off quite a bit about the beauty of Eath Wielders. I remember him leaving that night to sort it out with Meredith but he never told me the outcome. Guess they sorted it out..

"You are seriously vain." She had an amused smile on her face.

"I'm not! But c'mon. Every single person is wondering about that, Alex."

"Ever heard the saying, 'Two Foxes make a dog'?"

I squinted. "Where the hell did you hear that?"

She laughed. "Okay, I made it up. But I'm tired of every-one's shallowness."

"It's not shallowness, it's curiosity. Huge difference."

She pouted her duck lips. "Yeah, right." The bottle went to her mouth again.

"So, tell me a bit more about yourself." I really wanted to know the girl behind the glasses.

She squinted. "Why? We have plenty of time for that, don't you think?"

"Maybe I'm not as patient as everyone thinks I am."

"I'm not that interesting." She pointed at the glasses.

"You seriously just blame your appearance for not being an

interesting person? I wonder who the shallow one is now." I gulped my own beer. It earned me a glare.

"Fine, but don't say I didn't warn you," she said. "I love books, the kind that don't have illustrations. Jane Austen, Emily and Charlotte Brontë, stuff like that."

"Are those books?"

She sighed. "No, authors. Ever heard of *Pride and Prejudice*?"

"That cool zombie movie?" I was pulling her leg. Off course I knew *Pride and Prejudice*. Everyone knew that book.

She gave me a withering stare.

"I'm joking. I know *Pride and Prejudice*, *Wuthering Heights*, and what was the other one? *Jane Eyre*," I said the last one in my best snooty English accent.

"Ha! Not as daft as I thought you were, yes." She nodded and took another sip of her cider. "Told you." Her eyebrows raised again. "Not very interesting."

"Books aren't that bad. I never like them. I cannot sit still. I usually rent the DVD when the adaption comes out."

She groaned. "It's never the same."

"It's why it's called an adaption. I'm sure if they turn the movie into the actual book, we would have, like, nine-hour movies."

She laughed. "True."

"You like music?" I asked.

"Who doesn't like music?"

"Let me guess," I teased. "The classics."

She threw her head back and laughed. "No, I like Paramore, Muse, and Black Veil Brides."

"Ah," I shout animatedly. "See, not so boring after all. And art obviously."

"Yes, I love art." A dreamy expression stole across her face.

"So why do you think yourself as boring?"

She gave a mirthless laugh. "You really want me to answer that? I have bad people trying to kill me, Ethan. Ever since I was a baby. Believe me. Books, music, and art were the only choices."

"Sorry," I said. Of course she had a dark childhood. Running from place to place every few months, probably.

"Enough about me," she said. "What makes Ethan, well, Ethan? No, let's make this a challenge. What is the one bad thing you would like to change about yourself?"

I frowned. "The one bad thing about myself?" It was a strange question.

"Yep," she said. "And don't tell me you don't have something that annoys the crap out of yourself. Everyone has that one thing they either accepted or changed."

Nodding, I thought about it. I didn't take long. "I have this bad habit of labeling girls as animals."

She frowned.

"Like, when I meet or see a girl for the first time, they immediately get the character of an animal. Like, Sophie is a tiger. In the beginning, her claws always came out."

She laughed.

"Leanne is a pit bull, always protecting Annie, her Wielder, and Sophie. And your aunt, well, I don't know why but I see her as an owl."

She positively chortled at this. I couldn't help but to join in.

And then her words sliced me. "And I become the Ugly Duckling."

I spat beer. *Shit, she does know about that.* I closed my eyes. This was so embarrassing. My cheeks burned.

"Here." She handed me napkins. I reluctantly opened my eyes and started to clean foam on my shirt.

I finally looked at her as I wiped myself clean. "I'm sorry about that. It just..." I couldn't find the right word.

"Relax. You don't think I'm used to it by now?"

"Still, I didn't mean for it to get out of hand." I leaned back into my chair, feeling like an idiot. "No wonder you hate me."

She smiled. "I don't hate you, Ethan. It's like you said. I just don't know you."

ALEX

TONIGHT WASN'T SO BAD. Sure, he leached my energy as the night prolonged, but the laughter made up for it. And everything I discovered about him reinforced Cynthia's opinion that all the girls wanted him.

As much as I tried to hate Ethan Sutcliff, I couldn't. He was just a nice guy. We talked easily with one another. He seemed genuinely interested in knowing me, Alex Burgendorf. After a few hours, I felt bad for hiding my true form from him.

I wished I could tell him.

I didn't know when had been the last time I laughed this much.

Ariel was such a dance freak. She hardly came to the table and whenever she did, doofus and dwiddles and ogre followed her like lost pups.

It was as if there was a direct link that connected Ethan and my mind. He just laughed at his buddies, which made me laugh too.

He truly got me, and not just pretending because of my beauty, the way everyone pretended that night at the WABA Celebration. This time there was no beauty.

I didn't even want to think about that night anymore. I remembered the way he stared at me.

"Do you think your aunt will allow you to go upstairs with me? It's not so crowded and you can actually hear one another without screaming."

My heart stammered, but I had to play it cool. I shook my head. Whether it was no big deal, I didn't know, but I could always ask her. "Let me just go and tell her before she thinks Necrocretors kidnapped us both."

He smiled. I squeezed past him; the other side was still blocked by a couple who couldn't take their paws off each other. We had a bet on those two, to see how long they could last.

I found Ariel jumping up and down to a fast-paced song. How did her feet manage? Mine wanted to break and I'd only danced a few songs.

I grabbed her arm and, pointing emphatically at the stairs, yelled that Ethan wanted to find a place to talk. She nodded and kissed me on the lips. "Go," she mouthed with a wink.

I shook my head. She was strange when not under the supervision of my mother. Did she act like this while we were in her locket too?

Was she drunk at times, and maybe just once or twice forgot us somewhere? I could just imagine her retracing her steps, desperately trying to find the locket.

I found Ethan and nodded. He stood, took my arm gently with a little thrill of energy passing between us, and led me to the stairs way at the back of the club. They were barely lit as we climbed.

A drunk guy almost toppled on me. Ethan pushed him away with his one hand. "Watch it, buddy."

The guy apologized profusely. I shook my head.

Some people shouldn't drink.

On the landing, we found a second bar and a bunch to tables. Ethan was right. It was calmer up here. The music wasn't so in-your-face and the lights didn't pulse frenetically.

Ethan showed me a sofa to sit, then he went to buy us more drinks.

There were quite a lot of people up here, but at least it was not so overpowering.

I glanced out the tinted window, which overlooked the dance floor below. I found my aunt's yellow dress in no time. She was really having a good time.

In the second floor, people huddled together in small groups, speaking and drinking. Guys flirting with girls, others playing a game of pool along the opposite wall, others throwing darts at velvet targets.

Unimpeded, Ethan moved easily through them. He wasn't that popular here. Maybe he just didn't like Club V as much as his buddies did.

He finally reached me and handed me my cider.

Ethan spoke again. I was glad that this time we didn't have to scream to each other as before. Perhaps aided by our surroundings, the conversation took a turn to the deeper side.

He'd lost his mother at the age of ten. Necrocretors. They mistook him for an earth Wielder and she'd somehow bended from a light breeze a tornado that killed all their attackers and took her in the process.

"I'm so sorry, Ethan."

"It's not your fault."

His mother was dead because they thought he was me, and here he was not blaming me one bit. I would've been pissed off.

The reverent way he spoke about her made me realize that they'd had an extremely strong bond. I could tell he missed her a lot. Just imagining my life without my mom, even though she was annoyingly overprotective, was hard.

We spoke about birthday parties. How he'd celebrated his eleventh birthday one sneeze had made the trees smash through their windows, almost killing all his guests.

"Thank heavens they were all part of the Association," Ethan said with a laugh. "Can you imagine what would have happened if they were normal folks?" We were both laughing our asses off now.

Ethan dropped his voice in a great imitation of his father, explaining to a normal kid's mom and dad that trees had wanted to be part of his birthday too.

It was hilarious. I couldn't breathe.

My birthdays were boring. For the past sixteen years, always the same people. No other relatives. Not even aunt Ariel.

Someone grabbed me from behind. *Talk about the devil and you'll step on his tail.*

She pulled me up from the sofa. "You guys have talked enough. Come. It's dance time."

"Seriously?" Ethan sounded gloomy.

"Get your ass from that sofa, Mr. Sutcliff, or do you want me to use..." she wiggled her finger without saying the word *magic*.

Ethan leapt up. "I'm up." We all went back down with Ariel to the dance floor.

The night was super fun.

Just what I needed to get rid of all my long-bottled frustration and anger.

A slower song started to play. Ethan asked with a very traditional bow if he could dance with me. He was so sexy right now. He made me feel like Elizabeth Bennet going to dance with Mr. Darcy.

I curtseyed back and he took me by the waist and danced with me on one spot, deliciously slow. He twirled me out, which made me almost fall on my ass if it hadn't been for his crazy fast reflexes.

"Sorry," he said the fourth time he barely caught me before I hit the ground. "I seem to have that effect on you."

I laughed again, and just like that he kissed me.

What?

My stomach clenched as his kiss deepened. I could feel myself slipping. Then I remembered what this was. The Resistance.

This wasn't supposed to happen. Not with Ducky.

I pushed away and stared at him with huge eyes. He was grinning until he saw the look on my face.

"What?" he asked.

"Why did you do that?" I started to make my way to Ariel.

"Alex," he yelled after me as I pushed and squeezed through people to find that yellow dress to take me home.

This wasn't supposed to happen.

I touched my eyes. Yes, my glasses were still firmly on my head. Ducky was still in control. Why did he kiss me?

I found Ariel, grabbed her by the arm, and just pushed her until she stopped talking to a guy.

"Hey, what is going on?" she yelled. When she saw my face, she yelled goodbye to the dude.

"Sweetheart, what's the rush?" she asked. "Where is Ethan?"

"We have to go, right now." I was close to tears. Afraid and confused.

Why did he kiss me?

We reached the car in no time. Ariel took off as if the devil was chasing us. "Is it Necrocretors?" She sounded petrified.

I realized what I must have looked like. "I'm sorry. No. You can relax."

She swerved to the right and parked the car on the side of the road. "Then why, Alex? You almost gave me a heart attack. I should be driving yet. I haven't completely sobered up."

"I'm sorry."

"What happened?"

"He kissed me, okay? Me, *Ducky*." My voice was shrill.

Ariel just stared at me.

"Why did he have to go and do that?" I asked her in my famous whine.

"Oh, sweetheart." Ariel sighed. "When your mother decided to use the glamour, what was your actual reasoning behind this?"

I felt like such a failure. I was so weak.

"Oh, no," she said. "We should've never cast this glamour."

"I'm sorry that I wasn't honest about him." Tears filled in my eyes. I wanted to rip off my glasses.

"Don't." Aunt Ariel stopped me. "Deep breaths. Wait till we are home. Just... hang on."

I just stared out the window.

I felt like a failure, weak. Because the truth behind Ducky was simple. It wasn't to lure the Necrocretors away from me, to trick them. I knew the minute I found out Ethan was my Bender that I wasn't strong enough to face our biggest test. Judging by the way he stared at me that night, neither would he. I needed him to be.

Ethan Sutcliff was my weakness.

18

ALEX

I DIDN'T WANT to see Ethan. I couldn't. He wasn't supposed to kiss Ducky. He had to be the strong one to resist our test, but no, for some reason he fell for Ducky, the Ugly Duckling who had her night of glory. And oh, did she—I—take it with both hands.

Ethan phoned all day Sunday. Around the third time Mom came knocking on my door.

I was devastated. He shouldn't have kissed me. If I told Mom what happened, she would freak.

Ariel promised that she wouldn't tell Mom either, even though she thought we should.

"Sweetheart, this is getting silly," Mom said.

"It happened Thursday night. It's Sunday. You need to speak to that boy eventually."

I shook my head. She was assuming. I hated when people assumed.

"Okay, more time?" she asked and I nodded. "More time it is."

My door shut and I closed my eyes. I opened them immediately as Ethan and his lips on mine jumped into my mind.

Why couldn't I stop thinking about that stupid kiss?

Eventually I got up, took a bath, and went downstairs to eat something.

Ariel was in the kitchen. I thought I hated Mom's piteous smile, that compassionate look she got. And this time Ariel's smile was ten times worse than hers.

I ate supper, not speaking to anyone, and went back to my room and watch some TV. I must have fallen asleep because the next thing I knew, I was back in Club V, dancing with Ethan.

All innocent, he said that line. "I seem to have that effect on you."

I laughed, and his lips set me on fire all over again.

When we came up for air, it wasn't Ducky anymore but the real me.

The fear of Ethan finally discovering who was hiding behind Ducky was such a strong emotion, I jolted awake. I sat up, chest heaving, sweat dribbling down my face.

Mom was right. This was so stupid. I would have a strong chat with Ethan Sutcliff

And about that kiss... It could never happen again.

ETHAN

I WAS DANCING WITH ALEX. I had never enjoyed spending time with someone as much as I have enjoyed spending time with her tonight.

She forgave easily. I wasn't in the doghouse as I thought I would be when she discovered that it was me behind that horrible nickname.

Still I felt like a dog.

I didn't see her that way anymore. She was wrong about one thing. She wasn't uninteresting at all. She was full of life. She sparkled with easy laughter.

A slow song came up. I bowed like one of the characters from the classic novels at a ball. She curtseyed, which made me suppress my laugh again. She was silly too.

My arm encircled her waist and we moved with small steps. It was a devastatingly sad, wrist-slashing type of song that girls seemed to love. Our skin touched in a dozen places, more than it had all night. The same feeling she gave me that day in the gym bubbled in my gut.

I loved this feeling. It felt like home, like somewhere I belonged. I didn't have to make people like me. I didn't have to be the Golden Boy. I could just be me.

I twirled her out and she tripped on her feet. I moved fast and caught her before she fell. She was adorably clumsy.

I couldn't remember the last time when I'd felt so alive. It was my thirteenth birthday, I think. I twirled her out softly the next time, and again she almost fell. I caught her again, the maladroit thing.

She laughed as her head tipped back. And then something just clicked. I didn't know why, and I definitely didn't see it coming. But when I opened my eyes again, I kissed Alex.

Really kissed her.

Heat sizzled when our lips touched, and this overwhelming sense of rightness enveloped me. It was nice. The kiss deepened. I wanted more.

When it finally broke, I opened my eyes but it wasn't Alex staring back at me anymore. It was the girl I'd seen at the WABA Celebration. The Fox.

I jolted awake. *Just a dream.* The second time I'd had that dream.

I had no idea what it meant. Why did she keep taking Alex's

place all of a sudden? Was Alex right about me? Was I truly so vain, I had to imagine this girl because I couldn't picture myself with someone like Alex?

Someone like Alex? Jeez, listen to yourself. I was vain. An idiot too for thinking about Alex that way. She was an awesome girl.

Light seeped through my windows. I decided to go for a run. I pulled myself out of bed and got dressed, trying to shake the dream. I slipped out in the morning sun. The nights were starting to get that first hint of fall; a wave of goosebumps rolled over me until the sun's warmth soaked in.

I took the path past the lake. The light on the water and the fresh scent of pine needles helped clear my head.

I wanted to run passed the Buchman plantation, but the walls were so high, I doubted that I would be able to see Alex moving around in her room. So I cut it short a street before the plantation and head home.

I barely greeted Dad as I entered the house and ran up the steps two at a time back to my room.

A quick shower and a cinnamon-pecan crunch bar, and I was off to school.

Dad wanted to ask something but only got the door shutting as a reply.

I took the Jeep.

Today was football practice. I hoped to see Alex to apologize for that kiss.

Why did I kiss her? And was I truly sorry for that? I didn't feel sorry.

No doubt this was what the Association meant when they prattled on about the Resistance.

I didn't want to kiss her. I just had fun with her. Then why did I? *Did* I want to kiss her?

I felt so stupid letting these questions play on inside my

head. It made me feel like an insecure girl. I wasn't insecure by far... or a girl.

I reached the school grounds in no time. Alex was nowhere to be found.

I found her geeky friend who reminded me of a worm, but not in a bad way. A bookworm. Huge difference.

"It's Charlotte, right?" I asked.

"No, it's Cynthia." She didn't sound impressed that I didn't even know her name. "What do you want, Ethan?" There was that insecure backing away they always did.

"Have you seen Alex?"

"No, not today anyway. Why?"

"When you see her, can you please tell her I'm looking for her?" I walked to my locker across the hallway.

"Hey, you." Soph rushed up to me and hooked her arm with mine. She arched her back in that seductive way that she knew drove me crazy. "Where were you yesterday? We were waiting for you at the lake."

"Sorry, Soph. I was busy helping my father with the cars," I lied.

"Okay, so are we going to see you tonight?"

I squinted.

"The institute," she prompted.

"Yeah, I'm sure *I* will be there," I said.

She pulled her lower lip into a pout. "Screw her, Ethan. You don't need her." She gave me a hug. "We don't need them."

I sighed. I wished it were that easy. That someone could bottle the earth's essence into a lighter, like flames. Unfortunately, Sophie was wrong. I did need Alex. Otherwise I was just a normal human being like every other guy and girl in this school.

ALEX

I SPOTTED Ethan's back headed toward the cafeteria as I walked into school. Sophie was right next to him, her arm around his waist.

I wondered what she would do if she knew we had kissed. Would she still be as friendly as she was with him right now?

Stop it, Alex. You want him to forget about that kiss. You need to forget about that kiss, too.

I walked to my locker and found Cynthia with a huge smile on her face. "Ethan Sutcliff is looking for you," she said.

Yay, me.

"Seriously, I thought I was going to die when he spoke to me. Okay, so he didn't know my name, called me Charlotte, but still, he spoke to me."

I couldn't help but to laugh at Cynthia.

"So, you really train with him?"

I blinked. "Huh?"

"You said that's how you know him?"

"Oh, yes. I train with him." Gloom pervaded my tone.

"Are you okay?"

"I'm fine. I think I'm coming down with something." I hit my locker once on that spot. It swung open and I ducked out of the way, barely avoiding getting clobbered by it.

Cynthia stared at me with huge eyes.

Did my glasses fall off? I scrabbled at my face, but they were still in place. "What? Why are you looking at me like I grew a second head?"

"Nothing." She shook it off. "You avoided the locker."

I smiled as I got what she was saying. My reflexes were a bit faster than usual. "Yeah, going through it seven times a day, one ought to learn."

I packed my books for the first three periods and slammed the locker shut. I needed this day to be Ethan-free.

———

WHEN THE FINAL school bell rang, I thought for once that luck was on my side. I didn't run into Ethan once. I followed a line of students through the choked hallway. Just down the path, one flight of steps, into the SUV, and I'd be home free.

I got a whiff of the pull. It was what I called it... starting right now.

Ethan was a few steps away from me. I didn't need to look up to confirm it. My body was screaming it to me. It felt as if I was going to fall flat on my face and then I would never get up again.

"Alex," he said.

Cynthia sucked in breath as she spotted him.

"We need to talk, please," he begged.

I looked at Cynthia. "I'm late for Debate anyway."

I frowned. Since when did she start taking Debate after school? I felt like a bad friend. Never paying attention to what she was talking about. We waved and she jutted her chin toward Ethan, her googly eyes screaming, *Talk to that dreamboat!*

"Yeah, sure," I said to Ethan as she left.

"About Saturday," he whispered.

"Can we just pretend it never happened?"

He looked relieved. "Of course. I have no idea what came over me."

I gave him my best *you're-an-idiot* look. "Awesome. Now if you don't mind, I really need to get away from you. Otherwise, that tent-and-sleeping-bag idea of yours wouldn't sound so bad."

He laughed. "I'll see you later."

"Do I have a choice?" I called over my shoulder as I headed out.

"Not really."

I waved. "Then I'll see you later."

I slunk toward the SUV, where Louis was waiting. I could still feel Ethan's eyes on me.

I turned around as I reached the SUV. To my surprise, Ethan was nowhere in sight. Weird.

19

ETHAN

MEREDITH FINALLY AGREED to meet us in the woods. Everything just felt right out here.

I saw a very similar Jeep to Dad's, maybe a newer model, driving over the rocky path to where we waited.

I was glad that Alex had overcome her anger at the whole stupid kiss thing. I could have blamed the alcohol, but then again, I didn't have that many to start with. So I gave her a version of the truth. One of the many truths: I had no idea what came over me.

Telling her how I really felt—confused and uncertain—would only push her away.

A bald man climbed out from behind the steering wheel. Frederick's Bender, I was pretty sure. Alex and her mother climbed out from the passenger's side.

They were two completely different entities, Alex and her mom. Alex was pale, always hiding underneath hoodies. Her mother wore a flowy top and shorts, showing off sun-kissed skin.

Alex was short, her mom tall. Even Frederick was tall. Where Alex did come from with her round curves and thick, weak ankles?

I shook it away and walked to Dad, who'd made himself comfortable on a boulder.

Alex greeted Dad first and then grinned at me. "You ready for this?" She sounded jittery.

"It's going to be fine," I assured her.

She nodded. "This place is pretty great." Her pinched face filled with appreciative wonder as she took in the second-growth woods that sloped down for several miles and eventually ended at the lake. The carpet of lime-green ferns and spongy mosses and last year's old leaves held my favorite smell in the world— damp earth.

Above our heads towered a mix of maple, poplar, pine, oak, and the occasional white birch trunk or lacy hemlock needles. We were at the edge of a clearing about the size of a bedroom— not even big enough to completely break the canopy of branches overhead. It was lined with smaller, cheerful dogwoods and hawthorns.

Bald head waited on guard at the car, on the lookout for anything dangerous.

Meredith finally reached us. "Well, at least nothing will get torn into pieces when Ethan slips up this time," she said, following her daughter's gaze and taking in the woods.

"Excuse me?" Had I heard correctly? My father's shoulders shook as he covered his face.

"Oh, you're excused. Now, shall we begin?"

I got up from the rock and she took my spot.

No wonder Alex sneaked out with her aunt. It was hard to imagine that Ariel and Meredith were related. How did Dad fall in love with this prim, bossy woman?

Alex rolled her eyes at me playfully. My attention returned and we went together to the middle of the clearing.

A few extra trees here wouldn't make such a difference if something went wrong today.

We got ready. She held both her arms out for mine. This way had never worked before. "You sure this will work?"

"No," she admitted. "But it's the natural way, Ethan. We should always try the natural route."

The way she said it, made it sound as if our previous success was anything but natural. Did it hurt her the last time?

I gave her my arms. Our fingers gripped each other's arms tightly. I closed my eyes and Alex did the same.

For a long time, we just stood there. I felt a soft pull like I always did when Alex was near, but other than that, nothing happened. I open one eye to make sure that she hadn't fallen asleep. I just caught the end of a yawn.

I grunted, broke our grip, and took off my shirt.

"No, that won't..." she started to protest.

"Does it hurt, Alex?"

"What?" She looked confused.

"This way, does it hurt you in any way?"

"No." She sounded embarrassed, which I didn't get. "It's just that I can't control it."

I frowned. "You are not supposed to control it. That's my job."

She said nothing. Just took a deep breath.

"C'mon, if it's the only way you can do this, then so be it. I'll just find a way to deal with the energy thing."

We both glanced at her mom, who just gave her a what-are-you-waiting-for look.

She touched me like she did the other day in the gym. Very gently, with no confidence as she recited the words. It was unsuccessful.

The second time she attempted the spell, her touches were firmer, and I started to get a prickle where I really didn't want one. I forgot what else this spell awakens.

I really tried not to allow it to affect me. But I'd never had much control over what got me excited down there. No guys really did.

The fourth time she said the words, I had no choice. "Okay," I broke it before arousal got out of hand. How embarrassing if I got a full-on erection.

My eyes caught my father's as I pulled on my shirt. "What are we doing differently?" I asked Meredith.

"You broke away," she said. As if that wasn't clear enough.

"There has to be another way," I tried to make it clear that something was wrong with that spell.

She didn't catch the eagerness in my tone. "What's wrong with that way?"

"It's not always going to work," I said, stern.

She climbed off the boulder, folded her arms across her chest, and came toward me, frowning. "I don't understand. Why wouldn't it always work?"

I gave her a sheepish look. Behind her, Dad tried his best to suppress his laughter. Even Alex's shoulders vibrated with barely contained giggles. How did she have no idea what this was doing to me? Worse, how the hell was I going to break this down delicately?

She looked between Dad and me and back again. I raised my eyebrows. Still nothing. "Am I missing something?"

"Not at the moment, but I promise that another few minutes longer, everyone would get a clear picture of why that isn't working so well for me."

"*Working* for you?" she repeated in a snobbish Wielder-is-better-than-Bender tone. "I see."

"No, I promise you, you don't."

She shook her head. "I don't follow."

I gazed pointedly down at my pants. She reddened as understanding finally slammed into her. She whirled around, disgusted. "Jeff," she spat. "He's *your* son!"

Dad couldn't suppress his laughter anymore. He was folding himself in two. "What did you expect, Meredith? I told you before that doesn't always work the way you want."

"What doesn't work?" Alex asked.

Oh, please don't let her find out.

"Nothing for you to know. In the car."

"We're done?" both Alex and I demanded at the same time.

"Yes, you are done." Meredith sounded upset.

"Mer," my father said. "It's the most..."

"Fuck off Jeff," she yelled, and she turned around to face me. "And you, go take a cold shower," she hissed.

And with that she stomped to the SUV and climbed in.

I apologized with a facial expression to Alex, who stared at me through the window looking utterly befuddled. She shaped her fingers into the form of a gun against her head and pulled the trigger, pretending to blow her head off. I couldn't help but laugh as she fell on the back seat and the car pulled away.

ALEX

Mom refused to tell me what Ethan had told her, why she was so upset. Why didn't today work? When I asked her, she just made me promise never to try that spell again.

"Does it hurt him?" I asked.

"Yes," Mom cried. "I'm sorry I taught you that spell, baby. I should've thought it through."

"Something tells me that you are not being totally honest," I accused. "What is it, Mom? I deserve to know."

We arrived home. Louis pulled up in the courtyard and

before the gate was even shut behind us, Mom climbed out of the SUV. She was running away again. I followed her, rushing to keep pace with her huge strides.

I caught her in the doorway and grabbed her arm, pulling her to face me. "Just tell me."

"No, you don't need to know, and that is final. Just promise me, never again."

"What happened now?" Ariel sounded dismayed.

I stared with flaring nostrils at my mother. I took off my glasses and rushed up the steps, using my own legs to get me there faster. "How do I know never to use it again if you don't tell me what it does to him?" I yelled with each step I took.

Mom breathed hard and said to Ariel, "I need a cup of strong tea. You won't believe the day I had."

The day she had. Yeah, whatever. I slammed my bedroom door. I wished I had Ethan's number to find out what happened. Did I hurt him? Why was Mom so defensive? It was going to drive me to insanity all night long.

I took a shower, still stewing. When I came back to my room, Aunt Ariel was on my bed. She tapped on the spot in front of her.

I plunged down and just stared at her, towel drying my hair. I felt pissed off at everyone.

"Your mother told me what happened today." She wore a weird smile.

I'd had enough of this. "What is going on?" If mom won't tell me what happened today, then I would force it out of Ariel.

"You sure you want to know?"

"Just tell me. Did I really hurt him?"

Ariel laughed. "Oh, honey, I guess you could label it as pain. But no, it's not the hurting kind. For a woman at least, it's a magical type of pain."

"Huh?" I was even more confused.

Ariel giggled. "Okay, when you touch Ethan like that, it's not just your energy you are taking back from him. You are sort of stroking..." She made stroking movements, sighed, and contemplated her next words.

"Stroking?" I asked. And then just like that, I got it. I blushed scarlet. "Are you shitting me?"

Ariel snorted. "You think you're embarrassed? Try your mom."

She told me the whole story and I couldn't help but to feel bad for Mom. Especially when she followed Ethan's gaze to his pants.

I was such an idiot for not getting it sooner.

20

ETHAN

FOR THE NEXT few days we were back to square one, struggling to wield earth. Among the few times that Alex's hands did produce a sliver of a root or a vine, she would fall to the floor, spent.

Meredith turned all business. She was pushing Alex hard. Sometimes even Dad stepped in, saying we'd had enough. But Meredith cut him off so fast that he went back to sulk on his rock.

They ended up not speaking to one another, which only put more on Alex's shoulders.

"Again," Meredith would yell at Alex, touching her head, either to suppress a headache or wish more energy for Alex. Whatever she was doing, she didn't help much.

Alex kept pushing. Then her nose started to bleed. I looked at Dad in horror. "Meredith," he cried, exasperated.

"She'll be fine." Meredith sounded like someone possessed. She handed her a napkin.

"Alex, this has to..."

"I'm fine, Jeff," said Alex bravely. "I'm just tired." She sounded terrified. This bordered on abuse.

Meredith helped Alex up by the arm. "I'm sure we all agree that this training session is over."

I waved at Alex. She looked apologetic, but it wasn't her fault. I blamed her psycho mother.

That night, Dad had a hefty conversation with Meredith behind closed doors. I didn't hear much, but several times, I heard, "It's time!"

What was time? "Enough," I mouthed and went to bed. It was hard falling asleep. I never thought I would worry about someone like this. I should've gotten her number today. At least I would've known that she was safe.

At school the next day, I didn't see her. Was she even here today? I couldn't stop picturing her bloody nose.

That afternoon, they showed up for training. Everything went exact same, except the nosebleed.

"Okay, enough." I said. Alex looked like she was going to fall over any minute. She was as gray as the leaden sky overhead.

"You need to get your energy back. I suggest the other way." Both Alex and Meredith yelled no.

"Okay," I held my hands up in defense. "I take it the cat is out of the bag as to what happens."

A crimson flush spread over Alex's chest and throat, and two bright red spots colored her pale cheeks. "Can we please just try this way?"

"Is there any other way to do this?" I asked.

Alex sucked on her lips.

I laughed. "Why are you so embarrassed? It's not you with the problem."

"Stop, I really don't want that in the back of my mind for the next few hours."

"Oh, so you think about my erection."

"Ethan," Meredith exclaimed, scandalized.

"Someone has to break the tension you created here," I said, laughing.

"I created?"

I mimed zipping my mouth shut. Her spell. She created it. She got what I was saying. She lifted the heavy book she'd brought up in front of her face, studiously ignoring me.

"Alex, it's not the end of the world." She resembled a tomato that wasn't ripe yet. "In fact, it's most natural thing in the world."

"Tut tut," her mother chirped. "I want to hear nothing but bending, Ethan. Don't mess with my daughter's head."

I'd never seen Alex so embarrassed. She had to suppress her laughter a few times before we could regain our position.

I stripped off my shirt and crossed my fingers.

I wished it were true that after that, we magically wielded and bent because I cleared the air, but it wasn't. The wielding never came.

I was frustrated and I knew Alex was, too. She was tired. Nothing we tried blocked my drain on her energy. Alex had to find that balance herself. Until she did, training would be a waste of time.

When the sun started to set and Alex looked like she was about to fall asleep any moment, we called it a day.

I took out my phone as she gulped down her water and stood right next to her, pushing her name into my contacts. "Number?" I said.

She took my phone and keyed in her number.

"Send me yours and I'll save it." She picked up her backpack and staggered to the SUV.

"See you tomorrow Alex," I sang.

She waved, sort of. I laughed as even that looked like it wore her out.

I saw her a few times at school the next day, but we hardly

spoke. She would just wave, lower her head under her hoodie, and trudge on with her backpack slung from her shoulder. She always looked exhausted. I wondered what she would look like if she wasn't tired.

After football practice I had fifteen minutes left before meeting Alex and her mom in the woods. I took a quick shower and Dad actually honked the horn of his jeep.

That eager to see Meredith.

We waited at least another five minutes in our usual spot for them to arrive. Dad and I were surprised to see that Ariel tagged along today. She sported a cute gray two-piece and a straw hat. A hipflask stuck out of a satchel around her neck. Both my father and I laughed as she skipped her way toward us.

I look to see where Meredith was. She wasn't here. The air cleared immediately. It was as if she brought a suffocating vibe with her.

"What are you doing here?" my dad asked as he gave Ariel a hug.

"Meredith has an appointment she couldn't get out of. In fact," she said slyly, "she forgot it."

"Good," Alex said. "Two prune-free hours."

"Stop talking about your mother like that," Ariel scolded. "You know the rules. Only I can call her a prune."

I grinned at Alex. "Ready?"

"What, to waste your time?"

I laughed. She was really funny.

Training that day was still difficult. Once I thought she had it; the earth shook and something was about to happen.

All of us got excited. Especially me. But just like that, Alex gave in and fell to the ground, drained.

I grunted.

"Sorry." It was barely audible.

"It's not your fault." I lent her a hand.

My father didn't seem impressed today. Grunted a lot and shook his head a lot, as if his patience grew thinner and thinner every day.

Ariel had a worried expression on her face.

"Ariel, it's time," my father said.

"Time?" Ariel frowned.

"She doesn't have any strength and that thing is only taking more from her." He said through clenched teeth.

Hey! "I'm not a—"

"Stay out of this, Ethan," my father snapped.

I'm not a thing. I pouted.

"You know why we can't," Ariel insisted.

"He needs to learn how to bend earth. Ethan is the only one who will ever be able to protect her."

I frown at Alex, whose face was tipped up to the sky, eyes closed.

Ariel kicked a rock. "Discuss it with my sister."

"You do know that it drains her even more than what Ethan does?"

More than Ethan? "What are you talking about?"

"Let me handle this. It's something you should've known for a long time. Something about Alex."

"Jeff," Ariel shrieked.

I willed Alex to explain this, but she couldn't even meet my eyes.

"It's time, Ariel. Let Ethan learn the truth and for once let him learn how to bend earth. When would you prefer that he learn, when she is six feet under his own Element? It'll be too late then."

Whoa, that was grim. "What truth, Alex?" I was pissed now. "What is my father talking about?"

She looked at him in a scolding yet sad way.

"Just tell me. It's going to be okay."

"No, it's not," she cried. She spun around, throwing a silent temper tantrum.

"Talk to me," I begged. Distraught, she started pacing up and down. I touched her arm to make her stop. "What's going on?"

Tears shone in her eyes behind those glasses. Like huge owl eyes staring back at me. "For sixteen years, I lived in—"

"Alex," Ariel cut her off. "You don't have to do this." She strode toward her niece.

Alex held her hand in front of her. Ariel came to a halt. "No, Jeff is right. We should've told Ethan a long time ago."

"Told me what?" Was she sick, dying, what? I didn't like this.

"I'm an owl." Ariel said.

I frowned. "Wait, what?"

"I'm a shifter, an owl."

I remembered my dream about the owl, just before I met Alex.

"Ariel," Alex yelled. "Stop!"

Ariel closed her eyes. "Alex, think about this, please. Think about the reasons."

I frowned. Reasons? What reasons?

Alex shook her head. "I'm sorry that I didn't tell you sooner. My mother thought it would help keep me safe. Away from the Necrocretors. It has, so far. A long time. But it's also draining my ability. I'm just so tired and I can't do it anymore." She sounded frustrated as her gaze met her aunt's.

I watched my dad. He knew. He knew what they were hiding. I was so confused.

"You are not the only incubus in my life." Alex smiled.

I thought she was going to take off her hoodie and reveal a huge leech attached to her, something that fed off earth and somehow connected to her life force. A "kill it and you kill Alex too" sort of thing. But she just stood there. I didn't get it.

Then she took her glasses off.

In less than a second, she grew a head taller. Her pudgy middle shrank. Her short legs and flat ass turned into long, athletic legs and a plump ass. Her screwy buckteeth flattened to straight white ones behind plump lips. Her brown eyes shifted to a midnight blue.

I stepped back. Shock rolled over me in waves.

"I told you something didn't add up, son. It was her glasses."

I frowned at Alex. She took off her hoodie and revealed long, raven-dark hair. She looked up at me with midnight-blue eyes.

"You." It barely came out.

The Ugly Duckling was gone. Before me was unveiled the beautiful swan... the fox.

ALEX

HE JUST STOOD THERE. We were almost the same height. *Just say something. Anything.*

He shook his head like he was trying to clear water from his ears. His lips were set, curved down. I didn't like the look on him. It wasn't a scowl. It was filled with hurt, at being lied to.

"Say something," I said.

"What do you want me to say? That it's okay that you lied to me?"

"Ethan." His father got up from his rock.

"No. You don't get to 'Ethan' me. How long have you known about this, Dad?"

He closed his eyes. "You don't understand."

"You were supposed to have my back. All the time, mine.

Not your Wielder whom you haven't even seen for twenty years," he said through gritted teeth.

"It wasn't that easy."

"Whatever, dad."

"I'm sorry," I said.

"You are such a hypocrite," he spat.

"It's not like that, Ethan," Ariel started.

"No, don't worry, I get it." He sounded furious that we didn't trust him. As if we didn't give him a chance. He glared at me with those green eyes of his. It was the same color as the forest. "For some reason, I don't feel up to training anymore."

I looked at Ariel. *Please make him stop.* This wasn't how my unveiling went my head. It was supposed to be the opposite.

"Son."

"Don't worry. I'll find my own way home," he yelled and jogged down the path.

We all stared at him until he disappeared. I struggled to keep my tears at bay. A stray one rolled down my cheek. I dabbed it away.

"That went well," Ariel scolded Jeff.

"Don't you dare blame me. Your sister—"

"My sister did this for a reason, Jeff. What if Ethan never trusts her now? She was the one who was supposed to tell Ethan, not you."

Ariel shook with pure rage. She stormed over to me and put on my glasses. My body transformed. She flipped up my hood. "Don't be surprised if my sister wants to tear your head off tonight."

"She knows where to find me," Jeff said as if mom's wrath was no big deal.

We climbed into the SUV. Louis looked in the rearview at me as he switched on the ignition. The SUV started moving, but my eyes caught him staring at me every few seconds.

I sighed as I looked out the window with my knees resting on the back of Ariel's seat.

His gaze felt like Superman's, like it would incinerate me at any moment. "Give him time."

"So, he does speak," Ariel jeered.

Louis smirked.

I took a deep breath and stared out the window. I still felt like crying. Time seemed to be the one thing that I could give Ethan. But something told me it wasn't going to be enough. He was never going to forgive me for this. I saw it in his eyes today. I'd truly hurt him.

We got home and Ariel announced to Mom, "Well, the cat's out of the bag."

"Which cat are we talking about?" she asked climbed the stairs.

"He'll never talk to me again," I snapped.

"Which cat, Ariel?"

Nothing.

"Alex?"

"What!" I yelled. "Ethan knows." I slammed my door. Mom's fury erupted. I could hear her cussing and raging on.

I felt sorry for Jeff; I could tell he was on the phone when her voice got even louder and shriller. She was really losing it down there.

It went on and on and finally it stopped.

I texted Ethan: *I'm really sorry.*

And then: *I didn't mean for it to get out of hand. I wanted to tell you sooner but my mother…*

I hesitated, then typed, *Okay, fine. I didn't know how to tell you.*

I waited five minutes. *Just say something. Please.*

He didn't reply.

21

ALEX

FOR THE NEXT WEEK, I felt horrible.

I tried every day to get Ethan to text me back. He never responded. When I saw him at school, he pulled his hood over his head and walked on. He hardly looked at me.

I still had to wear the glasses, even though I hardly saw the point anymore. I would have gladly faced Necrocretors if I could only be back in Ethan's good graces.

I tried to speak to him several times, but the minute I got close, someone grabbed him and asked him something or Sophie was close by, so I just walk past. I didn't want to cause a scene.

In the afternoons I showed up at the woods like clockwork, but Ethan and Jeff never came. So I went home and called his house—since he wasn't bothering to pick up his cell.

Mom was still upset. "I don't know why he is so mad at you."

"Because we lied to him," I said with a sneer.

She kept muttering insults under her breath. Just then Jeff

picked up on the other line. I had to clap a hand over one ear to block her out.

"Can I please speak to Ethan?"

"Not today, Alex."

It was all Jeff said. *Not today.*

Three days later, before the final bell rang at school, I caught Ethan at his lockers, Sophie-free.

"Ethan, we need to speak," I begged.

He didn't even look at me. He closed his locker and walked away.

"Seriously, is this how it's going to be from now on?" I yelled after him with everyone staring. I glared back at them. They could stare as long as they wanted. This didn't concern them.

I was starting to give up. Fine, if he refused to acknowledge me, I would just do the same until he decided to fucking grow up. It wasn't just for him that mom conjured this stupid glamour. And I had received the brunt of the suffering it had caused. Not him.

The next day I walked into a nightmare. Every wall and locker in school was plastered with bright red posters. Each adorned with a big, unattractive picture of me. Surrounded by hearts. A smaller photo of Ethan sat at the bottom. Big white letters proclaimed, "STALKER ALERT."

I tore off the one from my locker and crumpled it up in a ball. I did that with every one I could reach. Rage warred with embarrassment; my hands trembled.

They had no idea what was going on between the two us, what this was about.

I fumed. It felt like smoke would pour out of my ears any second. I tried to calm down. A vibration ran through my fingers. I started to calm down and it disappeared.

"Have you seen this?" Cynthia's voice came from behind me.

"It's hard not to see it. It's everywhere around us." I was close to tears.

"No, not those." She hardly acknowledged the posters. She showed me what was on her phone.

Someone had recorded me confronting Ethan yesterday. In the hands of a gifted asshole, it now resembled a rap song. I looked pathetic.

I sighed and I hit my locker hard. *This is what happens when you are being a dick and do not fucking return text messages.* I was back to hating Ethan Sutcliff for being so fucking immature.

Maybe this was why Mom didn't tell him earlier. But no, that wasn't the truth. I didn't want to tell him.

My life at school was going to suck even more than it already did.

I got my books, shoved them into my bag, and closed my locker. Time to walk down the hall of shame. Literally.

ETHAN

THIS MORNING I had to admit, I felt bad for not acknowledging Alex when she tried to speak to me yesterday. I wondered how it must have felt to walk in and see this sea of red posters plastered with her own ugly face all over school.

I was just so fucking mad at her. I'd been searching for this girl everywhere, wondering who the hell she was. I'd stared at her like an ogre that night. And it turned out to be the one girl I didn't want it to be. Alex hiding under a glamour conjured by her demon mother.

Every time I shut my eyes, I saw those midnight-blue eyes begging me to say something.

This morning, those Stalker Alert posters wallpapered every

locker, every empty patch of space. Some of the papers lay on the floor, scuffed with dirty shoeprints.

"What is happening here?" Soph appeared out of nowhere, fluttering one in front of my face. I jerked back to avoid a papercut on my eyeballs.

"Nothing."

"Don't say it's nothing. What's going on between you two? Why aren't you talking to her?"

"I thought you would be happy, Soph. Why the million questions?"

Her expression was suspicious. "She tried to kiss you."

"Oh, please. *This* is what you want to fight about? Grow up." I stomped off to first period.

My phone beeped. I opened it. Oh, man, this was mean. It was a video only Frank and Debario could've made. An unflattering remix of her begging me to speak to her and me just walking away. It wasn't a great production, mixing her voice, repeating certain words, making her sound as if I was her moon and stars.

It was public. Already over a thousand views.

If only they knew who hid behind those glasses. Dad told me before how good Meredith was with glamours. I didn't think she was that good.

I closed the looping video. *It's not like that*, I wanted to say. But it didn't leave my mouth.

The day it was hard to avoid the posters everywhere. The janitors were certainly taking their sweet time getting rid of them. So much for the school's zero-tolerance policy on bullying. Alex was nowhere to be found.

I knew I should set this straight, but I was still so fucking upset. I just wanted to scream. Worst of all, I couldn't talk to any of my friends about it. As for the people who knew about the glamour, I didn't even want to see them. I couldn't.

Finally, the end bell rang. I raced out of there. *Screw football practice.* I wasn't in the mood.

Soph still wanted to talk but I shut her out. *Bet no one will make a video of this one,* I thought grimly.

"What is up with him?" Leanne asked.

"We had a fight this morning."

She always made it about her. Always.

"Must've been bad for him to miss practice." Leanne commented.

I ignored them both.

My eyes caught Louis's SUV. Alex opened the back door, hood concealing her face. She disappeared into the vehicle.

She should've told me earlier who she truly was. Then none of this would've happened. I wasn't ready to make amends. Not even close.

ALEX

I didn't speak to anyone when I got home from school. Just went straight to my room.

Taking off the glasses didn't even cheer me up anymore. Ethan liked Ducky more than he liked me. But he was pissed off with both of us.

I collapsed on my bed after chucking my backpack in the corner.

Fibbs brushed against me as if she was asking how my day was.

"Awful. Terrible. He just made it worse." I recounted my day. The poster, the video, everything. This was going to follow me till the end of my days.

My door opened. "Do you want to talk about it?" Mom asked.

When I glanced up, she had a crimson Stalker Alert poster in her hands. I shook my head.

"Okay," she said and my door closed.

Where did she even get that? Sometimes I wondered if she had a crystal ball to monitor my every move. But I knew she wasn't that kind of witch.

At some point, I must have drifted off.

A message alert from my phone woke me up. I opened my eyes. My room was dark.

I felt my way to my nightlight and switched it on. The side of my face felt numb. I stumbled over to my backpack and opened my phone.

It was from Ethan. Probably apologizing for what a jerk he was, or maybe a nasty jab, who knew? I chucked my phone away without opening the message.

After a while, though, curiosity burned. I retrieved my phone and opened it.

A multimedia text. A video.

Wary, I played it. If this was a copy of that godawful rap mix, I was going to throttle that boy. But it wasn't. It was dark, at first a bunch of jumbled images that meant nothing to me. Maybe he meant to send it to someone else.

It looked like some sort of a warehouse. The grainy camera passed conveyer belts and went through a set of doors covered with plastic sheets.

I was about to switch it off when I saw figures. Bodies.

My heart skipped a beat.

Ethan lay on the gray floor. Knocked out. Eyes closed. The screen panned slowly over him. Another body came into view, lying next to him. Cynthia? It didn't make any sense.

A harsh, robotic voice startled me. "You want to see them alive? Come to the Sugar mill, just off the interstate, 3020 State Avenue"

The sugar mill. Horror trickled through me. My entire being screamed that I should tell Mom.

"If you are smart," the robotic voice continued, "you'll come alone." The video cut off.

I knew immediately who was behind this. This the work of a Necrocretors.

Protecting my identity wasn't enough anymore. I had to save Ethan and Cynthia.

Someone had been watching me. Did they know who I really was? Had they been there in the woods when I showed Ethan who I really was? Surely Louis would've noticed it.

I got up, put my glasses on my face, and regarded Ducky in the mirror. Her face was contorted with fear.

"You know we have no choice," I whispered, feeling like a mentally ill person with split personalities. "They said we should come alone if we want them to live. They can't die. Not because of us."

I DRESSED in black from head to toe and climbed out my window. I perched on the sill, one leg in my room, the other dangling outside. I peered down at anything that could be of use. There, a potted ficus on the patio a story beneath me.

It would have to do.

I opened my hand and concentrated on Mom's potted plant. The ficus grew taller and taller, the woody trunks twirling around each other, until it reached me. I stepped out on the tree, which swayed unsteadily. I climbed down the ladder-like trunk and hopped to the patio below.

I wished that I could learn how to wield it back to its original size, but even if I could, there was no time. Not while Ethan and Cynthia's lives depended on me.

If I saved him—which the bastard didn't deserve—maybe he would see that I wasn't the enemy. Maybe he would stop making the whole glamour thing about him.

Okay, it actually was, since I was too weak to pass the Resistance. But I didn't want to think about that just now.

All I needed to concentrate on was saving Ethan and Cynthia, and figuring out how the hell I was going to do it all by myself.

ETHAN

I WAS TRYING to distract myself reading a bike magazine when a knock sounded on my door. I wasn't really into bikes, to be honest. I didn't even own one.

Dad entered. "Son," he started.

Piss off. I should've said it aloud, but my glare screamed it loud and clear.

"You need to stop. I made a mistake. I should've told you a long time ago."

My jaw muscles pumped.

Dad stood in my doorway, immovable.

I wanted to yell at him, tell him how disappointed I was and that I would never trust him again. I had no one in my corner. No one.

He came into my room and shut the door behind him. He pulled my desk chair out, positioned it by my bed, and sat. "What is really going on here, son?"

"Why do you think something else is going on?" I grumbled.

"I might not have had your back, Ethan. But I know you well."

I shook my head, frowning.

His tone was gentle. "You know her, don't you?"

"Yeah," I said. "She was at the WABA Celebration."

"And let me guess, she took your breath away."

My lip curled. "Why do they do that to us? Who makes these impossible rules? Why did they make us so incompatible? You know that invitation to her revealing at the Buchman invitation? I really wanted it to be her, the hot girl from the Celebration. But then I thought about it. Knowing that we wouldn't be together, to fight the Resistance, well, I was glad when my Wielder turned out to be Ducky."

Dad nodded. "I wish I had the answers. But you need to learn how to bend earth, how to connect with it again, how to protect her from Necrocretors. How to protect each other. Meredith told me the night of the Celebration, Necrocretors must have seen how earth showed up during your sparring match. They discovered that she was your Wielder. They tried to kill them that night."

A trickle of uncertainty teased me. "What?"

"Meredith was prepared. All of them were. Ariel protected her, but it was Necrocretors. Two of them. It was a close call. They will always try to kill her, Ethan. That's why I was begging Meredith to tell you the truth. To show you who she really was since the glamour blocks her ability to wield earth properly. But Meredith is convinced that the only reason there hasn't been another attack is the Necrocretors are still searching for the gorgeous girl. You need to get over this crap. *Of course* this is unfair. The world isn't fair. You need to shoulder your responsibility."

He made me sound like a coward. I wasn't. "It's not that, okay?" I got up and stood by the window with my arms folded across my chest. "I want to reconnect with earth more than you know, but I'm scared."

"Scared of what?"

"Failing the Resistance."

He nodded. He knew exactly what I meant. Alex was everything I ever wanted in a girl. Beautiful. Funny. Smart. And the only girl I couldn't have. Not unless I wanted her to destroy the world.

His phone rang and he answered it. "Jeff," he said. "Meredith, just calm down, you're not making any sense. Deep breaths."

My head snapped up.

"Now start from the top. And this time a bit slower." He frowned, listening intently. Color drained from his face. "No, Alex isn't here. Why would she be?" He got up and started pacing.

"Alex is gone?" I whispered. Tendrils of fear wrapped around my heart.

"A what?" he said, oblivious to me.

"Calm down. We'll be there in a sec." He hung up and put his phone in his jeans pocket.

"Alex is gone?" I repeated.

"She said something about a bad day, that Alex had locked herself in her room."

A twinge of guilt hit me. Those damn posters.

Dad continued, "Apparently when Frederick went outside for some fresh air, one of Meredith's potted plants had grown all the way to Alex's window. When they went to check, she was gone."

"What?" I couldn't believe it. "Maybe she's on her way here."

"Ariel is looking for her. She has some sort of a magical link to Alex. Meredith is waiting for us. They need your help too."

I nodded and followed him downstairs in a hurry. *Please be okay*, I prayed. If a Necrocretor found her, it would be all my fault.

22

ALEX

I SWITCHED my phone off in case Mom figured out I was gone and ruined the element of surprise by calling me.

That was, if I could pull off my plan at all.

The plan was... Well, I was still working that. It would come to me, or so I hoped. I couldn't let anything happen to Ethan or Cynthia.

I'd found my destination on my GPS and drawn a map before shutting off my phone. I realized it wasn't that far from the Buchman plantation. I had to borrow Louis's SUV as it was just South of the interstate.. He'd kill me for that. I didn't care.

Finding the sugar mill was slightly more difficult, but I made it. It was seriously south of the Interstate. You could see it a mile away. A squat, utilitarian building with a massive silver silo at one end and rows upon rows of south-facing windows. The car shook as I pulled over the railroad tracks to reach the parking lot. On closer inspection, it was three buildings joined together, with a long, angled tube for sugar to travel from one end to the other.

It was shut down, completely dark. I parked outside the gate and squeezed through an opening in the fence. It was a tight fit.

I prayed that with Ethan passed out, he wouldn't drain me so I would have enough strength to wield earth tonight.

I found the door unlocked. Hopefully it led to Ethan and Cynthia.

A wall of odors hit me, a mixture of rotting beets and molasses and rusty metal. Behind it all lingered the nauseating smell of a dead animal. I covered my mouth and nose with my sleeve as I tried to find the plastic-sheeted doorway I'd seen on the video. I crept along a processing line past scary-looking machinery, my eyes probing the darkness.

There it was, up ahead.

Ethan and Cynthia would be just behind it. I took a huge breath and pressed through creepy, dirty plastic.

I stood in the doorway, shaking, terrified of what I might find. *You can do this, Alex. It's not so hard.* Then why was my heart beating frantically? The mere idea of Ethan dead made me feel like I was going to die.

I took a few tentative steps forward. There was no sign of them.

In the video, they were right here in this packing area or whatever it was. I recognized the discarded, dust-covered paper sacks. Confused, I reached out and patted the pallet—as if that would make them magically appear. Where the hell were they? The dust wasn't even disturbed.

I didn't feel so good all of a sudden. My ears popped as if I was at high altitude. I worked my jaw. What was that low humming noise?

An invisible force picked me up. I gasped as my feet left the ground. Tossed like a rag doll, I flew all the way to the far wall. I covered my face and head. The wall connected hard with my body. Pain engulfed me. Something inside me cracked.

I crumpled down to the ground. Everything hurt. I groaned, unable to move. My ears were ringing. It sounded like bugs on a warm day as they baked in the sun's heat.

A voice started to laugh. I struggled to lift my head to see who it belonged to. "Poor little Alex," it said. Definitely male. He wasn't familiar, but he sounded as though he knew me well.

I tried to push myself up from the floor. Pain stabbed from my foot to my shoulder. I fell back. I almost cried out but I bit it back. I didn't want to reveal how bad it was.

"I'm here." I tried to get up again, using force on my injuries. "Now let my friends go."

He laughed. "You're as dumb as you are ugly." He was right in front of me, but it was too dark to see him. "Your friends were never here."

"What? No, I saw them. Right there. Where are they?" I hissed through my buck teeth.

The crackle of a hand radio. A woman's voice: "—just left the house. Over."

The man chuckled in response. "Don't worry," he crooned. "They won't make it in time." The radio fell silent. "If it makes you happy, Ethan isn't upset with you anymore."

Fear gripped me, giving me strength to sit up. "What are you talking about? Show yourself! Stop hiding like a coward."

A metal pipe connected with my body hard. I slammed up against the wall. My back burned as the rough surface and exposed nails scraped my skin. I tried not to scream, imagining my skin sloughing off.

The lead pipe hurtled at me again, knocking the breath out of me in a great whoosh. I pushed against it with all my might. My shoulder ached like mad but I wasn't going to give up. I realized it wasn't attached to anyone. It was manipulated by magic.

Then my attacker walked out from between two hulking

steel machines. He wore a military jacket that seemed too big for him, dark pants, and combat boots.

He gave me the creeps.

From the metal that pinned me against the wall, I knew what he was. He was a metal Wielder. Something I thought didn't exist anymore. Metal Wielders used to be part of Earth but due to another curse an earth warlock wielded, metal broke away. Some say it stabilizes and form on it's own, others say that it just died out a long time ago. But here he was, wielding metal as if it was as natural as breathing.

His one hand rose into the air. He flicked his wrist, baring his teeth. The pipe pressed harder into me. I gasped. Any minute now, my ribs were going to pierce my lungs.

"Your boyfriend is coming to save you, but he's too late."

I struggled to breathe. Dark blotches bloomed in my vision.

The metal pipe released. I crashed to the floor, gasping for breath, lungs burning, chest searing with pain. Blood filled my mouth.

Ethan wasn't here. It was a stupid trap and I fell for it. I wanted to weep. But then it hit me: Ethan wasn't here. There was no one to help me.

My attacker approached me where I lay in a heap of trembling limbs. He crouched down beside me. His hands closed around my neck. A viselike grip pulled me up to sit against the wall. I choked. His fingers prodded my esophagus. This was it. I was about to die.

He started to laugh. He was sick. Mentally ill. He gave me a sideways look to admire the pain I was in. I spat in his face. He didn't expect it. He wiped his eyes, releasing my throat for one glorious moment.

I jabbed him in the throat the way Louis and Dad had trained me. He gagged. I pushed myself up. My knee crashed hard into his chin. I kicked him repeatedly. "He's... not... my..." I brought my knee hard into his ribcage with. "Boyfriend!"

The kick must have hurt like hell. My leg did. He doubled over in agony.

"You think you won because you got me alone," I spat. "If you wanted me to be weak, you forgot the main ingredient." I opened my palms.

The ground beneath us started to shake as my Element seared through me. I could feel roots of long-ago-chopped trees lying dormant deep in the earth. They awakened eagerly. I concentrated harder. But with the glamour, concentrating like this drained me.

I couldn't even stop for a second to yank them off my face. There was no time. The Necrocretor would use any distraction to destroy me.

Then something unseen blocked me. As if the earth just clamped a lid on my ability. I didn't stop trying, though. I focused harder. A scream tore from my mouth. Blood dripped on the floor; my nose was bleeding again.

I had to stay alive.

The roots suddenly bucked wildly. Energy sparked everywhere like crazy static electricity. I ducked and dove as they came for me.

Something hit me in the head. I blacked out.

ETHAN

WE REACHED the plantation in no time. The car didn't even stop moving and I got out and rushed up the steps. The door opened to reveal a worried-looking Frederick.

"Glad you're here." He sounded grateful, something I never

thought Frederick would be. He led us to the basement. Meredith stood over a huge cauldron.

I squinted at the huge pewter pot. Steam roiled out of it, gliding over the edges and covering the floor. Along the walls, shelves upon shelves held glass bottles of what I only could assume were ingredients.

Dad cocked his head and raised his eyebrow.

Meredith add a pinch of some powder. A small explosion came from the cauldron. I jumped back as more smoke poured out, imbued with a soft earthy color. A caramel fragrance filled the room. She smiled. "Perfect." Only then did she look up. "Oh, Ethan." She gestured at me to come closer and turned her attention back to the cauldron.

As I neared I heard the liquid bubbling. She picked up a huge soup spoon. Huge was an understatement; the handle was half my length. She bottled some of the bright brown liquid. It smelled wonderful. Sweet. My stomach rumbled.

"It's not as hot as it looks. Drink this. Fast."

I eyed it skeptically as she shoved the bottle under my nose. "What will it do?"

"You are going to find Alex. Her glamour might protect her from your natural beacon, but this will help break through. It's a slam, a heightening of your natural ability to sense her."

I took the bottle and sniffed it. It smelled more irresistible than any caramel milkshake or pies. I downed the shot. She was right; it wasn't hot at all. It tasted like caramel too.

Meredith flicked her hand. A chair slammed into my knees from behind and took my feet out from under me. I fell into the chair just as my head started to spin uncontrollably. My face went numb. I opened my jaw. It felt detached.

"This is normal, Ethan," she assured me, no doubt seeing the panic on my face. "Just a little side effect." Her face, inches from mine, moved in and out of focus. "Concentrate on my voice."

The room spun. Nausea seized my gut.

"Don't throw up," she said. "Otherwise we'll have to start over."

I tried everything in my power to keep it in. Taking deep slow breaths, trying to focus on anything but the swirling in my head and gut. Blotches appeared in my vision. I panicked. "What's happening to me? I can't see."

"It's working!" Meredith sounded happy.

I didn't share her enthusiasm. "Meredith!" I yelled frantically. My sight went completely black.

"It's normal. Calm down." Meredith's voice answered me. "Deep breaths, Ethan. Tell us what you see."

"That is the problem, I don't see..."I paused. "Hang on." Faint light seeped through. It was dark. I struggled to make out where I was.

"Speak to me, Ethan."

"Meredith?" I was standing in a dark room. I turned around to find her. She wasn't there. I was alone. "How can I still hear you but not see you?"

"It's the spell. Where are you?"

"Hard to tell." A cold draft came from my left. I made out some long lines, maybe conveyer belts. "Some old factory, I think. I'm not sure."

"There is a bunch of old factories of main and south of the interstate.," my father suggested.

"Dad?" I smiled. This was so weird and freakin' awesome at the same time.

"Look for something with writing on it, son."

I heard a ruckus up ahead. "I think I hear something." I bolted toward the sound, describing everything I saw. A huge exit sign. A door covered in plastic that made me think of serial killer movies. This part of the building was in a state of disuse. Moss sprouted through the cracks of a worn-out concrete floor. "It's old, not in use anymore."

"I'm Googling," Frederick's voice said.

"A huge conveyer belt on my left. There is absolutely nothing with a logo." I walked further.

Metal clanged against metal. I gasped.

"What is it?" Meredith demanded.

I couldn't describe what I saw. Three huge trees punched through from the pavement. Alex was here, all right.

"Ethan, where is she?"

"She's close. Trees just destroyed the area I entered."

"Find my daughter and hurry up!"

"Meredith," Dad chided. "He's doing his best."

I jogged ahead. I struggle to breathe the further I ran. I didn't know what was guiding me but I hope it was toward Alex and not away from her. *C'mon, one clue. Where the hell am I?*

Fire lit up the scene in front of me. Then it died again. Then it flashed once more. "What the hell? Fireballs!"

The earth shook. She was fighting hard, wherever she was. I lost my balance. "I'm close," I said. I got up and pushed forward. I fell down again as the ground rippled. She was powerful.

Then she screamed. That agonizing, cut-through-the-bone sound sliced through my heart.

"No!" I yelled. Chaos broke loose. All my sparring at the institute kicked in. I ducked and dove as fireballs flew everywhere.

Metal beams hurtled toward me. The ones I couldn't duck sliced right through me as if I were a ghost. It felt awesome and weird at the same time.

I found Alex pinned against the far wall. Metal and fire attacked her from all sides. It seemed as if it couldn't reach her, though. Something, a shield I couldn't see, protected her.

She screamed. Her glasses were still on her face. She was Ducky. Why didn't she take them off? Metal pipes battered the invisible shield, trying to penetrate it. Flames licked too close to her in the shape of angry fists trying to rip the shield apart.

Then I saw them. Two Wielders. Their faces were hidden underneath deep hooded jackets. One a military jacket, the other a black parka. One was about my height, the other one a few heads shorter.

I ran at them. The need to make them pay for ever thinking of luring her to this place boiled in my blood. But I passed straight through them and fell hard to the floor. It was as if I wasn't even there.

"Where is my daughter?" Meredith screamed.

I looked up and through the window saw the outline of a flickering neon cheese wedge in the distance. I knew exactly where I was. "The sugar mill south of the interstate!"

Just then an owl coasted into the room and something invisible rushed passed me.

Déjà vu hit me. It was the same as in that dream, and the owl,it was the exact same owl.

The owl flew straight to the Wielder with the military jacket like a torpedo locked on target. Just before it reached him, it shifted into human form.

The woman punched and kicked with all her might. The metal clattered to the floor as the Wielder broke concentration. The fire redirected from Alex to the shifter. She ducked elegantly and shifted back into an owl as if it was the most natural thing in the world. The military jacket guy screamed in frustration, unable to get a hold on her. He fell forward without anyone pushing him and he screamed as a four scratch lines appears on his leg. He fights air, not knowing where the invisable creature is going to attack. The owl saw her opening and took it. She turned back into a human and kicked the shorter one, who barreled into crates a few feet away. She turned back into the owl just as the Metal Wielder thought he had her.

The fire Wielder ran away.

Oh, no, you're not getting away this easily. I followed.

He or she was fast, leaping over railings like nothing. Nevertheless, I followed. I hadn't felt this free or strong, maybe ever. Powered with super-speed and super-strength, I raced behind the Wielder. I didn't know how I did it, but I got hold of the parka forced the person to whirl around. I saw two red eyes before a cloud of green dust blew into my face.

It burned. I screamed. I covered my face, trying to shake the green powder out of my eyes. Footsteps got further and further from me. He or she was getting away.

"Ethan," Meredith's voice penetrated.

"My face!" I screamed.

"It's not real." The burning sensation cooled and vanished. Someone was shaking me by the shoulder. My vision came back. We were in the SUV. I was in the back. Dad hovered over me.

Frederick was in the driver's seat, Meredith in the passenger seat, and Louis beside Dad. "You did it, Ethan. We're almost there."

I frowned, confused and disoriented.

"I thought we lost you there for a minute. Where did you go?" Dad said.

"I followed one of them. They knew I was there."

"Did they blow green sand at you?" Meredith asked. "Is that what burned?"

I nodded.

The look on Meredith's face said it all. Not good.

Frederick touched her hand.

He looked at me in the rearview mirror. "What about Alex?"

"An owl... I know it sounds strange, but an owl came to her rescue, and there was something else, something I couldn't see that fight with the owl."

"Ariel." My father said as Meredith blew out a sigh of relieve. "They found her?"

"Wait, Ariel is really an owl?" I remembered her blurting out that she was an owl but I had dismissed it as a diversion and then forgotten it in my anger of Alex's deception.

"She was the shifter I used to tell you about," Dad said.

My mouth was agog at the memory of her attacking those Wielders. "She has some crazy moves."

Meredith smiled fondly, but it disappeared and was replaced with worry.

We just climbed off the Interstate and a few cross roads later, the old sugar mill. We jerked over the railroad tracks and Frederick pulled up next to Louis's SUV. His face was grim. "If we make it out of here, I'm going to rip her a new one for stealing that car."

Meredith was out first. Louis headed around the other side to cut off any escape attempts. I at top speed to where I knew Alex was pinned against the wall. Gunshots rang out. We ran faster.

Meredith wielded her fire and to my surprise I found my father bending it. He could still do that?

Louis put his hands in the air. "It's just me."

"No, no, no, no, no." Ariel's voice cried out. "Wake up, Alex."

"No!" Meredith screamed as she darted past me and toppled to the floor, clutching her chest.

I stopped. My heart was breaking into a thousand pieces.

Ariel knelt over a body that lay flat on the floor.

Dad came to a halt a few paces from me. Frederick darted

past Dad, screaming. He fell to his knees next to Meredith. Their daughter lay inert before them.

My mind went blank as I watched Ariel crying, Meredith screaming, and Frederick sobbing.

Louis stood behind them, with his gun-free hand against his forehead. Wondering the same I was. How could this be?

"Son, I'm so sorry," my father said and came over to wrap his arms around me.

I was too late. "This is all my fault."

Alex was dead.

23

ETHAN

TEARS PRICKED my eyes as my father held me tight. This wasn't real. She couldn't be dead.

She'd been alive when Ariel came. The other Wielder, I chased him or her away. She couldn't be dead.

Her mother gasped. "Baby," she wailed. "Frederick, I think she's still breathing!"

"Alex?" Ariel slapped her face a few times.

"Stop that!" Meredith scolded.

Frederick got up called an ambulance. When the call was over, he said, "We need to move her away from all this damage. We'll never explain this to the police. Ariel, get Clive on this." Louis picked Alex up while Frederick started dragging beams and machinery around. I went to help. With any luck, it would look like she'd fallen from the second story.

I hated this part of our existence. Always rearranging reality and using spells to hide evidence. Necrocretors weren't in the police system anyway.

More Beams fell and Frederick's hands engulved with

water. I wanted to bend earth but I couldn't. Alex was stone cold.

I couldn't see something, but I felt it. And so did Frederick. His water disappeared.

"Meredith," he yelled and ran toward the fallen structure.

He crouch down and lay his hand on nothing. Slowly a figure start to appear.

It was a big ass cat.

I gasped as the realization of what that thing was washed over me. It was a wisp and she was busy dying.

"No," Meredith and Ariel ran toward the cat.

They both fell down next to Frederick.

Ariel picked up her head and started to cry, so did Meredith.

"Please God, don't let this happen. Please."

I didn't understand. It was as if Meredith had more compassion for the cat then her own daughter.

"Fibbs," my father said.

"Ethan," Meredith spoke. "Are you sure the dust was green."

"Yeah," I sounded pretty sure. I mean I was farely close to when the fire wielder puffed it into my face.

"What is it, Mer," Ariel asked.

"She is only sleeping." Meredith sighed. "Ethan must have connected somehow with Fibbs and..."

"What?" I interrupted.

"It wasn't you that followed the other wielder. It was Fibbs. Earth Wielders can see through animal eyes but it take years for them to master the spell. I don't know how you made the connecton with our wisp, but somehow you did."

I could see through a huge ass cat's eyes. It would've been freak'n awesome if it wasn't for the fact that the big ass cat was knocked down. Dad approached, fiddling with a small electronic device in his hands. A phone.

"Dad, whose is that?"

"Alex, it looks like," he said.

Meredith grabbed the phone from my father's hands and punched really fast on the screen with her thumbs. She watched something intently. Then I heard it, a voice. It was kind of robotic, like it was tampered with. I'd bet those two guys who had created the rap video could manipulate it to discover what the real voice sounded like.

Dad and I both looked over Meredith shoulder. On the screen, I lay there sleeping. Or worse. I froze. Cynthia. The voice rasped, "You want to see them alive? The old sugar mill... If you are smart, you'll come alone." It was all I heard and then it

stopped.

"Mer," my father said softly. She turned around and pushed me hard.

"This is your fault. If you would have just spoken to her, this would've never happened, Ethan. She would have known it was a trick."

"It's not his fault." My father stepped in front of me. "I know you're upset, and what happened to Alex is awful. But get real. We would've never been here if you'd told him the truth from the beginning."

Frederick snapped his fingers for the phone. Meredith gave it to him. "Just go home, Jeff. Take your son with you. I can't deal with this right now."

"What?" Frederick whispered, watching the video. "You know who did this?" he yelled at me.

"Are you insane?" I bellowed. "You think I'd be standing here if I knew?"

He looked ready to breathe fire, never mind wield water. "Take the keys. We'll go in the ambulance. Just. Go."

"Don't do this," I begged.

"Ethan, go home," Frederick growled.

My father shook his head, staring at the floor with his hand on his hip. I stormed off. This was bullshit. *They're nice whenever they need me, but I'm not allowed to know if Alex is going to be okay?*

I would never forgive myself for what happened here tonight. I was supposed to protect her. I was such a failure. I let out a scream and kicked a metal beam. Pain radiated through my foot. I roared and punched the wall.

"Ethan!" Dad grabbed me and held me tight.

I grunted and screamed, wriggling to get loose.

"I know it hurts, but calm down. I promise you, we will find them, and they will pay."

THE NEXT FEW DAYS, rumors rampaged like wildfire through the school. The accident—a girl falling at the sugar mill was in all the newspapers. Everyone had their own version of things. Most people concluded that Alex had tried to commit suicide, which was the biggest bullshit ever.

I wasn't allowed to speak about it to anyone. Clive's orders. I was also not allowed to go and see her at the hospital. Meredith still blamed me for giving her the cold shoulder. Hell, I blamed myself for that too. I was a useless bender.

My friends were all sympathetic, the witch ones anyway. Even Soph suggested that she could sneak in and get the lowdown. I almost took her up on the offer, but then I remembered that nobody knew Alex's true form.

I leaned against Soph's locker. My eyes caught Cynthia,

Alex's dorky friend whom I'd called Charlotte. "Excuse me," I said to Soph.

I went up to Cynthia. "Hey. Are you okay?"

She nodded. "I know what everyone is saying, but I know Alex didn't do it because of those godforsaken posters."

The posters had mysteriously vanished overnight. *Oh sure, the school can react now.* I nodded, wishing I could tell her the truth.

"You wouldn't know if she's okay, would you?"

"Sorry, I wish I did," I said glumly. "But I'm sure her mom would let you go see her. She is at Friecs Emergency if you want to go say hi. Just tell her mom who you are. She'll tell you how she's doing."

She smiled. "Thank you, Ethan."

"No need." I walked away. I doubted that her mother would let Cynthia see her. But maybe, just maybe, I could get the lowdown through her.

I tried to not think about that night, but it was as if my brain was stuck on repeat.

I even dreamed about it, and that moment when I dived through those Wielders was ten times stronger than what it was through the spell. It always woke me up and always around two.

The next morning I found Cynthia again by her lockers. I went over to say hi and want to know if she went.

"She is still in ICU, they don't want me to see her. Her aunt said that she is hanging on. We should pray." Her eyes started to well up. It only made me feel more shittier then I was. I should've just answer Alex when she tried to phone me.

This was all my fault.

That night I truly struggle to fell asleep. I tried to punch my guilt away at the institute, but nothing worked. In fact I feel more tense then I were.

When I finally fell asleep I woke up with my phone ringing in my ear. I smiled as I saw Alex's number. Thank Heavens.

"Hey you, how are—"

"Ethan, it's me, Ariel." My hope fell back into my stomach.

"If you want to see her, you must come now. Meredith went home to get rest. She's been working on everyone's nerves, especially mine."

I wasn't even properly awake. What was she still doing up? "It's like two in the morning, Ariel."

"Sorry. I didn't realize it's so late."

"No," I said fast. "I'll be there in ten minutes."

I got up and pulled on a pair of jeans. I sneaked out of the house and into my Jeep and hightailed it to Friecs Emergency. Ariel texted me the floor number while I was en route. In less than fifteen minutes I was standing in the reception area.

I'm waiting, I texted Ariel.

A private room door slid open and a tired-looking Ariel slipped out. I gave her a hug. She clung to me. A part of me feel sorry for her. She was the only one who wanted her niece to be free.

"Is she okay?"

She broke the hug. Tears sparkled in her eyes. She shook her head and seemed to pull herself together. "Come." She gave the evening nurse a hundred and sneaked me in. She opened the sliding door and I quickly slipped through.

I wasn't expecting what lay on the bed. She was supposed to be beautiful Alex, not the Ugly Duckling. "I don't understand. Her glasses are off. Why does she still look like that?"

Ariel sighed. "The glamour burned into her face."

I remembered her scream. The agonizing, cut-through-the-bone scream. I closed my eyes. It wasn't because of the Wielders' Elements. It was the glamour.

"So, the glasses did this to her." Rage rose in my chest.

Here they were blaming me, making me feel shittier then I already did, and all this time it was the fucking glasses that should never have been wielded in the first place.

"Has she shown any sign of waking up or trying to change her appearance?"

"None whatsoever. They are actually speaking of DNR."

DNR: do not resuscitate. "*What?*" I roared.

"We don't know what Alex went through."

"She was fine, Ariel. I was there."

She nodded. "You were."

"Not like that. Meredith gave me a potion, one to help me track her. She was alive when you flew in." The corner of my lips curved slightly as I remembered the owl. "You know you saved her life? You have some crazy moves."

"Are you sure?"

I nodded. "Positive."

"I don't get it then. What happened?"

I shrugged. "I don't know. I followed the fire Wielder when he or she scrambled. I figured if I could at least see who was linked to all of this, I could help. But nothing." I wasn't in the mood to tell her about the green dust.

Ariel frowned. "Why isn't she waking up?"

"My father said he healed Meredith once. Can't I do the same for Alex?"

She squinted. "You would do that?"

Why was she even surprised? "Of course I would. It's my duty..."

She lifted her hand. "Not what I meant. I guess your dad didn't tell you about the aftereffects it has on Benders who heal their Wielders."

"Aftereffects?"

"Speak to your father, Ethan. Get all the facts before you offer something like that."

"So it's not far-fetched. I can heal her from this state. I can wake her up." In my mind, it was a done deal, aftereffects be damned.

"Yes, you can. But speak to your father, Ethan. You need to know everything."

I STAYED TILL AROUND FIVE. Outside the window, dawn was beginning to seep over the horizon. I gave Ariel some time to sleep while I keep guard.

When I got home, I found Dad on the phone. He looked relieved. "No, don't worry. He just walked in. Thank you, Clive. Yes, yes. I will. You too." He hung up. "Do you have any idea how worried I was?"

"C'mon, Dad, I'm eighteen."

"Almost eighteen," he corrected me.

I rolled my eyes. I was dead tired on my feet.

"Do I even ask where you were?"

"Sure." I took the chair at the breakfast nook. "I went to see Alex."

My father stared at me.

"What? Ariel phoned. She wanted to know if I wanted to see her. I did so I went." I used a flippant tone, like it was no big deal.

"You went?" Dad busied himself at the counter. The room filled with the heady scent of freshly roasted coffee.

I nodded. "Did you know that the glamour burned into her face?"

He took a huge breath. "So she's the ugly Alex without her glasses? Poor kid."

I nodded as he set a strong cup of coffee in front of me. "The doctors are talking about a DNR."

"What?" He sounded as shocked as I felt.

"Ariel said there is a way I could heal her, like you did with Meredith, and wake her up."

Dad's face froze. "Ariel did."

"Sort of," I said circumspectly. He looked very closed off. "I remembered you told me that you did it once. Saved Meredith's life."

"And she thinks it's a good idea?"

"Well, no. Actually the opposite."

Dad nodded. "She's right about that. You'll never be the same after you heal Alex."

"But can I? I mean, will it work?"

"Yes, but I am telling you to forget it."

"Dad, it's Alex. C'mon."

"And you are my son."

This took me by surprise. "She said something about aftereffects, that I needed to know everything before I say yes. What are they?"

He sighed. "Fine." He pulled out the opposite chair and sat down. "Alex will literally take about eighteen months off you. You will have the body of someone a year and six months older than you. You'll die earlier. That is what they do. The way she empowers you right now, that is going to stop and then the wheel is going to turn. They are ten times worse to us than what we are to them."

I sipped the bitter, hot liquid. "So let me get this straight. She will speed up my life cycle if I heal her."

"Another way to look at it. But yeah."

"It's worth it," I said decisively.

"It's not the only aftereffect."

"Then tell me! I don't see why I shouldn't be doing this," I insisted, adamant. I wanted Alex to wake up.

"You shouldn't, you really shouldn't. It messes with the

Resistance. It messes with both of you. Healing your Wielder, that magic is rare. One that works in a million ways and not one the same. Healing someone leaves a mark and the Resistance preys on that mark. It haunts your dreams and..." He stroked his face, a look of pure horror on it.

I was trying to understand what he was trying to say. I couldn't.

"Wet dreams Ethan. It's like wet dreams, just ten times worse."

"Oh," I said. "That's it?"

My father's body deflated as if I didn't see the big picture at all. "It's not just wet dreams. Both of you will experience the same dream at the same time. Making resisting each other much harder."

"Oh." I got what he was implying. "So, Alex will experience this wet dream with me."

He nodded. "There are no glamours in dreams."

"I see." I finally got what my father was so worried about and why he didn't want me to do this. I was going to have steamy hot sex in my dreams with Foxy Alex. Which almost put a smile on my face until I remembered what he said. Making the Resistance so much harder. I was already going to fail as is.

Still, I had no choice. I just had to save Alex.

24

"UNDER NO CIRCUMSTANCES WILL THAT HAPPEN," Meredith pronounced when Dad phoned her with my offer; she was still too upset to see me—or him for that matter.

I still blamed myself, of course. But for Meredith to just be blinded by the sex aspect and not the obvious upside of *her daughter actually waking up*... I didn't understand that. Classic Meredith. Going to extremes to protect her daughter but doing more damage than good.

"It's for the best, actually," Dad said.

"What?" I felt annoyed with the adults.

"Son, it's like you said. Even without the aftereffects, Resisting someone like Alex won't be easy. Now you want to go and make it harder."

My mouth hung agape. "If she doesn't wake up, there will be *nothing* to Resist, Dad. I'd rather face a near-impossible test than not have a Wielder at all. There is no loophole for me. I will die if I can't bend." Okay, a bit melodramatic. But I wanted this life. I was a Bender. This was our normal. "All you see is the aftereffects on me, isn't it?"

He sighed. "I don't want this fight for you."

"Dad, it's because of not wanting this fight for me that Alex is where she is in the first place!" I exclaimed. "I was a coward."

"I'll speak to Meredith again." He ruffled my messy blond hair. "When did you become so grown up?"

I flushed, startled and pleased by his words.

He turned around and pick up his cell again. I checked mine. Ariel hadn't called me with an update either.

My thoughts returned to the person I chased. Who was it? Did he or she keep tabs on Alex—if so, for how long? How the hell did that footage get created? Sure, it would have been easy to get one of me and change the background through image editing. But to get video of Cynthia lying next to me, they would've had to drug me.

It scared me. Not the fight, not protecting Alex, not bending earth. No, I was scared that whoever was keeping tabs on us was doing it close-range. Not knowing who that was that scared the living daylights out of me. It could be anyone.

For the next few days, Dad and Meredith had many phone calls. I heard their fights through walls, well, mainly his side anyway.

She wouldn't budge.

I didn't get this at all. I wasn't even considering the aftereffects anymore. I just wanted to see Alex walking and talking again, even if it was behind those beer-bottom glasses her mother conjured.

I should've answered her text. Even if it was just to say "I'm upset, leave me alone to deal with all of this."

Every time I closed my eyes I saw the Fox. She was far from an Ugly Duckling. *Who does that?* And then my mind would circled to the night of the WABA Celebration. The night I saw her for the very first time. She'd fainted when my earth came back. Or so Dad told me.

I tried to imagine her fainting. Doubtless she even made that look beautiful.

Beautiful. She was beautiful and now her mother is going to let her die because of it. She couldn't see what I saw. We'd find a way to Resist, not to fail. I'd rather die than watch Alex destroy this world.

Though if we did fail the Resistance, I probably would die. All the Wielders who went rogue and almost destroyed humanity as we knew it all had one thing in common: no Benders.

SATURDAY MORNING I woke up overhearing not just Dad's voice. No, this time I heard Meredith's shrill replies. Either my hearing had enhanced overnight, or Meredith was here. I jumped out of bed. If I could get Dad on board with my plan to heal Alex, then I could convince her too.

I yanked on a shirt and ran down the steps. The wooden floor thumped loudly underfoot and the conversation petered out.

I didn't just find Meredith. Ariel was there too. All three of them sat around the breakfast nook with cups of steaming coffee. Ariel smiled at me; her sister didn't even acknowledge me. She just stared at her coffee as though it had personally wronged her.

"Morning, son." Dad grabbed a mug to pour me some coffee too.

"Dad, Ariel, Meredith." I pulled out the chair next to Ariel.

"Ethan." Ariel was the only one who answered. She took another sip of her joe.

My eyes lingered for a few seconds on Meredith, but she

didn't even stir. A cold feeling wrapped around my heart. "How is Alex?"

"She's fine, still the same." Ariel was the only one speaking.

The fingers of fear released their grip and I could breathe again. Silence reigned.

Dad finally broke the ice. "Meredith."

"Jeff, you know how I feel about this."

"About what?" I interrupted, braving her glare. "Me wanting to wake Alex up? You've been there yourself, Meredith. If it weren't for my dad, you might be dead. Please, let me help."

She started to laugh. It was a tired, sarcastic sound. "And what then, Ethan?"

"I know about the dreams, okay? And I also know about the eighteen months she will zap from my life."

Meredith looked away guiltily.

I snorted. "It looks to me as if you are all focusing on the wrong things here. Yes, I know the dreams will probably be the hardest thing either of us will face, but let us face them. Give her the chance to face them and me the chance to Resist. Don't just give up and let her remain in a coma forever. Then the Necrocretors might as well have killed her the other night."

"Ethan!" My father sounded shocked.

"No, Jeff," Ariel said. "He's right. I've been saying this to Meredith for a while now and she doesn't want to listen. Alex isn't going to wake up by herself. If she doesn't come out of it, who knows what that glamour will do to her organs? Let Ethan help her. Let him heal her."

"I will be strong," I said, my voice husky. "I can prepare myself."

She looked at my dad, her expression bleak.

"Don't give me that look, Mer. I do feel like you do about all this. Ethan makes some strong points. I know the image in your head of my son is all hormones and charm, but I can promise you, he's more than that. He is set in his goals and will find a way to reach them with or without anyone's help. He is more mature about healing Alex than what the two of us were when faced with the same decision."

She scowled, but I could tell that she was contemplating it. A tear rushed down her face. Dad wiped it away with his thumb. She touched his hand. It felt as if I was intruding on a private moment. She was married, for crying out loud.

"Fine," she said.

Ariel did a double-take. My mouth fell open in surprise. "You mean you'll do it?"

"Yes, but you need to promise you will Resist her even in the dreams, Ethan."

"I promise," I said too fast.

She laughed. "We still have to worry about her other parent. I can promise you when it comes to a Bender's healing, Frederick is not going to be as lenient as I." She picked up her bag. "Thank you for the coffee."

Ariel got up too. "See you guys soon." It sounded more like a question than a statement.

The door closed and a few seconds later the car doors slammed, the ignition turned, and they were gone.

"So, Frederick won't do this."

"He won't like it, but you don't know Meredith. She gets her way. That was your answer, son. I just hope that you are as prepared as you say."

IT TOOK ANOTHER WEEK. Alex languished in that hospital bed for seven more rotten days.

At least I could go see her. Many nights, I sat vigil next to her bed with Ariel or sometimes Meredith. But then Frederick would come in and launch a full-on argument with me.

I hardly said anything to him, but it didn't stop him dragging my anger out of me. "She was a goner the minute she discovered that you were her Bender." He seethed.

"Frederick, stop." Meredith's voice broke.

An urge to hit him, that tingling sensation that warmed up my knuckles spread over my entire fist, seized me, but I fought it. I displayed to Meredith my remarkable sense of control, my ability to resist impulses, by not clobbering her husband. I just took a deep breath and walked past him. "I'll see you later," I said and left.

I went to the institute. I needed a workout to get rid of my bottled-up anger and Frederick's words that stuck in my mind like glue.

The workout had been going about an hour and a half when Mira found me. She said nothing. She just grabbed her gloves, took the place of the punching bag, and started coaching me. Another hour of that and I felt like the old me.

"Weekends this place is always so quiet," she said, unwrapping her knuckles. "Sedgwick still doesn't want to open on weekends. I've missed our Saturday sessions."

"Sorry I haven't been coming," I said, flexing my fingers. "Everything is insane at the moment."

She smiled and bumped my shoulder. We sat on the boxing ring with our legs dangling off the edge and arms hugging the elastic rope.

"So how is she?"

"She'll get there."

"How, Ethan? She's been in that coma for almost a month now."

I didn't reply. My mind was made up.

Mira knew me too well. "Are you insane?"

"You said it yourself. She's been in that coma for a month. She's at risk of brain damage or worse. I have the ability to heal her, Mira. I will do it. I will fight the aftereffects, too."

Her voice was harsh, that of my drill sergeant. "You won't succeed, Ethan. I know you're the Golden Boy, but those dreams are as real as you and me standing right here."

I had to admit that hearing it out of her mouth, at how real the dreams were, did scare me a little. I frowned. "How will I know what's a dream?"

"Exactly my point. Why do you think Wielders and Benders step over the line? Because they could no longer discern the difference between dream and reality."

I felt like a mountain climber facing Everest. "How long do they last?"

She sighed and looked away.

"How long?"

"As long as the affair in the dream lasts."

"What affair?" I was so confused.

"You won't be able to Resist. It always ends in a relationship between Bender and Wielder. In the dreams, it's safe, but it never stays that way. The dreams are never enough."

She sounded as if she was speaking from experience. "How do you know all this?"

She sighed. "I've been there. Why do you think I don't have a Wielder anymore? We stepped out of line. The Association made us split up."

"Wait, what?"

She smiled. "You think your father chose Siobhan through his accord? They got to him, Ethan. Made him see what Meredith was going to do to him. He had a back door, a second Wielder, but his case is unique. Those of us who don't have spare Wielders lying around lose our Wielders and never get another."

Pity welled up in me. Not just for her but my father too. I'd gone without a Wielder and knew how empty and painful it was to be cut off from my element. The Association made them split up.

"Why do you think there are so many Necrocretors? They didn't agree with the Association about the breakup. They ran away together."

"What happened to your Wielder?"

"Markus?" She smiled. "He married another witch. She wasn't of the Wielder race though. I think she's an Alchemist. The last I heard, he has a son."

I cringed. "And if we can't Resist, the Association will do the same to us."

She nodded.

The full weight of the danger I was facing settled on my chest like a heavy stone, crushing my ribcage. It wasn't just about Alex destroying the world anymore. I was risking losing her altogether. I had to save her somehow. I just had to find a way to resist her.

"Mira?" I had one more question.

She turned around as she was walking toward her office.

"If we find a way to Resist the dreams, how long do they test us before it stops?"

"They say around a month or so."

"Who is they?"

"The few who found a way were the same gender and straight."

25

THE DATE WAS SET and we were on the way. I realized I knew everything about healing and the aftereffects, but I had no idea how to heal this girl.

Dad and Meredith would walk me through it, step by step. Someone would always be close by. His tone was foreboding. I didn't want to ask what he meant about supervision.

I couldn't get what Mira had said out of my head. Why was this Resistance test so hard?

We arrived at the Buchman plantation. I started to get out of the Jeep into their manicured courtyard with its stupid fancy fountain, but Dad reached over me and shut the door.

Frederick walked down the steps carrying a duffel bag with Louis in tow. Meredith appeared in the doorway with her arms folded, glaring at her husband's back, shaking her head softly.

"Guess he didn't approve of this at all."

"Ethan, if she was my daughter and you weren't my son, I would act the same. I never thought I would say this, but this time I actually feel for Frederick."

"Dad, I said I'll be the strong one. I promised. Nothing's changed."

"Yeah, I know you will." He didn't take his eyes off the sports car that zoomed from one of the garages. They were so many doors, the building reminded me of stables, not a keeper of cars.

He spun past us and gravel sprayed against the Jeep. Dad flinched at the hollow pings. His jaw muscles pumped. "That was uncalled for."

"Asshole," I whispered.

We climbed out and walked up the steps to where Meredith awaited for us.

"So he left," Dad said.

"Yep, he asked me to choose. I chose my daughter." Her face was a thunderstorm.

"Choose?" he asked. She give him her signature raised eyebrow, and after a few seconds he started to laugh. "You gotta be shitting me. After all these years."

"Jeff, don't." She headed inside. "Come."

We followed her up the steps and once we were on the second story, she took us to a door. "The hospital dropped her off yesterday. Ariel prepared her for the healing early this morning. So she's ready." She smiled at me. "Now to get you ready."

"Great, what do you need me to do?" I said nervously.

"You did tell Ethan what he has to do, how the healing works, right?"

He squinted as if thinking hard. "No."

"C'mon, it can't be that bad. It's not like I'm going to have sex with her," I joked.

"No," Meredith said primly.

"Thank heavens. That would be awkward." It slipped out. Dad shook his head, embarrassed.

"What?" I shrugged at him.

"Let's just get you in there. Ariel is better at explaining this sort of thing than I am."

I WAS SITTING in Alex's bathroom. My foot tapped a wild tattoo in my nervousness. If they had told me everything the way Ariel just had, I might have had second thoughts about this. It was being supervised that made it so awkward.

I had to climb into bed with Alex. That wasn't even the freaky part. I couldn't wear thread of clothes. Yep, buck naked.

Ariel explained it using newborn babies. When they needed tender loving care, skin-to-skin contact healed their ails.

I had to hold Alex, who would also be naked, and recite a spell over and over out loud until I couldn't anymore.

That was when the others would carry on reciting the words. It was something that belonged in a horror movie about evil cults, not real life.

I jumped as a knock came at the door. "Ethan, you okay?" Ariel asked.

"Yeah, I'm fine." I didn't sound fine.

"You need more time?"

"No, I'm fine," I repeated.

Silence.

"You going to come out?" I could hear the smile in her tone.

"Yeah, in a minute," I said.

"Okay, so more time."

Shit, I wasn't fine. "Yep."

The door opened a moment later. Dad came in, laughing. "Son, what are you wearing?"

I looked down. I had Alex's Tinkerbelle bathrobe on. "I feel so naked, Dad."

"That's because you are. I know it's awkward, but it's the only way to bring Alex back."

"How the hell did you do this? Was it as bad as this?"

He wrinkled his nose. "I had Siobhan. No one else."

"Seriously, the other Wielder?" I tried to imagine if Sophie were here, calmly watching this. It made my skin crawl.

"We both wanted to save Mer. It was awkward as hell."

"It wasn't her aunt and mother."

He grinned. "True, but we are all you have."

"How long will this take?"

"It's awkward for the first ten minutes. Promise."

"Okay." I just wanted to get those horrible ten minutes over with. I got up. Dad handed me a towel, chortling. "Change into this."

I wrapped it around my waist and took off the robe. I hung it back on the hook behind Alex's door and came out.

Three pair of eyes stared at me. I touched my chest; Meredith looked away but Ariel stared. "I don't even know why you bother with the towel," she teased. "With that body, you can walk around naked and not feel an inch of shame."

"Ariel," Meredith scolded.

"What?" she shrugged.

"I can't take you anywhere." She studiously met my eyes and nothing further south. "Sorry about her. She has no filter."

I chuckled nervously and gestured at the bed. "So... I just climb in with her?" Alex lay on her back. The plush green comforter was drawn up to her chin.

"Yes." She lifted the covers revealing Alex.

We did this sort of side-step-dance past each other. She was more nervous than I was.

She closed her eyes and rushed over to her sister. My father sucked on his lips and shook his head. *Thanks for the support dad, seriously. Thumbs up to you.*

I climbed in and pulled the covers over myself, only then awkwardly unwrapping the towel. Ariel was already at my side of the bed, waiting for it. I handed her the towel.

I shifted toward Alex. I had no idea what to do next. Dad

stepped up. "Just pull her closer to you, Ethan. Hold her tight against your body."

"Not too tight," Meredith said in a strangled voice. Ariel snorted with laughter. "It's not funny," Meredith insisted.

"Don't pay attention to them. She was unconscious when I was where you are right now. Pull her closer and hold her, Ethan. You will find that she fits in your arms perfectly."

"Jeff," Meredith scolded.

"What? It's the truth."

I grabbed hold of Alex's limp arm and rolled her toward me without peeking. Her body was cool to the touch, too cool. I didn't think anymore. I wrapped my arms around her and held her tight. I was vividly aware of her breasts pressed against my pecs, her legs against mine. I willed everything to stay quiet between my legs.

Eight minutes to go. "Okay, what next?"

"You recite the following words. I know it's difficult, but it's a spell as old as time. There isn't a translation. Many spell-binders tried, but the original is all we have."

"Just give me the words," I said, annoyed.

She came to stand next to my father. "Okay, it goes like this:

"Curare Nunc
Autm pona inops dolor
Maneant modo poena, et non
Reverta"

WHAT THE HELL? I gave Dad a grave look.

"What it basically means is, 'I now heal the pain of this girl; disappear now pain, at my will.'" She squinted. "More or less.

It's the original tongue of the spellbinders, predating even Latin. Sue me if I have the meaning off a bit."

"You don't even know what it really means."

"It doesn't directly translate into English, Ethan." She huffed. "I doubt even spellbinders know what it truly means."

Alex's form was still very much all over mine. This was a lost cause. "Fine. Just say those words again."

By the third time, I was saying it with Meredith. By the fifth time had my pronunciation right and had memorized the words. The three of them said it with me. I closed my eyes. In my mind, I pictured them holding hands, sitting in a circle, swaying while reciting the words.

It was comical but I doubted they did it. I started to feel tired. Like, the tired I usually reached around a twenty-four-hour bender with no sleep.

Still I kept saying the words as my eyes grew heavier. Before I knew it, I fell asleep.

ALEX

I STILL FELT SLEEPY, but my body ached all over.

My senses slowly returned. It was warm in my bed, like Mom or aunt Ariel was sleeping next to me, our legs entwined. Then I realized the other person was naked.

My eyes flew open. A pair of pecs filled my vision. A guy's arm encircled me. His leg was draped over mine. What the hell?

I tried to think back. I'd screamed as my face burned. Something protected me from that Wielder's abilities. An invisible shield of mother earth herself.

I shifted slowly. I didn't want to wake up whoever I'd crawled into bed with. Why couldn't I remember? Was I possessed?

I pulled a few inches away and froze. Messy blond hair. Perfect nose. Suntanned skin. I checked out the pecks in front of my face. Yep, I'd know them anywhere. Holy fuck. It was Ethan.

My heartbeat went from calm to gallop in point-two seconds flat. The Resistance. I'd failed.

Someone was talking nearby. Sleepy words. The spellbinders' language.

I lifted my head. Mom was sitting in the chair. My eyes bugged out. What the actual hell? "Mom," I whispered loudly.

She looked up. Tears welled up in her eyes as she ran toward me.

"You're awake." She wiped a tear away as she touched my face.

I was naked in bed next to a guy. Why did I feel like the only grownup here? "I'm awake? God, Mom, get me out of here."

She nodded, ran to the bathroom, and came back with my Tinkerbelle robe. She lifted the covers. I wormed my way out of his monkey grip.

The last I knew, he was so upset with me he wouldn't even speak to me. Now I woke up with him naked in bed. What the hell? My mind reeled.

I almost toppled out of bed. Mom helped me up, put the robe around me as I pulled my arms through and tied the sash.

"Why am I naked?" I hissed through clenched teeth. "And why where you watching?" So embarrassing!

"It's not what you think." She tucked Ethan in almost fondly. This was beyond weird.

"I need coffee, and loads of it," she said and ran out. Why was she fleeing my questions?

I followed. "Mom, talk to me." I was still whispering. She just walked faster.

We neared the kitchen and I stopped as I heard Jeff's and Ariel's voices.

"What are you doing here?" Ariel shouted at Mom. Then she spotted me and dropped her cup, which shattered on the tile floor. She almost ran me over with a huge bear hug. "You're awake!"

She was the second person to say it like that.

"Is Ethan still asleep?" Jeff asked.

"You know he's up there?" I gasped, horrified. I felt a deep flush creep over my chest and face. "What the hell is going on?"

Ariel smiled. "Sit. It's a long story, girl."

MY MOUTH HUNG to the floor after Ariel, Mom, and Jeff took turns interrupting each other to fill me in.

My glamour had burned into my face. Doctors at the hospital had predicted that I wouldn't wake up. Ethan had healed me. He brought me back. That was why I found him buck-naked with me.

"What did Dad say about this?" I managed.

They all got quiet.

"Where is he?" I never thought I'd see my father and Jeff in the same house.

"He left, sweetheart. You father was dead-set against Ethan healing you."

"He... left?"

"I'm sorry." Mom got up and hugged me tight as Jeff plopped another pancake on my plate. I'd never been so hungry in my entire life.

"He didn't want Ethan to heal me?" I was disappointed.

She tucked a stray hair behind my ear. I was me again. The

glasses were nowhere to be found. Mom said I could go without them for as long as I wanted. "He didn't want the fight for you."

"What fight?"

She put her finger on my mouth. "Give me time to explain."

I nodded and then she told me an even scarier story.

26

ETHAN

I SNIFFED DEEPLY through my nostrils. My arms stretched above my head. I felt like I was rising from the dead.

Then it hit me. The last time my eyes were open. The humiliation, the awkwardness. The naked girl.

My eyes flew open. I lifted my head. "Dad?"

Nobody was in the room, including Alex. The pocket where she'd been felt desolate. My heart skipped a beat. She was awake. Alex woke up.

I leaped out of bed, grabbed my jeans, and yanked them on. I pulled my shirt over my head and opened her bedroom door.

It worked. I, Ethan Sutcliff, had it in me to heal my Wielder after all. I wasn't useless anymore.

The big old clock at the bottom of the stairs said it was nine. The daylight through the window said it was morning. I couldn't remember the last time I slept until nine.

Meredith was talking when I got to the kitchen. "I didn't want this for you, sweetheart, but I had no choice. You weren't going to wake up, and I don't know a spell that allows you to communicate with people in coma. Otherwise believe me, I would've used it."

"Mom," she grunted. It was the beautiful-Alex voice, the deeper one. Ducky had nasal twang. "You should've let me stay in that coma."

I halted just before I entered. I backed up a few paces. Hurt infused my being, trickling from scalp to toes. She didn't want me to heal her.

"I had no choice, Alex. I waited as long as I could, but there were serious risks in letting you stay down."

"You always have a choice. That's what you like to say, isn't it? You just sentenced me to death." A chair screeched.

Shit, she was going to come this way. I sprinted on my toes toward the front door and slipped out.

She didn't want me to save her. She saw this as a death sentence. Why? Because it was me?

All of a sudden I felt stupid, not brave. She didn't want to be saved. She preferred to die rather than face life.

Maybe it wasn't that she didn't want to be saved. Maybe she just didn't want to be saved by me.

I headed toward the courtyard gate.

ALEX

I WENT up to my room. My heart was breaking. Not only did Ethan lost something dearly trying to safe my life, 18months of his youth, Fibbs were lost to. She was hit with a sleeping curse, one as old as time itself and there were more casualties who died from it than woke up.

Not to mention the dreams—real, awkward, crazy dreams—would start soon. I wouldn't be myself. I'd throw myself on Ethan. It was the Resistance. I was horrified until Mom told me that she had no choice. Then I was just mad.

Necrocretors. Ariel should've warned Mom about the dreams. And about our kiss. I wouldn't be anywhere near strong enough to Resist Ethan if he tried his luck. I would give in.

The worst part was that Ethan knew all of this before he climbed into bed with me.

I had no idea how the hell I was going to face him, until she told me what he'd sacrificed for me. He was officially eighteen months older this morning.

I had to thank him, and then kick his ass. Why had he done something so stupid to just save me?

I opened my room and found my bed empty. My bathroom door was ajar; I checked it but it was unoccupied. Where the hell was he?

Then a wave of horror washed over me. He'd heard us talking. How much did he hear? I rushed out the door and down the stairs.

"Alex, what's wrong?"

"Ethan is gone," I yelled. Jeff's hand stopped and hovered, mid–pancake flip. "He must have heard something he didn't like just left."

"Calm down, maybe it's not such a bad thing, sweetheart. You can work with this."

"*Work with this?*" My voice climbed an octave. "Mom, the guy just saved my life."

"You want him to Resist you, Alex. Don't go look for him to explain. Let him be upset with you. When the dream period is over, you can patch things up."

"There is a time period?" That was good news.

"Yes, if you'd let me finish."

I sighed.

"Listen to your mother, Alex. I'll go see where he is," Jeff said. He pulled the skillet off the stove and headed to the guest bedroom. How many nights had he stayed here?

"Fine," I said, gloomy. "Whatever."

My relationship with Ethan seemed like it could never be normal one. My mother kept trying to manipulated it. Kept searching for the key to help us in the Resistance. Ethan would always be angry with me.

For some reason, I didn't like that very much.

MOM WOULDN'T LET me go to school. She wasn't ready. She also flatly forbid me from contacting my one and only friend there, since it was just complicate things.

Dad came home a week later and apologized profusely on his knees with a bouquet of white lilies and orange dahlias in his arms. Mom seemed unlikely to forgive him. Then he saw me. Tears streamed down his cheeks. He grabbed me tight and lifted me up, his form shaking.

My poor father. What had he gone through? I knew why he wanted me to stay in my coma. I wanted it too. Why couldn't she just listen to him?

I imagined the fight they must have had before he left. They were both so stubborn—a trait I had inherited. If I hadn't, I would've texted Ethan a long time ago.

I would've told him that he'd only heard a snippet of a hefty conversation, even though I didn't know which part exactly. He was assuming. I hated when people assumed.

Two weeks had passed. I didn't once dream of Ethan. A part of me thought that it was balderdash. Maybe they were just making a big fuss out of nothing. Our test would be face-to-face.

I really should just speak to him, text him and make

amends. Instead I texted Cynthia. If mom didn't want me to tex Ethan, well, I have to speak to someone.

"Hi, it's me. How are you? How is things at school."

It took about five minutes for my phone to beep. "Oh my word. Finally, you are back from the dead. I was so worried. How are you. When did you wake up."

I smiled.

"Early this morning. Soar throat and chest," I lied. To be honest I didn't know how one should feel after coming out of their coma. "Refreshed. Does that make any sense."

"Yes, it does. Ethan was worried. Why was Ethan worried again."

I send her a smiley, with the words typed next to it, he is an idiot.

We talked for the next few minutes. She told me what everyone at school was thinking, that I tried to committed suicide even though she knew I didn't, and then she asked me, did you?"

"No, offcourse not. I slipped and fell." I lied again. "I shouldn't have been there anyway but I like to go to the old Sugarmill to think."

I don't know how anyone could think there because of the horrible smell lingering in the air but it seems that she bought it.

"How does Ethan fit in all this," she asked.

"He doesn't. We are just sparring partners, remember."

"He acted more than just a worried sparring partner, Alex."

"Yeah, I heard. Sorry for the scare," I text.

"When are you coming back?"

"If it depends on my mom, never. But will let you know when."

We said goodbye and I lay on my bed and watched some TV. My eyes felt heavy.

Then a loud explosion on the TV jerked me awake. I looked

at the time. Ten o'clock. I picked up my phone and texted Ethan.

I need to tell you something. Please don't be mad. My mom never learns. I'm not going to play her stupid game anymore. I pushed send.

To my surprise my phone rang. I picked it up. "Hello?"

"Tell me what?" He sounded pissed off.

"Whatever you heard was out of context."

"Oh? What did I hear."

"I don't know, Ethan. But it couldn't be that good to leave without letting me thank you."

"Thank me?"

"Yes, of course." I felt surprised.

"I thought you didn't want to be saved."

I closed my eyes. "Out of context, remember? If you'd been there a few sentences before, I'm sure you would've heard the entire thing. You wouldn't have eavesdropped and left like a scared little boy."

"Scared little boy?" he repeated incredulously. "Nice. Go screw yourself, Alex."

The phone disconnected. I groaned. *Not what I meant!*

I had no choice but to go to his house and handle this face-to-face. I contemplated it. He was so resistant at the moment. Maybe it was safe. This was so stupid.

I walked to my window and opened it. Fresh, cold air blew in. It was getting chillier at night, a month later than the last time I had sneaked out of this window. The night was breathtakingly beautiful. An arc of stars glittered overhead.

I found Mom's plant on the ground below my window. It was small again. How the heck did she get it back to its original size? Or maybe it was a new one.

I held my hand palm out toward the ficus. It grew toward

me. I slid down it the same way I had with the previous one. I pulled my hood over my head and ran toward the gate.

Something sparkled in the moonlight. My old bike. Huh. I thought Dad had thrown it away.

Still I grabbed it and pushed it alongside me. I got to the gate and found the guards sleeping. I slipped through the gate. Only when I was out of sight did I climbed on my bike and start pedaling.

I didn't even know where Ethan lived, but I had this weird feeling inside me, guiding me to his house.

The lake was gorgeous this time of night. I wasn't even scared of Necrocretors anymore. I just wanted to speak to Ethan, force him see what a big misunderstanding this was, tell him that I was truly grateful that he'd saved my life.

I stopped in front of a house. His yellow Jeep was parked in the driveway. I threw my bike down. I even knew which room was his. *So weird*. Heart-shaped ivy spiraled up the gutter. I used it to get to his room.

I found him sitting behind his desk, chatting on his phone. Based on the sheepish smile on his lips, it was Sophie.

I opened his window and climbed in. Why was I here? *Because I need to get it through his thick skull that he's wrong.* Weird emotions of right and wrong warred in my gut.

Ethan's chair span around. He froze when he saw me standing by the window. "Soph, I'll speak to you later. My dad is calling me."

I gave him a raised eyebrow look which he didn't see.

He put down the phone, and looked at me not impressed. "What are you doing here?"

I gaped. "What am I doing here?" I parroted. "Seriously? You're being an idiot and I need to speak to you."

"If my dad catches you here…"

"What is he going to do?" I sneered. Who was I?

He narrowed his eyes at me.

"Look, it's stupid, okay? You only heard a part of the conversation." I sighed. "Obviously I'm glad you saved my life, but yes, I'm also upset."

"Why are you upset?"

"Cause I'm not as strong as everyone thinks I am, Ethan," I whispered. *Nope, scratch that. That is not what I wanted to say.* I'd wanted to say the reason was his loss of eighteen months.

"I don't understand."

I grunted, stared at the ceiling. *Eighteen months, Alex,* I guided myself. "I never had a weakness." *No, stop, what are you doing?* I couldn't stop. "Until I met you." I slammed my hands over my lips and closed my eyes. What just happened? This wasn't how it was supposed to go down in my mind, not at all.

I opened my eyes and found him staring at me, sucking in his lips, suppressing laughter. "So, I'm your weakness now."

I shook my head, my hands still clamped over my mouth.

He chuckled, pushed himself off his chair, and came closer. Stalking his prey was more like it.

My heart thundered in my chest. He took my hands gently off my mouth. I bit my lips so that I couldn't confirm his statement.

His eyebrows furrowed, making him look even sexier. "How the hell do you know where I live?"

I shrugged. I didn't trust the words that threatened to topple out of my mouth. It was as if they had a mind of their own.

Ethan stared at me. His eyes pulled me in. And then he grabbed my shirt and pulled me toward him and kissed me.

MY HEAD SPUN. His hands gripped hard around my butt. My legs twirled around his waist. He lifted me and set me on the desk, none too gently. I almost bit his tongue, warm and hot in my mouth.

I agree... if his father finds me, we'll be in so much shit.

His kiss broke. His lips traveled toward my neck.

Soft noises escaped my lips. *I need to stop, I NEED TO STOP NOW.* "Ethan, we should stop." I pushed him off me.

I opened my eyes and found his face inches from mine. That magnetic pull felt so much stronger. Why did I want him so badly? I shut my eyes tight, trying to dispel some of the pull he had on me. Nothing worked.

I looked at him again. His lips spread out in a gorgeous grin, and he laughed at me.

"It's not funny! This is serious."

"It's a dream, Alex. It's not real."

I squinted. "No."

"I can assure you. What happened when you fell asleep? What woke you up?" He stood in front of me, cupping my face. I couldn't think with him touching me like this.

"An explosion on the TV." It came out as if it was the hardest thing to say.

"You never woke up," he said in a reassuring tone. His lips found mine again. It was a hard, urgent, strong kiss that made my stomach flutter.

I didn't want to stop but I pushed him away again. "No," I shook my head. "I should leave." He bit his lower lip, looking like a model. I moaned uncomfortably. "It's too real."

"Trust me." He pushed himself against me. It felt so good. "It's a dream. You know exactly where I live, even though you've never been here before. Anything else that was weird tonight?"

My eyebrows knitted. I thought about it for a minute. The plant, the bike, the sleeping guard, finding his house... okay, it was too easy.

"It's a dream," he said again in a seductive tone, his lips inches from mine.

I grabbed him this time. So much for Resisting.

ETHAN

I DIDN'T KNOW how long this was going to last, but man, Alex was a damn good kisser. Her body was molded into perfection.

I heard Mira's voice in my head. "Dreams are never enough." I pulled Alex closer. This time it just had to be enough.

My lips wandered to her neck again. Her scent—something like hyacinth mixed with vanilla—was heady in my nose. I couldn't get enough of her. My hands filled with her soft curves and lean muscles... and it wasn't enough.

I pushed her hard against me. My pelvis started to move. Her breathing came fast, hard in my ears.

I wanted more.

A grunt tore from my mouth. I pulled her into me with my one hand while the other pulled at her shirt. Before we could think it through, her arms were above her head as I pulled it off and discarded it to the floor. She wore a tank top underneath.

My arms went up as she pulled off my shirt. She grunted as she saw my torso. I chuckled.

"It's not funny. I'm like Ariel in this dream world. No fucking filter." She kissed my chest. A tingle spread all over my body. My nipples hardened. Her lips set off a current rippling through my frame.

I tugged on her hair until my lips found hers. I kissed her hard. It didn't stop. I couldn't stop. I could kiss her forever.

It should've stopped, right before it began. Especially when she asked if I had protection. Any idiot would know that was the cutoff signal. Still I didn't stop.

Kissing and touching Alex was going to drive me insane. I realized it was nothing compared to being inside of her.

I didn't care about this omen hanging over us like a thundercloud. They would never break us apart. I was made for her, and she for me.

Being with Alex was the second thing I was truly good at. The first was being her Bender, her guardian. It was where I belonged. Right next to her, always were, since the day I took my first breath.

There had to be a way to make this work. And I would find it.

ALEX

"WAKE UP, SLEEPYHEAD." Ariel's voice barged in. I jumped out of bed. The memory of last night washed over me and... I stopped, looked around, me and blew out a gush of relief.

I stroked my hair. I was still wearing the same clothes I'd had on the night before. In the dream, Ethan ripped off my panties like someone possessed. Surreptitiously, I pulled the waistband of my pants back. My panties were in one piece.

Ethan was right; it was just a dream.

Ariel raised an eyebrow. "Ah," she teased. A knowing smile broke over her face.

"Ugh, that obvious?"

She walked over to me. "Baby it's written all over you." She touched my hair where it stuck up at an odd angle. "Ethan," she said. She tucked another strand behind my ear. "Ethan." She stroked the back of my hair. "Ethan."

"Stop that!" I slapped her hand away. "And don't you dare tell Mom." I felt like an idiot.

"My lips are sealed," she said. "I just need to know one thing. Did you know it was a dream?"

"Well," I wasn't going to tell her that the Ethan in my dream told me. That was my test. So I told her about the bike, the guard, my ability to find Ethan's place without knowing where he lived.

"I see. So you were the one who went to Ethan." Her tone make me feel like a slut.

"I had to talk to him," I said defensively. "He was being an idiot and I thought... Stop grinding me. I can't help it."

She laughed. "Go take a shower, a cold one."

How the hell was I ever going to look at Ethan now? I was glad we weren't on speaking terms.

After my cold shower, my phone beeped.

I picked it up, sure that it was Cynthia. I froze when I saw Ethan's number.

I opened it. A smiley face emoji. Nothing else.

I narrowed my eyes. Why the hell was he sending me smiley faces?

27

THE SMILEY FACE made me uncomfortable. He was supposed to be upset with me.

I went downstairs. Mom was cooking breakfast in the kitchen. I looked at the empty puffy pillow, huge puffy pillow, that was comfortably lying in it's steel stand.

I could feel Ariel's eyes on me and mine zeroed in on Ariel, who pretended reading the newspaper over my father's shoulder.

I felt so guilty because of that dream. Gosh it did feel so real.

"Good morning, sweetheart," my father said. He rose, kissed me on the cheek, and went over to the stove.

"Fibbs still asleep." I asked.

My mother nodded without looking at me while my dad kissed her on her temple. "You do know that we have staff who can prepare breakfast?" He pointed at the sunny side up eggs.

"I love making breakfast for my family," she said matter-of-factly.

Dad put up his hands in defense, grinning. "Just saying. No need to bite my head off." He grabbed a piece of bacon and popped it into his mouth as he walked away.

"He's friendly today," I said, grabbing a plate and approaching her like a supplicant. Mom hesitated, a pancake on the spatula. I was afraid to look at her. I just stared at the stupid pancake.

"Something is different about you this morning," she said.

Lie, Alex. Lie like you have never told a lie before. "Like what?" I said, louder than I intended.

"Why so defensive, Alex?"

"Because you're always insinuating things," I grumbled. I felt as if I could punch the wall. Why did it always seem like guilt was written on my face whenever I'd done something wrong?

"Did the dreams start?" she asked.

"No," I spat. "It's never going to start, either, because you and Jeff made sure of that." I slammed my plate on the counter and walked away.

"Alex." Mom followed me and grabbed my shoulder just as I got to the stairs.

"We did you two a favor. You had no idea how hard it is to Resist the test."

"That's not what I'm so upset about, Mom. We need to train. Ethan hardly knows how to bend earth. We need to let him bend earth with me, with this Alex." I tapped my chest. "And I guess it's never going to happen, because both of you are so freakin' scared we'll jump one another and make the same fucking mistakes you have."

I thought her eyes would explode. "Language!"

I stormed off to my room and slammed the door behind me. I would die if she ever found out that I was the one who went to Ethan. That I was the weak one. That I'd had sex for the first time, even though I didn't really. It was so complicated.

Nevertheless, I would die.

A faint knock came from my door. Ariel opened it, slipped in, and closed the door softly. "So, you're lying to her now."

"Are you insane? My mother can never know, Ariel. I'd never see him ever again." I lay flat on my bed, my ankles crossed, a magazine in my hands. "Don't look at me like that."

"Like what?"

"Like I'm... you know, someone who has a white liver."

Ariel threw her head back and laughed her great, snorting laugh.

"It's not funny," I muttered.

"Where did you hear that?"

"Girls talk in locker rooms too." I hid my embarrassment behind my magazine.

My bed shifted as she sat. "I'm sorry. I shouldn't laugh. We need to speak about that dream, Alex."

I groaned inwardly. At least it was Ariel and not Mom. "Can we just skip it, please? It's embarrassing enough without your help."

Ariel frowned. "Did Ethan even try to Resist?"

I stared at her. "Why did you make it sound as if he had a part in this dream?"

Ariel looked at me funny.

"Answer me," I insisted. "That was my dream and mine alone, right?"

"How is it that you didn't know this, Alex?"

"Didn't know what?" I was freaking out.

"Didn't your mom explain properly..." Her voice trailed off. "No, she didn't, because you threw a little bitch-fit when she woke you up, giving you another chance at life. You stormed off before she could finish explaining everything."

"Explaining what?" I said through gritted teeth.

A cold finger rushed up my spine. *Please don't say it was a two-way stream. I'll die.*

Ariel gave me an apologetic look. "That dream you had... Ethan had the exact same one."

"NO!" I howled at the ceiling. "So he was, like, there? Is that what you're trying to tell me?"

"Yes. He promised Meredith he would Resist you. She is going to wring his neck if she finds out."

"Then don't let her. She can never know."

"Oh? And what, the two of you are never going to let on?"

She had a point. It was written all over my face. Surely it must be written all over his too. For all I knew, Jeff had already figured it out.

"I doubt you comprehend the consequences. I've seen it with your mother and Jeff. I tried to talk her out of it, but she loved him so, so much. It's such a sad thing that the ones Wielders love the most are off-limits."

"It doesn't make any sense." I felt like crying. "We fit so well together."

There it was: that sympathetic smile I hated. "That's what Jeff said too."

"He did?"

"That day Ethan healed you. He had to hold you close. Jeff told him you would fit perfectly in his arms, like you were created just for him."

I didn't know if I loved hearing this... or hated it. "Why?"

"Why what? Jeff? Or the bigger issue."

My aunt really got me. Mom would've assumed and answered wrong. "The bigger issue."

"I don't know. Your mom used to think otherwise."

"Like?" I asked.

"That it was a curse cast by a strong witch whose Bender broke her heart, so she put this curse on him, but she didn't realize her tears fell into the potion she brewed." Ariel made it sound as if she'd personally witnessed this hypothetical witch.

Her voice was reverent. "And therefore her curse didn't just curse him, but every single Bender and Wielder ever to live from that day forward."

That made sense in a weird way.

"Don't." She must have spotted the hunger in my expression. "It's just a story your mother made up to justify what she and Jeff were doing. He saved her life, you know. I'm not talking about the way Ethan saved yours. He saved her life the day he chose Siobhan."

I frowned. "How can you say that? It broke her."

"It broke him too, Alex. If you haven't noticed, Jeff still loves her. It's like he never truly stopped. Like I said, it's a tragedy. Don't make the same mistakes. Put an end to this."

Tears pricked my eyes, but I nodded.

She left.

How the hell was I going to tell him that we couldn't be together? How could something feel so right and be so wrong? Worse, knowing he'd experienced the exact same dream, how was I ever going to look at Ethan now?

My phone beeped. I knew now why he'd sent me that stupid smiley face. We'd practically ripped each other apart last night in our weirdly connected dreams. I picked up my phone and saw a gazillion messages.

WTF, Ethan.

I opened the first one: *Hey, sleepyhead, you're up?*

I cringed. He was calling me names now.

Talk to me. Then: *Why aren't you talking to me?*

The rest were more or less the same. Ethan Hottie Sutcliff, insecure.

Please don't let this be awkward. Otherwise how are we going to train this afternoon?

My eyebrows rose. How the hell did he manage to get her to say yes to training while we were still in the danger period post-healing? The minute she saw us together, she'd know I'd lied to her. I was screwed.

I didn't know, okay? I typed.

My phone chirped after few seconds. *Didn't know what?*

That we were having the same dream. I sounded like an idiot.

Seconds spun out. *LOL. It's okay. Now you know.*

What are we doing, Ethan?

We'll figure it out, came his quick reply. *Just don't be all awkward and don't expect me to apologize like last time. I wasn't even sorry then, I just had to tell you that so you'd stop ignoring me.*

My eyes bugged out in shock. *Wait, you actually liked Ducky?*

His next text was fast. *Yes, I like spending time with you. Why was it so hard to imagine, Alex? Because you didn't think she was beautiful?*

That's not what I said. My thumbs punched the touchscreen hard. But I wanted to scream, "Yes! She was supposed to protect me from you!"

I waited for a reply, fiddling with the slick pages of my magazine. Finally he said, *So I'm really your weakness.*

I screamed silently. *Just forget about that dream.*

Are you insane? he wrote. *That was like the best dream ever. Heck no.*

I started to laugh. *Fine, don't. But stop grinding me about it. You sound like my mom.*

My phone beeped cheerily. *Meredith knows?*

No, I shot back quickly so he wouldn't panic. Then I wrote a longer reply: *But it's only a matter of time. Jeff must not have told you that much about my mother. You can't lie to her. You can't hide anything from her. It's like she was born with a third eye, the all-seeing eye. So yes, she will discover this and she will probably wield another spell where you won't be able to visit my dreams.*

Beep. *I'm not the one visiting your dreams, Alex. The way I remember it, you climbed through my window.* He was teasing me again.

Do you want me to put the phone down? I demanded. *Promise me training won't be awkward.*

As I waited for his message, my mind went to Fibbs again. I missed her. Mother told me that Ethan saw through her eyes, how did he even manage to do that.

I miss her purr, I miss pulling my fingers through her thick coat.

Finally his reply came. *As long as you promise not to show up with a sheepish grin on your face.*

No problem, I promised.

Cool, he wrote. *Me too.*

Like you promised my mother you'd resist me? I goaded him.

Silence. Then: *How do you know about that?*

Ariel.

Ariel knows?

A sly smile appeared on my face. *Ariel is the one everyone struggles to fool. It's like she just sees right through you. She knows everything, Ethan. And I mean everything.*

ETHAN

A STUPID SMILE was plastered on my face as I looked at the phone in my hand.

I couldn't get her out of my head. I wondered if last night had been as amazing for her as it was for me.

The dreams would never be enough. I kept hearing Mira saying it over and over in my head. It had to be enough. We had to make it enough. I could never lose her the way Mira lost Marcus.

Dad knocked on my door.

I tried to wipe the grin off my face. "It's open."

Dad's face popped in. "I just got off the phone with Meredith. She thinks it's fine idea to train this afternoon." He sighed. "I just hope..."

"Hope what?" I was fed up with everything they kept doing to keep Alex and me apart.

"That seeing her doesn't kick-start the dreams."

"The dreams? Dad, we have bigger things to worry about, like how to keep Alex safe. I need to train with her, bend properly. Otherwise, the next time I promise we won't be so lucky."

Embarrassment lined his face. "Er, you're right, son. Sorry. I shouldn't listen to Mer." He closed my door. His footsteps pounded his retreat on the hardwood hallway floor.

He was so going to kill me when the truth came out.

We could never let them see how we really felt about each other. But at least it got me what I wanted. Real time with Alex.

———

IT WAS ALMOST THREE. I'd told Alex to erase my texts. There could be no trace that we were speaking consistently to each other. If I could, I would keep it a secret till the day I died.

I thought I would feel guilty for cheating on Soph. Okay, dreaming about another girl wasn't really cheating, even if you were ripping all her clothes off just to get your hands on her perfectly sculpted body and... I grunted. I couldn't get Alex's naked body out of my head.

I took another cold shower, hoping Dad wouldn't ask why I took so many showers. Maybe he'd assume that it was a teenager thing.

About Soph, though... nope, not a twinge of guilt. In fact, quite the opposite. I felt guilty thinking about Soph, like I was cheating on Alex. So weird.

Around four, we drove to the clearing in the woods where we'd been training before Alex got hurt. I hadn't trained with her for more than a month. I hoped somehow we could train through the glamour. Hopefully Ducky, as Alex called her, had lost some of her power and Alex would wield her earth more easily.

We arrived first and waited for ages on the boulder. I scraped lichen off the rough gray surface and aimlessly picked the resulting bits out of the half-moons of my close-clipped fingernails.

"That anxious to see her, Ethan?" Dad asked.

Shit, fuck, play it cool. "I haven't trained for more than a month with her, Dad. So yes, I would like to finally learn how to bend earth."

"Not what I meant." He shook his head. "Damn frustrated teenagers."

Play it cool, Ethan. Just play it cool. "Will Alex be able to wield her abilities better now with the glamour?"

"Glamour?" he asked as if he had no idea. "Oh, you mean the glasses."

I nodded.

"Didn't I tell you? You're not going to train with that Alex anymore. From now on, it'll be the real one."

I froze and swallowed hard. "What?"

His eyes trained on me. "Oh yes, Meredith thinks it's time you start bending earth. I agree."

My voice was strangled. "Have you *seen* Alex?"

My father squinted, and then he got it. He chuckled. "I told you a million times, Ethan: earth Wielders are beautiful."

"Beautiful is an understatement," I grumbled.

"Are you scared of the Resistance?"

"A little," I said with a sigh. "But I have to face Alex eventually right?"

"If you feel you're not ready, then—"

"Are you kidding me? Heck no. Let's try."

"Okay." He thumped me hard on the back.

Just then we heard an engine. I glanced over my shoulder to see Louis's SUV coming to a halt underneath the trees. Three guards climbed out, followed by Meredith. Then the back door opened.

Alex was wearing a skintight pair of black running pants with a pair of expensive athletic shoes and a black hoodie that clung to her body perfectly.

I gave Dad a helpless shrug. Did she want to make this harder than it was? He raised his eyebrow.

"Good afternoon, Ethan," Meredith greeted me. She came over and settled close to Dad on the boulder.

"Hey," Alex said with a wave.

"Hey," I replied. *Don't smile, just don't smile.* "I'm doing this with *Alex.*" That didn't come out right.

Brow furrowed, she looked at my dad. "Yes, your father didn't tell you?"

"It slipped my mind," he said. I smiled. *Play it cool, Ethan.*

"Fine, maybe now we can get somewhere." I aimed for sounding like the pissed-off Ethan Meredith wanted me to be.

"You sure you're ready for this?"

"Been waiting for a while now," I said without breaking a sweat.

"Okay, Golden Boy," Alex said.

I couldn't help but to smile.

She took the spot opposite me, the trees arching over us, the sky blue and worry-free, unlike my nerves. This time, though, we didn't touch each other's arms. She stood several feet away from me.

"Alex, take it easy," her mother said. Something told me that this training session was going to be one I would never forget.

She took off her hoodie. Long, raven curls fell from underneath. She opened her palms. A slight rumble came from deep below the earth. "Let's see if you remember how to do this," Alex said with a taunting smile. She flicked her hands.

Roots, perfectly controlled, not too big and not too small, sprouted from the earth. They twirled around her. She was breathtakingly beautiful.

"Ethan, whenever you're ready." She brought me out of it.

I remembered that I actually had to bend. I opened my palms and concentrated on the roots. I felt my connection with earth. It was like a drug. One I couldn't get enough of. It rippled through my entire being, filled me up.

The roots wove in on one another, twirling and curling at my will. I wielded them into whatever I wanted them to do.

My father cheered behind me. I was doing it like I'd done it every day of my life. Maybe bending was like riding a bike—something your body never forgot how to do.

Alex added more. Vibrant yellow and pink flowers. Vines. Leaf-covered branches. Graceful, pliant reeds. Everything was coming my way. I didn't have a picture in my head yet of where I wanted it to go; nevertheless, whatever it became, it would be a lot of fun to create.

It started to look more or less like a web, which gave me an idea. Two big trees with nice straight trunks grew a few feet apart, right behind Alex. A good foundation for my idea. I bent the tips of a few roots toward each of them. They twirled around the trunks and slowly pulled the web into the space between the two sturdy trunks.

More roots twirled around the two trees. Alex looked

around to see what it was I was busy conjuring with my bending technique. It was a web or a slingshot. It looked strong.

The roots grew through each other, entwining to form a thick platform. I bit my lip, concentrating, forcing a few roots around others that weren't as strong in some places. The weak spots were connected with me somehow; I felt all of them.

My hands bent the earth to fill all those spots, strengthening the base of the slingshot. With every flick of my wrist, the roots moved where I wanted them.

I flourished my wrist again—and no root came. I flicked harder. There were no more roots. I pouted at Alex. "You're breaking the creation!"

Dad and Meredith laughed.

Alex stared at my creation with her beautiful mouth agape. She'd broken concentration. She blushed. "Sorry," she said. "How did you do that?"

"It's what I do. Bending is my game and Ethan is my name."

"Is that supposed to be some sort of an introduction?"

We both laughed.

Dad and Meredith slid down off the boulder and approached us. "What is it?" Meredith sounded excited.

"Don't diss it. I had to make something from scratch," I joked.

Meredith smiled. She actually smiled at me.

Dad circled the giant slingshot, his face impressed as he appraised it.

I was proud of my masterpiece.

"This is really strong, Meredith." He smiled and leaned against it. Then he went to the far side and pulled with all his might.

I was nervous. There were still so many weak spots. The base stretched as he pulled it, but it wasn't breaking.

"I'm impressed, son."

"Will it be able to handle, let's say, fire?"

Alex soured at her mother's words. She blew out some air and shook her head. As if she was telling me something important. I would never be enough in her mother's eyes. Never strong enough to protect her daughter, never good enough to bend her earth, never smart enough, never enough.

I smiled at Meredith. "There is only one way to find out."

28

ETHAN

WHEN THE WORDS left my mouth, the challenge weighed heavier than I thought. I'd seen Dad bending fire before—and that was just from his Zippo lighter. We'd gotten a tiny dose of it just a month ago at the sugar mill.

Meredith's hands were aflame. First the tips of her fingers, then her palms, her wrists, and slowly running up both her arms until it consumed her entire freakin' body. Her eyes glowed red.

I stared at her in horror.

"What are you waiting for, Jeff? Want to teach your son never to underestimate a fire team?"

Dad chuckled and flicked his palm. Flames burned in Dad's palms. Brighter, hotter than I was used to seeing from him.

The element began to take over. It was Dad's drug too. He looked at me and Alex. "If I were you two, I'd make my slingshot stronger."

Alex smiled at her mom. "You up for this?"

"You bet," she said.

Vines, moss, and small plants bearing flowers shot from the ground. My hands already guiding them to fill the weak spots.

For the next half hour, Dad and Meredith hurled fireballs and gouts of flame at our creation. They tried with everything they had to get our slingshot to break.

Alex fed me earth. I never imagined I would feel this power in between my palms again. I had never felt so alive.

I fortified the slingshot as I swung from root to root, sliding down treetops, using all my power to escape Meredith and Dad's wrath.

I didn't know the old man still had it in him. I had to admit, this was a different side of Jeff Sutcliff. He was a fire god.

He never forgot the power of a Wielder. Okay, so he'd had a loophole all these years with his Zippo, but it wasn't the same. He wielded with impeccable force.

Then two hot geysers poured from his hands. They looked like he'd sprouted two new orange-and-yellow arms. They shook the slingshot.

In response, earth roared from Alex. It sprouted everywhere. The ground shook beneath our feet. At first I bent it, but it got to be too much. It was sort of blocking all my attempts to reach her.

What was this?

"Jeff, stop!" Meredith yelled. I found an opening through one of the branches and swung down a wildly flinging tree root to the ground.

Dad's fire died down. Meredith's too. But Alex earth was still breaking through the ground. Her eyes were white. The beautiful midnight blue was gone.

"Ethan, do something!" Meredith yelled.

I glared at her. Oh, so now I was good enough? It felt like

Meredith had two different personalities. The one she desperately tried to hide only came out when Dad was nearby.

I tried to get closer to Alex.

She couldn't stop. *How does a Bender control this?* Earth curled around her, suffocating her. She was drowning in her own element.

"Ethan!" Meredith screamed. Dad pushed her out of the roots' path to safety.

I ran on a thick branch and dove into the cocoon that trapped Alex.

I gasped at what I saw.

Brilliant green light glowed all around her. Bright fairy lights floated everywhere, giving off just enough light to see the magnificent white-and-pink flowers growing in the hollow. The roots below me looked like giant, diamond-studded beanstalks.

I ducked as a root came out of nowhere. It brought me out of my admiration and I remember what was actually going on. I slid down the vines that grew against the edges of her cocoon. How the hell would the Association cover this unnatural cave?

Think, Ethan. You need to control Alex's ability. In every darkness, light was the answer. I needed sunlight.

I pushed with my left hand. The opening expanded marginally. I concentrated harder. I pushed all my energy forward, trying to break through the clutches of earth that wanted to trap Alex and feed off her.

It felt as if I was about to explode with all the strength inside me. My body weakened. And then a force pushed through. It pulled me into the light and I broke through the surface into the bright light. I fell to the ground, hard. I hit my head on something solid and passed out.

ALEX

WE WERE WINNING. Ethan was part monkey. He had moves—not just the amazingly delicious ones from last night, either. I marveled as he swung and jumped from one branch to another, understanding the way I wielded to a T.

It was like he was in my head and knew where the next source of nature would show up. I relished working with him as a team. Nothing—not even last night—had ever felt so right.

Mom and Jeff tried to destroy our slingshot. Ethan protected it with all his might. And power poured through every fiber of my being.

Jeff shot one fireball after another, straight into the core of the slingshot. It all sent them right back. Mom caught them with her wielding techniques and fed Jeff new, stronger fireballs.

I had to wield more. Earth poured out of me. I was pushing myself like never before.

Two arms of flame blazed from Jeff. Something inside me knew that I needed more power. That those flaming arms he was bending would destroy Ethan's masterpiece.

Young branches shot from the earth. In the distance I heard a click of a button. A switch that wasn't supposed to get flipped.

Too much earth roiled everywhere. It sprang out the ground with incredible strength and power. It tightened around my legs, running up like snakes. The ground shook and heaved. I couldn't scream. I had no voice.

I started to panic. The more I struggled, the tighter the roots squeezed.

Mom screamed at Jeff to stop, but she sounded far away. She yelled at Ethan to do something.

I couldn't breathe. Everything started to go dark.

But the weird thing was, I felt Ethan close. I hoped that he would be smart enough to get us both out of here.

The earth was still feeding off me. I thought we had an agreement, but I remembered the click. It was the sound of me stepping over the line. Did I break the accord with my element?

Wielding should have been a natural thing.

I'd pushed it today for the wrong reasons. Mother earth was teaching me a lesson: I wasn't in control. I would never fully be in control.

My windpipe tightened.

Black blotches danced in my sight. My head felt woozy, like I was flying. Lightheaded. For the first time, I understood that word. How it felt when my brain didn't get oxygen.

The earth was strangling me for breaking the agreement we had. One I didn't remember signing.

Then I felt it.

Light. Light was always the answer. An uncontrollable force shook my core, threatening to break my body into a million pieces.

WHEN AWARENESS CAME BACK, I felt oddly out of place. My throat was sore; I reached up and felt bandages. I looked around. I was in a gleaming metal box, surrounded by beeping and blinking equipment. Mom was seated beside the stretcher on which I lay.

"Sweetheart?"

"How long was..." I coughed, unable to talk.

"Don't speak. You took a nasty fall."

"Ma'am, we need to take her to the emergency room to make sure she's fine."

Mom patted my arm. "Tell Ethan she's okay."

Sirens wailed overhead. A door closed. Mom hunched over me, smiling.

On my other side, a paramedic—a youthful, energetic dude

with close-cropped brown hair—did his thing. He studied the machines. "It looks like she's out of danger, but she needs clearance from a doctor."

Mom nodded and stroked my hair back to kiss my forehead.

How were we going to explain this to the doctors? Who was I? I looked like me and not Ducky. They knew Ducky.

"What happened, exactly?" the paramedic asked Mom, who just shook her head. She started to cry. "Can we not speak about this now?"

It was an act for the paramedics. Although I knew she was shaken up, she was much stronger than this woman she was playing.

The paramedic bought it. I closed my eyes. I listening to the earsplitting siren as we sped toward the hospital.

Was Ethan okay? The last thing I remembered was light seeping through.

Light was always the answer to beat darkness.

29

THEY ADMITTED ME THAT NIGHT. Mom claimed I was her niece from my father's side. Dad met us at the hospital and pretended that he was trying to get a hold of my mother. He explained to the doctor that she was on a cruise in the Bahamas.

Ethan couldn't come to visit, because, well, how the heck were they going to explain that? He practically lived at the hospital the last time I was here.

I just wanted to sleep.

I WOKE up in my own bedroom. It was dark. My throat was still sore. I had no idea how my parents got me back home. They probably called one of the Association doctors and sorted everything out.

I rolled over. A faint tapping noise on my window broke the quiet.

What the hell?

I pushed myself up from the bed and went to my window.

Ethan lurked behind the bushes. My father would kill him if he found him here.

"Wield the earth," he whispered loudly. A smile broke on my face. I shook my head. But stupidly, I wielded the earth anyway. He jumped on the tree that grew up toward my window.

I had to admit, it was quite sexy watching him dangle on the giant plant.

I flinched. I knew what this was. It wasn't real. I knew it because of that ficus. After that night that I snuck away, Dad remove all the plants close to my room, including the ficus.

I was still in the hospital. Based on the way Ethan looked at me—as if I were his favorite food—told me that he knew what this was too.

He jumped swiftly through my window. His feet hardly touched the ground before he smashed into me. Our lips met vigorously.

I didn't care about Aunt Ariel's warnings anymore. I wanted him so fiercely. My legs twirled around his waist as he lifted me up and toppled with me to my bed.

My nostrils filled with his signature smell, something musky and earthy spiked with peppermint. His presence clouded my mind. Giddy, I laughed into the hollow of his collarbone.

"How are you feeling?" He looked down at me.

"Right now?" I took off my neck brace and threw it off my bed. "Not a single ounce of pain." I pulled his head toward me and we kissed again.

I wasn't going to stop. I knew he wasn't either. We didn't have the strength to stay away from one another. If dreams were all we had, I wanted them.

I WOKE the next morning with the brace around my neck. Light streamed into the too-white room.

"Alex?" Mom's voice was merely a whisper. "How are you feeling?"

"Like I've been squeezed by million branches," I croaked.

"Not funny," she scolded.

I sighed, my thoughts lingering on the dream. When I was with him, I didn't want to leave. I didn't want to be the strong one. I wanted him.

But in the morning, I felt like an idiot. I had failed once again. This would be the end of both of us if we didn't stop.

"How is Ethan?" I asked, focusing at last on her face.

"He's fine." She smiled. "For a minute, I thought he wouldn't be able to get to you, but I must admit, he came through."

"Mom, you can just say it. My Bender is just as much of a kickass god as yours."

She laughed softly. "That's what worries me."

"Stop. We'll be fine."

"You sure? He sneaked in last night or early this morning and brought you that." She pointed.

I couldn't turn my head, so she leaned over me and grabbed something. It was the fluffiest teddy bear I'd ever seen. I squinted at its too-long ears. "Is that a bear or a rabbit?"

Mom laughed again. "Perhaps it's a rabbit that wants to be a bear."

We both laughed. Well, I started, but pain stabbed through my neck. I winced. Mom tried to help and make me feel comfortable.

"He's just worried. Without me, he can't bend shit," I lied.

Mom scowled. "Language."

Fear overwhelmed me. "What if Ethan doesn't get to me in time... next time? What then, Mom?"

She sighed. "You shouldn't push yourself like that, but you haven't trained with all your power before, honey. When you're better, I suggest hard training with Ethan, so you can learn how to control what you wield, how much to wield."

It sounded like a great plan, and the only one we had. But why did I have this horrible feeling that spending time with Ethan would be the nail in my coffin?

ETHAN

NOT SEEING Alex at school was hard. Sophie's constant yapping in my ear about how Alex should face everything again, didn't make any of this any easier either. I knew she didn't mean it in a harsh way, as she put voice to her concerns the other day. It had nothing to do with Alex this time. Ever since I got the taste of my element, and we spoken a few times after my training with Alex, she knew that I was becoming my old self again. The Ethan all of them fell in love with. The Ethan from the beginning, the leader, the one that wow everyone with his cool bend. She missed that Ethan, and she was assuming that was why I was so grumpy lately. Not seeing Alex at school did have its toll on me.

I wondered if her glasses didn't have anything to do with it. Why wasn't her mother sending her to school. Was the glamour broken? Did she not want to conjure another? All of them made sense, but it also meant that I would never see Ducky in school ever again, and I know why she didn't send the real Alex either. The Necrocretors. Bodies of girls still showed up. They were unrecognizable, but I know they were link to Alex. My father and Meredith spoke in secret about it. Or he thinks it was in secret. He still has no idea that I heard them the other night, or just him speaking to her. There was still something and not just from him, but from her too.

This Bender, Wielder relationship thing was just so wrong. We should be able to be with one another, we were made for each other.

Joe connect hard with my body as the ball was still firmly gripped inside my hand.

Again!

The wistle blow and I felt Coach frustration behind his blow. "Ethan, what is wrong with you lately," he yelled close by as Joe give me a hand.

He grab frame on my helmet and pulled me slightly to and fro. "You need to get your head into the game. Where are you son."

"Sorry, coach." I yelled back. "It won't happen again." But for some reason I knew that it was a lie. Not seeing Alex was making me crazy.

When the wistle blows, I was happy to just have this training session over. We all started gunning for the lockers when coach yelled. "Where are you think you going? Practice until Ethan get the plays right. In two weeks is the homecoming game."

Groans and moans come from every single one of the guys. I knew they were cussing me secretely in their heads, heck some of them threw invisable daggers at me with their looks.

I never thought that I would say this, but I hate being the quarter back of Sky View High.

WE FINISHED AROUND SEVEN. There wasn't even time to text Alex to tell her that I wasn't going to make this afternoon's training. She was going to be so fucking upset with me.

Ryan dropped me off at home. Of all the days I told dad that he could take my Jeep for a check up.

"Sorry about this afternoon," I felt bad.

"Hey," Ryan said. "It's okay. I know you have a lot on your mind."

The one side of my mouth curved slightly. If only he knew how much.

I watched him drove off until I walked into the house.

"Ethan," dad's voice came from the lounge.

"I know, coach forced a late practice. I'm sorry, I tried to let you know." Dad was sitting on the couch. He looked at me over his shoulder.

"My phone battery died. I'm sorry." I did sound sincere.

"You okay?"

I sighed. "No. I'm not." I came to sit on the couch and just pull my hands through my hair.

"Did the dreams start."

"No," I said way to hastily and looked away immediately. "I just wish I could train more with Alex. It's like I'm never going to get there. Maybe I should just give up football—"

"Stop! You are being way too hard on yourself. Alex will understand. Meredith will too, eventually. We have to blend in. It might be something that Meredith forgot a long time about, but she will understand. Don't give up football Ethan. You are good at it. You and Alex will get there. Go take a shower. I'll phone Meredith."

I got upstairs, plugged my phone into the charger and waited till it was on one percent. I switched on my phone and watched it come back to live. Messages seeped through. All of them were from Sophie. Not one belonged to Alex.

I didn't even read Sophie's and texted Alex immediately.

I'm so sorry I was stuck in late football training. Coach didn't want us to text. I'll make it up. Sorry.

I waited a few minutes. She didn't reply and felt angry again for not being able to spend real time with her. The dreams were great, don't get me wrong, but not able to see her for real, was taking it's toll on me.

ALEX

I STARED at his stupid text. He didn't show today and now I know why. Football season.

Something tells me that I was going to take a back seat now. Our training was going to take strain. Mom wasn't very happy until Jeff phoned and told her what happened. Ethan was stuck with extra football training.

I didn't know what to text him back. I didn't want to text him anything but a part of me didn't want him to know that I was upset either. It felt so stupid for me to feel this angry.

It's fine. I understand. I typed back and pressed the sent button.

I text Cynthia back. Mom still doesn't know that I started speaking to her. She really wanted to know why I wasn't at school yet.

One can only play the hurting ego part for so long.

So I texted her back that my mother didn't want me to go back yet.

It wasn't that. Mom conjured the glamour again. She was afraid this time, not me.

She didn't want me to wear the glamour, or she wasn't ready for me to become Ducky again.

I would give anything to just go. To see Ethan in real life, apart from our training.

I wondered what school life would be like. Would he sit with me and Cynthia, or would he still be around Sophie.

Their relationship bothered me. She was still his girlfriend. And what was I? A test he failed.

"Have you find out what is wrong with Ethan?" She asked.

"Not many kids knew that Coach was Cynthia's dad and don't ask me how, but he asked her to find out if she could discover what was wrong with Ethan. It was news to me, and lately I didn't want to ask him negative things. I just want to be with him, and our dreams was the only time we get to truly be with one another.

"Nope, why, he still acting weird."

"My dad just came home literally minutes ago. He said Ethan's head is not in the game."

I frown. I closed Cynthia's messages and open Ethan's. "What is going on with you lately?"

He didn't answer my previous text and don't know why he would answer this one.

Then my phone buzz. "Nothing, why?"

What do I say now, that Cynthia is coach daughter and he asked her to find out. "Roomers say that your head is not in the game." I texted back.

He didn't text me back.

I closed his text and open Cynthia's. "I don't know. I haven't seen him in a while." Which was a lie.

"You still train with him right."

"Sometimes," I lied again. "It's football season remember."

"Yeah, dad is calling. SUL"

I smiled. See you Later.

My phone buzz and Ethan's name flashed on the screen.

"Hey," I picked up and wish I didn't sound so somber as I felt.

"Hi," he said back. He didn't sound so good himself. "It was my fault that the training took so long. I'm so sorry."

"Why do you say it's your fault."

"Because the roomers are true. My head is not in the game. I tried to tell my father that I should quit and just focus on training with you, but he said blending in was just as important then bending. And football is blending."

I laughed. Bending and blending. "Sorry to hear that. But we'll get there, eventually."

"Please don't make me feel crappier then I already do. Tomorrow is out too. Another late training session for homecoming.".."

"Go Falcons." I sounded not impressed.

"Sorry, I should've been there this afternoon."

"It's okay. I just wish I could go back to school but my mother still doesn't want to budge."

"Yeah, I get the feeling. I would feel much more at ease if you were here."

My lips curved up unvoluntary. So he does worry about me. "Me too."

"What is that supposed to mean?"

"Alex," mom called.

"I got to go. I'll speak to you later."

"Alex?" he still asked but I cut him off.

I felt better after his small revelation of me not being at school makes him feel worried.

I least he cared about me. I hope.

ETHAN

THE NEXTFEW DAY, Alex and I trained hard every single second we could. It was earth wielding in the first degree, like nobody had wielded earth in the history of earth Wielders.

I learned more training with Alex in the past two weeks than I learned about bending my entire life.

She was a natural. Her power was solid.

There were times when our eyes would meet, times when I thought I saw the girl who spent every night with me in my dreams. But she hid that part masterfully, not just from me, but from Jeff and Meredith too. Sometimes I wondered if Alex really did dream with me, or if it was just my hormones.

Sophie didn't like the new me that much. She hated that I was so short with her, and that we almost never kiss anymore.

I felt bad at times that I couldn't hid better, the way Alex did. But I really loved Alex. I didn't want to be with Sophie anymore.

She was annoying me like hell and the more time I spend with Alex, the more I knew Soph and I had seriously not a lot in common accept being Wielders.

We fought tonight over text. She wanted to know why I was so out of it. Why my mind was so occupied. What was going on.

So I told her, half the truth. I worried about Alex. She shoud've been at school already.

"But you practice with her every day, Ethan."

"It's a different type of worry," I typed back.

"Different as in how? I don't understand."

"I'm not going to fight with you over this. She is my Wielder, I'm her bender. You have to deal with that Soph."

"Oh, like you have dealt wih Sam. Goodnight Ethan."

I didn't text back. I wasn't in the mood. I just wanted to go to bed.

Every single night was the same, I drifted off and then something startled me awake: Sophie on the phone, Dad barging into the room, or a cat in heat yowling on the roof, a trash can crashing over.

I usually made my way to Alex's house. There were only a few times that I woke up and found her in my room. The other nights, I couldn't wait to get to her.

She became my everything.

It was intense, yet felt free. Easy and hard at the same time. It was enough but at the same time, I wanted more. More of Alex.

I didn't want to even imagine what Meredith and my Dad went through. Mira and Markus too. I couldn't imagine my life without Alex. She was now a part of me.

We were once again in her room. She dozed with her head on my bare chest.

The past few weeks we'd learned so much from one another. Shared our pasts. I recounted exactly what it had felt like when I lost my element at fourteen. How I'd had to find another way to still do what I loved, to feel unbreakable and powerful without the one thing that made me feel that way.

She'd shared how her parents had kept her safe all these years.

"You what?" I'd asked her incredulously.

"I lived in Ariel's locket."

"Her locket, like the one around her neck?"

She'd nodded. "She kept us safe all those years, she and Fibbs."

I felt bad the minute she said Fibbs name. Not ones have I asked her how their wisp was doing? She got hurt with Alex that night. I haven't seen her since. "How is Fibbs."

She had rolled onto her stomach and rested her arms on my chest.

"Fibbs—" she looked around— when she looked back her eyes were filled with tears.

"No, your mother said that she was just sleeping."

"She is still, but Clive said if she's not going to wake up soon, she's going to disappear and we will never see her again."

I stroke her face. "I'm so sorry." I pulled her closer to me and just held her tight. "If you want to know something cool. When your mother gave me that potion to go and find you, I saw through Fibbs eyes. I never felt that powerful or that fast my entie life, Alex. Fibbs will wake up. She is strong."

She smiled. "My mom told me."

I NODDED. "I didn't even know we could do that."

"I did, but my mom doesn't want to teach me the spell. Or want me to have used it on our wisp. Your lucky."

"She really love you, Alex. All of us do."

I kissed her again. I hated how the conversation about Fibbs made her feel. I wanted to hear her laughter again.

I'd grabbed her and pushed myself atop her again, ducking underneath the covers to seek the soft flesh of her hips with my mouth.

Finally she'd laughed softly, music in my ears.

We somehow spoke more about wisps, what they truly are to witches. Then I remember something. "I dreamed about one." I'd frowned as it hit me. The dream. I's witnessed the day Ariel had freed Alex and her family. It was Ariel who dragged the castle out of her locket. Fibbs was the wisp that had chased me.

"What is it?"

I'd smiled. "I don't know how to explain it, but I think I dreamed about the night your aunt freed you."

Her eyebrows raised. "You did? That is so freaky, yet so fucking cool." She pulled me on top of her. It was how our dream conversations went: a little getting know one another sandwiched between a lot of grabbing and kissing.

Feeling the touch of her skin on mine, how could this be a dream? It felt so real.

THE DREAMS always went by too fast. I found myself staring at her. Our dream was about to end. It always does with the ray of first sunlight. Alex was stunning, even when she was sleeping. She looked like an angel, strands of raven hair falling across her smooth face. I picked up her hand and kissed her knuckles.

This was the part where I couldn't get enough of her. Her hyacinth-vanilla scent, her warmth, the softness of her skin.

I buried her hand inside mine and found her midnight blue eyes staring at me. "Did I wake you?" I chuckle; we weren't technically awake.

"Nope." She propped herself up on her arm, covering her nakedness with the sheet.

I rolled over on my side. Something on her face wasn't right. "What is it?"

Her smile vanished. Her expression became sad.

"Don't say it's nothing, Alex. What is bothering you? If you say the dreams, I'm going to pull you over my lap and I'm going to spank you."

She squinted. "You'll do *what*?"

I laughed, lowered my head, kissed her lips, and pulled back. Our eyes lingered on one another. "What's bothering you, Ducky?"

She smiled. "I'm scared you are going to spank me."

"You really don't like spending time with me like this."

"You know that isn't the truth. But we can't deny what we are going to do to one another eventually."

"We'll be fine, Alex."

"Will we?" She sat up in bed, yanking the sheet to cover herself, animated with anxious energy.

I sighed. "We're being careful. Nobody suspects a thing. You are way too good at that."

She got up and took the sheet with her. She sat at the edge of her bed. The long slope of her naked back faced me. I ran a finger along her spine. I pushed myself closer to her and brushed my lips over her shoulders.

"And what about Sophie, Ethan?"

Hearing that name here in this space jarred me unpleasantly. "What about Sophie?" I felt pissed off all of a sudden. She was the last one I wanted to talk about when I was with Alex.

"Are you still seeing her?"

I took a deep breath and looked away. "She's my cover."

Her lips spread in a thin smile. "And what do you tell her when she asks about the dreams? You lie to her too?" She got up and wrapped the blanket around her body.

"Are you seriously fighting with me because of Sophie? I don't lie to her, Alex, and I'm not lying to you. You want me to break up with Sophie now? Is that it?"

"You are unbelievable," she hissed. "I'm not... ugh."

I felt like a jerk. "I didn't mean it like that, okay?" I went over to her. "We both know there's no filter in these dreams. Sometimes words come out differently than how we mean them."

She glared at me.

"Just talk to me." I balled my fists. "Tell me what you want me to do."

"That's precisely it, Ethan. Nothing. Because we can't do anything in the real world. I want more and I can't have more." She was yelling now. "I can't do this anymore with you."

Dread struck me hard in the chest. "Wait, what?"

"I'm waking up."

Before I could retort that she could never ever even think about breaking up with me, I was standing alone in her room. She was back in reality.

When I woke up myself, the first thing I picked up was my phone. She could not break up with me.

ALEX

I TOUCHED my phone screen and found Cynthia's name quickly. I wanted to text her about what a jerk Ethan has been. How he was cheating on Sophie. I stopped.

I couldn't share it with her. She has no idea about the dreams, about Ethan, about what I truly looked like.

Such a great friend I turned out to be.

I was sure that she would find it in her heart to forgive me when I do come clean. I just had no idea how to explain it to her.

I closed the texts we had been secretely sending one another over the passed week. She wanted to come over so badly. I wanted her to come over too, it was just my mother had no idea that we spoke.

My heart was breaking. Not just because of lying to my best friend, but about Ethan.

I knew it was stupid fighting with him about Sophie, but I couldn't stop myself. We couldn't do this anymore.

Ariel's words from yesterday haunted me.

Mom still refused to let me go back to school. So, Ariel had found me at pool.

"Hey, you," Ariel said, flipping her towel out on the deck chair. She was wearing one of those swimsuits that looked like a bikini in the back but was a one-piece in the front. She plopped down with her shades resting on her head. "So." She glanced back to the house to see if anyone was within earshot. "How are the dreams?"

I told her how Ethan had dreamed about the day she'd freed us.

"He what?" she asked. I repeated it. But she said nothing, just sat there looking perplexed. No, thunderstruck.

"What is it?" I had to know.

"There was really someone there," she finally breathed. "Fibbs and I thought there was. She even chased someone and came back and told me it was a shimmer."

"What's a shimmer?"

"Someone like Ethan. Huh. I thought they didn't exist."

I shifted in my stiff deck hair. "So, that really happened. He was there."

"Sort of," she said. "Wait, you guys speak a lot in your dreams? It's not just..."

"No, heck." My tone was disgusted. I frowned. "One thing I don't get: how the hell doesn't a Wielder know that they are dreaming?"

Her face darkened. "It's going to get worse, Alex. You need to stop it now, while you can."

"Why do I have to stop? It's just dreams. I'm technically still a virgin." I said that last part softly.

She took a huge breath. "I wish it would just stay at dreams, Alex, but they never do. That's when it becomes a huge fucking problem."

"What is that supposed to mean?"

"Your mother and Jeff did the dream thing for a long time. Almost a year. It gets harder. Later they tried to take it to the next level and not get affected."

"Affected?"

She slipped off her flip-flops. "Meredith and Jeff was dead sure that somehow they were the ones who would find a way to be with one another and not lose it."

I knew where she was taking this suddenly. I didn't want to listen.

"She was just as blind as you are now, Alex," Ariel said sternly. I got up to leave but she pulled me by the hand because she didn't want to yell after me and let mom hear.

I jerked my arm away from her. "We aren't Mom and Jeff. We can control this."

"What if you're wrong, Alex? What then? You going to run away, become Necrocretors? Or wait, you will realize why it's against the law, only when Ethan is dead?"

I froze. "What did you say?"

Her face turned soft. Compassion filled her eyes. She looked sad. "Sit. I'm not being the sour grape here, baby. I worry about the two of you. It's the truth. Why do you think your mother and Jeff ended?"

She started telling me a different story after I relented. The one that nobody wanted to tell me.

What happened to Wielders and Benders who broke the rules, when the dreams weren't enough? I knew that most of them devolved into the Necrocrecy race, but none of them ended with a happily ever after.

For some reason, I would morph into Ethan's succubus. I would drain all his energy, his strength, even his youth.

"Benders who go rogue with their Wielders never see their fortieth birthday. They rarely see their thirtieth."

I got it. My love, me being intimate with him, would destroy Ethan completely if it moved from the dreams. Dreams that wouldn't be enough in the end.

Ariel believed that someone had told Jeff the truth. My mother was convinced that she would find a way for them to be together without the deadly effects her love had on Jeff. She refused to believe that she was killing him.

Ariel had fought with her ferociously. She kept catching Jeff sneaking out of her apartment just as she would flew in from her nightly owlish endeavors.

Mom was blind to all of it.

I would not just kill Ethan at the end, but I would lose myself too. I would become an insane witch. I'd crave more and more power to fill the gaping hole Ethan's death would tear in me. I would kill Benders just to get that power. But unfortunately, in my situation, there wouldn't be other earth Benders for me to use.

To live, not just for me, but for Ethan too, I had no choice but to break it off with him.

It wasn't easy.

My body shook as I pulled the covers over my face. It hurt so badly.

My phone buzzed from my nightstand. I lifted the covers and saw Ethan's name flashing on my screen. I slid the option to ignore the call.

A horrible feeling gnawed at my core, at my soul, ripping everything in its wake to shreds.

How on earth was I going to be okay? I didn't know. But I had to do this. I had no choice. It was time for me to be the strong one.

I had to pass this test, because Ethan dying was not an option.

30

ALEX

ETHAN TRIED to call me the entire day. I ignored all his calls and text messages.

How was I going to stand strong and tell him no?

It was like we were under a spell... But no. I had fallen in love with Ethan, before I even knew I had.

I wished I could say that he didn't show up in my dreams, but Ethan was very set in what he wanted, and I was one of those things.

He threw pebbles at my window for a long time. I buried my head under a pillow.

I cannot fail. Eventually the dreams will die out. Hopefully.

"Alex," he started yelling, loudly enough that my dream-parents would wake up. This was something I feared incoherently; I didn't know what impact it would have on real life if they did.

And then, as if fear was a person, Dad's voice overpowered the backyard. "Ethan, is that you?"

I woke up in a cold sweat. I was in my room. I jumped out of bed and ran to the window. Outside it was pitch dark. No one lurked in the bushes, throwing pebbles at my window. I opened my door an inch. Dad's snores traveled down the hall.

I breathed again.

Then as I was about to close the door, my father stopped snoring. I hear his voice in the background, gruffly telling my mother to wake up.

"What?" she asked, her voice thick with sleep.

I couldn't make out what he said, until he spoke a name: Ethan.

"HOW LONG?" Mom roared. Smoke seemed likely to pour from her ears any minute now.

The entire household sat around the table in the kitchen. By the way she was yelling, even the neighbors would know that I was dreaming about Ethan Sutcliff.

"Does Jeff know?" she asked.

I just stared at her. I said nothing. Not a word.

"Answer me!"

"I don't know," I said sullenly. "What do you want me to say? You should've listened to Daddy and let me sleep."

"Don't you dare give me that nonsense, Alex." How long has this been going on?"

I crossed my arms over my chest. "It's dreams, nothing more."

"You think that this is innocent?" she shrieked. "It's not. You want to lose your Bender."

"She didn't do anything wrong, sweetheart," Dad piped up. "Ethan was trying to get her to wake up."

"Dad, just stop, please," I begged. He was going to be so disappointed.

Mom gaped at him. "You are so easily manipulated by that girl." She pointed her finger at me.

"Excuse me?" My father sounded upset.

Good. If they were fighting my mother wasn't fighting with me. I tried to get up.

"Sit down," she cried. "I'm not done with you." She looked at my father again. "It's been more than a month, you idiot. If she was so innocent, the dreams would've been over."

Understanding clicked into place in Dad's eyes. His gaze cut over to me.

I sank in my chair. *Please just kill me now.*

"Is this true?"

"Dad, please. I'm not going to have a Sex-Ed discussion with you."

"Alex, how long has this been going on?"

"It was just dreams. It's over now, okay? Could you please just get off my back? Telling him that I can't do it anymore wasn't easy, but I did it." I gave Mom a scathing look. "Something even *you* couldn't do."

Mom froze in shock, and I took the opening to flee to my room. I didn't care if they fought about the past. They should just leave me alone.

I collapsed on my bed.

Whoever made the rules between Benders and Wielders must have been smoking something. Because I was beginning to realize one: they made it nearly impossible to Resist each another.

The minute I wanted to be good, something bad happened. I was never going to pass this test.

ETHAN

THE CAT WAS out of the bag. I was in deep shit.

How was I supposed to know that one of her parents could wake up in this dreams and catch us? I got such a big telling-off from Meredith the following day, I doubted she would ever let me see Alex again.

It was a mess. All because Alex was jealous of Sophie. She wouldn't even answer my calls.

When Meredith left, I threw myself down on the sofa in the living room. I figured Dad was next in line to light into me. But he just looked at me with plenty of compassion. "Is it over?" he asked.

I shrugged.

He looked weary. "It needs to be over. You can't win this. Nobody can."

"Why?" My foot connected hard with the coffee table, and the only thing it did was tipped over. My anger felt way stronger than that. "Why would anyone give us a perfect mate but forbid us to be together? Were they drunk when it came to Wielders and Benders?"

"I know how you feel. I've been there, Ethan. I know it's not easy. It feels as if your entire world is crashing down. But it needs to be over."

How could he ask that of me? "It's unfair and I don't understand why we can't be with one another. It makes no sense."

He rubbed his temples. "Give me a minute. I'll show you." He left and went up to his room.

Baffled, I watched him go. Did he have evidence all these years and never told me? He came back with a tattered old box, about the size of the throw pillows beside me. He settled on the couch. The leather creaked under his weight. He placed the box between us.

"What lies within is for your eyes only. You can't tell

Meredith or Alex about what I'm going to show you, Ethan."
His face was grave.

I nodded.

"Meredith and me, we were going to run away together. She
was so convinced that some long-ago witch had cast a curse on
the Wielders and Benders. Like you, she refused to believe that
we weren't made for each other."

I frowned. That didn't sound like Meredith.

He lifted the lid and took out a stack of photographs. He
showed me the first one and I jumped up off the sofa as if it
was hot.

He threw one after the other onto the coffee table, the one I
kicked over a few seconds ago, and Dad just pasiently picked it
up again, like a grisly card dealer. All of them looked the same.
Gray mummies. Corpses casted in gray cement. "What is this?"
Overcome by morbid curiosity, I sat and took the photos he
offered.

"It's what they do to us, slowly. Over a period of five to ten
years."

Terror clenched my heart. "Five to ten years."

"Remember when I told you that she would start taking
energy from you?"

I nodded.

"It happens when you sleep with one another, and I'm not
talking about the dreams. Reality. Being with them is like taking
ecstasy. You are on another level, one that humans like us can't
handle. I remember being so out of it, but at the same time
loving every single moment. It is the best drug I've ever experienced. Yet it was the worst drug on this planet." He took out
other pictures.

Men and woman who were still alive, but looked as if they
were taking drugs, getting abused. Bloody gashes from shoulder
to navel, purple and green bruises mottling their flesh.

"She wasn't just giving me the best sex I ever had, the best love, the most perfect love. She was doing this to me too, and I refused to acknowledge it. I said I was stronger than the others when she wanted to stop." He looked somber. "We both believed with all of our hearts that she had proof of a curse. But there was none. It was the Resistance addling our brains." He tapped on the photos of gaunt, injured Benders.

I was speechless, absorbing these images.

"Why do you think they run away and become Necrocretors, Ethan?" He fingered the worn corner of one photo. "I know you think that you and Alex are stronger. I've been there. But earth Wielders and Benders have it the worst of all the other Elements. You must stop seeing Alex."

I shook my head and I push myself off the chair.

"I can't. I can't leave her."

"You have no choice, son. Did you think I wanted to choose Siobhan? I didn't. I loved Meredith with every inch of who I was. I wanted to be with her so badly. The minute our love became a physical reality, the Association knew. The Sentinels knew."

"Wait, the Sentinels?"

"They are not just a bunch of hocus pocus, they exist.They know everything, Ethan. They have people who can see things others can't, know things they can't possibly know. The dream world is the only place where your love is safe, but it's never enough."

The second person to use those words: *the dreams are never enough.*

"Alex finally understood, son. You need to grasp it too."

I didn't want to listen. "So, what happened after they discovered that you broke the law?"

My father stroked his face thoughtfully. "They came for me. I didn't even know they were watching. They took me in as if I was a criminal. They showed me pictures like these, just fresher and more nightmarish. They told me the havoc a Bender's love wreaked. How our bodies couldn't handle it. How Wielders literally sucked us dry. How Wielders couldn't handle all the power. It was like a drug to them too and they wanted more; they changed and became monsters. She never wanted to hurt me, but by the end, she wouldn't have cared. Our power is what changes them, Ethan." He reached across the box of horrors and seized my shoulders. "Promise me that this will stop. Please."

"It's why you chose Siobhan."

"I had to, not just for my sake but for Meredith's too. I couldn't watch her destroy herself and others because she wanted more after I'd be gone. Why do you think the Necrocretors so unstoppable? There isn't a single Bender or guardian in their ranks that they love, because they killed them a long time ago."

It was silent. My hands trembled. I had the uncanny sense that I could smell decaying flesh from the box between us.

"Just think about it," Dad said, gathering up the photos and replacing them. "I can't force you to do the right thing. But I hope you will make the right decision before it's too late."

He got up and left.

I LAY IN MY BED, staring at the ceiling. This was so unfair. I knew how I felt about Alex. It wasn't something super visual, though everyone thought it was.

It wasn't just a button I could switch off.

I still had to protect her. Necrocretors would make a fresh attempt at any time. I still had to train with her.

I finally understood why this was the hardest test ever. The ones who made it, well, some of them are not pairs anymore.

It was nearly impossible to pass. They were always there, even when they were not there.

It wasn't fair. For some reason I felt angry at Alex. She just gave up on us. The dreams were safe. Why did she had to go and ignore me?

The dreams were perfect, and she went and fucked it all up.

31

ALEX

TRAINING STOPPED. This time it wasn't my mother who stopped it. It was Ethan. He refused to speak to me. He claimed it was all his football games, but it was a lie and we all knew it. Not that I blamed him. I wouldn't speak to me either.

I still secretly message Cynthia. She was very understanding, still not knowing about Ethan and me, but understanding on other matters, like my reason why she couldn't come and visit. I told her that my mother took me away. She thinks we are somewhere on an island. I hate lying to her.

I missed her.

I missed him.

I didn't know how I was going to do any of this.

One positive thing came out of this: Clive gave the final report that there were no Necrocretors in the area. Not up at the school in the mountains and not near Sky View High. Mom felt confident enough to send me back to school. Sort of.

I had to go back as Ducky, at first I thought that my parents were really playing on death's doorstep, cause the Necrocretors knew what Ducky looked like and that I was the Earth Wielder. But Dad sure believed there was no Necrocretors around, and now, I had to play the part as every single one of my friends know Ducky was the daughter of Frederick and Meredith.

Mom shared all this with me over dinner. I pushed lasagna around on my plate as I listened. Whoever was keeping tabs on us was long gone and under the impression that I was dead, he'd said. Mom gave me Ducky's glasses and sat on my bed as I put on the glamour.

I could still feel the pain of her searing into my skin. It still haunted me. Ethan used to make it better. I took off the glasses and looked at Mom.

"You can do it, Alex. You know the drill. Protect your true identity at all times." She sprinkled a bit of parmesan cheese on her own plate; she would keep doing this until it was all gone, obsessively adding cheese every few bites.

"What if they are still close by?"

"We would've picked up a trail. Clive promised me that there wasn't anyone with that power around. And Louis done his own little investigation.

I shoveled another bite of pasta and ricotta into my mouth.

"Are you going to be okay to be in such proximity to Ethan?"

I gulped. "He hates my guts. I doubt he'll try anything."

"That's not what I meant, Alex. I do know how you feel about him. I was there a long time ago, remember?"

I nodded. "I'll be fine." I gave her a fake smile. "I'm just exhausted. I guess trying not to fall asleep wasn't such a great plan after all."

She took out a beautiful golden necklace from her back pocket and put it around my neck. "This will protect you." A small cross glittered on a simple chain. Mom wasn't the religious type.

"It has a tracker inside."

I rolled my eyes. Of course it was just another cover-up, another prop. I pushed my plate away. I was no longer hungry.

I crawled into bed. Moonlight shone through my window. It was such a beautiful night. I couldn't believe that I was going back into my cage tomorrow. I knew that I shouldn't look at it that way, but it felt like it. Ducky wasn't just a protector anymore. She was my trap too.

I finally dozed off.

It was strange how empty my dreams were now.

They were still there. I woke up as if I didn't fall asleep. Sometimes I wondered if I was asleep. They were starting to become so real. Like whoever created these dreams had realized the flaws and was slowly fixing all of them. I could understand how Mom and Jeff didn't know when it was real and when they were dreaming.

I still had the urge to phone Ethan or go to him sometimes, especially at night, before I went to bed. But then I had no idea whether it was because I was asleep or if I really wanted to see him.

It was confusing.

So I stayed in my room, and I guessed Ethan stayed in his, fighting the Resistance with me. Something we were doing together.

When my alarm rang, I woke up. It felt as if I didn't sleep at all. Being awake inside my dreams wasn't fun.

Mom brought me today to school. "Are you sure you will be okay, sweetheart?" Concerned, laced with fear.

A part of her was still wary of sending me to school. But Louis promised her that they had searched town with a fine-toothed comb. No trace of Necrocretors was found.

I nodded and gave her the widest smile I could muster. I just needed to get back to my life. Even if the last time I was here, I was being labeled a stalker. I couldn't fathom what rumors had evolved in the wake of my injury and nearly two weeks- absence.

I hoped they were laying it on thick with the severity of my injuries. Making those idiots who wanted a laugh feel like shit.

I climbed out of the SUV and headed to the main entrance of the school building. Everyone I passed stared at me. Whispered to one another.

"I thought she was dead."

"C'mon. It wasn't that bad. I heard they moved."

"Well, guess the stalker's back. We should warn Ethan."

A girl slapped the guy who had said that. The guy winced. "You heard what the principal said. No more calling her that."

I took a deep breath and opened the door.

Just my luck, the first person who I saw was none other than Ethan Sutcliff.

Our eyes lingered on one another. He looked away first. Hurt, anger was written all over his posture. "I need to go. See you later," he said to the girl next to him. Only then did I register her presence, a bleach-blonde maniac. Sophie glared.

I pulled my hood over my head. Maybe coming back here wasn't such a good idea.

THE ENTIRE SCHOOL was advertising homecoming Posters hung from the ceilings and wallpapered the lockers, a welcome reprieve from the last posters I'd seen like that.

Voting polls were everywhere. Ethan's face was plastered on all of them, Sophie's too, with a brunette who was probably her rival.

There was even a poster of Ethan on my locker. I tore it off, balled it up, and threw it on the ground. I hit the locker hard on the dent and it opened.

I started shuffling books, thinking through which ones I needed between now and lunch.

Something hard connected with my body. I almost lost my balance.

"You're back!" Cynthia yelled. I flinched and wrapped one arm around her with caution.

"I thought you were still lying somewhere on an island," she yelled at the top of her lungs. Then she pounded me hard. "Why didn't you call me?"

"We came in late last night, and sorry. I guess I didn't want to wake you." I lied again.

It felt good to have someone like Cynthia. Through all this, she didn't think ones that the roomers of why I tried to kill myself was true. The bell rang. We both made our way to our first calls, Maths.

THE DAY GALLOPED BY. I received many fake greetings —"glad you're okay" and "so happy you're not dead" and "oh thank goodness you're back—from people I had never spoken to. I was legend, but in the worst way possible. Someone to be pitied. Someone who was weak and worthless.

I couldn't wait for the final bell to ring.

When it came, I couldn't get to my locker fast enough. I hit the locker hard and it swung open. I packed my books quickly and slammed it shut. Sophie appeared where the locker door had been, leaning against the one next to mine with her arms folded across her ample bosom.

I jumped. "What do you want?" I said as I slung the heavy bag over my shoulder.

She grabbed my shirt collar and pulled me close. "What's going on?" Her face was inches from mine.

"Nothing," I said back in the same dangerous tone she used.

"Ethan has been in a terrible mood lately. Judging by the way he ran away from you, I would say it was something that you did."

"If you can't handle your boyfriend's mood, Sophie, don't take it out on me. He's just my Bender, not my everything." I said as softly as I could. I made to walk away.

She grabbed my arm tight and pulled me to face her again. "You don't want to mess with me, little girl. Tell me why my boyfriend is in such a bad mood. Now."

I yanked my arm out of her grasp. *He is pissed off because I told him no more screwing each other in our dreams...* I wondered what she would say if I told her that. But I didn't.

"Look, we had a disagreement. Training hasn't gone so well lately."

She huffed. "It can't be that." She sneered.

"Then what do you want to hear?" I said. "What would make you leave me alone?"

She curled her lip. "Fine, go. But I will find out, Ugly Duckling. And believe me, my wrath is something you don't want to face."

I couldn't help it: I snorted. "Whatever you say, Malibu Barbie." I turned on my heel and left her in my tracks.

Her wrath. Could she even spell that word? Did my appearance really fool everyone who knew what I really was?

Did they really think I was this pathetic little earth Wielder who just don't have the strength to wield her element properly?

Her wrath. Laughing, I opened the door to go home where I could just be myself.

The Alex that few really knew.

32

ETHAN

I WAS livid with Soph when I discovered that she had confronted Alex.

Whe had a huge fight and it just slipped out, the words. "I'm done, we are through?"

Sophie's eyes grew. "Through. Are you breaking up with me? Why? What have I done?"

"It's not you, okay."

"Oh, you seriously going with that stupid excuse."

"It's the truth, Sophia, what do you want me to tell you."

"The truth?"

I just stared at her. "You wouldn't understand, so just let it go."

"NO!" Sophie yelled. "It's not that simple. What about homecoming?"

"I don't care, I'm not going, find someone else."

"But you are nominated for king, Ethan. I know that you do care, even if it's just a little."

"Oh yeah, This is me not caring." I turned and walked away.

"Ethan," she yelled but I just disappeared through the ocean of people.

It was a weird feeling I felt. I thought that at least I would feel loss or sadness, but I felt nothing.

One night I was reading a health magazine on my bed and heard a noise outside. Someone was climbing up my gutter. For a hopeful second, I thought it was Alex.

We were sort of back on speaking terms. Well, not really. She apologized, I said I understood, and that was where it stayed. But really, we didn't interact other than training.

She complimented me more than usual, but messages never came at night.

Soph appeared outside my window and not Alex. I let her in and she threw herself at me.

"Stop it," I said and pushed her off. "It's over, Sophie."

She stepped back. Her jaw was set, arms folded. She didn't look happy this time. "You still playing that card."

"It's not a card. It's over."

She shook her head as tears welled up in her eyes. Urgh, I hated it when she cries.

"Don't please," I begged.

"Don't what, cry." She yelled at me. "What happened, and don't tell me that I wouldn't understand."

"Fine." I sighed. "I met someone else."

She gaped at me. "Who."

"Does it matter," I asked.

Then it was like a bulb went off above her head.

"You gotto be shitting me." She chuckled. "You seriuolsy leaving me for Alex."

"Don't." I said. She had no idea who the real Alex was.

"I don't believe this." She said and had a weird awkward

smile on her face. "You seriously choosing someone like Alex over me. I can be with anyone Etan, but I chose you. You think Sam didn't try. He had. But we cannot be together. She is going to kill you."

"I don't care."

She shook her head. "She is going to kill you. You need to let her go. Don't push every one away. You are smarter than that."

I didn't care. I didn't said anything either as well.

"You don't need to make up your mind right now, but please, just think about it." She left and that was it.

I fell on my bed.

I missed Alex, but I did think about what Soph was saying.

The next day, I tried to act a bit friendlier toward everyone, including Soph. I gave her a hug and apologize for how I acted.

She accepted.

She struggled with the fact that we couldn't be together anymore,, but at least she was still willing to be my friend.

For a while I felt a little less suffocated.

Who knew where I would be next year? College maybe, or closer to home because of Alex... who wanted nothing to do with me whatsoever. The dreams finally stopped. It would've been enough. I was so sure of it, yet she just threw it away.

The chants came from the hall. The pep rally was already starting. I was part of the homecoming comitee. I should've actually been there, lifting up spirits.

For years I dreamt of this day, finally being a senior, part of the homecoming comitee, and to run out wearing my football jersey as varsity's quarterback, yet I don't give a shit about any of this anymore. It all seems so little after everything that happened.

I actually have no idea how to lift up spirits, I mean how does one lift up a spirit when you feel like shit.

I stopped in front of coache's office. He wasn't going to like what I have to say.

I knocked twice.

"Enter," his voice came from inside. He should've been at the pep rally, but for some reason he doesn't like it either.

I opened his door and he was surprised to see me.

"Ethan,"

"Coach," I sighed and looked down at the floor. I had no idea how to break this to him.

"No," he shook his head and got up from behind his desk. "There is no way you are quitting the team."

"I cannot play, coach. I'm sorry. You have to play Joe. I just can't." I didn't give him time to talk me out of it. I loved football, I still do, my heart was just not in it at this moment.

"Ethan," he yelled after me and I walked faster.

I found my jeep and just decided to go for a drive.

MY PHONE RANG a few hours later. After the million text messages I received from Ryan, and Joe, and Sophie. Everyone seem to wonder the same thing.

I picked up without looking who the caller was.

"You quit football," Sophie's voice was on the other side. I don't know why this pained me so much that it was her voice and not Alex's.

"So what."

"Ethan," she stopped. Probably had no words for what I'd done.

"What is it Soph."

"Why are you doing this?"

"I don't have time for anything else. I have to learn how to protect Alex properly and my football is in the way of us training."

"She is seriously behind all of this."

"It's my decision, not hers." I put down the phone.

I know she doesn't understand. A part of me was still speechless at what I did. It's weird to describe it.

The knock on my bedroom door made me look up. My father's figure was leaning against the frame. "You quit football?"

I shrugged.

"Ethan," he had that disapproval tone in his voice

"Dad, please, not today."

He didn't push further.

"Are you atleast going to the game tonight."

"I'll be there."

My father left. I know he didn't understand my action just like the rest, or maybe he did.

My priorities changed. I was an earth bender, and with that comes certain obligations like protecting Alex and the only way to do that, and do it well is if I train more with her.

AROUND SEVEN I parked the jeep in the parking lot. I could hear cheers and chants already coming from the crowd.

Tonight I was supposed to run out wearing the quarterback jersey but it will be Joe, Sky View High's new varsity quarterback. I didn't know how many people knew about the change, I guess a lot as a few of my friends were dumbstrucked as I quit the team.

I pulled on my hoody over my head and buried my hands in my sleeves. I doubt Alex would be here tonight.

I was still so upset with her, but I knew I couldn't ignore her the way I had that last time. If something had to happen to her again, I wouldn't be able to live with it.

A couple was kissing right underneath the bleacher. They didn't even notice me. I walked passed them and just stood in one of the entry ways. Away from the crowd but where I could still see the game.

The crowds were going crazy and the guys, my team, or used to be mine a few hours back, crashed through the white homecoming banner with Joe as their leader. He was wearing his helmet already. Probably way too excited for tonight's game.

I was super excited for him. But apart of me regret it completely.

ALEX

I sat in the cold with a hot chocolate in my hands, trying to warm up. At least I wasn't alone. Cynthia was right next to me.

She was oddly quiet tonight and I didn't know how to handle it. I feel like an intruder asking her what is wrong, or if she is okay? Sometimes I wonder if I seriously was friend material.

I don't know how to treat one to begin with. I doubt lying was part of it and I was lying to Cynthia on a daily basis.

"Are you okay," I finally asked.

"Yeah, I just feel a bit down. Maybe it's the flue, I don't know. Maybe I should just go home."

"And be all by yourself."

She looks at me weird. "Your father, being the coach. Is there anyone waiting for you at home besides him."

"Oh, no. I guess I can wait. It's not that bad."

I smiled. "I would miss you if you go now." I said. I love her company. She was the only one really giving Ducky a chance.

The band was playing a new song and the cheerleaders were going crazy as the football team came running out.

They were playing the varsity team of one of the close by colleges/schools.

It's tradition apparently. What do I know, I was stuck for sixteen years in my aunts locket.

I took a deep breath as I saw Etan running through the banner with his team behind him.

Why was he being so difficult.

I missed him, I truly did but I had to be the responsible one as he clearly wasn't.

Everyone cheered with the cheerleaders as paper flutter and a team of jocks threw helmets and jump on one another.

Ethan seemed different though.

"Is it just me, or did Ethan bulk up."

"You notice it too." I look at Cynthia.

"Yeah, odd."

Huh? I frown. What happened. Was it a spell or something.

The game started and everyone sat on the edge of their seats to see what is happening.

Ethan messed up, many booed, but somehow he got it back on track, caught the ball and sprint forward.

Something was seriously off about him.

"Pass out the ball, idiot." One of the student in front of us yelled.

I wanted to kick his back, or mess my hot cocoa on him for calling Ethan an idiot. But he somehow saved that play too and the team ended up scoring.

The band played and everyone congratulated Ethan and the guy who scored.

The guy in front of us was super quiet now, in fact he forgot about the name calling.

We sat back down as the second play started.

It wasn't a touch down and something strange was happening with Ethan. It was as if he was tired. His feet started dragging and he struggled to take off his helmet.

My heart beat like the band's drums, and nobody seems to notice it, until he fell down to the floor. Then someone screamed.

ETHAN

EVERYTHING STOPPED.

I watched as Joe fell to the floor. He didn't look so good a few minutes ago and I know he was fit. He could last at least two full games. He trained hard as he always been the back up quarter back.

The minute he hit the ground, something awful rushed through my body.

Was that meant for me. He was wearing my jersey, as I literally didn't gave coach the time to order Joe his own with a number one on.

I sprinted as fast as I could to him, and everyone was crowding him.

The school medic was already at his side.

"Joe," I yelled and fell literally next to him.

"C'mon buddy talk to me."

He didn't answer.

"Give him some space." The doctor tried to get us to just back up slightly.

Joe still didn't move.

Coach finally reached us. He also asked us to give Joe some space.

His eyes caught mine briefly, the horror reflect back to mine. This could've been me.

"Does anyone smell that," the doctor asked.

I tried. I couldn't smell anything. Unless....

I looked at the doctor again. I never noticed it before but I could swear I saw a yellow tint in his iris. And the only supernatural race that has the ability to smell that sharp, was werewolves.

He begged us to step back.

"What smell," coach insisted.

"I'm not sure," the doc said, "but I have to send it to the labs."

He touched Joe slightly in the neck and then his face went blank.

He shook his head.

No. It cannot be.

I walked away, dased. Realising what this truly meant. The only thing I could think off was that the jersey carried some sort of deadly substance and through the sweat, Joe's body finally vape it up and it got into his blood stream.

Whatever was on that jearsey was meant for me.

ALEX

ETHAN DIDN'T LOOK SO good. He was in shock. I felt better, felt as if I could breath. The minute I saw him running out, I knew it wasn't him. That was why he looked different tonight, because it literally wasn't him.

The game was stopped.

Some girls cupped their mouths, many voiced their concerns.

What the hell was happening.

My eyes stayed on Ethan he looked worried and then he started to run back.

"We should go," Cynthia said.

"You think?" I sounded worried.

"I should've go the minute I wanted to. I really do not feel well, Alex."

"Okay," I nodded. Not sure why she didn't want to stay to find out.

Then I heard his voice. "Alex," he sounded worried.

I looked down at him. "Just give me a minute," I looked at Cynthia and she nodded.

I went down to Ethan. "We need to go, it's not save."

I still wanted to hit him for scaring me like this, but the urgency in his voice put me on full alert.

"What do you mean."

"Joe is dead. Whoever killed him wanted to kill me. That jearsey is mine."

"Why are you not playing tonight?" I asked.

"Because I quit this afternoon."

I stared at him. "Why?"

"It doesn't matter now, does it. If I didn't that would've been me?"

He sounded and looked horrid. "Please, it's not save here, you need to come with me."

I looked at Cynthia, she was gone. I wanted to go and look for her, but Ethan pulled me by my arm.

"Please, I have one job to do and that is keeping you save," he spoke softly. "Now let me do that?"

I nodded and I went with him.

We rushed to where I assume his jeep was parked when a figure was coming toward us.

Ethan pushed me behind him. I hated how he thinks I cannot defend myself.

But when Louis stepped out from the dark, I felt safe.

"It's fine, Ethan, I have it from here."

"Yeah," Ethan's eye twitched. I didn't understand it. "What is the password."

I squinted at him. "What?"

"Shush, Alex. The Password Louis."

Louis didn't say anything. Then he grunt and literally went for Ethan.

In less then two seconds they were in a full on fight.

I didn't know what to do. Why would Louis fight Ethan and why did Ethan ask for a password. What was this.

"Alex, Run." Ethan yelled as Louis got him in a grip and I just ran. I knew my father's Bender. Why did he attack mine. That was Ethan. I felt him. The current always been there, maybe not as strong as before, but the pull was always present. It was him, unless....a cold finger run up my spine.

Unless that wasn't Louis.

A firm grip grabbed me and pulled me down. His hand was over my mouth.

"It's okay Alex," my father's voice said. "It's me."

I wanted to believe him but I couldn't.

He let go of his hand over my mouth.

"Ethan," I said.

"Jeff is on his way."

"Louis."

"It's not him. Whatever happened here tonight, is the work of the Necrocretors, we need to go."

I didn't like the tone but I left with him.

Our SUV stopped and my mother rushed out, hugged me tightly and walked with me to the back of the car.

She opened the door when Ariel came swooping in. She literally attack my mom, changed into her self. "Run, Alex, it's not your parents," and back into an owl.

She kept attacking my mother.

My father grabbed me again. And I thrust my palm into his nose and my knee connected with his groin. He folded double.

"I'm so sorry if it's really you daddy, but right now. I can't trust anyone."

I ran back to where I left Ethan.

How was it not my parents.

I wanted to cry, not because I was sad or scared. Okay, I was scared, but not cry scared. I was confused, and it was so frustrating and overwhelming. I should know my parents. My mind yelled.

Ethan grabbed me again. I felt the pull.

"What is happening."

"Necrocretors." My dad, or whover my dad was confirmed that. Holy crap, was my mom and dad really okay.

We reached Ethan's truck and he spun away the minute we got in.

"Stap yourself in, Alex." He yelled.

My arms and hands followed his orders but my mind was realing. "Why did they look like my parents, and Louis."

"They are called Changelings, Shifters. They are not like your aunt."

"I know which kind you are talking about. Are you sure."

"They attacked us. They killed Joe, thinking it was me. I need to get you to safety."

We reached the interstate and was almost leaving Billings completely when he took another off road.

I knew it was Ethan you cannot fake the pull, that much I know.

We reached a house, that only had a porchlight on.

Ethan looked everywhere around us as we climbed out and rushed up the porch.

"What place is this?"

"It's one of the safe havens. Someone will come and get us here."

"Ethan, how do you know to trust them."

"I will tell you inside."

He pressed a code and locks shifted open.

We went inside and now all we can do was to wait.

ETHAN'S PHONE rang five minutes later. It sounded like my mother. He asked for the password and she must have given it to him.

I didn't even know about a stupid password.

Anger filled me again. Why didn't I know about this. And why was this happening.

The first one to arrive was my real parents and Ariel. My mom hugged me tightly.

"I'm so sorry sweetheart." She kissed me on my head.

My dad just hugged the both of us. I couldn't help but to look at him limping or a bloody nose. He didn't have any of those. It was really imposters. I almost left with them.

My knees gave in and my mother help me to the nearest chair.

It was as if reality finally kicked in.

"I know it's scary." My mother said as Ariel came waltzing in.

I got up and flung my arms around her.

"I was so worried that I wouldn't get to you in time. When I saw them almost tricking you," Ariel spoke fast.

"Don't. Please." I begged her to stop, just imagining what could've been if she didn't showed up when she did.

"The locket doesn't seem so stupid now anymore does it."

"I don't want to go back."

"At least you are safe."

"I don't' want to go back, please. I can't."

She saw something in my eyes. I don't know if it was my frustration with that damn make believe world or if it was my begging. But I'm done hiding.

I punched the guy that looked like my dad. I gave him a blood nose.

I just need a stupid password too.

33

ETHAN

JOE'S MEMORIAL was a few days after homecoming game. Homecoming was canceled for now until an arrest was made.

Clive and his officers swept the entire school and lockers trying to find the culprit.

They didn't leave any tracks whatsoever.

To make matters worse, I was always on edge. Not just when it comes to protecting Alex but just on edge. It was as if I was waiting for danger, which wasn't a way to live.

A part of me wished Alex would take her family's offer and just go back into the locket. She's safe there and I will help Ariel guarding it until she is twenty one and her ability stable.

But Alex was stuborn. She didn't want to go back.

I couldn't lose her again, not like that.

What makes it so harder was that training with Alex, bending her earth, felt like the most natural thing in the world. It was weird and perfect simultaneously.

When we actually wielded and bent, we were the old us, pasts forgotten, joking and laughing together. The minute it stopped, she would climb back into that beautiful shell of hers and not say a word. It was as if nothing happened a few days ago. And as if nothing happened between us.

Oh sure, she'd send a text later, just one, saying "Well done with training" or "I didn't know you could do that." I usually replied with a smiley face or the blushing emoji.

Meredith didn't glare at me the way she used to anymore. That wanted to decapitate me with her laser beams from her eyeballs stare was gone. I geuss she only see the guy that desperately tried to keep her daughter safe now.

AFTER A WEEK, life was starting to feel normal again.

It was sad how everyone just forgot about Joe. There were still memorial flowers and a cross on the field laid for him.

I refused to pick my jearsey. Someone trying to kill me, if that wasn't an eye opener, then nothing would be.

The only constant reminder of what was looming over us, was the front page of every single newspaper.

Everyone that comes to a realization of who Alex was, end up dying. Then it would be quiet for a while, until they figure it out again.

She wasn't safe here, but then again, would she be anywhere else.

At least here she was close to not only her Bender but to head quarters too.

By the third natural disaster plastered on the front page Meredith stopped training session even though dad told her that it was stupid. Now, if any other time, was the most crucial to train with one another. Now that they were near.

Bodies showed up, if not half composed in the forest, washing up a few states in the lakes and rivers.

It was screaming the work of vampires needing to feed and other supernatural.

"Etan," Sophie yelled. By the tone of her voice I would say she tried to get my attention a couple of times now.

I gave her a blank stare. And shrugged. "Will you go with me to homecoming. And before you say no, I know you care."

I sighed.

"As friends, offcourse."

"Fine," I gave up and by the surprised look on Sophie's face, I would say that she didn't expected that at all.

I STOOD in front of the mirror, eyeing my tuxedo. In less than five minutes the limo that I had agreed to share with Garret and Ryan would arrive.

We should not be going at all. This was way to soon for the homecoming dance.

My entire body tingle, but I told Soph yes, I would go with her.

My phone beeped. I picked it up from my dresser. It was a text from Alex. I opened it as my heartbeat rose slightly.

Enjoy tonight.

I asked her to come with me, but she declined. It was a long shot anyway, but had to try. There were so many times I imagined what it would be like if I show up with the real Alex. I was positive that Sophie would understand why, but Alex was the opposite of what witches truly were. She wasn't vain and she was far from showing off.

I stare at her text again.

I hated this. These texts felt so fake. I could tell she wanted to say more. I sent her a smiley face back and tried to put it out of my mind.

In less than ten minutes we would go pick up the girls, our dates. Sophie—who had convinced me to go with her after all—was first.

I could just imagine the number of pics her mother, Barbs, was going to take. She was an air Bender, like Leanne. Soph's father was a metal Bender. They were almost as rare as earth Benders; only a few of them were scattered across the world.

My door opened and Dad walked in. The corners of his lips curved and he appraised me.

I rolled my eyes at his sentimentality. "Dad, c'mon. It's not the first time I've worn a tux."

"No, it's not," he said. "It's got to do with the amount of times I'm still going to see that. I can't help but think about the one who wanted to be here to see this day so badly."

My mother.

Everything was so focused on Alex and Meredith, part of me had begun to doubt if he ever loved my mother. My doubts vanished at the sight of his sad smile. A knot formed in my throat. If she had lived, how different might things have been?

I puffed out my chest gruffly. "So how do I look."

"Soph is not going to be able to take her eyes off you."

I huffed. I didn't want it to be Soph.

Just then a car honked, breaking this I said goodbye to my father.

"C'mon, one picture." He took out his disposable camera.

"Fine, just one." I opened my jacket to reveal my cummerbund and leaned against the door frame. A tongue-in-cheek impersonation of a model in a cologne ad.

Dad laughed and snapped a few pictures. "Serious now," he said. I obliged, closed my jacket, put my hands in my pockets, and plastered on a fake smile while the camera clicked away.

The limo honked insistently. I rushed down the stairs.

"Enjoy," he yelled after me.

Outside, the limo door opened. Garret and Ryan each had a beer in their hands.

"It's party time, dude," Garret exclaimed. He popped the tab on a tall can and handed it to me. Ice from the cooler clung to the sides.

Engine purring, the limo pulled away.

"Isn't this ride sick?" Ryan said. "Look." He fiddled with some buttons and switches. Multicolored lights flashed in the cab. Hell, prom could've been held right here.

At Sophie's house, I climbed out.

"Please, dude, don't take too long. Rayne is going to kill me if I am late." Garret waggled the champagne bottle that had been chilling for the girls.

I shook my head. Rayne was like the first date he ever got, poor girl. I hope she knew what she got herself in to.

I rang the bell at Soph's gate and was admitted. Their house was gorgeous. It was well known that Metal Benders weren't only rare but smart too. Soph's dad owned a big chain of businesses in hydraulics and big machines and whatnot. He tried one time to get me interested in studying his field. He was really doing well for himself.

I still had to decide what I wanted to do.

The door opened and Barbara, Soph's mother, greeted me with a friendly smile. "Ethan, we haven't seen you in such a long time. Come in."

I walked in. Something about her Barbara's comment told me that Sophie didn't tell her mother about our break up.

"Sophie will be a down shortly," she said. "Sophie, honey, Ethan is here," she called as she climbed the stairs. As she reached the top, Sophie appeared.

She wore a gorgeous pink dress that hugged her sculpted body tight. It was sleeveless with a scandalously low neckline. It complimenting her body around ever curve and all I could think about was Alex.

I shook myself from this thought of what Alex would've looked like tonight if she was my date and not Sophie.

I smiled at her. Her beautiful blonde hair was taken up at the one side while the rest fall in beautiful curls over her shoulders.

When she reached me, she gave me a kiss on my cheek.

I handed her the corsage that was in my hand and put it gently on her wrist. A white lily and pink roses. I put it on Soph's wrist. Barbs took pictures of the two of us as Mr. Rutter came into the foyer.

"Ethan." He reached out his hand and I took it. "Long time no see."

"Sorry I haven't been around. Things have been a little crazy."

He clapped me on the shoulder. "It's all good. As long as you learn how to bend properly."

"Finally," I joked. I just wanted to get out of the Rutters' house and get tonight over with.

"Mom, enough pictures," Soph complained. She dragged me by the arm to the door.

I said goodnight and promised to look after Sophie.

"Enjoy the evening, sweetheart," her mother called while her dad mumbled something I didn't quite catch. We escaped.

Garret opened the door of the limo from the inside and Soph climbed in.

"Oh my freakin' word. Is this for real?" she squealed.

Garret chortled and popped the champagne. He grabbed one of the flutes and poured Soph a glass. She accepted it and downed it too fast. She handed him back the glass, already wanting more.

We stopped at Leanne's next. The redheaded pit bull was Ryan's date.

Last it was Garret's date, Rihanna. She was as smart as they could come with long dark hair and specs resting on her nose. But tonight she exchanged the specs for contacts and I had to admit, I never noticed the color of Rihanna's eyes until tonight. They were a dark grey. Actually beautiful..

The girls chattered over each other. A headache formed in my temples before we even arrived at the function hall. It was a cool venue, perched right next to the lake, opposite side where I lived. There was a lonely dock and a boathouse. No doubt many couples were going to go to the dock house later.

Twinkling lights showed the way to the entrance. It was elegant.

Inside, dozens of round tables clustered around a buffet and a big dance floor awaited under flashing colored lights. We were in for a nice dinner first, and then the party would start. A night of celebration. We were finally graduating.

And I wasn't in the mood for any of it.

ALEX

I COULDN'T HELP but to think of Ethan the entire night. It was homecoming and I decided not to go. There were way too many reports via Clive that Necrocretors were acting up again and the insident at the rally proofed it.

I texted him but he just replied with a stupid emoji like always. We weren't really talking yet, but he didn't ignore my texts this time.

Soph was damn lucky. She had everything going for her. Everything.

I tried to read a book, but all the male characters appeared to be Ethan. Ethan with long hair, Ethan with dark hair, Ethan with no hair. I discarded the book with an exasperated sigh and watched TV.

A knock came from my door. "Enter," I called.

I waited. Nobody came in. With knitted eyebrows, I got up and went to my door. Another knock.

For some reason, I paused.

I closed my eyes and took a deep breath. *You are safe Alex, everyone who has kept you safe for 16 years is in this house.*

I opened the door and found Cynthia. Why didn't Mom call me down?

"Oh, hi." She had a huge smile on her face and her eyes looked extra big behind her goggle-like glasses.

I gestured for her to enter. "What are you doing here?"

"Oh, your mom invited me. Thought it was a good idea to come and be with you, what with missing homecoming and all."

My mom?

I froze. *I'm not wearing my glamour.*

Cynthia knew? How?

Cynthia started to laugh. "Yeah, I fucked up a bit there, didn't I?"

Fucked up? My mind reeled. Something didn't feel right with the smile that was lingering on Cynthia's smile. It felt wrong. My heart started to pound for no reason. I struggle to breathe.

My hand was still on the doorknob. I had to get out of here and I opened the door .

A mighty force hurled against my door. It slammed. There came the distinct sound of the deadbolt sliding into place. An invisible hand turned me around, pinned me to the door, and lifted me up. My feet dangled. A tight grip squeezed around my throat. An even tighter grip of horror seized my lungs.

"I knew I should've left it. But no, your father's stupid bald-headed freak had to go and kill him." Cynthia—sweet, friendly Cynthia—sounded downright sinister.

Not a peep came out of me. *Killed whom?*

"Your mother is one smart woman. Disguising you behind a pair of glasses. Something we have in common." She started to pace. "The glamour is the reason we couldn't find you as fast as I wanted, because it dampens your magic. The same way you couldn't track mine. I knew what Ethan was, but I had no idea where you fit into the story. I put two and two together when you destroyed the 'club.'" She finger quoted.

I tried to summon earth, to get the force around my neck to ease. Nothing happened.

Cynthia laughed again. "Oh, Alex. Still so much to learn." She took off her glasses. Cynthia disappeared. A woman in her mid-twenties, skinny with oily dark hair and two sizes too small clothes took her place. "I can feel it, you know. You begging for your power. It's not going to come, Alex. There is a glamour wielded around us. You see, this is where I differ from other Wielders. I was born the runt. A family of Spellbinders. David was like me, the only one who understood me. My family never did. He freed me."

Who the hell was David? I want to tell her that my mother was exceptional at spellbinding too, but I couldn't get this grip around my throat to loosen. I grunted with futile effort.

"What you took from me cannot be replaced. I thought you were dead." My body flew from the wall and crashed into my desk chair. The metal sprang to life and wrapped around my wrists. A piece of metal from my dresser slapped over my mouth.

I whimpered. I couldn't move.

She jumped on top of me and looked into my eyes.

How was I so blind to not see the metal Wielder behind the

glasses? But then again, she didn't see the earth Wielder behind Ducky's..

"I'm not Dave," she carried on. "I told him on numerous occasions that he should stop playing games. He always loved the fear, teasing it out of his victims. Me, I went straight for the kill." A sad smile darkened her face. She touched my cheek with a fingertip and I shuddered. "Not this time. You will pay for his death. My ship will finally come in, not that it matters anymore. You will pay for what your father has done. I want him to suffer the way I am suffering now."

I tried desperately to call my earth, to get this thing off my lips. I squirmed to get her off me, and she laughed. Why didn't my mother hear? I know it was glamour, but she was good at spells.

"Poor Alex," Cynthia said.

My door opened. I bucked and heaved to no avail. Cynthia looked behind her. My mother. Hope fluttered in my chest. Help was here!

But Mom looked in the direction of my window. Without paying me any mind, she closed the door and walked toward my bed, where a still figure lay. It was me, but it wasn't really me.

Cynthia jumped off me.

I jerked and wriggled to break free. Mom didn't look at me once. She didn't even turn her head. She was too busy trying to get the fake Alex's attention.

Cynthia went and settled on the bed, next to where I lay. Mom was oblivious to her presence. I screamed behind my metal gag.

"Alex," Mom said. To my surprise, fake-Alex woke up.

"Mom?" Cynthia spoke for me. Fake Alex even sounded like me. "Is everything okay?" She lay it on thick. I never took her for such a drama queen.

"I don't know." My mother sighed. "Something feels out of place."

"What do you mean?" Cynthia sounded more serious. Yeah, my mother wasn't that stupid. Bitch.

Mom went to my window. She looked out and closed the curtain. She smiled. "How are you doing?"

Cynthia shrugged; fake-Alex shrugged. She played me well. She must have been monitoring me closely for ages, learning my habits and gestures. A sick wave of fresh fear rolled over me.

"Okay." Mom sounded nervous. She knew something was wrong. Did she sense the glamour?

A huge smile spread on Cynthia's face as she watched Mom retreating toward the door.

Mom! I yelled inside my head. I grunted and jumped and kicked. Nothing got her attention.

She put her hand on the doorknob. I made as much noise as possible, begging a higher power to make her see me. To see past the glamour, to realize what the hell was happening under her own roof.

She looked up. Her eyes zeroed on mine. I froze. She was looking straight at me. Yet she still opened the door and walked out.

"Goodnight, sweetheart," she said cheerily.

"Night, Mom," Cynthia sang as the door shut.

She jumped off my bed with an evil laugh. Fake-Alex disappeared.

"See? I should've been a Spellbinder, not the runt." She leaned with her hand on back armrest of the chair. Our faces were inches apart.

"And tonight, everyone will see that. He is going to be so pleased with me." She smiled at a thought or a memory, whatever sick sadistic thought was playing through her mind.

"You won't be there to see it, but he is going to rule all the super naturals. Not just the Necrocretors."

She smiled again. "Hmph. Are you ready to confess your sins, Alex?"

My breath came fast through my nostrils. Confess what?

I was going to die. Right here under the roof of the people who had kept me safe my whole life.

34

I WAITED for it to end. I closed my eyes and thought happy thoughts. There was nothing I had to confess.

Cynthia didn't agree, though. But nothing she did to me would make me fear her more than she already had. "Confess!" she yelled. When I didn't answer, her arm swung back and struck me in the face hard. Pain radiated through my jaw.

I imagined the corpse Mom and Dad would find. It would be covered with bruises and blood. Beaten to a pulp. Unrecognizable. Like those many victims in the newspaper lately.

Hopelessness suffused through me. I had really believed that Mom saw me. I thought that she knew it wasn't really me on that bed. But I was alone.

"Wakey, wakey, sleepyhead. It's not time yet to say nighty night!"

The door crashed open.

"What the fuck?" Cynthia flew off me as a breaking spell poured from Mom's lips. Dad and Louis were already on top of Cynthia.

"Baby," Mom cried, her voice strained. She knelt in front of my chair. "Oh, please, God, help us."

Her lips moved fast. Sizzling heat wrapped around us. The metal plate vanished from my lips. The metal loosened from my wrists. Mom touched my cheek and spoke:

> *"Curare Nunc*
> *Autem poena inops dolor*
> *Maneant modo poena, et non*
> *Reverta."*

She chanted the words over and over. I'd heard them before. But where, I didn't know. Slowly the pain lessened. I didn't know what the words meant. Only the oldest and most powerful spells were still in the old language.

It was a healing spell.

I felt almost myself again. "Mom?" It barely came out. She embraced me.

Dad and Louis were overpowering Cynthia. How did she even get past them tonight without being noticed?

"I knew something was wrong tonight." Mom tucked my hair behind my ear. "Sorry baby."

I smiled tiredly. "You came. It's all that matters."

The entire house rumbled. The windows shattered. Mom threw her body over mine. An inexorable force pulled me toward the wall. Her lips moved fast; a spell rang in the air.

Dad, Louis, and Cynthia hurtled toward us.

Electricity sparked off the invisible shield that Mom was busy conjuring around us.

I caught something out of the corner of my eye. A ball of flames, fire so tall that it cloaked the walls, the floor, the ceiling. Flames I doubted Dad would be able to kill with his water.

Mom screamed an incantation.

Then I felt the blow.

The walls Mom's protection spell didn't reach exploded. They caved out. Light blasted through. Flames burst outside.

Mom's voice got softer and softer. She was drained. Her eyes drooped. The wall started be consumed. Heat pouring inside. Another explosion hit as her spell waned. Everything shook. My teeth clattered. My bones rattled. My ears rang.

The flames were dying. My curtains barely burned.

My head felt as if it was going to explode. Everything slowed down. Ashes drifted in slow-motion to the ground.

Mom was still, her eyes closed. Dad too. A couple of feet away was Louis, also knocked out or worse. Beside him lay Cynthia, whose eyes were very much open.

She got up and untied herself fast. The last thing I saw was her climbing out my window, one shoe missing, and disappearing into the night.

ETHAN

WE FINISHED DESSERT. The band struck up a tune. Everyone got up and moved to the dance floor. Soph pulled me by the arm to join her.

As I took that first step, I felt a jab of force. Alarmed, I glanced at Soph. She felt it too. Something in me took control. I dove, taking her with me.

The windows shattered as I covered her with my body. Agonized screams rent the air. The earth rumbled like an angry beast waking up.

Chairs toppled. Tables fell. Drums clattered. The PA system emitted a terrible whine of feedback that sliced through my eardrums. Tuxedoed and sequined prom-goers scrambled for cover.

Everything went eerily still.

I got up amid the chaos and lent Soph a hand.

A few girls close by sobbed in terror. One was pinned under a table, her date working to help her out from under it. Another had blood pouring down her face. Some students were badly hurt.

A few guys try to comfort them. Eighty percent of the rest ran around like jerks finding a way to save their own fucking necks.

"Calm down!" one of the chaperones yelled.

"Ethan," said Soph. "Did that come from Alex?"

"No, it felt like a natural disaster," I said.

Just then my phone rang. Ariel's name flashed on my screen. A horrible foreboding exploded in the pit of my stomach.

"Yes?" I answered fast, dragging Soph toward the wall.

"Ethan, you need to come." The connection screeched in my ears.

"What?" I yelled. "Come again?"

More static. I could barely hear Ariel's voice.

"Ariel!" I yelled.

The connection went dead.

I looked at my phone. My hand was shaking. Okay, so I was wrong. This did come from Alex.

I caught something in the corner of my eye. I looked out the window to the lake. Terror crashed through me.

Earthquakes always went hand in hand with one thing: water.

Loads and loads of water. A wall of it was marching our way.

My mind worked fast, on over time. There were way too many innocents here. There was no time to hide.

"Leanne!" I yelled.

"Not without Annie," she was smart, she knew exactly what

I was thinking. To block the water with her air. "Our only hope is the roof."

I nodded. I wouldn't be able to bend without Alex either.

"Run!" I yelled, pulling Sophie with me. We had to get onto the roof, but how?

"Get outside now," Ryan and Garret was already taking action and starting to help the girls who took off their shoes.

We were all running.

Outside their chances for survival was stronger then being trapped inside.

I decided on a spell. One that Mia taught me a long time ago. Although I weren't a spell binder, magic still ran through my veins and we could summon some encantations if needed.

I would need all of my friends for this.

"Ryan, Sophie, Leanne, I need your help." My hands were already up facing the lake. I knew that wave was out there, if not already summoned, it will be shortly.

"Garret, get the others on the roof or trees, high up."

"What about you?"

"We will be fine."

Leanne took my left and Soph my right, Ryan was next to her.

"What is the plan, Etan. We are not witches."

"We are they fucking Guardians. It will work. Just have faith."

"Blocking spell". I started to recite the words, over and over.

"You got to be shitting me," Soph said through clench teeth.

I ignored it and yelled the words harder. Now was not the time for her to argue, we all need to concentrate.

Ryan was starting to say the words next to me, and so were Leanne.

By the fourth verse Soph finally said it as well.

The wave groaned as it started to form and porch lights by

the boat house were the first to drown. It was crashing over the dock, running up towards us, just tons and tons of water. Behind it, another humungous wave.

We were yelling the words now.

Seeing the wave made my mind spun like crazy, desperately rolling over and discarding plan after plan to get out of this alive. All I needed to do was to buy time for the others to reach the roof or the big oak trees that grew everywhere around the hall. For us, without our Wielders, we didn't have a chance. And there wasn't nearly enough time to get to a tree.

"Sorry dude," Ryan was the first to break, then Leanne was not standing beside me anymore.

"Etan," Soph yelled.

The wave was coming and it wasn't going to stop.

I let down my hands and hugged her body tight waiting for the wave.

Water droplets splatted on my face. I hugged Soph tighter, bracing myself, waiting for gallons of water to take us. Nothing happened.

My arms were still wrapped around Soph. We weren't wet.

Water washed past us, over our heads, taking chairs and tables toward the exit. Lights flickered weakly. Water groaned. Abruptly it was pitch dark.

I heard a flick. Soph lit her lighter. It shone brightly. She looked as perplexed as I felt. The spell, it worked.

A chuckle escaped my lips.

"It worked." Soph said as a smile tugged at the corner of her lips.

"It had to." .

Then the wall of water rippled. It was about to break.

"We need to get out of here," Soph said.

"How?" If I knew how, I would. But she was right. If the water crashed through this protective wall, we'd drown.

Water dripped through the invisible barrier. It wasn't strong. Soph grabbed me again and kissed me. *Seriously, woman?*

"I love you," she breathed against my face.

But all I wanted to be with was Alex.

I held her tight and shut my eyes as the whole opened. Waiting for the impact.

No impact came. Footsteps tapped nearby. Someone grunted. I opened my eyes and saw Ryan with his fire in his palms. Flung over his shoulder was a body. He was dry, walking as if the building wasn't flooded. "A little help please?"

I felt a tinge of anger, because he left like a coward, but

I rushed forward and grabbed the body—Garret.

Blood pumped from a cut above Ryan's eye and soaked his white shirt a garish crimson.

"I told you it would work." I sounded angry.

"It didn't work." He grunted back.

Then behind Ryan, Leanne appeared, her hands twirling, wielding air. How?

"Move your ass!" Annie's voice came from way at the back.. What was she doing here? How the fuck did she get here so fast?

"Annie, I don't know how you know, but fuck am I glad to see you."

"Yeah, yeah, you can thank me later."

"What is the deal with Garret." I asked as I put him on the ground. Then an awful thought hit me like that tidal wave was supposed to. "They didn't make it, did they?"

"I got them to safety, but they all got a lot of questions," Annie said while feeding air to Leanne.

A heavy weight expelled from my shoulders. It was fine, we could deal with the concequences. At least they are alive. It was all that mattered. "Head quarters can fix that."

"I found Garret closeby," Annie said. And Ryan just jumped in our bubble before the water struck."

Soph's curls were a mess, her shoes gone. My jacket was shredded; I shrugged out of it.

Garret started to come to as Leanne and Annie closed the underwater tunnel, this bubble they wielded.

"Oh, shit," Soph said. "Do something before he sees!"

He was normal. He couldn't know about our powers. He wouldn't understand. Ryan kicked Garret as hard as he could. He passed out.

I didn't know how long Leanne and Annie could keep it up. The water still roared above our heads. I had no idea whether we'd get out of this alive.

To make matters worse, Alex was in danger. She wouldn't wield her element like that if danger wasn't near. Why did Ariel call me? I had to get out of here. Fast.

SOME TIME LATER, a groan came from the other side of the bubble, from the water. I never feared the water element until tonight.

"Leanne, we have to get out of here." Annie's hands were moving in a circular motion so rapid, they were a blur.

Leanne nodded and started to push against the water with her air. It made a slight dent. She blew her hair out of eyes, lifted the damp hem of her dress, and tied it into a big knot. Resituated, she solidified her stance and pushed again. I could tell she was using all her strength.

My heart felt like it was going to explode from its panicked tempo.

She was forming another tunnel. One that hopefully led out of here. Annie nudged at me to go first.

I didn't hesitate. I grabbed Garret, who was still stone-cold, and flung him over my shoulder. I strode into the tunnel behind Leanne.

ALEX

I woke up with wind caressing my face. The last thing I remembered was getting attacked by someone who used my element against me. I never even knew that was possible. It knocked me out with something summoned from deep down.

I was outside, in the bitingly cold air. Around my waist, my element swirled like snakes. The roots' grip was tight. Moss crept along my arms and tickled my neck.

Beneath my feet, a giant beanstalk trailed from my bedroom, way, way below where I dangled in the air.

Then I fell.

The roots were still cinched around my waist. It didn't let me go or lose strength.

I flung out my hand and tried to wield my own element. Anything that could save me from this fall. But I was cut off completely.

The wind tore at me, ripping the breath from my lungs. The earth inched nearer to the half-moon shapes of my eyes. They stung. I hurtled downward and waited for the death-delivering impact with the ground.

I never felt so weak, so helpless.

Then it stopped abruptly. A terrible force yanked me backward, threatening to break me in half. My heart thundered. I was merely a handbreadth from the ground, hovering in the air.

At once, I got launched into the heavens again. Nausea twisted my gut.

What was this and why was it toying with me?

I remembered what Cynthia said: David liked to toy with

his prey, but she killed hers immediately. She could've killed me if she wanted to.

As I zoomed through the sky, I thought about geeky Cynthia, my first-ever friend outside my family. Was there a part of her that could've truly been my friend?

No, she tried to kill you, stupid.

I came to an abrupt midair halt. Another stab of pain ran through me. Tears welled up in my eyes from the agony. I didn't know how long I could hold on.

"Just say the word Alex. And it's all over."

I gathered the little strength I had left. "You won't get my ability, ever." I yelled as hard as I could.

The force let me fall again.. Sooner or later, I wasn't going to stop. I was going to be torn into pieces and die.

ETHAN

Leanne got us out of the building, her tunnel was strong, and we actually walked on water for a bit, as it lead to one of the big oaks that grew close to the hallway.

I climbed into the tree, a few branches higher while Garret was still flung over my shoulder. Damn he was heavy.

When I was a few branches up, I put him down and went back down to lend a hand to Soph who was climbing out next and Ryan.

Annie and Leanne made a jump for the tree and our bubble just disappeared with the water flowing with a force past us.

Was it going to stop.

Plenty of screams for help came from nearby trees. There were even shadowy figures on the roof top. It was hard to make out in this darkness how many, but some made it to the roof.

"Etan," Annie said. "You sure Head Quarters would deal

with what they saw," she nod toward the others that was in the trees and on the roof.

"They will," I put my hand on her shoulder. "You did great tonight, Annie. If you didn't show tonight, who knows where we would've been."

A small, unsure smile played on her lips.

I looked at the lake. Its water wasn't descending. I didn't even fathom that the lake held so much water to begin with.

"You know what to do?" Annie stood right behind Leanne.

"We aren't strong enough!"

"With that attitude, we won't be," she sang.

My mother was an air Bender, just like Leanne. But I never saw her in full form with her Wielder.

Garret still laid limply over the branch. He'd wake with the biggest headache, but that was the least of my concerns. It was the questions he'd no doubt have.

Annie spun her arms in large circles faster and faster. The wind grew stronger and stronger as Annie wielded her element powerfully.

"Everyone hold on, strong wind is coming." Ryan yelled to the others so that they at least took caution.

Soph lay down on Garret to keep him from falling and Ryan and I held on to Annie and Leanne.

A grunt left Annie's mouth. "Leanne."

"Not yet," Leanne said.

More wind came and we clung to the tree harder. Soph and Ryan took the lead and used all their strength to not get blown out of the tree and into the inky depths of water. We all did.

What the hell was Leanne waiting for?

"Leanne!" Annie yelled again.

Leanne lifted her hands in complicated, forceful movement. She started to blow as hard as she could. Like she was showing the water to stop, blowing it back to calmness. Back to its home.

I struggled to keep my eyes open..

She needed more power from Annie, a strong dose of air. The water levels lowered.

A strong current poured from Annie and Leanne, pushing the water back to the lake. I watched in awe while holding as tightly as I could on to Annie.. Leanne bent the water with the mere gesture of blowing with her mouth.

Ten minutes later, the water receded to ankle height. Leanne stopped and almost fell..

Ryan was holding her tightly. "I got you," he said and started pulling her up the same time I pulled up Annie.

I couldn't help but hugging her. She was after all the hero of tonight, her and her kick ass bender.

I could feel her legs giving in, and her body going limp. When I broke the hug, her eyes lolled in their sockets.

Ryan put Leanne on one of the branches, she too was stone cold.

"What now," Soph crouched next to Anne as I lay her down on to a branch too. We can't just leave them here." I jumped down the tree. My shoes were covered in water.

"Drop her Ryan," I said and he let go of Leanne. I caught her and lay her gently near the tree. Annie was next and then Soph. Garret was last and Ryan took the jump himself.

"I have to go, But you stay with them, Soph. If danger comes, use your element. There is no time trying to hide it now. I have to go to the Buchman plantation."

"Are you insane?" She was beyond herself.

"I have no choice. Phone Sam. Phone everyone that can help. And try to help as many of the others you can.. They're probably terrified..."

"Yes, of us." She sounded frantic.

"I don't have time to argue with you," I yelled. "Just do as I say."

Her lips thinned. Whether it was because I was going to Alex or whether she thought I was insane, I didn't really care at the moment.

I looked at Ryan. "You coming or staying?"

He looked agitated. "You know I'm in. Whatever happens, Ethan. I'll back you up."

Gratitude welled up in my chest. "Okay."

Everything around us was either askew or fucked up. The number one question that I had to get an answer to was how the hell we were going to get to the plantation.

35

ETHAN

THE ONCE-ROMANTIC BOAT dock was in shambles. Ryan and I ran out onto it, arms outstretched for balance. Several boats had overturned or were flooded. We hopped in to two promising ones—a sloop, but its mast was shattered and I couldn't adjust the main sail (and didn't really know how anyway), and a pontoon that was unharmed, but the engine locked and the keys nowhere on board.

Boat after boat had its problems. Hope was starting to disappear.

"Etan," Ryan yelled from up ahead.

At the end of the dock, he found a pair of Jet Skis in decent condition.

I hopped out of the one boat on to the next and onto the next one again until I reached Ryan.

It looked like they had been swept out of the boat house. We had to hotwire the engine—a handy but shady skill of Ryan's—and soon we were zipping along the water toward the plantation.

The water wasn't very deep. It roared as it flooded back into the lake. How the hell the current was still so strong after Annie and Leanne were knocked out... well, it showed how powerful those two were if they put their minds to it.

A frigid breeze slowed us down. I tried to block it, but it was no use. So I endured the angry wind and pushed forward.

I was glad when we saw the houses that bordered the shore were intact. I didn't want to know what destruction the mini-tsunami had wreaked on the environs.

The Buchman plantation was just a few miles up.

No doubts that the Necrocretors was behind this. I told Dad that I didn't want to go tonight. Not what happened at the rally.

The only mind easing thought I had was that Frederick was a water wielder, he would have protected his family.

He might have just had a ball.

I yanked hard on the Jet Ski, forcing it to leap out of the water. It skidded on wet grass and came to a halt. Ryan was a few seconds behind me.

The scent of crushed vegetation filled my senses, along with the vaguely dirty smell of lake water.

I dropped the Jet Ski and ran toward the plantation, taking a shortcut between the houses. Everything looked different at night.

A metallic click preceded the flick of a Zippo and a faint whiff of naphtha. Ryan manipulated his fire to light our path.

Everything around us was destroyed. People climbing down from rooftops. Debris and broken furniture lay scattered over the ground. Trees lay their sides, their suffering twinging my heartstrings. The only ones that made it were the gigantic oaks.

We didn't falter. I leaped over a few obstacles in the road, running as fast as I could to the plantation. It was a good two-to-three-mile run. The damage lessened as the distance melted underfoot.

Alex just had to be fine.

For some reason, I couldn't get that afternoon she'd over-tapped her power to wield earth out of my head. This quake had been stronger. Worry roiled in the pit of my stomach.

I started to feel a strong source. She was alive, at least; it was her I was feeling.

Everywhere my feet touched the ground, grass sprouted. I felt it before I lifted each foot to take the next step. This was the kind of bending I hadn't attempted since I was a kid. I was getting closer.

Alex was probably scared out of her mind. How the heck was Clive going to deal with this?

I didn't have to look behind me to know that Ryan was still there. I could hear him, panting, no, gasping as I touched things along the way. Plants that had been uprooted and knocked over. As I touched them they righted themselves and revived. Flowers bloomed in full glory. This was my element, what I couldn't live without. This power.

I finally had it back.

The streetlights were all dark. Ryan expanded his fire.

"Make sure nobody sees it," I said over my shoulder.

"There's is nobody here," he said in that *chill, dude* tone of his.

I halted. High, vine-covered walls blocked our way. The plantation. It was totally dark.

We struggled to find the entrance. It was blanketed with green leaves, moss, and roots. We shrugged and climbed the wall. On the other side, a huge structure had replaced the elegant castle. It was just a hulking mass covered with plants and green leaves. A cave of earth.

"What the fuck?" Ryan regarded the structure with huge, round eyes.

We walk with caution toward it, past an old fountain with a

huge tree growing from it. It was the same courtyard as always. It was the same elegant fountain. Destroyed. The garden was gone, the garages, the cars... That cave-like bulk was their house, swallowed by the earth element.

I ran up where I knew the stairs were. The essence of the earth tingled in my hands. The hairs on my arms raised. This was formidable wielding. *Alex, what the hell happened?*

We couldn't get in. Roots completely blocked the doorways. Ryan used his fire to burn them out of the way. I bent every weed I could. At last we managed to find a hole and slip through. Sweat beaded our brows from exertion and the heat of the flames. Already the hole was closing fast with new plants.

I felt like we'd stepped into the Amazon. Trees and plants grew thickly in the foyer. Flowers as big as my face greeted me. Vines covered every inch of wall. As we moved forward, I lost my bearings; I didn't know if we were in the kitchen or the living room. I had only ever been here in my dreams.

"What is that?" Ryan asked, pointing.

Five large cocoons were suspended from the ceiling. They were big. Human-sized. They looked straight out of the movie *Aliens.* As if they had been spun by impossibly huge spiders. Goo dripped from the bottoms onto the fern-carpeted floor.

"What *is* that?" I echoed.

We moved closer, with caution. "Keep your eyes open. We need to find Meredith, Frederick, anyone." I spoke without taking my eyes off those cocoons. "And stay away from those."

I wanted to yell, but at the same time, I didn't want to give our position away if this was the work of Necrocretors.

Where the hell were her parents and Louis?

Something swished above us. One of the cocoons was rocking back and forth. Ryan and I scrambled back. Disgust washed over me. The smell was like something acidic, something bad. Something plunked to our feet.

"Help," a male voice croaked. On the ground was a blob of goo... that covered a person. "Ethan," said the goo-covered person.

Peering at it, I said, "Louis?"

"Alex! She's outside. Best go to her window."

Understanding trickled over me. Those cocoons contained people. Ariel, Frederick, Meredith, and...

Louis struggled to free himself. "Ryan, stay and help me get them out before it's too late." I wondered how he knew Ryan's name.

Ryan obliged, kneeling beside him to help pull away the stringy stuff. Louis was as big as an ox; nobody would mess with him. Not even plants that swallowed people.

"Ethan, go to Alex. But be careful. We don't know how many more Necrocretors are on their way."

"Necrocretors are here? Offcourse they are." Urgency filled me. I ran toward the stairs to get to Alex. Why did Alex trap her parents with vines? Was she trying to save them and just lose control?

The stairs were half-destroyed; I bent vines where I had to. The ridiculous image of the *Batman* villain Poison Ivy's lair popped into my head. I had to tamp down the urge to giggle nervously. I had to jump the last few steps onto the second-floor landing, as there was a huge fucking hole. I misjudged and barely caught the other side.

Dangling from the landing, I cleared my mind and tried to preserve my strength. *Bend earth, Ethan.* It was strange how that voice sounded like my mother's. As if she was guiding me from the grave.

I let go with one hand and pointed it toward a root that lay dormant on the floor like a lazy anaconda. It started to move. I concentrate harder, pulling from Alex's nearby energy. Why was this so hard? Because Alex lost it again. She couldn't control this. Was it too much for both of us?

I tried again. It took all my willpower. My strength waned. The root barely moved. I wasn't going to be able to hold on much longer.

My fingers strained and popped. I stopped bending and tried to catch the beam with my other hand. It was just out of my reach. *C'mon, Ethan.* One finger slipped off the ledge. Then another. I was holding on with three.

I pictured in slow motion how I'd fall and shatter every bone in my body.

An arm reached out and grabbed me just as my fingers gave way.

I saw the silhouette of a male. "Dad?" I said. "How the hell?"

"Let's get you up and I'll tell you how the hell." He struggled to haul me up.

"C'mon, put some muscle in it, old man."

He grinned; his teeth glowed like Chiclets in the darkness. "Now is not the time to tease me about my age, son."

He grunted and pulled. I slowly rose. When my shoulders reached the ledge, I grabbed on and helped to pull myself over the ledge. We collapsed in a sweaty tangle of limbs onto what was left of the landing. It was covered with thick leaves and greenery. Nothing looked familiar in the flame that sparked in his palm.

"How did you get here, Dad?" I asked. I didn't dare ask if our house had survived the lake.

"I felt Meredith wielding her fire. It. was intense. I dropped everything and was headed here, when the earthquake hit. It was chaos. Panic kicked in among our neighbors as the lake rocked and a huge wave formed. I knew it was moving toward you guys and did whatever I could to get to you, son."

"Wait, what?"

He gave me a one-armed hug. "I know at times you've felt like I didn't have your back. But I found Sophie, Sam, Annie, and Leanne. They told me you were here."

I marveled. "Dad, how fast did you get here?"

My father looked at me. And then he started to laugh. I'd never heard him laugh like that before. It sounded... wrong.

Then I realized...

This wasn't my father.

I dove out of the way the moment a fireball left the impostor's hand. I skidded around the corner, my mind spinning to understand this latest development. The only thing I could think of was that I was facing a Changeling.

Changelings were a sort of shifter. Contrary to popular belief, they were not just fairy babies swapped for normal ones. They were beings who could change into any human form—but not into animals. Changelings were hideous in their natural form. Their true appearance was always that of a person whose face had been devoured by wolves. It was the price they paid to become anyone.

They usually took on the recent memories of the person they morphed into. My real dad was worried, then. Where the hell was my father?

Not now, I told myself sternly. *Your number one concern should be Alex. Dad will be fine.*

I hated Necrocretors. And I hated shifters. Well, actually, shifters were fucking cool, especially Ariel. But I hated these sort of shifters, the rogue ones.

I tried to summon the earth. It was too powerful for me to grasp. Some roots slithered halfheartedly as they tried to connect to my will. But that was all.

The Changeling came closer. I covered myself with the

earth. Plants, moss, flowers, they all started to cloak me from this thing that pretended to be my dad.

He was right in front of me, casting his hungry gaze about. As long as he was in my father's form, he would be able to throw fire.

He passed. Time to strike.

I jumped out of my hiding spot, clutching a long, thin, bendable vine. I landed on his back. I twisted the vine around his neck and started to pull.

I fought the terrible sense of wrongness that I was choking my own dad.

He slumped backward into the plants that covered the walls, trying to shake me loose or maybe pierce me with a thorn. But I held tight and every sharp thorn shrank away.

He gurgled. His face flickered. It was alternating between many faces really fast. All the forms he ever took in his life. It was a shifter, all right. Before he died, he morphed into his true form.

I let go of the vine. His corpse fell like a sack of flour on the floor. Ugly fucker. I kicked him once for good measure.

I ran toward the roof. I had to find Alex.

36

ETHAN

I FOUND ALEX'S ROOM. The place where I practically lived every night.

The door was covered with vines. Although I couldn't break through them, I could guide them to move so that I could get through the door.

Inside, her room looked like a rain forest. A gaping fissure had replaced her bedroom window. I wasn't alone; a man stood nearby, partially concealed by trees.

With weary steps, I crept toward the intruder. A man. He was big, with dark, oily hair and hands that ended in giant beanstalks. He was waving these wildly; the beanstalks snaked outside and did his bidding with violent speed.

Faint screams set off alarm bells in my soul. Alex.

Where did they come from? It sounded like she was in the sky but rapidly approaching. But that made no sense. Did it?

I coaxed leaves and vines to conceal me. Unseen, I reached the crack in her wall. I could finally see what was happening outside.

Alex was falling fast. Attached to those giant beanstalk arms. The ones attached to the grim puppet master in the room with me.

My heart dropped to my stomach. No way was I going to reach her. I didn't want to look, to know that I had failed her. I tried to bend more earth than I already had, but something blocked us and I was unable to do anything more than the tiny coaxing I had done so far.

But wait. She stopped just inches from the ground. *Not dead!* Anguished screams tore from her lips. She grunted out in pain. How could she not be dead, and then I saw how close it stopped from the ground.

The guy threw his head back and laughed. Why were all Necrocretors so crazy?

"It can all stop, Alex. Just say the words. I give you my powers, then I can consume your heart and gain all your powers. Your parents will get a swift execution, you have my word."

"What the fuck," I whispered.

"Never," Alex cried. She was tired, barely hanging on.

The guy grunted.

A second later, the giant hand that held her flicked. Her body flung back into the sky as if attached to a cruel giant's bull-whip. Screaming, she ascended. I winced, realizing her eardrums were in danger of popping at those speeds.

My gaze shifted to her attacker. He was still laughing, enjoying every second of his sadistic game. He was the one controlling this.

He was an earth Wielder. It was impossible, yet there he stood, wielding earth. He said he need her ability, eat her heart... I couldn't think further just imagining it.

Still, he was twenty times stronger then the two of us.

My mind tried to make sense of what he said. Taking powers. At once, everything made sense. Why all the other earth Wielders were hunted like animals. *He* was the reason they all died. He somehow usurped all the earth's power.

The giant beanstalk descended again. I didn't think anymore and I didn't care if we were strong enough or notI just ran. I jumped through the hole in the wall and grabbed the giant beanstalk.

"What have we here?" the man said, cackling theatrically. Nothing escaped him. "Is that your Bender?"

He shook the beanstalk and I almost fell off, but I clung tight. The vines that enfolded around Alex body loosened and cinched tightly around my leg.

The beanstalk shook again. My teeth rattled and the world turned upside down. The psychopath was reeling me in. Soon I was inches from his face. Blood rushed to the top of my head.

"If it isn't Ethan Sutcliff. Come to save the day, are we?" he mocked me.

"Who are you?" I demanded.

He laughed.

"Who are you?" I yelled.

He frowned as if he didn't expect my ferocity. "I would be more careful with my tone, Mr. Sutcliff."

Rage burned hot in my chest. "I'm not afraid of you."

"You should be. Your future is literally hanging from a branch. It only obeys me now. One tiny squeeze..." He squeezed his fist and Alex screamed. He laughed. "I'm sure you get what I'm saying. You have nothing to bargain with."

My fingers tingled. Heck, my entire body started to vibrate. A scream ripped from my mouth.

"What are you trying to do?" he said with mock concern.

I ignored him and concentrated hard on the giant root right behind him. Another grunt left me. Something wet—blood— dripped from my nose.

"What the...?" The root folded around him and knocked him to the ground. He was unconscious.

The grip around me immediately loosened. I grabbed another branch to avoid falling on my ass.

Did I just make that happen?

I concentrated on my earth element. Now that the psychopath was out, it was easy to bend earth to my will.

I got to Alex just as the grip around her went lax. I grabbed her arm just in time. Vines and roots formed a hammock behind her and lowered her gently to the ground.

A minute ago, they wanted to squeeze the life out of her; now they were gentle.

I knelt beside her and touched her face. Her eyes were closed, but she was still breathing. I lay my hand on her and started chanting the words her mother had taught me.

She needed healing. I didn't care this time how bad the dreams would be. She needed to be okay.

ALEX

I dreamed that Ethan came to my rescue. I must have been close to death, as I knew they'd already taken care of him.

Victor, the psychopath that wanted my earth, told me that.

Who knew that one of the earth Wielder had found a way to cheat Mother Nature and Father Time? He was easily pushing four hundredyears, yet he looked like a man in his mid-thirties.

My body was breaking. The abrupt stops, yanks, tugs. The incessant whiplash combined with sheer, unadulterated terror. My element refused to heed my call. I wasn't strong enough to match this guy.

Something jabbed my face. What now? More jabs. And

then a voice called my name. It sounded like Ethan. Was I dreaming... or dead?

"Alex, c'mon, open your eyes," he said. I opened my eyes. I felt so tired. I just wanted to sleep.

Then it hit me. I didn't feel pain anymore.

"That's it," he encouraged. "Wake up. I can't do this alone."

"Do what alone?" At once the entire evening replayed in my mind.

Cynthia who wasn't Cynthia but another woman hiding like me behind a pair of glasses. She almost killed me.

And Victor.

I came wide awake with a great, shuddering gasp. Ethan was right beside me, cradling my head in his lap. "You came!" I wanted to kiss him.

"You know I always will." He sounded sincere.

Just then, something clasped my foot and yanked me hard. "Not again."

Ethan roared. A root sprouted from nowhere.

Ethan was bending.

I concentrated on wielding him earth. The two roots fought like two eagles in the air. Snapping at one another. I was caught in the middle. I ducked one of them that zoomed fast past me, and again as it retreated. I had to get away from it.

The grip around my foot let go. I tumbled toward the ground. I grabbed the nearest thing that zoomed past, a root, and slowed my terrible fall. I rolled a few times, got up, and made my way to where Ethan had been.

He was gone.

I heard his voice from my bedroom. Victor's too. They were battling in close quarters. I scrambled up the vines and crawled inside.

Ethan had somehow shielded himself from Victor's force. Victor's face was contorted with pure hatred.

And then I realized it: Ethan wasn't shielding himself; he was bending Victor's earth. How was that possible?

Understanding clicked. Jeff had two Wielders, the only Bender in history with that quirk.

Could it have been passed down. His only son just bend two wielders Earth.

Mine and Victor's. The only problem was that Victor wasn't in awe the way I am. Still, Ethan was barely trained and couldn't match Victor's power. I needed to find a way to fortify him.

I swung from trunks to root to vine like a monkey to get to his side. I darted past Victor and kicked him as hard as I could. Louis at least taught me everything I know about close combat.

He smashed against the wall.

I landed feet from Ethan. He stared at me. "What?" I shrugged. "I've got moves too."

The corner of his lips curved. Together we watched Victor stagger to his feet. "Doesn't this guy ever die?" Ethan grabbed my hand and ran toward where the door used to be. We crashed through a wall and fell a few feet. I wielded and he bent; branches and roots caught us before we hit the floor.

I was hopelessly turned around and couldn't make out shit. What part of the house was this? We hid, but some of the plants start to snapping at us like yap-yap dogs, giving away our location.

Ethan fled, my arm still gripped in his hand. "Move, Alex," he yelled.

He was still wearing his tux or part of it. His jacket and tie was gone. This was still homecoming night. The absurdity of it all struck me and distracted me long enough that I didn't see the vine reaching for my ankle until it was too late. "Ethan!" It snatched me up.

Ethan grabbed hold of the vine. It threw us both in the

opposite direction. We thudded against the wall. Excruciating pain radiated through me. I wanted to lose consciousness, but I held on.

Victor attacked Ethan by trying to suffocate him with the veins that was wrapped tightly around Ethan's body. He'd figured out what Ethan could do. Having a Bender again wasn't on his agenda.

I tried to push myself up, but my leg... I gasped, seeing it for the first time. A root stuck into one side of my calf and out the other side. It went straight through muscle. It hurt like a bitch. Somehow the sight of it made the pain rear its head.

Precious seconds lost, I sought Ethan. He was stone-cold. I willed him to open his eyes. *He can't die!*

I tried to wield my element, but nothing came.

Ethan opened his eyes just as Victor was going in for the kill shot. He bent Victor's earth.

Both used all the strength they had. Ethan appeared to be a worthy match.

The vines ease and Ethan freed himself.

Although Ethan was wily and fast, Victor was more experienced. He knocked Ethan on the head and smashed him into the wall repeatedly.

"C'mon, Alex," I groaned, pulling at the root lodged in my calf. Sharp pain knifed me, but I kept struggling.

My wielding power didn't come close to Victor's, but I couldn't let Ethan die. I needed him more than he needed me. I finally pulled the bloody thing out of my leg with a silent scream. It hurt like nothing I'd ever experienced.

With shaking hands, I shredded my shirt and tied a makeshift tourniquet above the knee just like mom had taught me.With other pieces of my shirt I tied a tight bandage over the double holes in my calf.

When flow of blood slowed, I grabbed the vines to pull

myself up and, staying concealed, hobbled over to Ethan. Every step was pure agony on my pierced muscle.

"Oh, Alex," Victor sang, abandoning Ethan where he lay knocked out. "Come out, come out, wherever you are."

Always playing games. I hate games.

I ducked as a vine whipped past me. He knew exactly where I was. The vine missed me by inches. I wasn't so lucky with the second one. It slammed into me and I came crashing against the far wall. Immediately it threw me against the same wall where Ethan lay.

Suddenly fire burst right in front of me. Victor screamed, enraged. He cussed slightly but regain his perky self fast."Mer, is that you?" His mocking scream devolved into a chilling, amused laughter. "I should've known that situating your cocoon so close to your true love would get you out of that sticky situation."

No one replied.

I crawled toward Ethan. He leaned against the wall. He looked on the verge of death. "No, no, no, no." I said. "Don't you dare." I slapped him on his cheek. His eyes barely opened.

"Ethan Sutcliff, you are not going to die. Just..."

My mother screamed. Startled, I looked up and saw her through the thick vegetation. Victor was squeezing a branch around her. Blood trickled out of her mouth.

"No!" I screamed, tears in my eyes.

Ethan was half dead, Mom was dying, and I couldn't protect any of them.

I didn't know why I did what I did next. But everything seemed as if it was coming to an end. Nothing mattered anymore.

I pressed my lips on Ethan's and kissed him like I'd never kissed him before.

37

ETHAN'S LIPS MOVED. It was a wince at first, and I kissed him more gently. Then he started kissing me back. He was waking up, perhaps realizing this wasn't one of our dreams. This was real. I was sitting on his lap kissing him.

Breaking the law. Dooming us both.

His kiss became greedy as if he was gaining energy from me, and I from him. It wasn't like everyone warned us. This... this was different.

His hands cupped my face and the back of my head. He pulled me tighter against him.

Mom's screams died out. Victor's laughter faded. It was just the two of us. Kissing.

I felt so selfish, yet so selfless at the same time. I felt like a failure and yet a part of me felt as if I was succeeding. Guilty yet free.

I wanted more.

The power-up came first. I felt like a succubus. Ethan didn't stop either. I couldn't. I wanted more and then somehow it stopped. It wasn't me and it didn't feel like him. Something pulled us apart. Something that couldn't be seen. Power, and loads of it.

My back arched. Ethan's hands caught me so I didn't fall. Blinding, brilliant light poured out of me. It was too bright. I tried to close my eyes but couldn't. My eyes stung.

This, this was the reason our love was forbidden.

I screamed. Power seared through my being. Power that wanted to break me into a zillion pieces. Ethan was the only thing keeping me together. Keeping me from shattering.

He screamed too. Power coursed through both of us. When it finally died, the dark returned. We were both spent.

I couldn't keep my eyes open. Ethan's were already closed. I connected hard with his body as I fell over. It was time to die.

Everything went black.

ETHAN

I opened my eyes and found myself surrounded by four clean walls. Silence reigned the semidarkness, with only a soft beep mimicking my heartbeat. I was wearing a hospital gown. Small, round, gel pads were attached to my chest. Dad was seated in a chair near my bed. We were in the hospital.

My throat was dry. I felt like I'd been run over by a truck. Twice.

The old man woke up, perhaps because of the change in my heart rate. "Ethan!" He jumped up and came to the bed. "Son." His voice broke as he gently ruffled my messy hair. He rested his forehead against mine. He took a shuddering breath. For some reason this annoyed me like hell.

Everything came back to me at once. I sat up and winced. My ribs, my chest, every single bone in my body. The monitor chirped incessantly.

"Son, calm down." He rested a hand on my shoulder. "You're safe."

"Where is Alex, Dad?"

He didn't respond.

"Where is Alex?" I exclaimed.

"She's fine," he said hurriedly. "Don't worry. You just need some rest."

"What are you not telling me?" I insisted. "You paused. Is she hurt?"

"Sorry, I didn't mean to worry you. You just need to rest. We can worry about the rest when you are better."

"Tell me, Dad," I demanded. "Now."

"Ethan..." He stroked his head as tears welled up in his eyes. If Alex was fine, why was he so upset? Then it hit me. "It's Meredith," I breathed.

I remembered what happened. I was still half-conscious, still clinging to wakefulness, waiting for Alex to do her thing. Her mother was screaming. That shrill scream would haunt my dreams for a long time to come.

"Is it Meredith, Dad?"

He nodded. "She's in a coma, on ventilators. She isn't going to make it. Frederick even asked me to try healing her. I can't reach her. No one can."

Her loss hurt more than I thought it would.

"How is Alex?" I had to know.

"Woke up a few hours after the ordeal. When she saw you... I've never seen anyone so traumatized. She blames herself for what happened. Said this was the punishment for stepping over the line."

I frowned, confused. "Dad, nothing happened.."

I didn't tell him about the kiss, scared they would yanked us apart again. Even as she leached my strength, she returned fresh energy to me. A loop, filling one another with strength, creating more energy for us both to revive. It was nothing like he'd warned me. I wasn't sucked dry.

"Ethan, you destroyed the plantation."

My mouth hung open. "What?"

"The last thing I remember was darkness. Getting sucked up in a cocoon. Louis cut me out. Meredith lay next to me, covered in goo. I heard Victor hurling you from wall to wall upstairs, but I couldn't get to you. That was when Meredith heard Alex cry out in pain."

His eyes shone. "The next thing I saw Meredith wasn't next to me anymore. God, she loved her daughter."

I absorbed this in reverent silence.

"I followed her upstairs, too weak to do anything but watch. She connected hard with Victor. She formed a fireball, but then Victor grabbed her. He was killing her, killing everything. It got so cold. So dark. The air, it got thin and unbreathable."

I nodded. I'd felt that moment too, from deep within my stupor. The moment I knew we were all going to die.

"A bright light poured out of Alex. A beacon." The edges of his lips curved up. "Light," he said. "It's the key to destroy darkness. The only problem was that not a lot of people can sustain light like that." He sighed. "It must have destroyed Victor.." His face was grim. "It had to."

"Wait you didn't find a body."

He didn't answer my question just kept telling me what happened. "Everything shattered—the walls, the forest inside, everything just collapsed, that is how I know that Victor perished. The plantation will never be resurrected."

"You and Louis found Meredith."

My father nodded. " We dragged you three out of the rubble. We tried everything. Maybe the only time Frederick and I ever been a hundred percent united. Louis says you helped

Alex somehow. That's why you were out for two weeks, and she was up and running after a few hours."

"Two weeks." I blinked.

He smiled. "Soph is good for you, Ethan. Stick with her."

I groaned. "Dad, don't."

"Alex will kill you. Please."

I shut my eyes. He knew exactly what had happened. How we managed to shine that impossible light. It wasn't just Alex's light. It the two of us combined. The way we felt when we were together. *How can something feel so right yet be so wrong?*

ALEX

Ethan was finally awake.

Two weeks. He was out for two weeks.

This, this was why we weren't supposed to be together. I wasn't good for him. I would end up killing him.

Mom languished. Jeff had tried to heal her four times now. Nothing. Nothing happened.

Even Dad supported Jeff's healing. He would do anything to get Mom back. So would I.

First Fibbs and now mom. I cannot lose Ethan too.

I had no choice but to go and visit himtoday. Jeff said he was asking for me.

I shouldn't have kissed him. I thought we were going to die. How the hell did I know that bright light would come out? Light that destroyed Victor, or that is what Clive said. There was no body. If it wasn't for that light, none of us would've survived.

I was standing in front of my closet. I put on five different tops, two pairs of jeans. Nothing worked.

The gape in my whole was fixed. There wasn't even a mark. It was a potion made by a very clever alchemist in Head Quarters. It fixed me up in a matter of hours. The rest, well it was a bit more trickier to fix.

Clive let everyone believed that it was a natural disaster that destroyed the hall, and everyone that voiced paranoia of what they saw, the got a wiff of the forgetting spell too. It was only us that knew the truth of what was behind this.

A couple of Necrocretors was caught, the rest they still search for them. Cynthia being one of them.

I stared at my closet again.

I wanted to go as me, but but Sophie would be there. She didn't know my true form. She wouldn't understand... or maybe she would, all too well.

Dad thought it would be best to go as Ducky. In case there were other Necrocretors scouting the area, lingering nearby, watching us from afar.

I hated Necrocretors. They made life so difficult. And why? Just because they wanted things they couldn't have. *Join the club,* I thought bitterly.

I put on my glasses and Ducky appeared. She was the last thing conjured by my mom. Could be the last I have of her.

Don't think like that Alex.

I took a huge breath, tied up her dry, blond hair in a bun. Added lip gloss. Shrugged.

This was as good as she got.

RYAN AND SOPHIE were with Ethan in his room. They were laughing, making jokes. Ethan told them to stop through gritted teeth. He was chuckling, though. A good sign.

I hide by the door, not read to go in.

I felt like an invader and decided to leave.

"Alex," Ryan's voice called after me.

Shit, fuck. I took a deep breath. "I can come back later." I turned and saw Ryan's figure leaning against the doorway. He was smiling from ear to ear.

I wondered if Ryan knew about me, my true appearance. He was much nicer to me suddenly. "C'mon. Soph and I need something to eat anyway."

I went into the room and found Ethan, arm tight around his body, bruised skin. I looked to the ground as guilt rushed through me.

Ryan dragged Sophie out by her arm. She protested but her mood was so cheerful, she allowed it. She even greeted me as she passed. "Ethan, I'll bring you something other than jelly and custard to eat."

He laughed and shooed her away.

Once they were gone, he asked me in a low voice, "You still wearing those stupid glasses?"

A smile tugged at the corner of my lips. "Dad thinks it's for the best, until all the danger has passed." I finally looked at him again.

His face fell. "I'm sorry about your mother."

Heartache threatened to consume me, and tears started to welled up. "Yeah, me, too."

"Alex?"

"Don't, Ethan. I shouldn't have done that." I sat down on the edge of the bed, close to him.

"If you hadn't, we'd be dead."

"I could've killed you." My voice went up an octave. "Why do you think I was up and running in a few hours and you were stone-cold for two weeks?" I felt like crying.

"I woke up," he said as if it was nothing.

I huffed and laughed all at once. It sounded stupid. I managed to wipe a stray tear away. "I don't know how else to say this, but..."

"Shh." He placed a finger on my lips. My entire body tingled but I tried not to let on. "I know it's forbidden, okay?" He smiled. "I know we can never be together. I'm not stupid, Alex. I know you could kill me, that you suck my youth. But I'm here. I'm not going anywhere. I don't care what anyone says."

"Ethan," I said a bit too loud. What was wrong with him?

"I'm not finished," he interrupted. "I know everything, Alex. And I also know that something this good, the way I feel when I'm with you, *can't* be wrong. Alex, we fit like a two-piece puzzle."

I couldn't help it. Tears pricked my eyes. This was the blindness that my mother had fallen into. Jeff had been the strong one. I had to emulate him.

"I know what you are going to say," he continued. "My dad says your mom was as stubborn as an ox. You got it from her, you know."

"Is." My throat constricted. "She *is* stubborn."

His face filled with sadness. "Sorry."

I tried to smile but couldn't.

"Alex." He squeezed my hand. "Whatever you want. I'll be there, no matter what. But I'm not going to wait for you to realize it. I can't force you to fight this with me if you don't want to, Alex."

"It's not..."

"You're scared. I get it. I am too. But I'm willing to fight for what I want." His face darkened. "You aren't."

What didn't he get? "There's no way to fight this. Everyone who tries ends up a Necrocretors or dead."

"They weren't earth Wielders."

Just then Ryan and Sophie walked back into the room. I got up, wiped my tears lingering on my cheeks, and choked out a goodbye as I hurried to the door.

"Leaving so soon?" Sophie sounded friendly. Too friendly.

"Yeah, Ethan's in great hands. I need to see my mom."

"Sorry to hear about her," Sophie said and I nodded.

I could still hear their whispers as I left. Ethan laughed. Why was he doing this to me? He knew the law. Why was he so eager to break it? He was so stupid. In the end if anything ever happened to him, it would break me completely. I would become like Victor.

Worse, I would be worse than Victor. I just knew it.

38

ALEX

LIFE MOVED ON. But Ethan meant every word he said. Dad wasn't mom, and he told me that no matter what we tried, the glamour was not an option anymore. He let me stay at home, he even gave the option of going back to school. We didn't care about the Necrocretors anymore. Dad strongly believed that they would be gone for a while. We scared them more then they scared us.

I stayed at home. My tutors took their old posts again. Teaching me once more.

Ethan came every afternoon. We practiced together in the woods privately. He was friendly like always, but he didn't push. He gave me space and didn't even seem guilty when Soph called and he flirted with her.

"What time do you want me to pick you up?" He covered the phone and waved at me. "Enjoy your weekend," he mouthed.

I smiled. "You, too." I walked to Louis's SUV.

Why was he doing this to me? He had no idea how I felt

about him. I knew I should let him go. Let him be with Sophie, but it was driving me crazy.

I didn't want to share him with anyone.

I finally knew how Mom and Siobhan felt.

Tonight Sky View High was throwing another homecoming because the first had ended in disaster. Dad was invited too; he'd financed many of the projects to help get the city back up and running. But it would take years for Billings to be what it used to be.

Louis took me back to the new house.

It wasn't as big as the Buchman plantation, but it was fancy. Dad was on the phone as I walked in. I leaned over and kissed him.

Ariel was preparing something to eat. The smell of sautéing onions filled my nostrils. She gave me a look, one that I ignored. There was no reason to tell them how I felt. It was no use. We could never be together. And Ethan had made it clear that he wasn't going to wait for me.

I wanted my mom. I rushed up to her room.

The hospital had released her, though she showed no sign of improving. With the home nurse and all the medical equipment Dad hired, the doctor didn't see why Mom couldn't come home.

Something in my chest broke when I saw her fragile body on the bed. Fibbs lied next to her. She haven't woken up either. I padded over to mom's side. I put her handagainst my cheek. I would give anything to hear her voice.

All that advice of hers I used to scorn would have been music to my ears now.

Ethan had released me. I'd turned out to be the one who couldn't let him go. I didn't want to. But what was the use in fighting. Where could we go? To whom could we complain? We were the highest power there was, and we had no answers. The Sentinels were no help.

If I had a shred of evidence that we could make it without him dying and me turning into a monster, I wouldn't have given it a second thought. I wanted so badly to be with him. I shook with sobs. I ached to hear Mom's advice on the matter. I missed her. I was so tired.

Someone touched my shoulder. I wiped my tears with my sleeve. It was Dad. "What's wrong, sweetheart?" He settled on the edge of the bed. Stroking mom's cheek gently and then Fibbs.

It was no use speaking to him. He disliked Ethan more than my mother had. Mute, I shook my head.

He sighed. "It's about Ethan, isn't it?"

"Dad, lay off. He isn't making it hard anymore, okay?"

He smiled. "I know he isn't. Louis gives me the breakdown every night about your training." He gazed at his wife with tenderness in his eyes. "She would kill me if she knew what I'm about to tell you now."

I straightened. "What are you talking about?"

Tears filled his eyes. His Adam's apple bobbed as he swallowed hard. "I loved her so damn much and I knew. I knew if she knew the truth, she would leave me."

"Dad?" I touched his arm.

He sniffed. "I lied to her before we got married. I knew if she ever found out, she would go straight back."

"Straight back?"

"To Jeff. But I can't do it this time."

My brow furrowed. "I don't understand."

"Your mother wasn't far off when she suspected that someone had cursed the Wielders. There is someone who can help. Someone very powerful, someone who has all the answers, the way to break it. I knew this before Jeff chose Siobhan. I could've reached out to her, but I stalled because I wanted your mother for myself. So, I took my time. Your mother was destroyed, heartbroken in the wake of their breakup. I saw my chance. I lied and told her there wasn't a way."

My heart thundered in my chest. Hope flickered through my being. "Dad, what are you saying?"

He regarded me. "I'm not going to make the same mistake I made with her, sweetheart. There is someone who I think that can help."

ETHAN

I SCRUTINIZED myself in the mirror. A second chance athomecoming..

I couldn't get Alex out of my mind. I tried so hard to be happy again, to be good to Soph. But at night it was always Alex. My heart desired her with every single beat.

I couldn't imagine how hard it was for my father. To have let go of Meredith, and to find a way to love again, like he had with my mother. Even Siobhan's death must've taken a part of his soul. It seems like nothing we do, love is just not in the cards for us. How did he do it?

No limo this time; I took the Jeep.

Frederick had donated a fortune to help the families who lost loved ones that night.

Around ten people died.

Eight of them were with us that night at homecoming. Not everyone made it to safety and Annie didn't take it so lightly. She blamed herself. She was only one person. She saved so many.

The last few weeks had been an endless parade of funerals and moments of silence.

THE VENUE WAS the community event hall far from the lake.

The rather plain, utilitarian building was fixed up nicely. A flight of stairs led down to the small ballroom area. It wasn't big enough for a sit-down meal. I saw that as a plus, personally. Just the party side with light finger foods and punch.

I walked in with Soph attached to my arm, looking radiant. She knew that I was hiding something from her. Something that revolved around Alex. Her true form. Ryan saw it that night at the plantation. How I don't know, he just asked me and put two and two quickly together that the ugly duckling was in fact a beautiful swan.

Ryan almost spoke out of turn and Soph caught it, wanting to know badly what I was hiding from her.

Still, I haven't told her.

We stopped for some photos and grabbed two flutes of punch as we reached the bottom.

Almost everyone was here.

The last few weeks had been an endless parade of funerals and moments of silence.

My eyes fell on Garret. Unlike the others whose memories got changed, our group decided to shield Garret from it. He knew now what we are and somehow found it to be exceptionally cool. If I knew it was going to follow with a gazillion questions about the supernatural, I would've choose otherwise.

WE TOLD him as little as we could without putting his life in danger with the Sentinels and that was enough.

Now whenever something didn't make sense and we couldn't explain it, we just said it was on a need-to-know basis. He accepted this. Leanne had a lot of fun with Garret, though.

Soph and I stood by them and waited for the night to begin.

I surveyed all my friends as they joked with one another. Soph squeezed my arm as she laughed at Ryan and Garret.

I grabbed another flute as a waiter passed. With any luck, the pranksters, Wes and Phil, had already spiked it. I couldn't tell.

I was still up for homecoming king. Soph and Jessica were up for queen.

To my surprise, Frederick took the stage.. My stomach fluttered just thinking about Alex, but she was nowhere to be seen. I craned my neck. Nor was Ducky here.

Frederick thanked everyone for inviting him to this beautiful establishment and apologized for the disaster that ruined our first homecoming and caused death and sadness.

Funny how his eyes lingered on us when he raised his glass and said, "In times of need, true heroes arrived."

Everyone applauded.

Principal Warren made some announcements and when he mentioned the crowning of tonight's king and queen, everyone went wild.

They started with the girl.

"Sophie Stutter." Her face lit up with victory and she strutted to the stage like a tigress. Jess didn't love it; she stomped out the back door.

"A bit of a drama queen that one," Annie said. Garrett brought her with this time, in case another disaster decided to hit us.

I just laughed.

Soph made a little acceptance speech, which elicited a few laughs. She accepted her sparkly tiara with a huge grin.

Principal Warren then announced the king. Me. I collected my crown, forgoing a speech. I had to open the dance floor with Soph.

Frederick lingered on the edges of the dance floor. He chatted with one of the chaperones.

"Are you in some sort of trouble with Frederick?" Soph asked, catching me staring at him.

"No, I think we finally found mutual ground."

She smiled. "I see. Would you rather dance with him?"

I laughed. "No." *I would kill to dance with his daughter, but she isn't here.*

She kept glancing at the door. I followed her gaze but saw nothing. "What is it?"

"Just making sure that a six-foot wave isn't coming for us."

I smiled. "Alex promised she'd behave."

Others joined us as I climbed back into my shell.

"I'm too scared to ask anymore," she said.

"What?"

"You know what. You've changed so much, Ethan. I'm sorry. I know it has nothing to do with me, but I need to know. How?" she stopped. I knew what she was trying to say. I saw it in her posture. She felt bad just thinking and wondering about it. "How did Alex manage. I know Ryan knows. Just tell me."

"Soph, it doesn't matter..."

"Don't say that. You are not the Ethan I knew. It's like she became your entire world...Ugly duckling," she chuckled that unbelievable laugh of hers.

I put my finger on her lips as tears glistened in Soph's eyes.

"Everything isn't what it seems okay." I smiled softly.

She sighed. "When are you going to tell me." She nagged.

"It's not my story to tell Soph." I looked at Fredericck again. "I'll be okay."

She huffed. Looked up at me. This time there was an irritation and a bit of frustration behind those blue eyes. "Every time I mention her name, Ryan's eyes light up like a Christmas tree and yours too. What is it about her that I don't see?"

"Nothing." I dipped her in time with the music.

"Please tell me," she begged.

A few guys made a commotion, pointing at the stairs and making lewd gestures.

Ariel had just walked in and aroused their... attention. Ariel was here. She was here?

Soph looked too. "You know her?"

I nodded. "It's Alex's aunt. She probably came with Frederick."

"That is Alex' aunt." She sounded skeptical.

"Yeah," I chuckled.

The song finally ended. We went to the punch bowl. Soph stood to the side, giggling at something Leanne said. I scooped Soph a fresh drink and caught the distinct whiff of champagne. *Thank goodness.*

Ryan and Garret were also there getting fresh drinks.

"Holy fuck," Garret exclaimed suddenly.

Ryan spit out his punch.

"Who the hell is that?" someone else asked.

My heart sank in my stomach. Ryan raised his eyebrow at me. I knew without looking who was causing all the fuss. She came.

I turned around and found Alex, not Ducky, the real Alex on the stairs. Raven curls poured like water over her shoulders. A glittering silver gown with a scooped back and an elegant neckline hugged her perfect curves.

Frederick went to take her hand. She accepted it, beaming.

"Who is that?" Leanne demanded.

Ryan cleared his throat and looked away.

"She is fucking hot," Garret said.

"Guess Frederick didn't seem use for her glamour anymore."

"The Necrocretors are gone. She has nothing to fear anymore."

"Ethan," Soph said, "you know her?"

I sighed. "Yeah, Soph. I know her. We all do."

She huffed. "Glamour." More tears lingered in her eyes. "I'm so stupid." She said barely audible. "Let me guess. This was what you couldn't tell me, isn't it?"

I felt so stupid. She looked wounded.

"I don't get it," prompted Leanne. "What glamour."

"It's Alex." Soph set her drink down so hard, liquid sloshed over the rim. She stalked off.

Leanne gaped at me. "Alex who?"

"Burgendorf? The Ugly Duckling?" Garret stammered.

Ryan slapped him on the back in confirmation.

His eyes bugged out. "How?"

"Need to know basis, Garret," we both intoned.

"What?" Leanne said softly. She stormed after Soph, ever the pit bull.

"That is Alex?" Garret repeated, incredulous.

I shook my head. He was my curse now.

Alex's eyes found mine. I smiled and looked away. What was she doing here? When I looked at her again she was still watching me.

I smiled, knowing what she was doing. I walked over to her and greeted Ariel.

"Don't you look handsome?" she said appreciatively.

"Thank you." I bowed. "And may I say you look just as exquisite?"

"Oh, excuse me. Good luck, Alex," she said playfully.

Alex laughed. "May I have this dance?" she asked me. I followed her out onto the dance floor.

She fit perfectly in my arms. We barely lifted our feet,

gliding across the dance floor like we were made to be together. Because we were.

Everyone was staring at her. She was stunning. "You're popular" I commented..

Her laugh tinkled in my ear.

"They're all wondering who this foxy lady is."

She laughed. "So that's the animal you've christened me with. Foxy?"

I smiled. "Told you, it's a bad habit."

She laughed and I dipped her. She didn't stumble in this form. She was the definition of grace.

"Why are you here, Alex?" I asked as I lifted her back up.

"Taking a chance on something my father told meabout.."

I smiled. "Taking a chance for how long?"

She shrugged. "Until we find Mother Nature and get the answer we need."

I stumbled but recovered the tempo. "What?"

Her laughter was like chimes. "Yes, apparently she's real. She's the only one who has the answers. If there is a curse, a potion we need to drink before doing that thing you loved so much while I arched my back."

Heat rose in my cheeks.

"Dad said she exists and he is one of the best researchers I know. If there is something, she'll know. If you are willing to take this chance with me..."

Hope flooded my veins with almost the same amount of energy as a good earth wielding. I didn't even let her finish. I lifted her up and embraced her tight.

She wrapped her arms around me. "I'll take that as a yes," she said.

"A million times yes." I couldn't stop smiling.

She smiled with those midnight blues of hers. "You're not

the only one who was struggling Ethan. I meant every word I said that night. When I said you were my weakness."

"I'm your weakness?" I scoffed. "It didn't look like it."

"I know. One of us had to be the smart one, Ethan."

I arched a brow. "Oh, so now I'm the dummy?"

She shook her head. "However you want to look at it. To be honest, I don't care what you are, as long as you are with me."

This was what joy felt like. Light and happiness poured through me. Grinning like an idiot, I pinched myself to make sure this wasn't a dream.

"Whatever you say, Foxy. Can we at least party tonight?"

"Yeah, sure." She sounded unsure of my question.

"Awesome, cause something tells me Mother Nature's location isn't on Google Maps."

She threw her head back and laughed.

I wrapped my arms around her and dipped her one last time.

Our lips hovered a millimeter apart for a few seconds. Then they finally met.

ABOUT THE AUTHOR

Kristin Ping lives with her family in South Africa. She has been writing for the past eight years and dabbled in many genres using different pen names.
Hinder, a *Benders* novel, is one of the *Guardians of Monsters* series.

For more information please visit
www.kristinpingbooks.com